FALCON FIRE

ERIK A. OTTO

eBook Rev 1.1 April 15th, 2024

Print ISBN: 9781732136168

Cover design by Erikas Perl.

❀ Created with Vellum

HEMISPHERIC MAPS

Venus NoPo

VENUS NOPO
EQUATORIAL WASTES
BETAR CITY
BETAR
NORTHERN BASIN
KILLIAN
TETHUS
NORTH POLE
TAWNY STATION
CHALKLEY
TETHUS CITY
NEWIK
QUELWAY
HIGHPORT
ATLAR
ISHTAR
LAKSHMI PLATEAU
LAKSHMI CENTRAL
MAXWELL MONTES
APHRODITE
DURRAH'S OCEAN
OATAR
MILLIAS
ELEVATED LAND MASS
HIGH ALTITUDE MASSIF
BIOCRAWLER CHANNELS
SHUNT TOWER METROPOLIS
TOWNSHIP
SMALL SETTLEMENT

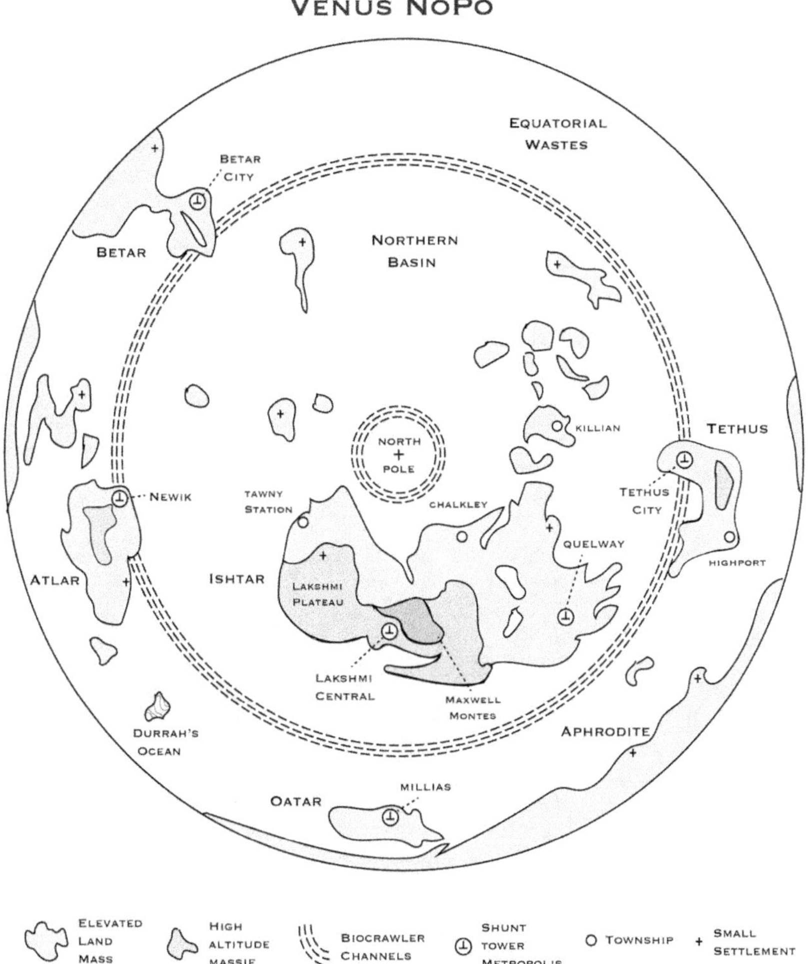

Venus SoPo

GRAFFI
DIONE
SENA
NAVKA
TYKE
MONTKEROT
CLIFTON
RYKERS
TOWN RUIN
SAMAR
CITY
ENJO
REDROCK
THEMIS
LADA
EASTBOROUGH
REDROCK
CITY
WESTBOROUGH
PYRE
SOUTH
POLE
BASU
SCORPIO
SOUTHERN
BASIN
EQUATORIAL
WASTES
IMDAR
VAS
CITY
LAE'S
OCEAN
ARTEMIS
APHRODITE PLATEAU
ELEVATED
LAND
MASS
HIGH
ALTITUDE
MASSIF
BIOCRAWLER
CHANNELS
SHUNT
TOWER
METROPOLIS
TOWNSHIP
SMALL
SETTLEMENT

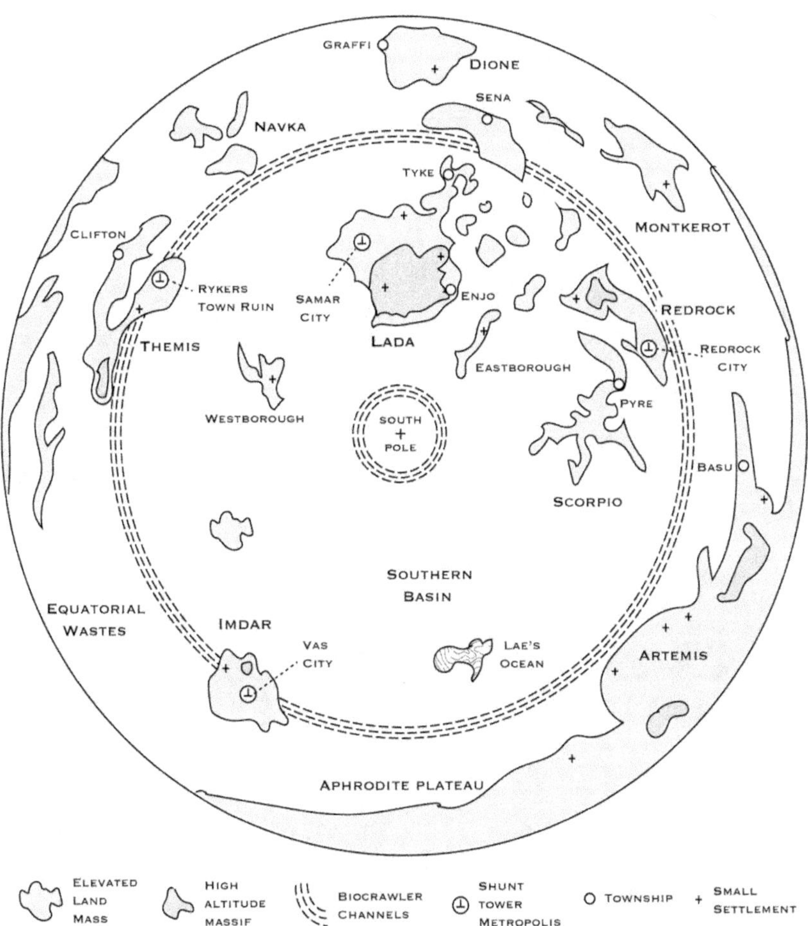

PART I

NEW ASSIGNMENTS

$$1$$

THE RACKSHACK

The *Rackshack* was an interplanetary transport ferry. Hix had been on one before, as a set-piece in *Sky Gate*, but it wasn't the same. The set-piece designers weren't too concerned with realism.

There were no plush seats or moody nooks for discreet conversations, nor were there exposed gantries allowing enough latitude to enact a sultry pose or make a speech to the crew. It was also far removed from a maintenance shuttle or even a First Colony dirigible, which were spartan but spacious, and often big enough to get lost in.

In fact, the *Rackshack*'s name was quite fitting. Hix and the other prisoners were packed together like fattened pheasants prepped for slaughter, manacled within slatted cages. There was a prisoner on either side of him, and he had the privilege of looking at the backsides of another row of prisoners stacked ahead of them. Their cages turned along a winding conveyor belt that revolved through the main hold until prisoners were eventually removed by a mechanical arm and placed into a tight vestibule, where they could take care of bodily functions like eating, replacing their wet bags—diapers, essentially—and if time allowed, running on a treadmill. Then they were prodded back onto the conveyor for another twelve hours.

It was humane enough—at least according to the reformer who'd corralled them onto the *Rackshack* at the Venus orbital station—because they had vid screens to watch. The vids certainly did help pass the time, although they were almost all shows Hix had seen before.

The prisoners adjacent to Hix weren't much help. The one on his left was a hedonite named Dez. Dez had a bony frame and deep-socketed eyes. He was missing a finger on one hand, the result of a machine accident, according to him.

It was hard to know for sure, but Dez was probably a gull. He chose to watch both *Toreno Run* and *Sky Gate*, and he would nudge Hix with a sharp elbow everytime Hix was featured in a scene, grinning and winking at him in some sort of attempt at male bonding. It was as if he was affirming Hix was living the hedonite dream, oblivious to how at odds this was with their current situation. Other times, Dez would ask about how much Hix worked on his lats, or spout off about *Onslaught* scores, or go on about all the flashy Samar City peacocks Hix must have "tagged".

Hix was more interested in the neighbor on his right. He had red, close-cropped hair. His skin was pale, with no mottling or discoloration, and his fingers were soft and creamy, the color of white magnesite cabochons. He wouldn't make eye contact. At first, all Hix got from him was his name—Tolquist—and that he just wanted some peace and quiet.

Hix suspected there weren't many reformers in the *Rackshack*—probably no more than a handful out of the hundred or so prisoners. It was a guess, based on appearances, but in Tolquist's case he would bet on it. The white fingers, the lack of scarring: it was pretty obvious. His name, though—what a mouthful—that sealed the deal.

Hix gave him his peace and quiet for the first few hours, and then said, "You know, Tolquist, we're not as bad as you think."

"What do you mean?"

"Hedonites. *Heeds.* Whatever you want to call us. You'll need... friends where we're going, don't you think?"

Tolquist didn't answer at first. It took him about a minute to speak. "I'm a climate scientist," he said.

"I'm an actor," Hix said.

"I know," Tolquist said. He still hadn't made eye contact. He was staring at a blank vid screen.

"I can help you," Hix said.

This earned him a sideways glance. "How can you possibly help me?"

"I know people."

"Like who?"

Hix turned and smiled thinly at him, with just the right amount of assurance. It was enough, for now. Tolquist would have to mull it over.

Alliances were delicate, especially in their inception. Hix's sister Mel once had a gull security guard she'd been leaning on. She'd called him a soft-boiled egg. "There could be some yolk in him," she'd said, "but if I grip too tightly he'll just go to goo in my hand."

Three days into the trip, they lost gravity while the craft re-oriented. Hix had been warned to not eat or drink during the maneuver. That part was easy, as they were locked into their cages, without any food leftovers, and no belongings to speak of. After the spin, the retroburners ignited and gravity returned.

The cage began revolving along the conveyor again, and people went back to their vids.

Eventually, the pressure started to build. Hix's pulse became audible in his ear.

"My chest feels funny," Dez said. He was no longer elbowing Hix or even making much conversation. Instead, he spent a lot of time squirming in his cage.

"The G-forces are increasing," Hix said. "They'll be flexing the thrusters as we get closer to Earth orbit."

Dez stared at him blankly.

"It'll get worse before it gets better," Hix elaborated.

The man diagonally opposite Hix convulsed in his cage, ejecting a wad of vomit from his mouth. The strong G-forces quickly recoiled the chunky liquid back to massage the side of the man's face and drip off into the rows of cages behind him. A couple of drops hit Tolquist's cheek, and he shuddered. Hix suspected the vomiting man hadn't adhered to the dietary restrictions imposed on him after his last dismount from the conveyor.

A waft of the man's hot, acidic breath hit Hix. It was liable to bring up more vomit from others.

Tolquist's pasty complexion had lost even more color.

"You okay, Tolquist?" Hix asked.

"I'll be fine."

"Close your eyes and pretend you're flying."

"What?"

"The G-forces are tough in confined spaces. It feels oppressive, like the walls are crushing you. If you pretend you're flying over the Northern Basin, or maybe paragliding off of the Lakshmi Plateau, it's not as bad."

Tolquist only frowned at him. A few minutes later, however, he had his eyes firmly shut. He said, "How do you know this?"

"I'm a pilot."

Dez blurted out the infamous tag line: "Go get em', Falcon Fire."

"In the vids," Tolquist said.

"Not just in the vids," Hix said. "Ten stars."

Tolquist couldn't suppress a scowl. Ten stars was the highest rating, achieved by less than five percent of pilots. Tolquist clearly didn't believe him.

Eventually the G-forces dissipated, reversed temporarily, and faded to nothing. The conveyor ratcheted around to drop them into the airlock where they'd entered days before. On the other side of the airlock, in place of the CP Station hangar, was a large open bay. On the far side of the bay, several hundred feet away, there was a viewing port showing a field of stars, and the arcs of several large rings that made up the superstructure of Kanto—the space station that orbited Earth. It was Hix's first view of space—of outside—in five days.

They were told to line up against the bulkhead. A woman whisked close by Hix on her way to join the line. "Out of my way, you twisted slag," she said as she breezed past his ear.

He didn't respond, but he did get a good look at her. Her arms were lean, accented with taut muscles, the result of rigorous training. She had fine eyebrows and high cheekbones. Red dot tattoos lined her shaved head from front to back—a common pattern for security guildsmen back on Venus. Hix tried to memorize the serial number stenciled on her shirt.

Two heavy-set men strolled among the group and attached circular metal spans around their wrists. Ten others—reformers, by the look of their buttery faces—floated along a guide rail to line up in front of them. These ten had coveralls with *Kanto* stenciled across their chest. When the prisoners were all outfitted with cuffs, one of the heavy-set men pressed something on his comm and they were pulled against the bulkhead by their wrists. It must have been some kind of magnetic force field.

The Kanto Station reformers walked up to the line of prisoners, the soles of their magnetic boots slapping in double taps against the metal floor paneling. They analyzed the group, scanning tablet information cross-referenced to the serial numbers emblazoned on each of their shirts. Often the reformers would move closer to examine the eyes, teeth or limbs of a prisoner. At times they would even touch their forearms, massage their biceps or quads, or even grip their buttocks.

Something about the way they were touching the prisoners made Hix's heart beat more rapidly. They were exerting pressure that was too weak to be testing muscle strength, general fitness or even to act as part of a medical examination. It had to be something else—something perverse.

The same thing had happened to him when he was young, when he was with Mel. He was standing in front of a man, who was grinning at him. "The Director," Mel had called him. "He made films." The Director had slick, oily hair, and a face that was creased from smiling too much. He'd told Hix to take off his shirt, to flex his "little muscles". He'd grabbed his behind, just like the guards were doing down the line.

Two Kanto reformers moved rapidly in his direction. One was an older woman, probably mid-fifties, with short, peppered hair and a transparent mask covering her nose and mouth. Maybe it was the smell? They hadn't changed their wet bags since they docked. The other one was tall and skinny, with jerky movements and an angular body. His attention was focused on a tablet, while the woman was scanning the prisoners. They paused near Hix.

"These are the more skilled ones," the skinny reformer said. "Ma'am, there's a climate scientist." He spoke with a measure of surprise. "A reformer by the name of Tolquist Spitzaner, lineage 42b."

"Well, let's snatch him up quick," the woman said. She yawned and glanced down at her own tablet. Tolquist's wrist made a snapping noise and he began floating away from the wall. The skinny reformer pulled him back to the railing and gave him magnetic boots to put on.

"We still need a machinist," the skinny one said, "and we could use a co-pilot."

"Okay," the woman said. She seemed woefully uninterested. Her eyes strayed back toward the view port showing the station rings.

"There are six pilots and eight machinists," the skinny one said. "Should I go through the—"

"Just pick them," she interrupted. She made a revolving motion with her hand.

Hix interrupted. "I would like to volunteer for the co-pilot position." While he couldn't be sure it was in his interests to be selected as a pilot, generally speaking it was probably better than the alternatives. His logic was that if he was selected, he was considered useful, and if he was useful, he was less expendable. Also, his intuition told him he didn't want to be selected by the other Kanto reformers, based on their perverse selection criteria.

The woman frowned. "I recognize this one."

"Falcon Fire," Dez said beside him, smiling and nodding.

She rolled her eyes. "Ahh, yes, from *Sky Gate*. No thanks. We need real pilots. I'm sure the others would appreciate a vid star, though." She gestured down the line. One of the prisoners was fighting back with his free arm, pushing away the reformer in front of him. They gave him an electric shock with a prodding device, and he slumped down.

Back in his youth, that time with the Director, that's what Mel had done. She'd fought back. When the Director grabbed his buttocks she'd slapped him in the face and kicked him in the crotch. She'd told him to "fuck right off," and chased him out the door.

They couldn't do that here.

The skinny reformer gestured to a broad-shouldered woman with deep green eyes close by in the lineup. "I recommend this one for machinist. Name's Nia Imdar-Bae. Not the best performance ratings, but she's got coring experience."

"What's her crime?"

"Theft. She stole a few torches and a material scanner. There's two others with better performance ratings, but one's an addict and the other has violent tendencies."

"Works for me," the older woman said. "Let's grab the co-pilot and get out of here."

The skinny one was typing away on his tablet, pushing down and swiping. He was taking a while. The old woman was fidgeting.

"What's the hold up, Sonders?" the woman asked.

The skinny one—Sonders—was looking squeamish. He said, "Ma'am, as I have explained before, piloting is an important contributor to mission risk mitigation. It behooves us to have quality pilots."

"So?"

"This one, the one who volunteered, his profession isn't listed as a pilot, but he has the best simulation score of the bunch. Ninety-eight percent."

That drew her attention. Tolquist's eyes opened wide as well.

"You—Tolquist," the woman said. "You were cooped up next to him. What do you think of him?"

"I... is he really is a ten star pilot?"

"Yes," Sonders responded.

Tolquist frowned, looked down and muttered, "He was helpful."

"His crime?" the woman asked, turning to Sonders.

"Dirigible theft, First Colony larceny, and attempted manslaughter. The manslaughter charge was not verified. It's listed as probable."

"Wow." The woman's eyebrows raised. "That's quite a rap. I suppose once you pluck a dirigible there's no going back. Might as well jump to murder."

"Allegedly," Hix said.

That got a laugh from her. "This one knows some big words," she said. She held her chin and looked him up and down. "You really did a joyride in a dirigible?"

"Yes, ma'am."

"Why? Are you a loon?"

"To impress a girl."

She smirked and shook her head. Then she seemed distracted by looking down the line of other captives, and by scanning Sonders's tablet device.

When Hix was young, after the Director had left, Mel had said, "Don't worry. Things have a way of working out." Mel had worked hard to give him his shot. There had been another Director, and another, and the fourth one took him in. He starred in a show about a boy with a pet spider, and was admitted to the Vas-Lumina film school in Samar City.

That one time, at least, Mel had been so right.

But now she was in the flow, and he had to get back to her. He was a prisoner, and there were forty-six million miles between them, but he would find a way.

Finally, the old woman looked up from the tablet device. She stared back at Hix again, a sour look on her face. "You're sure you want this one?"

Sonders said, "As I've explained before, the psychanthropic assessment states that risks of insubordination are minor in relation to the danger of the mission itself. Of the many variances of mission parameters, piloting—"

"Is the biggest," she finished for him. "Yes, you tell me all the time. Fine, take him. At least he'll be entertaining. Let's get them cleaned up before we brief them."

Hix's wrist clicked, and he floated off the wall. Sonders gave him a pair of magnetic boots.

Hix slid on the boots while the others watched. He glanced down the line at the hedonite criminals that had been selected by the other reformers. Their eyes were downcast.

He hoped he'd made the right choice to volunteer.

They began moving toward the exit, under the viewport showing the coiled rings churning in their bed of stars. He kept his head up high as he walked out of the bay, into Kanto Station.

2

THE BIG BEETLE

The scanner probed Neeva's naked skin with its red light, chirping repeatedly like a stuttering sparrow. When it finished a green sign illuminated, reading *Clear*. Neeva washed her hands thoroughly in the sink for good measure. A rack of beige tight-fitting rec suits revolved and stopped with her size directly in front of her. She put one on.

The door opened to a glass-walled corridor illuminated by brilliant sunlight. On one side was a biopen filled with tall grasses and bushes. A herd of obese ostriches were ambling around with their stick legs barely supporting their rounded torsos, some of them hovering near a hole in the far wall where their mash would be delivered. On the other side of the corridor was a proper aviary, with larks and robins circling tall trees. The ecochamber featured two ponds and walls of perforated, feces-laden basalt for roosting.

The corridor branched off in two directions. Neeva stayed to the left, keeping near the aviary.

She played with the tacti device in her hand as she walked. It was a shiny ball, covered in studs, with a feathery tail attached to its end. The textures would deliver sensations, and the sensations would deliver thoughts—often soothing, sometimes stimulating. Her parents had given it to her, but Grandpa said it was a bad habit. "You'll tame it eventually," Grandpa would say, "just like you tamed your exams."

She pocketed the tacti device in her rec suit.

The glass enclosures flanking her fell away to reveal Chronach's Park, the largest unfettered expanse of greenery in the Big Beetle. A dense deciduous forest spread out on either side. There were a few older folks in tight-fitting rec suits walking along the path through the woods. Their eyes were glued to the ground, and their ears filled with speaker buds. They paid her no mind.

She reached a shallow slope leading up to an observation point cleared of trees, an arboreal bald spot on the head of the biocrawler's vegetative sprawl. Here she could look out across the park and see many of its features. Chronach's Waterfall was to the north, the Gray Cliffs to the west, and the many spherical viewing pods that hung down from between the biocrawler's array of sunlight filtration panels above her.

The Big Beetle was the largest biocrawler in NoPo, cruising along with the forty-degree latitude congregation at six miles an hour to keep in sync with Venus's rotation. As the name suggested, the vehicle was shaped like a beetle's shell, though without any semblance of legs. It was immense—three miles long and one mile in width, driving forward on huge caterpillar treads. At one point it had been the flagship of the crawglodyte fleet—a monument to the now-defunct anti-Verdara movement. This meant that although it was lavish and beautiful, it was also ripe with inefficiencies and contributed little of agricultural value. The Verdarists were always eager to point out that, per unit volume, the degree of genetic diversity and caloric output was less than forty percent of the more efficient crawlers.

With plenty of hilly green spaces, comfortable animal paddocks and rest areas, it had its uses. These outer-latitude crawlers were popular for retired reformers because the green space was so plentiful that it was like a kind of runner-up award for not achieving Verdara before they died. And it didn't hurt that there were only a few hedonites about, mainly just support staff for power maintenance and other basic services. Entertainment was brought in on occasion.

When she reached the western end of the park, the path wound through additional enclosed ecochambers, which were mostly controlled vegetative systems without animal paddocks. Finally, she veered right into another expansive chamber, where a plush rolling meadow led down to a pond. Neeva found Grandpa by the water, peering into its depths and supporting his weight on his cane.

"Ah, Neeva, my sweet girl, how are you?" He hugged her and held her shoulders, looking her over with a smile. His gray beard was neat and trim but his hair was stringy. It seemed thinner every time she saw him.

"I'm well, Grandpa, and you?"

"This old heart is still beating. Come, let's walk."

They took the path that circled the pond. He was moving quickly, using his cane for periodic support rather than a crutch.

"It was such a nice service for Shawna," he said. "She would have been happy with it."

"Thanks, Grandpa."

"How are you feeling?"

It had been a month since Shawna's death, but the mention of her name still sent a pulse of anguish through Neeva's chest, one that was often followed with bitter anger. But Grandpa didn't need to know about that.

"I think about it all the time," she said. "Signs I might have missed, things I should have said to warn Shawna. Although now that Hix has been sent away, I do feel some closure. There will always be open leads I'd like to explore, but I'm ready to get back to work."

Grandpa nodded. "Don't let the arbitrary actions of some half-wit hedonite get to you. I also warned your sister but I sure didn't imagine their relationship could have ended in this way. Anyway, you've done what you can. In terms of work, I'll talk to Fisker. Maybe there's something we can do to help ease you back into things."

"Thank you Grandpa, but I'd prefer you didn't."

"I insist, Neeva. Please let this old man be useful for something."

Neeva didn't like the idea of Grandpa calling in favors for her, but she supposed there was no harm in it, especially if it made him happy.

Grandpa said, "Remember your importance, Neeva. You need to stay on track, and although this incident with Shawna has been tragic and terrible, it will help prepare you for what you'll see—for what you'll become. You should be ready soon."

"I know," she said.

She was to be a Keeper of First Colony heritage, just as Grandpa had been, and her great grandfather before him. She remembered vividly the day when Grandpa had told her. "It's you," he'd said, pointing a crooked finger at her. "You'll be the Keeper, Neeva. You're the one who will be given these gifts, and you're the one who will bear this burden."

A blue jay fluttered down in front of them, stopping on a branch before flitting away. It brought a childish smile to Grandpa's face.

Neeva said, "I'm still not sure why you chose me over Shawna, or Bethany, or even Gerrick."

"Your exam scores, for one, but Bethany scored higher, so it was more than that. When you all did the LC treasure hunt together, you stayed afterward to figure out why you missed some of the clues. You would *always* stay later, and do more, and ask the most questions. You were always looking for that... what did you call it? Oh, I remember—that *little detail*. And look at you now. One of the youngest inspectors we've ever had. Should I go on?"

"Yes, I work hard, but that doesn't infer any kind of moral superiority. I haven't done anything special."

He stopped walking and put a hand on her shoulder. "Oh, but you will, my dear. There is much we need to do to reach Verdara. We've made a lot of promises. It will be up to you to keep them." A subtle grin pulled at his lips.

She could only frown and nod her head.

He nudged her shoulder with his hand. "Come on, Neeva! It's exciting!"

She allowed herself to reciprocate his smile.

They continued on until he stopped by a large tree next to a pitted outcrop of smooth basalt. He peered under the overhang and pointed with his cane. "You see this?"

There was a faint greenish tint on the base of the stone. "Yes," she said.

"It's a type of fungus. Do you know they found fungi in the equatorial wastes?"

"What? Where?"

"Near one of the newly-formed basin lakes. Nothing like this, of course. It was a kind of Aspergillus, they think."

"How is that possible?"

"They don't know. Maybe it was an escaped spore from the biocrawlers that mutated. These spores are tenacious, Neeva. Once there were microbes in the lakes, it was only a matter of time before something would grow out of water. Fungi are some of the heartiest organisms, and most able to withstand the atmosphere—in the shaded areas, at least."

"And so?" she asked, knowing this was a lead-in to some topic he wanted to discuss. Many people were fooled into thinking Grandpa was carefree with his running commentaries, but she'd learned a long time ago that he was too focused to make statements that were truly random. It was unlikely that he would just happen across this fungi by accident, for example. In fact, it could have been the main reason he'd wanted to meet her in this ecochamber.

He smiled. "I'm telling you because we have to hurry. The hedonite protests in SoPo are distracting the council. If we don't impress upon them the need to apply more resources to the task, we won't be able to reach the Verdara soon enough. We're far enough along with atmospheric composition and temperature reduction that Venus will find its own Verdara, using this fungus or the microbes or some other form of life, and the planet will be taken over. An alternative biome could take hold, one that will contaminate the ecological pool we've planned for a thousand years."

It made sense. They simply couldn't unleash the Verdara in a controlled way until they had finished terraforming, so any locally evolving ecologies could become quite a nuisance in the meantime. But there were still so many challenges to achieving Verdara. They needed more water and hydrogen from the belt, and efforts to adapt plants to the Venusian day-lengths had so far been fruitless.

"So this is your way of kicking me in the behind?"

Grandpa laughed. "I would never," he said sarcastically, "but in truth, I know there's not much you can do about it, for the moment. I'm just saying you should keep your head on straight, because we'll need it when your Keeper title is granted."

Neeva only nodded.

They made their way along the path in silence. A swampy area was revealed beyond the pond, where seagulls and finches swooped down all around them, feeding in the waters or the nearby grasses. From there Grandpa led her to an arched bridge made of real wooden beams. An old couple stood at the top of the arc, holding hands and leaning over the railing, looking down toward another part of the pond.

Grandpa said, "Maybe you should grow your hair out? You have such a pretty face."

Neeva resisted the urge to roll her eyes. She'd always worn her hair short. It was a simple black patch matted against her skull, discreet and easy to manage. Sometimes Grandpa said she looked "too reformed", as if it might hinder her in finding a mate. This, from one of the staunchest defenders of the Reformer Doctrine.

"I like it like this," she said.

"Any lucky men I should know about?"

"I'm seeing Celia," she said.

His brow furrowed. "Oh yes," he said. "I forgot."

Beyond the bridge a man in a dark blue uniform stood at attention. He was tall, with a v-shaped torso and rippling muscles—an enforcer.

"Mr. Nash," the man said, nodding. "The usual today?"

"Yes, thank you, Kirrick." Grandpa passed him his ID chip, which Kirrick poked into his scanner. It flashed *Randol Nash lineage 4a verified*.

They left Kirrick behind and proceeded along the water's edge, past a grove of trees where several benches could be found. Fishing poles were perched next to a stump by the shoreline, already fixed with tackle. The still waters of the pond were occasionally disturbed by the ripples of fish swimming underneath.

Grandpa grabbed a rod and hobbled over to sit on one of the benches.

Neeva looked at her comm. She still needed to catch up on hundreds of unread messages. Fishing seemed a capricious waste of time, and decadent as well. The average Venusian would have to pay half a year's salary just to eat a real fish dinner. To actually sit down and fish for one probably cost twice as much.

When she looked up, Grandpa's eyes were fixed upon her.

"I know what you're thinking," he said, "but if we didn't have this to aspire to, maybe we wouldn't aspire at all. The crawglodytes—for all their bizarre rituals and flaws—had that right. The Big Beetle shows us who we are, and better yet, who we want to be."

"I understand," she said, but she still didn't join him at the bench.

Grandpa sighed, and his eyes softened. "I know you need to get back, but first stay with me, Neeva. Indulge this old man who's stuck in the past, and together we can imagine our future."

She took a breath, forced a smile, and sat down next to him.

3

THE HABITAT

The center fuselage of Kanto Station glistened along its surface. Heeds liked to call the fuselage *the snake* because the winding cylindrical curvature made it look like a white snake with rectangular scales raised periodically along its length. It seemed to be rolling along this axis, but it was actually an optical illusion caused by Hix's relative position. In reality the twelfth ring—the ring he was on—was circling around the snake.

Kanto Station was huge. Twenty-two other rings revolved around the snake, stacking into space in front and behind him. Rings one and two housed the non-criminal reformers. These two rings featured more numerous outcroppings with lounges and open rec areas, and ports for shuttlecraft. Another ring was in a state of disassembly, buzzing with automated welders and construction drones. Yet another was only a half arc. Charred struts still stuck out where some unspoken incident had destroyed the other half of the ring.

Hix could adjust his perspective by focusing on the surrounding stars flitting past. The Earth came into view, accompanied by the starfield. It was less "earthy" than he imagined—more yellow than brown. Only the occasional tan swirl spiraled across a spectrum of mustard shades. It looked like a perfectly rounded scoop of butter crunch pudding careening across his line of sight.

If only the surface *was* made of pudding. It was a broiling tempest of deadly carbon dioxide gas, acids and vaporized metals, with average temperatures of over five hundred degrees Kelvin. Many held out hope there were pockets of breathable air, or chambers of less toxic atmosphere deep underground, but this was just the typical cooing of gull hedonites. The owls—or those Hix suspected were owls—hadn't said a word, which led him to believe the rumors weren't true.

Pru asked, "You eager to fly again, Falcon Fire?"

Her question pulled his gaze away from the overhead viewport. Pru was the hedonite that had tagged him with the Mantle callsign "twisted slag" in the selection hangar when they'd first arrived on Kanto. Her red-studded head tattoo was partially obscured by brown stubble. She was sitting across from him in the mess hall, chewing on a gelatinous slab of cherry protein.

He did miss flying. It was one of the few times he felt free, and in control, but there were too many uncertainties about his mission for him to be excited about it.

"Not really," was all he said.

"But it's so colorful," she said, grinning and looking up as Earth swung past again. She was being facetious. Pru acted like a gull, but every once in a while she said something that made him question that. Of course, he didn't have much evidence, since they'd only met twice. She'd spoken tersely each time, all Mantle business, and was otherwise tight-lipped.

"You flyboys gonna do us proud—I know it." She said it with a smile.

Besides some slow-moving projects that were underway to build atmospheric dirigibles, the surface coring missions were the main reason they were all there, so anyone assigned to those missions had a certain level of importance, including Hix. But so far, besides Pru, it seemed that the heeds on the twelfth ring could care less about the coring mission crews. They cared more about murderball and carousing in the rec sections on the fourth ring.

"What are the sanitation folks like?" he asked.

"Typical heeds—penguins full of piss and pomp. They talk of skinning the orange down there—or maybe it's more of an apricot?" She paused, thoughtful about her rhetorical question. "But it's a real bore otherwise. The seventh ring, where I'm stationed, is only about a third full, so time passes slow. How about you?"

"The *Zephyr Spear* crew are fine. We've only met three times to talk about the missions. We've been on the simulators for the last few days in preparation, but most of that is individual training."

Pru took a final bite of her slab of cherry protein, chewed it fervently, and pushed away her tray. "You ready for today?" Her words were muffled by the food in her mouth.

Hix frowned and nodded. "Yeah, I'm ready." They weren't supposed to talk about it in public. She had to be a gull.

A loud crash drew his attention across the mess hall. A tall hedonite named Mak had pounded his hand on the table. The person opposite him, a barrel-chested man with a droopy beard, was named Jin. Jin threw up Mak's tray, spraying him with yellow liquid and purple noodles. The two of them grappled and landed together on the tabletop, their arms flailing into each other's sides. The hedonites nearby stood up and backed away.

Two guards with dark orange helmets and black nylon suits were stationed at the mess hall entrance. They were clearly watching the fight but did nothing to intervene. The rest of the mess hall also watched with interest, including Hix.

It looked like Jin was winning. He threw Mak off after some well-placed kidney shots. While Mak was kneeling over on the floor, holding his back, Jin punched him in the side of the head, knocking him to the floor.

Jin was about to continue laying into him, but he paused, visibly restraining himself. His eyes were bulging and blood-infused saliva was dripping out of the corner of his mouth. It was a good choice.

Security would let heed prisoners "play", but if they killed or maimed another prisoner punishment would be immediate reclamation.

Jin's blazing eyes darted about the room. "Mak here forgets who's boss," he said. "Now who's gonna skin this bitch-of-a-planet with me?"

"Yut-yoh!" a man from Jin's table cried out

"You're damn well right!" said a woman across the hall.

"This planet is *ours*. Yut-yoh!" said another.

Yut-yoh was a chant spectators would call out when Jin's murderball team played on Venus. More people in the room got to their feet and nodded, joining in.

Here on Kanto Station, Jin was a meal prep admin clerk. It wasn't a bad vocation, from Hix's perspective. He had minimal interaction with the reformer guards, and it wasn't dangerous. Despite this unimportant position, among the hedonite prisoners he had quite a following. He'd been one of the better murderball players back on Venus, and he'd parlayed his fame into establishing tribal popularity on the twelfth ring. From what Hix could see, there were only three others with as many in their tribe, and one of them was Mak. That would change, after today.

Hix stroked his chin as he watched the others' reactions to Jin. For the moment no one looked like they wanted to counter him, so Hix stood up and joined the rest. "Yut-yoh," he called out. Several others followed after Hix, including Pru.

Eventually, Mak limped away and out of the mess hall, bent and holding his back. The chants died down, but every once in a while there would be revelry from Jin's table. Jin would pump his fist. Ra ra. They were going to tame the planet.

It was highly unlikely.

Or at least, that's what Hix had learned from the reformers on the *Zephyr Spear*. Oh, sure, they had given him assurances about the structural tolerances of the vessel, and about the many resources they had to explore the planet—certainly enough for hundreds of coring missions.

But there was a saying about reformers: *You learn more from the questions they don't answer.* In this case, there were too many, like how long they had been running missions, and how many missions had failed. Plus, Hix knew that the simulations were lacking. He had run thousands of piloting sims back home. The Venusian sims could accommodate almost any variance, and any unusual maneuvers. Here, though, when mission variances were pushed to the limit, the simulation would simply say *not enough data* and reboot.

Needless to say, it didn't give him a good feeling about his first mission. It also made him wonder if he'd made the wrong choice about pushing for the co-pilot spot on the *Zephyr Spear*. Many of the other prisoners may have been in undignified roles, but dying was also pretty undignified.

He tried to push these thoughts aside. For today, at least, he had more immediate concerns.

He stood up and said, "It's time."

"Sure is," Pru responded.

He left Pru at the table, delivered his empty tray to the return rack, and entered the interior promenade.

The promenade was a broad avenue that circled around the twelfth ring. Through the transparent floor near the mess hall, all the rings of the station were visible. Further along the promenade, the floor became an opaque gray, and the walls were made up of nondescript light blue paneling, the guts of the ring hidden behind them. The blue was probably intended to promote some form of psychanthropic calm. Box droids would occasionally skim along and dutifully open up the panels for maintenance or restocking of supplies. Otherwise, the only break in the monotony was the artboards placed every hundred feet.

Most of these artboards were Venusian nature scenes, as if their reformer wardens felt it necessary to remind them what they were missing, to exacerbate their punishment. One of the images was a rough textured painting of Venusian soil. It was topographical, depicting white magnesite sands, red-brown basalt massifs and volcanic flows in three-dimensional form. Hix ran his fingers over the undulations of the artboard as he walked past.

The next artboard was a depiction of the steep canals that channeled down Maxwell Montes, with cascading flourishes of water. The canals were lined with ample foliage. It was a common rendering—a vision of the Verdara that they were constantly chasing. Or, at least, that most reformers were chasing. To heeds it was just another symbol of capricious resource use when they could be improving the SoPo tenements, or expanding the biocrawler network.

Other pieces he passed were simple depictions of roses, or fleets of dirigibles, or the Bicanthem Towers in SoPo. The primary media was paint, but often art-putty was applied, and a few were digitally rendered. Two pieces he passed were depictions of vid stars. Hix wasn't featured, thankfully, even though one of his co-stars was portrayed prominently: Ana "the Swan". She had a mischievous look on her face, and her long orange braids flailed in all directions behind her. Most heeds believed Hix and her had been in a year-long relationship. Many others thought they had a child together. The truth was they barely knew each other.

Hix was a prisoner, forty-six million miles from home, but at least he didn't have to deal with the constant media attention.

There was one last installation just before the fourth spoke junction. It was a depiction of an outdoor walkway near Samar City named Tree Walk. Tree Walk was a garden of fake flowers and trees made of acid-resistant plastics. Like the Maxwell Montes canals installation, it was a promise of what was to come. He had to admit, the piece was masterfully done. On the left, the flowers looked wilted into sickly shapes, gray and flaccid, but as you kept walking to the right along the walkway, more and more color and rigidity was imbued into the plants. By the time you reached the rightmost extent of the placement, the verdure was bursting off the canvas. It was funny, because the artwork was so much more beautiful than the real thing.

He'd been to the real Tree Walk with Shawna. He hadn't really wanted to go, but how could he say no? How could he tell her that these flowers, these trees, weren't beauty to him, they were insulting?

A plastic flower isn't a promise. A plastic flower is a mirage—a weaponized mirage.

She'd marveled at the flowers and trees, even though she'd certainly seen real flowers and trees in the biocrawlers countless times. She could see things in that fake plastic that Hix couldn't. He had many talents, but Shawna's imagination exceeded his by a fair margin.

She would have appreciated this installation, probably more than anyone here on Kanto Station.

He clenched his teeth and moved on.

Lon was waiting for him at the entrance to spoke four, a frown on his face. Earphones and an entertainment visor were dangling from a string around his neck. Slick ice-white hair contrasted with his dapper, dark blazer. He was one of the few people that insisted on wearing his Venusian clothes rather than the typical standard-issue Kanto coveralls. He said it was a form of silent rebellion, but more likely it was because Lon liked to remind people of his former gravitas. He'd been a music mogul in Samar City.

"Can we..." Lon spun a pointed finger in the direction of his mouth.

"Yes," Hix replied, "there's no audio or video surveillance on this spoke."

Lon tilted his head, pondering for a moment, then asked, "Where's Pru?"

"She'll meet us soon. I thought it best we split up. She's taking spoke three."

Lon nodded slowly. "Okay." He had a way of saying "okay" that was drawn out, as if he was testing out the sound of the word.

Hix began climbing up the ladder into the spoke, reaching up toward Kanto's main fuselage. Lon took up the rear.

"Why can't we meet down on the promenade if there's no surveillance?" Lon asked.

"People could walk by. Even in the spokes and shunts there could be passersby. In the habitats we can ensure complete privacy. They're soundproof."

They pushed off the ladder into an adjoining passageway.

These shunts had no art installations and lacked the soothing interior skin of the promenade. In fact, obtrusive boxes of ducts and wires were laid bare for all to see. Periodically, airlock doors with neighboring control panels marked each habitat location.

The habitat modules were docked between the ring spokes along auxiliary shunts that connected them to an inner contour of the ring. There were hundreds of the modules across the many rings, and most were being preserved for the eventual emigration to upper atmospheric stations on Earth.

They stopped at Habitat 34C.

Hix checked his comm to confirm his program was running. He turned to the airlock control panel, blocking Lon's view with his body as he entered his fake credentials.

The airlock belched at them and shifted open. A second interior airlock door opened in sequence.

"Where did you learn that?" Lon asked as they entered the intake area. It was a utilitarian space with a few extra atmosphere suits, tools, and control panels. There were hard-formed benches on each side to sit on.

Hix hinged his body slowly to a sitting position near the internal airlock door. "You know, from waterholing," he said. "Kanto Station isn't that different from the systems on Venus. It's the same old First Colony software, with similar weak points."

It was mostly true. Lon stared blankly as he took a seat across from Hix.

Hix elaborated. "Waterholing is like creating a fake interface, one the reformers expect to use normally, and then capturing credentials as they plug it into the layer you've created."

Lon squinted but also allowed him a forgiving nod of under-standing.

Pru's red-beaded head popped out around the airlock bulkhead. Her approach had been extremely quiet. She sat next to Hix without a word.

"Well?" Lon asked after they had sat in silence for a moment. "Aren't you going to close the airlock?"

"Eti's still on her way."

"Eti?" Lon's eyes lit up. "Why is that toucan coming?"

"I'm sorry, I thought you'd agreed..." Hix shrugged.

Lon looked livid. "Agreed? With her?"

"Don't you think we need her?" Hix asked.

Lon did consider it, but only for a moment. "Of course not, that..."

He trailed off as Eti made her presence known by moving her ample frame into the airlock doorway. She was well over six feet tall, with blocky shoulders and a dimpled, jutting jaw. It was hard to tell how much she'd heard. Judging by her one raised eyebrow, it had been enough.

"You're always so welcoming, Lon," she said with a half-hearted grin.

Lon's complexion darkened.

"And sorry I'm late," Eti continued. "The access door to twelfth was locked, so I had to wait for help. There was nobody around on the snake, and there's only a few of us in twentieth to begin with. Spooky."

It was true that many areas in Kanto Station were hauntingly devoid of activity. Pru had a purview of all the personnel manifests for sanitation management, and she'd told Hix that less than a quarter was actually occupied. Many of the rings had rebuilt interiors that had become convoluted mazes of faux walls, and three of them were off limits due to "decompression danger." Other rings without any real structural issues had nobody living in them, and served no real purpose.

"Thank you both for coming," Hix said. He tapped the airlock control panel and the door closed behind Eti. She ignored the available seat next to Lon and instead found another at the far end of the airlock. There she stretched her long arms behind her head and adopted a smug countenance.

Hix waited to see if Lon or Eti would be willing to open the conversation, but they were silent.

"Look," Hix said, "it's going to get savage soon. It couldn't be more obvious, with Jin here on the twelfth ring. He just neutralized Mak. And you know that Rav is also quietly rallying gulls on the seventh ring. There's about five other would-be chiefs, across the four most populated heed rings, and there's both of you. This isn't like the Samar City tenements, where you've got weeks to strategize and make your play. So I figured we'd better make sure we can get things under control, or a lot of us are going to get sent to the clam. Maybe the four of us should work together so that we can at least stay in the game."

When there was no immediate reaction, Hix raised his voice ever so slightly to drill in his conclusion. "We can't afford to not talk."

Lon was squinting at Hix.

Eti broke the silence. "Okay, let's hear it. What's your plan, Falcon man?" Her expression was still uncompromisingly smug.

"I don't have one. I'm just one guy, or maybe there's two of us, if you count Pru. But you can't tell me you haven't been planning something."

Lon cast a snide look across the airlock at Eti. Neither of them spoke.

Finally, Eti looked at her fingernails and said, "I'm not worried, honestly. There's thirty of us in the twentieth."

"How many of those do you have with you—loyal?" Hix asked.

"Seven, but I'm working on the rest."

Lon rolled his eyes. "Why are we even talking? Sorry Hix, this was a waste of time. I doubt—"

"That's just one ring, you prissy penguin," Eti said.

"What?"

"I wasn't finished. Those are just my followers in the twentieth ring."

"How many more do you have?"

"Not sure *why we are even talking*, as you say."

"I've got plenty," Lon countered, "and one of them is on the fifth ring—a reformer."

"How much is plenty?"

Lon squirmed. His nose wrinkled as if he'd caught the scent of a dead animal.

Hix guessed they would banter for a while, trying to reveal just enough to convince the other of their importance, but not enough to show all their cards. It seemed like a good time to make his play. He pressed his comm app, and the device buzzed at him. He'd made it loud enough to interrupt their conversation.

He pretended to look down at his comm display. "I placed a sensor by the shunts," he said. "Somebody just went by it on one of the spokes. I have to go check to make sure they're not coming this way. You can keep talking. I'll be right back."

He stood up, but waited to make sure they'd acknowledged him. He couldn't very well just run out. Lon looked annoyed, and Eti's expression was unreadable.

"First the habitat credentials, and now *sensors*?" Lon said. "Who invited the reformer?"

Hix laughed, but he cut it short, because Lon wasn't smiling. Lon had his hand up, signaling he wasn't quite finished. He said, "You know, I heard there's some Mantle dredges here on the station. They're the only heeds I know of that mess with First Colony tech. Is there something you're not telling us?"

The words hung in the air. Eti raised an eyebrow and turned to Hix with a look of curiosity.

Pru said, "What the heck is a Mantle? Anyway, I saw him water-dump, or whatever, the reformer guy to get his password over in a fifth ring parlor. It was somethin' else. The guy was so mesmerized by getting Falcon Fire's autograph he didn't even blink."

"It's water*hole*, Pru," Hix said.

"Whatever."

"I got the sensor from our ship, the *Zephyr Spear*," Hix explained. "The climate scientist—a reformer named Tolquist—showed me how to use it. It's just a motion sensor, slightly tweaked."

Lon had opened up his comm. He was probably looking up Tolquist on Kanto's directory, checking Hix's story.

Hix allowed him a moment. "Anyway, I'd better go check." He

pointed toward the airlock exit, wrinkling his forehead into a frown, as if to suggest their conversation was silly.

Eti stared back, and Lon finally looked up from his comm. Hix's heart beat like a resonant bass drum in his chest, escalating to a crescendo he thought must be audible to everyone in the cramped airlock. Even if they didn't hear it, his pulsing neck was surely visible, along with the sweat glistening on his temple.

But they didn't notice. Or maybe they didn't care.

"Sure, go ahead," Eti said, swatting him away with her hand. Lon squinted again, but didn't object.

Hix opened the two airlock doors and exited. Pru followed. "Just in case Falcon Fire needs some muscle," she said. "They make 'em look tough in vids, but really he's a peacock."

Once outside, Hix immediately ported his comm to the habitat terminal. Lon and Eti had gone quiet. They were probably waiting for him before they continued debating. That was fine, as long as they did, in fact, wait.

The program ran quickly. First, he switched habitat communications off permanently, then he disabled any manual overrides to the flight sequence. He checked the program twice. There had been no security sweeps, as far as he could tell.

Pru waited patiently behind him.

He tapped the *Execute* icon.

The inner hatch of the airlock slid shut. A second later, the outer hatch slid shut too.

Lon came to the thick glass porthole window, his hands up in a quizzical gesture and his face a mask of annoyance. Pru shrugged her shoulders while Hix scanned the active program on the terminal again. It was working.

Red lights starting flashing behind Lon in the habitat airlock.

"Let's go," Hix said, and he began walking down the shunt toward spoke four. Lon was pounding on the window and yelling, but there was no sound.

"How much time do we have?" Pru asked.

"It will launch toward the surface in thirteen minutes. Be in your room by then. Remember your alibi."

"Why do I need an alibi? Me and Rav have been playing *Onslaught* the whole time." She smiled at him. He didn't smile back.

Hix had never met Rav, but according to Pru he was Mantle. Hix had no choice but to believe it, because his sister Mel was in the flow.

They began climbing down the rungs of spoke four toward the promenade.

"What will happen to them down there?" Pru asked.

There was no anxiety in her tone. She looked mildly curious, as if this were a game—as if she was asking about the outcome of a murderball match.

"Landing and life support systems have been disabled, but they won't make it that far anyway. It will be quick."

When they reached the promenade, without another word, Hix turned away from Pru and began heading back toward his room.

Twenty-seven minutes later, after the alarms sounded, and communication protocols failed, the bridge of the first ring of Kanto Station watched as Habitat 34C entered Earth's atmosphere on a descent trajectory angle that was twenty degrees too steep.

It was incinerated in less than a minute.

4

FISKER

Neeva was moving at a steady clip through the huge six-story hall known as the LC emporium. It was one of the main hubs of business activity in Lakshmi Central, lined with both shops and offices, and also provided access to the shunt tower.

Lakshmi Central, more commonly known as LC, was the most populous city on Venus, with over a million inhabitants. It occupied the center of the Lakshmi Plateau in NoPo. LC wasn't a continuous cityscape of undulating buildings, but rather two hundred or so skinny, twenty-story towers shooting out of the plateau, and only a few other developed areas surrounding them. Most of the actual city was under the surface in wide passageways and cavernous urban centers. It was thought that eventually, during the Verdara, the plateau on the surface would be used for parks and agriculture. Much of the landscape had already been organized into ecological plots and waterways, even though the Verdara was still decades away.

The prevailing feature over this sprawl of needle-like towers was directly above her; the Lakshmi atmospheric shunt tower. It was in the geometric center of the city—a huge cylinder a thousand feet in diameter that shot up into the upper reaches of the Venusian mesosphere. Over the years, given the central location and economic necessity of atmospheric access, a number of structures had been stacked against the base of the shunt tower, and as LC shunt tower real estate became more in demand, tubular outcroppings kept climbing up, revolving hundreds of stories above the base like aggressive vines. Many of the uppermost buildings splintered from the main shunt pillar at an angle, giving the tower the appearance of a growing fern, where the leaves were dotted with pinpoints of light. The fern was where some of the most prized office spaces in LC were located.

She joined the line for the crowded shunt tower lifts. Ambitious young reformers maneuvered around her, many of them showing their best plumage. For the men, this manifested in the flaunting of ripples of muscle evident under stretched netted shirts. Many had hairstyles that were just as sculpted. The latest fashion trend—which as usual had begun with some hedonite vid star and migrated to the rest of the population—was to have triangular fins of hair, firmly gelled in place, jutting out from the peak of their scalps. These fins were often died orange, purple or pink. The women had more varieties, sometimes with multiple braids, each with different color combinations. They wore flowing gowns with revealing slits.

It was at times like these that Neeva would wonder about her calling. Grandpa said that she was special, but she sure didn't feel special in this zoo of vanity. Her hair was conspicuously bland, and she was wearing a conservative PDA atmospheric suit. It was standard issue, emblazoned with split blue and yellow circles on her collar, and the torso was banded with shiny silver lines, making the fabric look almost aquatic, like sunlight reflecting off the top of a pool.

She was a fish out of water, floundering in a garden of flowers.

The lift door opened, and she pushed in with the next wave of reformers.

"Welcome back," Griffith said. Griffith was a pale-faced cadet with big ears. He was standing across from her, talking through the crowd. "And so sorry about what happened to Shawna."

"Thanks Griffith," she said. She tried to avoid his eyes.

The lift stopped and passengers peeled out in front of her. She walked across the lobby and through the open cubicles toward her office. Her door was open, and someone was sitting in her chair.

"Hello?" She knocked on the glass of the open door. It was sun-season, so light shone through the full-length filtered windows, basking the chairs and tables in a golden hue.

The woman spun around. She had shoulder-length blue hair and was wearing a white blouse. "Oh, hello, Neeva," she said. "I'm Pettina. So sorry to hear about your sister. There have been some changes since you went on leave. Fisker can explain."

"Okay, thanks." Neeva offered a tight smile and walked up the hall toward Fisker's office. His door was open.

Fisker's broad back was leaning over the terminal in the center of the room, his dark eyes intent on digesting his display screen. His office was a glass bubble that extended out of the one of the lower leaves of the fern, overlooking the Lakshmi Plateau below. He had pulled the shutters above his head, but the light still projected across the floor in yellow shards through slitted apertures. Tablets were stacked into towers on several tables. Fisker hated the inefficiency of having to navigate through a cluttered tablet interface, so instead he kept a number of different devices with committed apps for each activity. It seemed to be an excessive use of Planetary Defense resources, but one allowed of his position.

"Neeva, welcome back," Fisker said, before she could knock. "Please come in."

She sat down across from him.

He offered a compassionate grimace. "How are you?"

"I'm fine. The ceremony was low key, but I think that's how Shawna would have liked it. And I've come to terms with how we've handled the situation with Hix. We're all ready to move on."

"Good, good. I've heard from your grandfather—Randol—and extended my condolences as well."

"Oh yes, sorry about that," Neeva said. "He has a hard time staying retired, and I really don't want any preferential treatment."

"Don't be silly. I'm happy to get advice from a First Colony Keeper and former executive officer any day, and we did talk about other things. Besides, I was the one who called him."

It was curious that Fisker had called Grandpa first, and Neeva wondered what the "other things" could be, but she decided not to pry.

"So are you rearranging the office?" she asked.

"Pardon me?"

"Someone named Pettina is sitting in my chair."

"Oh, yes, I see." Fisker winced and looked down. When he looked back at her he was focused—too focused. He had that staid look that occupied his face when he was recounting some snippet of oratory he had prepared in advance.

"Neeva, I'm sorry, but you've been demoted to Junior Inspector," he said, "and transferred, in fact."

For a moment it felt as if she was in zero G. Her mouth opened ever so slightly, but she composed herself and closed it again.

Grandpa wasn't kidding about not giving her preferential treatment.

"It's important for you to know it's not because of your long leave, or anything you did on assignment. I actually fought against the determination, citing your near-perfect work history."

Her eyes darted back and forth. "What determination?" she asked. "From whom?"

Fisker squirmed in his seat.

There was only one possible explanation. "It was the vids interview," she said, "what I said about Hix's sentencing."

He nodded gravely. "In particular, what you said about a sterner punishment being warranted."

"That was taken out of context. My point was that it could be worthwhile for the investigation to continue. I suggested we might want to do more digging because a sterner punishment may be warranted, or we may find leads to accomplices."

Fisker put his hands up, as if she was about to strike him. "I'm just saying, it made you come off as biased. Maybe we should never have allowed you on the case, being the victim's sister and all. I'm sure you understand that in a matter as high profile as this—a hedonite vid star murdering a member of a single-digit-lineage family—there can be political consequences if things get distorted by the media."

"The media took my comments out of context," she repeated.

"Maybe you shouldn't have said anything at all?"

Neeva bit her lip. Her comments had been earnest. She'd hoped they might persuade the council to continue the investigation. And yes, she was biased, but only insofar as she wanted to ensure justice was served for Shawna.

"And who exactly *determined* this anyway?" she asked. She could only think of two people that would have the gall to push for her demotion on the Executive Council.

"That's not important, and besides, I have a feeling you'll be back in no time. I made sure you were given a role suited to your skill set, where you can really shine. You're still an inspector, and you still report to me. You will be without an office temporarily, but you won't be sitting around typing memos anyway. Your first assignment will be important and will require extensive travel."

She sat in silence for a moment, still numb from the news of her demotion. She just didn't have the energy to protest. Now she realized why Fisker had called Grandpa. He must have wanted to tell him about the "determination" to control the release of the bad news. If Grandpa hadn't objected, there wasn't much she could do. Maybe Grandpa thought it would be good for her, whatever this new assignment was.

Her seat was uncomfortable, and the office around her felt small and claustrophobic. She reached for her tacti device in her pocket and touched the smooth curvature of the metal ball. Above all else, she wanted to leave.

"What's my first assignment?" she asked.

Fisker smiled at her and handed her one of the tablets stacked on his desk.

The train torpedoed southward at close to the speed of sound. Occasionally it would tilt up or down to accommodate the contours of the Venusian topography. It was traveling on top of one of the many transglobal power lines that generated Venus's artificial magnetosphere.

The landscape alternated between textures of white and pink magnesite. Some of these were wave formations made up of fine powder blown into place, others were solidified into a plane, with cracks propagating throughout, and still others were a jumble of more solid craggy formations protruding from the surface. There were a few hardened lava fields, black and swelling onto the fields of white magnesite, like scabs on the surface of skin. And for the first time, Neeva saw one of the newly-formed bodies of water—Durrah's Ocean.

The name was aspirational, because it was more the size of a large lake. Or rather, that's what she'd been told. It was hard to tell how big it was, because she could only see it in the far distance, well below the huge support pillars that lifted the conduit line above the basin. But it was there, a real body of water reflecting the creamy sky, a lake that would eventually expand to become a sea, and then an ocean. Someday, anyway.

Neeva's watch-comm chirped at her, taking her attention away from the window. It was Celia. She tapped the *Accept* icon.

"How's the ride so far?" Celia asked.

"Fine. I just saw Durrah's Ocean."

"Really? You know people pay good money to see that. You didn't tell me you were going on vacation."

"You don't have to try to make me feel better. I've come to terms with the new job, even though I'm not so sure I agree with how they made the *determination*."

"You're never going to use that word the same way again, are you?"

Neeva's lips curled into a grin. "I'm not sure I've made that *determination* quite yet."

"So what's the assignment?"

Celia had asked two times already, even though Neeva had said it was confidential. It was her way of teasing. "Nice try," Neeva said.

"Oh, come on. It has nothing to do with the hedonite riots? Why else would they send you to the other side of the planet?"

"You know I can't talk about it."

"I know."

"I'll also have a chance to look for Hix's sister, Mel. I think that's one reason I was given this assignment. Grandpa couldn't save my job, but he at least helped me find one where I could look for her."

There was dead air for a moment. Celia said, "Neeva, what's the point? Hix is gone. I'm not sure it's healthy to keep obsessing over Shawna's death. And besides, didn't they already search for Mel?"

"Yes, but the SoPo inspectors can be sloppy, and they never gave me a high enough budgetary clearance to do a thorough search. If we locate her, it could help us find out more about Hix, and in turn improve the psychanthropic analysis of his motives."

"You said yourself they didn't need his sister for that. What could they possibly turn up that will change things? Didn't you say the psychanthropic algorithms were conclusive?"

"Yes, on commandeering the dirigible, but there was uncertainty around the manslaughter charge."

"It sounds like it won't change the sentencing, so does it really matter?"

"It matters to me."

Things had been tense with Celia during the investigation. She hated the way Neeva was so wrapped up in it, physically and emotionally.

"I understand," Celia responded after a moment of quiet. "I was just hoping we could put it behind us, that's all."

It was probably best to change the subject. "How are things up in LC?" Neeva asked. "Anyone stop by?"

"Nobody. It's lonely here without you. Rocket's chirps sound much more melancholy than usual."

"I still don't agree with your characterization of Rocket's chirping. Birds don't have that range of emotion. They can't be melancholy."

"Maybe it's me who's melancholy," Celia countered. "Maybe Rocket is channeling me."

"I think you're losing it. Maybe you should see someone."

"I'm seeing you."

"You think the owner of a melancholy bird is going to help you? You're mistaken."

There was a snuffling sound that could have been attributed to laughter.

Neeva said, "Thanks for calling."

"Of course. I'll let you go. I look forward to hearing nothing about your assignment."

"Very funny."

"And Neeva..."

"What?"

"Be careful down there."

"I will."

5

CHOOSE LIFE

Kanto Station's security brigade launched an investigation into the habitat incident. People were questioned, and the habitats were patrolled. They blared harsh warnings over the intercom about immediate reclamation for anyone found to be responsible.

Hix wasn't worried. It was only Lon and Eti's closest acquaintances that were questioned, and a few other people in habitat maintenance—no one who'd seen Pru or Hix with them, as far as he knew. His program should have left no trace. The only loose end was the reformer he'd waterholed, but he probably had no idea his credentials were used, and certainly not by Hix.

The investigation didn't last long. It was just too easy for them to blame Eti and Lon—too easy to assume they were just stupid hedonites who didn't know any better.

Sometimes reformers were more gullible than gulls.

"It's always better to choose life."

That's what Dad had said. When faced with a choice, you choose the option that gives you a better chance at living.

It's harder than it sounds. Dad learned that the hard way.

Hix didn't have many memories of his parents. For his mom, his only recollection was from a picture of her dancing in a club with clusters of tangled hair shooting out from the centrifuge of whatever move she was performing. There was also a song she used to sing to him when he was little. It was called "The Loneliest Borough", about a family that was cut off from the rest of their tenement by a cave-in. Mom was your typical wild hedonite, but she also had a deeply spiritual side. She was involved with the pyrolytes from a young age, and she was selected to go to the ceremony when Hix was only five. Mel said later that dad thought it was just a hobby—a spiritual sidebar— and had never thought she would actually go.

When Mom did go, Dad lied about the ceremony. He said she was going on a long journey to LC—that she would be watching them from afar. Hix was happy for her at the time, even though he missed her. But Mel was crying, and Hix realized something wasn't quite right about what Mom was doing, or about what Dad was telling them. That's when Mel first started changing. Even though she was only eight years old, her disposition turned darker with the burden of Mom's death.

Hix couldn't blame Dad for not explaining the ceremony. How do you tell a child that their Mom purposefully stood in front of an oncoming pyroclastic cloud until she was burnt to a crisp? It was better this way.

So they were alone with Dad, and it was peaceful for a while. Those years were full of study, and playful imagination, and weren't punctuated by starker events like the years to come. Dad was a sanitation engineer at the Redrock Massif Fusion Reactor. In this case, that didn't mean "janitor". Sure, they had to take care to keep things clean, but were also responsible for containing fusion byproducts, including tritiated water, and that depended on sophisticated transport systems and logistics.

One day Dad brought home two fifty-gallon bottles of water. They were the expensive kind, like you might buy in the fancy First Colony neighborhoods in Samar City. Hix and Mel made cylindrical stems and rounded bases out of cardboard, attached them to their water cups, and pretended to drink the water like crawglodyte wine.

The next day, Dad carted in a much bigger shipment of water in the middle of the night. Half of Hix's room was filled with bulbous plastic, three containers high. Hix would shine flashlights through the bottles and watch the rainbows scatter throughout the room. Dad said that they had to drink this water from then on, and cook with it too. A few days later, they were bathing with it as well.

Dad said it was cleaner water. He said they were being extra healthy so they could be "super" kids. They were told to not drink the water at school.

A few days later Hix came home from school and Mel was there, alone. He could tell from her eyes that she'd been crying, like the day Dad said Mom went away to LC. She said Dad had an accident and now he wasn't feeling well. She took Hix to the infirmary, and Dad was there. It was packed with hundreds of people. Hix had never seen people's skin turn shades of green and blue before. Dad tried to hug him, but it was more of a pat on the back, and then he fell asleep.

When they arrived back at home, Mel said that Dad was going to visit Mom in LC, and that they needed to move to Samar City for a while. She said it would be fun.

Hix believed her, but he knew she wasn't telling him everything. Even as a child, he knew it had something to do with the water.

It was only much later that Mel told him the truth. Dad suspected one of the workers had accidentally dumped tritiated water near the community well. He knew it would leach into the water supply. She said something about beta radiation, and that it would cause sickness for everyone.

Dad eventually confronted the plant manager about it—an elected official and reformer named Varleman who didn't know anything about fusion reactors. Varleman blamed the entire sanitary staff, including Dad. They made them test the water, but it was already contaminated. Dad was forced to drink from the place of highest concentration, as a punishment. Varleman probably didn't even know it was a death sentence. He didn't know that most of the people in their tenement were going to die anyway.

But by confronting the plant manager, Dad had broken his own rule. He felt some compunction to call out the danger to everyone else, when he should have been focused on saving himself. He made the wrong choice, that one time, and it cost him his life.

Years later, Hix would read about the Redrock Fusion Reactor Tragedy. Seven hundred dead, but there was no mention of the cover-up, or the radiation. The vids said it was bacterial food contamination. Hix would ask Mel about it and she would hush him. "Don't talk about it anymore," she would say. "You never know who's listening."

That was how it was in the tenements. Piecemeal information, spurious causalities, uncertain allegiances, and the actual truth was ever elusive. Morality and emotion blur together. Social justice is a mirage—a set piece that changes with each scene.

So Hix took what his father said in earnest. It would be best to put his energy into a single focus. You do what you can to survive.

"It's always better to choose life."

6

EASTBOROUGH

Neeva's shuttle lifted off, scorching the already-black landing pad with its down jets. The X92 copters weren't very economical—the new rotary blade copters would have been more fuel-efficient—but some reformers still worried that the evolving atmospheric conditions could compromise lateral stability. It was silly, and the rotary copters had their fair share of issues. They were jerky and if you pulled off too fast the pitch was hard to control.

X92s were also expensive, but none of Neeva's PDA officer peers in Enjo seemed to care when she booked it. Even a junior inspector was of high enough rank to deflect any scrutiny from local governance, and hedonite tribal representatives cared little about such practical matters.

The Enjo Executive Suites hotel receded from view behind her. It was a large, pyramidal building sticking out of the warehouse-style admin complex like a red fang. The major north-south conduit and train track she'd arrived on receded into the horizon behind it.

The sky was full of orange and purple tones that were slowly overcoming twilight. Dawn days were a beautiful time to fly.

After escaping the relative cleanliness of the Lada massif, the ground fell away to reveal the great basin underneath them. Here, the

Venusian surface had turned gray with a layer of fine ash, and the horizon morphed into a dark haze. Both were the result of a volcano that was spewing its contents in the distance. The prevailing winds were pulling ash away from Enjo, for the time being.

"How far to the mine?" Neeva asked the pilot. He was sitting next to her, gnawing off a piece of sheck—a red, gummy substance that SoPo hedonites chewed on to stay alert. He had a tattoo on his arm that looked like a circle with needles arrayed around it, pointing inwards. A stencil across his breast read *Bam Jam*, which was presumably some kind of nickname.

"Not far at all," he said amid noshing sounds. "Just sit back and admire the view."

"There's a view?" Neeva flashed her eyes at the distant wall of ash.

He laughed. "Yeah, not so much out there, but we'll pass over the major dirigible soon."

It became evident a few minutes later—a huge ovoid that tapered to a stubby nose in the front, lying askew on the tilted gradient of the plane. As they came closer, Neeva realized that "huge" was an understatement. It must have been a mile long. Dunes of gray magnesite were pushed up against the hull. In some places, the hull gaped open, partially filled with sedimentary rock. Lights still dotted the sides, congregating in sections, but large swaths were unlit and looked abandoned.

As they passed over it, a round dome became visible, jutting out from the top of the dirigible—the fusion reactor. Dozens of power conduit tubes reached out from it, draping over the sides of the hull to stretch in every direction onto the surrounding plain, like the legs of some giant insect that had taken up residence inside. The greatest concentration of lights were near the reactor, and new, less-weathered rectangular structures appeared to have been bolted around the circumference.

"Have you ever been to the reactor?" she asked the pilot.

"I go from time to time," he said, still chewing his sheck-gum intermittently, "usually porting recorders, energy auditors, and engineers."

"Is there much left to see from the First Colony days?"

"I don't know. I did a tour once. Much of it's roped off, so I'm sure some of it is preserved. Or it could be it's just falling apart. I'd rather see one that's still flying, if I had the chance."

Neeva wondered if Grandpa had ever been inside a major dirigible. There were only a handful still aloft, but they were hard to access, and as far as she knew this was the only one that hadn't been disassembled after landing. She might even learn something that Grandpa didn't know, which would be a first.

"Do they still offer tours?" she asked.

"I think so. Ask at the hotel."

The copter banked and turned north, following one of the power conduits that extended from the reactor. A flurry of ash began pelting the shuttle. Bam Jam was unperturbed.

A raised plateau became visible in the distance, along the line of the conduit. The vertical face was marked with windows and lined with external elevator tubes. The area was windswept, with magnesite dunes in places; in others, the underlying brown basalt was laid bare. Two great roads dotted with transport vehicles forked off from a large basin that ate into the plateau, heading north and east.

The main activity in the mining facility took place in a large courtyard carved out of the rock, where transport vehicles came and went. Conveyors circulated heavy rock into the building, then carried it out as a refined grade of sand on the other side. There were fifty-odd people milling around the work area.

The copter descended and veered to land on a lit circle next to a blocky slit-windowed tower on the surface of the plateau.

"Hey, you know I do tours as well, if you're interested." Bam Jam was looking back, a grin on his face.

"Thanks," Neeva said, smiling in return. "I'll let you know." She was well aware he could mean *tour* in a more carnal sense. She would never accept, of course, but it was a good rule of thumb to always keep people invested in her wellbeing, especially while in SoPo.

She fastened her breathing mask, sealed it, exited from the rear hatch and descended the unfolding stairs. A dusty wind blew particles of ash and grains of magnesite across her transparent faceplate.

Gorman was walking out from the building to greet her. He was wearing a reformer-issue atmospheric suit, but his mask was a cheaper conical variety that only covered his mouth and nose. Over his eyes he wore what looked almost like swimming goggles. He appeared different than on the video footage she'd seen, but it was probably only because his hair—once well-coiffed and slicked back—was flailing in the wind, and his green irises were barely visible behind his goggles.

He pointed at his head. "Sorry—mask's broken. Let's get inside."

She followed him into the facility by way of a double airlock system. It was trapping a fair amount of external sediment, something you would never see in NoPo, but this was a mining facility so Neeva didn't expect much decorum. They removed their masks and Gorman escorted her across an entry bay lined with rows of worn-down atmospheric suits, crates and energy packs. They continued along a railing overlooking a broad indoor lane with service vehicles running up and down it. There was a faint rubbery smell in the air.

After waiting to cross a traffic tube, they passed over a gantry and entered a suite of offices. Here, a mix of reformers and hedonites toiled on tablets and monitors. Gorman led her to his glass-encased office overlooking another outdoor work area. His view of the outside revealed a huge pile of excavated Venusian soil surrounded by cranes, trucks and processing machines busy at work extracting silica.

"Welcome to Eastborough, Inspector," he said with a smile. He gestured to the seat before his desk while he took his own.

"Thank you for meeting with me," she responded.

A slim young man with a shaved head walked into the room. He looked to be about twenty years old, if that, and he was wearing a PDA-issue atmospheric suit. When he came close he extended his fist and opened his hand, palm up and fingers flaring out. It was the First Colony fist-to-seed greeting, otherwise known as "Verdara's promise". It was supposed to be gesture of friendship and giving, but it had become more of an affirmation of loyalty usually reserved for formal situations.

Neeva returned the gesture in kind.

"I've asked Anuvant Renshaw 98c here to join us," Gorman explained. "He might be able to help."

"That's fine," she said.

Anuvant took a seat next to her. His hands were cradled together, his back stiff.

Gorman said, "Can I ask why you've come all this way? We've had the SoPo inspectors visit several times already. I'm happy to host you anytime, of course, but they seem to have the matter well in hand."

"NoPo Intelligence wants more direct insight into the matter," Neeva explained. "The SoPo inspectors don't always apply the right processes for novel situations."

"Is there something novel about this situation?"

"Three dead enforcers, four dead hedonites, and an entire mining settlement gone missing? I don't recall ever—"

"No, I know, the severity of the situation is higher than usual, but this is still just a hedonite disciplinary issue—more of an accident than anything else. There was a heated argument, emotions ran high, there was a scuffle, and people fled for fear of the consequences. It's all in the SoPo inspector's report. There is also a psychographic assessment of the event from the symbionts."

"Good, then I won't be here long." She smiled politely.

"I'm sorry if I don't sound welcoming, Inspector. I don't have many staff to help me here, I've spent countless hours with the SoPo team already, and I'm down a whole settlement."

"I will try not to be too much of an imposition."

He nodded and sat back in his chair. "Fine. How can I help you, then?"

"Why don't we begin with the video and audio? If you give me the files I can look at them in my own time."

"We don't have any."

"You don't have... any?"

Gorman shrugged his shoulders in an exasperated fashion. It was only now that his hair was beginning to settle on his head. Perhaps it had been statically charged by the wind. "Inspector, SoPo is ninety percent heeds, so we have to make certain accommodations to keep the peace. We have surveillance coverage for key mining operations, train and shuttle ports, shunt towers, and a few large shopping areas, but these are the exceptions, not the rule. In fact, it's outlawed to monitor any living areas, gardens or communal gathering areas."

"Don't you think that could result in more crime?"

"No Inspector, the opposite is true. Heeds would be incensed if they knew they were being watched. They value their privacy and independence above all else, and they certainly don't want us breathing down their necks. Besides, there would be so many petty crimes to manage—too many. It's better if they self-police, at least for the little things, so that we don't cause any more tension than necessary."

"In that case, how about the list of settlers?"

"You should already have that. It's with the psychanthropic assessment in the report from the SoPo inspectors."

"Yes, that lists the victims, and the eye-witnesses, but not the settlers who fled."

"The settlers who fled? There are hundreds."

"Well, maybe I will be here for a while after all."

Gorman's brow furrowed in frustration. "Do you really intend to try to *find* these people? They've surely melted away into the tunnel tenements and distant archipelagos of SoPo. If you go poking around it could cause—"

"Why do you think I'm here, Gorman, if not to investigate this matter thoroughly?"

His jaw clenched and he shook his head. He shifted in his seat and opened his hands to her. "Fine, I'll have them sent to you. Bam Jam will take you to the scene of the crime. And Anuvant will assist you with anything else. Sorry, but Anuvant is all I can afford."

Anuvant smiled at her. It was too eager—a smile that told her he might be more of a hindrance than a help.

She nodded and stood up. "Thank you for your assistance,

Director Gorman." She splayed her hand once again in the fist-to-seed salute.

He returned the gesture and eyed her warily.

After a short jump in the X92, Bam Jam dropped Neeva and Anuvant off at an access port near the Eastborough 13 settlement. At the port entrance there was a car reserved for mining operations. Anuvant commandeered it into the tunnel system.

She used the time in transit to review the list of fleeing settlers Gorman had provided. Many names were missing, and those that were included had limited information. Was this normal for SoPo? They didn't even keep track of where people were living. No wonder it was so difficult to keep the peace.

They reached the end of a circuitous array of tunnels to arrive at electrified security wire blocking the entrance to the abandoned settlement.

Anuvant disarmed it with a tap on his tablet and they proceeded on foot, ducking under the inert security wire. They were still on a main thoroughfare but it was clear of people or vehicles.

"So what brought you south?" Neeva asked Anuvant.

"I'm in PDA officer training. I decided to do my internship at the mine."

She tried to keep her face devoid of expression. Gorman hadn't even given her a fully-trained PDA officer.

Anuvant was scanning a map of the settlement on his tablet. Icons were flashing on the surface. "The town square is just up here," he said. "That's where the conflict began."

Ahead of them, a curvature in the tunnel darkened to shadow. Anuvant turned on a light on the back of his tablet to provide illumination.

The town square was a hollowed-out cavern, several hundred feet across, with a large skylight at the apex, although at the current time it provided little ambient light through the sooty atmosphere. In the center of the cavern was an intersection of several roads, with parking areas inset into the cavern walls. Lining the square was an all-purpose Multimat store, a semicircular amphitheater, and a number of other small shops and restaurants.

"Did the SoPo inspector team shut off the power?" Anuvant asked. He was tapping on the tablet, bringing up the facility reports to determine the answer for himself.

Neeva looked around. There were lampposts but no light fixtures. The walls looked to have had track lighting at one time, but the lights had been removed. In some places there were gouges in the wall, as if they had been attacked with sharp objects.

"It says here," Anuvant said, scrolling his screen, "that the entire settlement was scoured of anything of value, including light fixtures, glassware, clothing, tablets, and other personal belongings. Even cars were hijacked."

"Allegedly."

"Pardon me?"

"You're telling me what the eyewitnesses told you, so it is not a verified fact. Until a fact is verified, it is an alleged fact."

"I understand. Apologies."

At least he was respectful.

"So what would they do with all this pilfered merchandise?" she asked.

"They will probably pawn them for food or credits in other settlements."

"You can do that here?"

"That's what I've heard. It's also cited in some of the eyewitness testimonies."

"Even so, pretty thorough for a bunch of panicking hedonites, don't you think?" Neeva gestured to the area around them, and felt at a notch cut into the wall.

Anuvant shrugged. "These mining settlements are very poor, only a step above the deep tunnel tenements in Samar City. Virtually everyone gets the same standard wage, so just a little more means a better quality of life, even if it's temporary."

Neeva nodded. It made some sense, and it also exposed how different hedonite society had become in the two poles. In the north they had socio-economic disparities, sure, but she knew of no black market networks for selling stolen goods.

"So where did it all begin?" Neeva looked over Anuvant's shoulder at his tablet.

"Just over here." He pointed at the Multimat entrance, where there was a corresponding cluster of icons on his tablet map. "The accident happened right next to the entrance."

Anuvant went to stand at the location he'd indicated. "The girl was hit by the car," he continued. "She was injured and her father threw a punch at the driver when he got out to help. According to witnesses, the driver looked intoxicated—he was slurring and walking unsteadily. Then the local enforcer—and there was only one of them in the square at the time—tried to break it up. Someone pulled him off, right here." He pointed at the ground. "And a full brawl broke loose. The enforcer lost his helmet and struck his head here." He pointed to the sidewalk.

Neeva remembered from the reports that the enforcer security guard had a significant gash in his head, but there was no blood anywhere on the ground. The sanitary units must have thoroughly cleansed the area.

Anuvant said, "That's when the full riot began, and there were no more enforcer security guards left in Eastborough to stop it. Five enforcers did come from neighboring settlements, but a barrier was thrown across the road. The rioters overturned their vehicle there." He pointed to a non-descript patch of road leading into the town square. A large, disconnected guardrail was bent askew, halfway into the road. "The rioters assaulted the enforcers and fled, after taking anything of value. The whole settlement took what they could from their quarters as well, perhaps fearing retribution."

"Allegedly," Neeva said.

"Apologies. Yes, ma'am, all this is based on eyewitness reports. Allegedly."

Neeva pondered the situation and strolled around the scene, occasionally stopping to glance at Anuvant's tablet. Nothing else jumped out at her as being extraordinary. But the flight of the entire settlement still didn't tie in to the incident. It seemed excessive. There had to be something other than a traffic accident and scuffle. Maybe there had been some prior grudge or conflict that had been unearthed between the people involved.

"What do the local hedonites do for fun around here?" she asked.

"They watch vids. Murderball tournaments are popular. They have parties of all kinds. Also they play a lot of *Onslaught*."

"I saw an *Onslaught* billboard outside the hotel. Is that a game? We don't have that in NoPo."

"Yes, computer sim. It's quite well done. It takes place in the future, during the Verdara. You have to protect your settlement from invading Martians who are trying to take our resources. People form teams, which sometimes meet up in real life to strategize, or to celebrate a victory."

"Could a conflict in this game be a cause of contention, something that might cause a riot?"

"Well, yes, but so could murderball, or racquetball, even a game of cards. Fights and conflict are the norm with SoPo hedonites. It's almost like another form of entertainment."

"How do you know *Onslaught* so well?"

"Yes, well... I've played it from time to time, ma'am."

"You play a hedonite game? It must be good."

He nodded sheepishly.

With their examination of the square exhausted, Anuvant led her into the settlement dormitories. Some artwork still remained, and stale food, but everything of value had been taken. Chairs weren't arranged properly, drawers were left open, and beds were left unmade. Neeva took her time, walking through the entire settlement. Anuvant would fidget, and ask benign questions about reformer projects in the north. He was patient enough.

After several hours, she made it back to the town square and sat down in one of the seats in an empty cafe. She played with her tacti device in her pocket while she mulled over the evidence.

"My tablet is almost out of battery," Anuvant said.

"I guess I've seen enough."

Anuvant smiled politely. They began walking back through the tunnel toward their car.

"So what's next?" Anuvant asked.

"We need to find Zae Samar-Nia."

Anuvant frowned and checked his tablet, no doubt reviewing the list of settlers Gorman had provided.

His frown deepened. "If I may, Inspector, I don't understand why we would look for this woman. There are quite a few others on this list, many with criminal records. It says here that Zae Samar-Nia is a mining team lead with two children. She is also a town council member and is known as an upstanding member of the community."

"You're right. She seems to be the least likely to commit a criminal act. She had a great position here, and a lot of friends."

Anuvant still looked confused.

Neeva explained, "There was no reason for her to flee, and yet she did. I need to find out why."

7

MORE THAN EXERCISE

Hix strolled through the fifth ring promenade, his swim bag over his shoulder. He passed other hedonites with flushed faces, fresh off their morning exertions. An older man with long braids said, "Hey, it's Hix from *Toreno Run*." His companion, a skinny, one-armed woman said, "Go get 'em Falcon Fire". Hix offered a nod and wry smile in return.

When he was sufficiently distant, his smile faded. He inhaled a long breath through flared nostrils.

He passed by a gathering of twenty people that didn't recognize him. Or perhaps they weren't paying attention. They were watching a murderball tournament in a glass-encased gym that was offset to the ring. He stopped for a moment, trying to not stand in the line of sight of the other spectators.

There was one player remaining on the white team, and one left on the green. The green team player threw the ball off the wall and the remaining white team member managed to catch it. He faked a throw, causing the white team player to jump in the air. With his opponent's evasive action revealed, the green team player quickly disabled his magnetic boots with a throw to his legs when he landed. He followed up by running and shoulder-checking the unmoored player into one of the death pits—ten-foot deep holes in the floor. It had a padded bottom, but the walls still hurt. A few people cheered as the white team player ricocheted off the pit walls to the bottom in defeat.

Hix moved on.

The fifth ring promenade was more thoughtfully decorated than the twelfth ring. The floor, ceiling and side panels all seemed to glow with iridescence—waves of blue, red and green that shifted with his perspective. The width of the promenade was at least twice that of the twelfth ring, and there were more frequent offshoots into plush rooms. This was because the fifth ring was originally intended for the reformer guards and administrators, just like the fourth ring. Given all the excess space in Kanto Station, at some point the wardens had given it up to the hedonite prisoners and retreated to the first two rings. Now the fifth ring was used as a place for sport and gaming, a more wholesome adaptation than the fourth ring.

Of the many hedonite stereotypes, the one about being physical creatures was mostly true, and in the fifth ring it was evident. The murderball courts, racquetball courts, swimming lanes and weight rooms along the ring promenade were often fully occupied, and usually one or more sporting contests with numerous spectators were taking place.

Hix reached the pool, which was another offshoot to the main promenade. He had to wait twenty minutes for an open lane. Its occupant was only too happy to relinquish it when she saw who was waiting. She was about his age, with prominent dimples and a ready smile. She gave him a sultry up-and-down glance as she toweled off. "Falcon Fire," she said.

He looked down his nose and winked, just like his character, Captain Zak, would have done. "Colonel Riley," he said, role-playing.

She walked away but glanced back at him over her shoulder as she left for the changing room.

His response was instinctual, a habit born of ensuring his fans were happy, but it was also off-putting. He knew nothing of this woman, so it felt disingenuous. The other stars loved the press conferences, the photo shoots, and the parties, but they all felt like work to Hix.

"Heeds have limited currency," Mel once told him. "You use what you have."

He swam, lap after lap, for an hour. It was more than exercise—it was escapism. Here he could avoid his fans and disconnect from reality—he could float in the foreign ether that made up his mind. He imagined himself on another world, in a distant solar system, tumbling through lakes, rivers, and oceans. He'd told Mel about his visions and she'd scoffed at him, calling him a Verdara-lover, but this wasn't that. It wasn't a Venus of the future, it was a place without reformers. It was a world devoid of people, except for him and Mel.

When he was finished he went to the sauna, despite the fact that his body was hot from his exertions. It was empty, so he twisted the heat gauge, sat down, and closed his eyes. His heart was still pounding and his muscles were replete with lactic acid.

Saunas were a funny thing. Most hedonites thought they were silly reformer diversions, especially those hedonites who worked in the outer atmosphere in construction or maintenance jobs. Why subject yourself to even more oppressive heat?

Maybe that was why Hix liked them. It reminded him of when he was younger, before all the fame, and before he was recruited into Mantle, when he was working with Mel in outer maintenance. They had to fly shuttles into the Artemis volcanic region, working at the highest atmospheric suit tolerances next to cooling lava flows. Often, if there was extensive damage on a magnetic conduit line or a planned water culvert, they would have to stay for hours. Much of the return shuttle ride would be spent quipping about who smelled worse. Mel had let him try the shuttle copter controls; a stinky hedonite kid who'd been complaining all day.

"I thought I might find you here," someone said, breaking him out of his reverie.

The man who had entered sat mostly naked across from him, with a small towel wrapped around his waist and long orange braids extending down to his shoulders. He was grinning, and when his mouth was open Hix could see his teeth were chipped, leaving one of them sharp and jagged. A tattoo of a black hawk stretched across his neck, which wasn't unusual. Many heeds had bird tattoos somewhere on their bodies. His bare chest also exposed a mark on his upper left pectoral. It was a circle of scar tissue, ridged and flaring out in places, like the outline of a burning sun.

"I know, I know," the man said, tracking Hix's gaze to his scar, "it's a bit of an eyesore. A pipe exploded, and part of it impaled me." He closed his eyes. "I dream about it sometimes. It was so vivid and real, being stuck for hours with only my own agony to keep me company. This dream plagued me, until I let it become a part of me." He opened his eyes. "I am Rav, part heed, part scalding pipe. What do you dream about, Hix?"

"Home," Hix said.

Rav rolled his eyes. "How boring," he said.

"What do you want?" Hix asked.

"I want to make sure I don't end up atomized in Earth's atmosphere, for one."

Hix clenched his teeth and frowned. He pointed up at the ceiling.

"I wouldn't be that irresponsible," Rav said. "There are no sensors here."

"How do you know?"

Rav frowned. "That's like Captain Zak asking a cadet to teach him how to fly. I learned it the same way you did, in Wik's little academy."

It was probably true, but it was hard to know for sure. Most Mantle members were just errand boys. Very few had full technical training.

Either way, Rav's question didn't make much sense. "Why would I be a threat to you?" Hix asked. "I did what you asked—or at least, what Pru asked. I'm in the flow."

"Well yes, you did what I asked, but this isn't like Samar City where Wik's disciples are watching out for us, and can hunt us down if we go astray. Maybe you want to get rid of me, or even expose me. You've been under the bright lamps of the inspectors. Who knows what kind of gobble-talk they've pumped into your flyboy brain."

Hix shook his head. "I doubt they even know we exist. And besides, if I was a traitor, they would have kept me on Venus in order to expose Mantle. They wouldn't send me to Earth, of all places."

Rav contemplated his statement. He smiled and wagged his finger. "Yes, more witty repartee from Falcon Fire. I love it. Then he goes and blows up the enemy fighter craft." Rav pretended he was holding onto a gun placement, gyrating his hands as if firing on an enemy target.

People would often emulate Hix's most popular vid scenes, and it usually didn't bother him, but for some reason he found Rav's impression particularly grating.

"Why Lon and Eti?" Hix asked.

"They were poking around, asking about Mantle, so they definitely knew *something*."

"It wasn't because you needed their people for your own tribe?"

Rav smiled. "Yes, and that too."

"So what are you planning?"

"On surviving, for one, but also Mantle business."

"You mean your business."

"No, my friend. I've been in contact."

"How?"

"I'm not one to kiss and tell."

He might, however, be one to kiss and *lie* about it, but Hix didn't say as much. Instead, he said, "What *can* you tell me?"

"That Wik is appreciative of your silence, and would like you to help me."

"Help you do what?"

"We need access to the first and second rings. You're going to help me get it."

"What kind of access?"

"Full security clearance. We need to be able to get in and out quick."

"Why?"

Rav puckered his lips at Hix and shook his head.

It was infuriating, but not surprising. This was how it was with

Mantle owls. And on that account, Hix could be fairly certain Rav was no gull—recruiting a significant tribe and his knowledge of sensors was enough proof of that. As to his motivation, and the claims he made, Hix was less certain.

In the end it didn't really matter. Rav had probably recruited many of Lon and Eti's wayward tribes already. Even if Rav had only been able to add a quarter of them to his growing band of followers, he would be a force to be reckoned with.

In other words, if Hix defied him, he was dead.

"I guess I can try," Hix said.

"That's what I like to hear," Rav smiled, showing his chipped tooth again.

Rav shifted his position, leaned back and closed his eyes. Hix stayed alert.

Not more than a minute later, Rav opened his eyes, sighed and stood up. "Well, this has been nice."

"What happens next?"

"When's your first coring mission?"

"In two days."

Rav tilted his head to one side. "Let's talk after that. I'll send Pru."

Rav opened the door. Before he stepped out he turned to Hix and winked. "Go get 'em, Falcon Fire."

8

———

ZAE SAMAR-NIA

Zae Samar-Nia hadn't been hiding, per se, but it still wasn't easy to find her. It took Neeva a while just to locate her worker ID number, because it wasn't in the Eastborough 13 manifest. To make matters worse, hedonites had worker numbers that weren't always documented in PDA records, and the numbers were often transcribed incorrectly. Neeva had to track down an old foreman to get it, and then check with SoPo PDA to see if it was, in fact, real.

Once they had Zae's ID number, Neeva had Anuvant ask around and check local manifests at three mining sites, to see if she had worked at other mines in the past. He came up with a couple leads, including yet another foreman Zae used to work for.

They found her with this foreman in a crew in Imdar, on the opposite side of SoPo. The mining company had a couple active video feeds of the construction site, and Neeva saw a feed of a woman working for this foreman that met Zae's description. She had taken a demotion to crew leader, second in command of a mining team, below the foreman.

It would take time to get to Imdar, so Neeva knew she'd better make her other stop in the Lada Massif before they left.

Mel Redrock-Ora's old apartment wasn't far from Neeva's hotel. Neeva didn't take the X92 this time, and she went alone. Even though Fisker had given her his blessing, she felt that she needed to be economical, given that it wasn't really official Planetary Defense business anymore.

She traveled two tram stops north along the main Lada route, where she stopped and changed trams at the Samar City outer junction. The outer line arced around the northern outskirts of Samar City—the largest SoPo metropolis. On the tram there were only a handful of people, all preoccupied or in trances of some kind. Most appeared to be hedonites wearing work coveralls or administrative attire.

The line was elevated two stories above the ground, and traveled along the circumference of the original First Colony imprint of the city. Below it was a large highway that arced along in tandem with the tracks. On Neeva's right the cityscape was airy and spacious, with huge columns supporting transparent containment overlays hundreds of feet in the air. Buildings reached up to the ceiling, supported mostly by pillars of carved igneous bricks and imprinted with leaf-patterned siding panels. Broad avenues reached into the center of the city periodically, lined with motorized carts.

To her left loomed a great wall of basalt. Near the base it looked like giant worms had bored holes into it. These led to the many tunnel tenements that served as suburban communities for hedonites.

Neeva disembarked at the next stop, and walked down the exit staircase. A comm buzzed at her. It was Celia.

"Tell me you're not going alone," Celia said.

"I've got a friend with me." Neeva felt at the bulge in the small of her back, tucked neatly under the blazer she was wearing.

"You're going to get yourself killed."

"You're too paranoid. I'm not going to harass anyone. They could care less about a lone inspector walking through their neighborhood. These people have enough to deal with."

Neeva turned into one of the dimly lit tunnels at the base of the wall. A man passed on her right. He was tall, with sunken eyes, made darker by the shadowy surroundings. He was mumbling a tune, and paid her no mind.

"Do you want to talk about this?" Celia asked.

"Why would I want to talk?"

Celia sighed. "Because you're looking for something you can't find. Shawna isn't going to be redeemed if you learn more about Hix. It's not going to change anything."

"No, this isn't about personal closure. This is business—a loose end on an investigation so that the file is complete."

There was a pause. "Why don't we talk about it later? I miss you."

"I miss you too. Give Rocket a chirp for me."

The line disconnected.

It was true that these tenements, including the one where Mel lived, were known to be sketchy. But it was early in the morning, and most hedonites would be working. It would be much more dangerous to be out during the rowdier evening hours.

A few twists and turns later, she arrived at a nondescript door in a small vestibule. Neeva deactivated the SoPo inspector lock and opened the door.

It was musty and smelled rank, like unwashed clothing. Brown and beige checkered wallpaper covered the walls. Two couches with depressed cushions kept a small vid screen company in the middle of the room, before a basic-looking kitchen. There was no art on the walls. If Neeva recalled correctly, no artwork had been taken by the inspection team, because there wasn't any when they first arrived, which suggested that Mel had probably moved out of her own volition.

And yet there was a picture in the bedroom and a couple of rusty and cheap-looking diamond necklaces hung on a hook. The picture was of Hix and Mel together, her in a short black dress and him in a tan suit. His hair was dyed an electric blue color, without the brown roots that had been evident when Neeva had interrogated him. They were smiling and waving during what looked like the opening night ceremony for a new vid. A number of photographers were crammed together in a cordoned-off area behind them.

In the closets and drawers were a few remaining shirts and pants. These were on the sultry side, with tassels and netting, but not that unusual for hedonites. Most of it was tattered or stained. Mel had probably taken the best and left the rest.

Neeva's first pass revealed little, but she wasn't disappointed. She had known the most likely outcome would be that she would come away with nothing, and she was fine with that.

She did find something interesting, eventually. After combing all the rooms, sifting through the drawers and even moving the furniture, she tapped on the walls. She even probed near the ceiling and the floor. There was a hollow sound in one area, so she pushed and found a seam in the wallpaper. There, behind the wall, was a small shoebox-sized hidden compartment... with nothing in it.

Maybe it wasn't that interesting. Many hedonites dug hidden compartments into their walls. The basalt rock was soft in places, and with enough friction it would eventually erode. Heeds could hide valuables, or anything that they'd want hidden.

Neeva shone her flashlight in the hole again and noticed a sparkle in the corner. At first she thought it might be more worthless diamonds, but looking closely she saw a white powder with something reflective in it, but no more than a few particles. Nevertheless, she photographed it, and also took a sample to take back to the lab. It was probably nothing—the leftovers of a hit of Tetra, or some jewelry remnant.

She sat on Mel's bed and massaged the rough sheets while staring at the picture of Mel and Hix. She didn't have a good bearing on where to place Mel in her mind relative to other hedonites, or even relative to Hix. This living space, this vessel for Mel's life, was so meager it couldn't even produce a shadow of its former occupant. Indeed, the symbiont's psychanthropic report was sparse on Mel. It identified her as a typical hedonite, with a slightly higher probability of drug addiction and petty crime. This apartment search would only reinforce that conclusion.

And there wasn't anything remarkable that might read through to Hix.

Maybe Celia was right. Maybe Neeva had expected to find something more. All she wanted was a feeling, a range of emotion she could ascribe to this woman so she could craft the right narrative in her mind—a narrative that might explain Hix's actions.

But it was proving elusive.

She stood up and walked out.

Before she locked the door, she hesitated. She returned to the bedroom, snagged the picture of Mel and Hix, and left again.

No one would miss it.

The next day, Neeva and Anuvant took an early dirigible transport from Samar City to Vas City in Imdar. It was a pleasant seven-hour automated ride through the stratosphere from shunt tower to shunt tower, courtesy of centuries-old First Colony engineering.

In Vas City they reached out to a few people in the Imdar construction corps working on silica and other mineral extraction teams, to see if they knew Zae. Neeva was directed to a kid on Zae's new crew who ran errands. Under his dandruff-sprinkled coif of purple hair, his face was white with fear at the sight of Neeva's PDA uniform. He provided the whereabouts of Zae's home readily.

Neeva and Anuvant made their way there immediately. It was possible the kid could tip Zae off, and Zae might flee again if she found out that a NoPo inspector was after her.

Vas City was more affluent than the area around Eastborough 13.

This was predominantly because these caverns had been carved out by the First Colonists to accommodate atmospheric shunt tower operations. The elegant and more spacious designs of the support trusses and pillars featured sculpted leaves and calligraphy-embossed stencils. The area was also an administrative center, which lifted it up economically.

Zae's home was far away from the shunt tower, where new abodes had been blasted out of the rock in the last hundred years to accommodate hedonite population pressures.

The tunnels became more dungeon-like the farther they went from the shunt tower. After navigating a number of steep grades and tight curves, they parked at an open bank of apartments stacked up toward a faux skylight. They zigzagged up the stairs to Zae's apartment and tapped on the doorbell. A hollow gong sounded on the other side of the door.

The stucco façade that contoured the door was presumably intended to make the abode a little more welcoming than a cave. Neeva touched it and a piece crumbled off. She rubbed the stony pellet between her fingers as she waited.

"Do these units have a back door?" she asked Anuvant.

He was scrolling on his tablet. "It's not shown on the Vas City municipal plans, but hedonite contractors sometimes took liberties in the tenements and didn't always follow first colony building codes."

"Of course they did."

The young boy who opened the door was in the middle of a sentence. "Ven, you little..." The words got stuck in his mouth when he saw Neeva and Anuvant. His dark hair was a bowl-cut, and his face sported a fiendish grin, though it faded rapidly when he saw their PDA uniforms.

Neeva said, "Is your mother home, son? Don't worry, she's not in trouble."

"Mom!" the boy yelled, and he ran into the apartment.

From the open doorway Neeva could see the whole living space, which was small, maybe four hundred square feet, about the same size as Mel's one-bedroom apartment. It was open plan, with a kitchen, a counter, and a small table. Tattered cushions stitched into arrow patterns were scattered on the floor. Zae was lying on the cushions with a young girl who had a bowl cut similar to the boy's. Zae stood up, a measure of caution in her eyes, her hands holding the girl's shoulders protectively.

"Mik, Rho," she said, "to the bedroom, right away." Zae guided the children toward the back firmly.

"What's this all about?" Zae said as she joined Neeva and Anuvant at the door. She was wearing scuffed coveralls. Her hair was oily, marked with faded red dye, and pulled back into a ponytail. The chemical smell of the antiseptic that the miners used wafted toward Neeva when Zae reached the entrance.

"Mrs. Samar-Nia," Neeva said, "I'm a PDA inspector, here on behalf of Eastborough Mining Operations. If you don't mind, we'd like to ask you some questions about what happened two weeks ago, when everyone fled Eastborough 13."

"I don't gotta answer any questions," Zae said. Her hand was gripping the door firmly, as if she was prepared to shut it on them at any moment.

Neeva smiled at her. "That's right."

Zae frowned, and looked them up and down. "You're northern 'formers?"

"Yes, although technically Anuvant here is an intern at the mine. You aren't in any trouble. We just want to ask some questions, and we'll be on our way."

"Let's see your ID," Zae said.

Neeva provided her ID token, which Zae swiped in her comm. Her eyes widened, and she said, "Okay, five minutes."

Neeva had been hoping they would be invited inside, but maybe she should be thankful Zae was willing to answer any questions at all. "Mrs. Samar-Nia, can you tell me what happened that night in the Eastborough settlement?"

"We were at home, just minding our own business, when we heard yelling in the halls. People said they were leaving because there'd been a savage fight. We went to the town square. There were lots of people talking—real heated like, because of the injured 'form-ers. One was dead, we could see. There was blood, sure and true. People started skippin' out."

"Did you see anything else in the square? What were people doing?"

"Swearing, mostly. Getting pushy. Wasn't a place for me and the kids, so we left."

"You didn't see anything else?"

Zae looked down, and up again. Her brow creased. "No."

"Did you say anything to the people gathered there?"

"Me?"

"Yes. I came to talk to you because you were on the settlement council. People would have listened to you."

"No."

"Why not?"

"Cause I was *scared*, that's why. Who knew how the 'formers were gonna take it? Beg my pardon, ma'am. And the whole community was leaving. I wasn't about to stick around."

"Will you go back?"

"No. It's a bad place. I got a new job."

"I'm sure you could get your old job back. It's better pay, and a nicer home—twice the size, I believe."

"It's a *bad* place. Look, I think your five minutes are up. If you don't mind, I have kids to take care of." She edged the door to a half-closed position.

"Of course, Mrs. Samar-Nia. Thank you for your time."

Zae closed the door on them.

Anuvant was looking at Neeva, one eyebrow raised.

"Let's go," she said, heading down the stairs to the car.

"So what now?" Anuvant asked.

"Just a moment," Neeva said as she opened her tablet interface.

"Who else is on your list?" Anuvant asked. "I have a few other names if you need them."

She didn't respond. Anuvant tired of waiting for an answer and sat in the car.

"We aren't finished here," Neeva said. She kept working on her tablet.

Anuvant exited the car. "What do you mean? We don't have a warrant. What can we do?"

"Hedonites are predisposed to be liars, but they aren't stupid, Anuvant."

"What do you mean by that?"

"I mean, this woman comes off as a bit slow, but I don't think she is. She wouldn't have this position, or the job she has, if she wasn't at least reasonably intelligent. So this talk about it being a *bad place* is likely just nonsense—hedonite hand-waving. She's hiding something. I think some other factor is holding her back from talking. And besides, she didn't mention people were stealing things from the square. Everything was pilfered, including items from her own home. We had eyewitness reports of stealing, so she's withholding evidence."

"But I still don't understand what we can do about it. We don't have a warrant."

"We do now." She flashed her screen at him, showing the official doc that had just been sent to her. "The NoPo symbionts processed it for me. They agreed that she is likely withholding evidence, and that she is demonstrating a high probability of fraudulent behavior. Let's go."

Anuvant was shocked into inaction for a moment, his eyebrows raised. Eventually, he caught up with her on the stairs.

Neeva pressed the doorbell again.

"What is it now?" Zae asked, opening the door to reveal her mask of annoyance.

"I have a warrant, thank you very much." Neeva flashed the document at her. "If you can please step aside, we will search the premises. Anuvant, please start with the bedrooms and I will meet you back here."

Zae's annoyance withered into a tight, deadpan look. Anuvant made his way toward the back of the apartment, donning rubber gloves from his pocket as he walked.

Instead of venturing farther into the room, Neeva lingered at the entrance, making a show of lifting a cushion and opening a drawer. "You see, Zae," she said, "we're pretty sure you're lying to us."

She let her words simmer as she moved toward the kitchen. "So here's how this works: we may find something, or we may not. We'll see. Even if we don't, the symbionts have given me the prerogative of putting a monitor on you for up to a month."

"What kind of monitor?"

"A standard biomonitor. One where we track your movements, and record video and audio." Neeva was opening kitchen cupboards, looking inside plastic cups, tapping on the walls to search for hollow spots.

She glanced back to see that Zae's eyes had widened.

"What do you want from me?" Zae asked.

Neeva stopped searching and turned, but chose not to respond for a moment. It was better not to answer right away, to let Zae imagine the consequences of this turn of events. Beneath Zae's stony veneer, the tension would be mounting.

"You know what I want," Neeva said, her eyes darting back to Zae. "I want you to answer our questions truthfully."

There was moment of silence as Neeva returned to her search.

Eventually, Zae said, "You must know how it all works."

"I'm a naïve NoPo reformer. Why don't you enlighten me?"

Zae shook her head. Her brow furrowed in contemplation. She was looking for a way out. "Go to the Hock Pocket—in Lada Skid-dado. That's where everyone sells their stuff. I'm not part of that... I just do what I'm told."

"What stuff?"

Zae shook her head.

"Part of what? Who tells you what do to?"

Zae shook her head again.

"Did someone tell you to leave the settlement? Is there someone pressuring you—threatening you?"

Zae's jaw clenched. "Leave me alone," she said. "Leave *us* alone. I've given you more than you deserve."

Anuvant returned from the bedrooms.

"Well?" Neeva asked.

"Nothing," he said. "Should we call in a forensic team?"

Neeva held her chin. "No. I don't think there's any need for that. Maybe we should commission a monitor for Mrs. Samar-Nia, though."

Zae's mouth gaped open. "I gave you what you wanted!"

Neeva was about to tell her *too bad*, that a month shouldn't be too much of an inconvenience, but Zae's reaction shouldn't have been so strong, so vehement. Maybe more importantly, Anuvant had gone sheet white. Neeva was missing something here, and it made her hold her tongue.

"Well, I suppose I'll think about it," Neeva said, watching the reactions of Zae and Anuvant carefully. "But let's be clear. You definitely did not give me what I wanted—yet. I suppose I can wait until we go to this Hock Pocket place, but I doubt it will answer my questions."

"Jib, at the Pocket," Zae said. "You find him. He knows." She looked frightened. Was it real, though? It was hard to say.

"We'll see," Neeva said. "Come on, Anuvant."

They made to leave. Zae didn't say goodbye. Neither did Neeva.

Just before they entered the car, Zae's son Mik ran out from a dark passage. He was carrying a storage cube.

Neeva shrunk away. "Whoa, stop right there," she said. She had one hand reaching around her back, fingering the handle of her blaster.

Thankfully, the boy did stop. He placed the container on the ground. "Please don't hurt my mom," he said.

"Don't worry, we're not—"

But he was already running away, into the shadows of an adjoining tunnel.

Neeva cautiously approached the container and glanced inside its open top. Inside was a rounded, ornate light fixture, with S-shaped arcs and frosty glass, probably taken from a lamppost. Littered around it were wall reflectors and metal cups. It must have been scavenged from the Eastborough site.

It was almost too easy.

"See, that wasn't so hard," she said to Anuvant.

His response was a confused frown.

Anuvant was quiet on the way back to the shunt tower. His gaze was anchored to the hypnotizing lights that lined the tunnels.

Neeva felt good about the lead and the new evidence, but something about the experience made her feel sullied. It wasn't Zae's premises, or the smell. It was what Zae had said. "Leave *us* alone." It was so defiant, and laced with hatred.

"Why do you think she had that reaction about the monitor?" Neeva asked.

Anuvant finally shared a sideways glance, but only for an instant before he looked away. "Down here, they call the monitors *time bombs.*"

"Why is that?"

"Because you only have so long until they take them off."

"No kidding?" she said sarcastically.

He didn't comment. He still wouldn't look at her.

"Nothing happens when you take it off," Neeva said. "You're free to go about your business, as long as you didn't tamper with the monitor."

His expression was pained.

"Spit it out," she said.

"I only know of two times people had to wear monitors at the mine. One went missing afterward, and was never found. The other was beaten to death and left in an excavation tunnel. That's when we stopped using them."

A wave of nervous energy coursed through her chest. "Oh," she said.

That was why Anuvant had blanched at the suggestion of the monitor. That was why Zae was so compliant, and why her kid gave up her stash of stolen items. The monitor would have been a death sentence. Anyone who wore one was seen as tainted—considered a tool of the PDA.

Neeva had just threatened to kill Zae, and she hadn't even realized it.

9

A BON VOYAGE PARTY

Hix's first coring mission was less than twenty-four hours away, and it was customary to celebrate beforehand, so the hedonites on his ring held a sort of bon voyage party for him.

Music blared in the background, a mix of high-tempo percussion and ambient synth rifts. Space had been cleared for a dance floor in the mess hall, with tables pushed to the side. A dozen hedonites thrashed about, flailing multicolored braided hair or gyrating their hips. Hix sat on a chair, his head bobbing to the rhythm, one hand cradled around a frosty glass of spiced gin mixed with synthetic lime flavoring.

"Hey Falcon Fire, show me how you burn it up." It was Pru, rolling a finger at him from the edge of the dance floor. She had mostly been dancing by herself, but occasionally she moved away to bounce around in the more frenetic center.

He smiled but shook his head. He didn't dance that night, even though he wanted to. He wasn't flashy. No, he was the handsome pilot seen on the films *Toreno Run* and *Sky Gate*, stoic and assured. It would be out of character.

Pru had been drinking—a lot—but it didn't seem to change her disposition. She would still easily deflect any of his questions about

Rav. He would just have to wait until after his mission to learn more about his next job.

When Hix was young, not more than twelve, he would go to parties like these with Mel. Those parties felt worlds away, often in the deepest tunnels of abandoned First Colony settlements of Tyke, at other times in upscale apartments in Samar City. He would dance, but only a little, and Mel wouldn't let him drink. Mel would tell him to sit down and watch—to be quiet and not talk to anyone.

"Learn," she'd told him, "to be better than them. Learn what is real and what is not. To leave this place, you must first learn to be like them, but never, ever *become* them."

So that's what he did. He would sit just like he was sitting now, and stare, watching people for hours. He saw how they made conversation, how they used their hands and facial expressions to influence others, how they made each other feel good, or envious, or jealous. He learned how they would show off with a boisterous laugh, or an exaggerated smile, how they would retreat when frustrated, or afraid. He could tell when they were flirting, or boasting. Sometimes they were genuine, but most of the time the room was a colorful landscape of posturing and posing.

Meanwhile, Mel would dance. She would mingle. He watched her just as much as the others She would drink, too. Sometimes, after draping herself over a man, or a woman, she would leave to go to a room in the back.

"Aren't you becoming one of them?" he once asked her, when they were on their way home in the small hours of the night. She was walking funny, with a staggered gait.

"Never," she said, laughing at him. "Don't be a gull."

But he didn't laugh with her, because by then he'd learned enough to know what was real and what was not.

10

THE HOCK POCKET

After the encounter with Zae, Neeva felt like she needed to molt and grow a new skin. She had almost sentenced an innocent woman to death. Inadvertently, yes, but incompetence was no excuse. She'd been careless. She'd been overconfident.

At least she'd found the evidence of settlement stripping, and she could add that to the file. She could say that the SoPo inspectors did their job just fine, and she could return home.

But no, there was something more here, something she was missing, and so if she went home she would quite clearly be giving up. Grandpa didn't choose her to be the next Keeper because she gave up. You make mistakes and you learn from them. Then you move on.

She vowed to do better.

The Hock Pocket was in a seedy outskirt of Samar City called Skiddado. Neeva had heard of the area before, up in NoPo. People would smell a waft of strong cologne or perfume and label the wearer a "Skiddado slut."

Neeva had questioned her SoPo inspector peers about the Hock Pocket. They'd told her what to expect, who'd been there before, and the wide-ranging history of local crime. She'd questioned other people they'd referred her to, and still others, at random, on the streets of Samar City. It helped her strategize an approach.

A few of the SoPo agents had said it could be dangerous, so she commissioned a Special Ops Enforcer named Egan. Special Ops were elite military police who spent most of their time training in readiness for combat operations.

Egan was strong—almost too strong. His arms were rippling veiny bulges, and his chest was as thick as a First Colony structural pillar. His body stretched his civilian clothes so much that he was conspicuous. Neeva bought him a ratty sweatshirt and linen pants to cover his climate suit. It helped to at least partially conceal the juggernaught that he was.

While she was at it, Neeva also bought new clothing for her and Anuvant. She had a temporary tattoo of the Lava Launchers murderball team placed on her neck, and her nose studded. She also dyed her hair purple, a popular color among hedonites, and wore a tight-fitting leotard, underneath baggy pants and a vest to conceal her blaster. Anuvant seemed morose about the requirement, but he also dyed his hair stubble to a bleached blonde color, and agreed to wear a sleeveless T-shirt. He looked like he was made of toothpicks when he stood next to Egan.

Skiddado wasn't too far from Mel's place; just two more stops along the Samar City latitudinal tram line. The access tunnel was busy, but it wasn't until they reached the main Skiddado square that the place overwhelmed Neeva's senses.

It was jammed with people. Most noticeable were scantily-clad woman and men posing suggestively, their eyes searching the crowds. Others were talking, haggling or hustling across the main thoroughfare. Fragrant perfumes, colognes, incense, and other less determinate smells wafted into her nostrils, drawn by people rushing to and fro in front of them. Flashing lights and colorful graffiti adorned the ceiling, and music of every variety pumped out from mini-shops carved into the rock walls.

The three of them moved through the crowd quickly, jostling with the occasional hedonite passersby. At one point Anuvant was side-swiped, causing him to almost drop the covered box he was carrying, after juggling it around for a brief moment. The local hedonites paid no attention. Packs pushing through in a sort of standing wrestling match was the norm. Neeva and Anuvant continued on until they reached the leftmost offshoot tunnel. They flowed into a stream of humanity heading deeper into the bowels of Skiddado.

A turn here, a turn there, and the foot traffic lessened. People moved more slowly, more cautiously. Hedonite eyes that were once glazed, or staring at the feet in front of them, became stickier, adhering to the trio just a little longer than normal. Their passage pivoted more than a few heads.

They reached Annex C12. This was a larger hall—once a three-way intersection that had been hollowed out by a hedonite contractor to allow for a few shops, stores and businesses in the wall across from them, including the Hock Pocket. These buildings all went up four stories, and had balconies lining the length of the annex. Two pairs of men were on these balconies, wearing black and glancing down upon the annex activity occasionally.

"Ma'am," Egan said quietly. "I can't be sure, but those men appear to be some kind of security." His words came out a bit rushed. It could have been nerves, but she'd noticed this about him before. It was like he was the shy kid in school, he'd been asked to speak in front of the class, and he couldn't get the words out fast enough.

"Thanks," she responded.

Before approaching the shops, Neeva kneeled down, ostensibly to clean off her shoe, while nonchalantly placing a node droid firmly in a seam of the rubbery pathway. If anyone found the device it would appear to be a tarnished silver sphere, much like a miniature petanque ball, but in reality it had several hidden cameras, remote telemetry, paralyzing darts, and could sprout wings and fly on command.

They walked into the Hock Pocket.

Inside there were all sorts of items adorning the walls: musical instruments, kitchen appliances, sporting equipment, colorful masks, and more. Neeva couldn't help letting her finger pass over the blue velvet on the side of a drum set as they walked in. It sent a tingle up her spine. Two hedonite youths were clustered around a monitor, fiddling with controllers, playing some kind of computer game. On the screen the players were firing at paratroopers jumping down on undulating hills of green grass.

"That's *Onslaught*," Anuvant said quietly. The game interface looked close enough to the ad she'd seen near her hotel. The display changed to feature a camouflaged woman hurtling over hedges in a lush garden, a blaster in her hand. Around the main window were vignettes with maps, statistics and character attributes.

The three of them headed to the back where there was a short man with a distinctly round head who was eyeing them from atop a tall stool.

"How can I help yez?" he asked.

Neeva pulled up a chair and rubbed her head. "Real hectic out there today. You been to the square?"

"No, what's up?"

"Just busy is all. Anyway, we've got some kitch to hock."

"Let's see it."

Anuvant tilted the box so that the man could look inside. It contained the items that Zae's son had given them.

"You mind if I take it to the back?" the man said. "I can only price 'em if I check on our inventory of similar stuff."

"Sure," Anuvant said.

"Actually," Neeva interjected. "I do mind. Can't you just take a picture or somethin'?"

"Of course, but I'm no vulture, if that's what you're worried about. The box is probably worth more than what's inside it." The man offered a broad smile.

She grinned back at him. "All the more reason not to give you the box."

The man frowned, took out his tablet, snapped a photo of the contents of the box, and went through a doorway to the back of the shop.

It didn't take long. He came back to the counter and said, "Seventy credits should do it."

Neeva had thought he would offer no more than twenty. Considering these didn't look like high-value items, and many of them would probably need to be recycled, seventy was more than a fair amount—a week's work for the average hedonite laborer—but she wasn't about to question the offer.

She scratched her chin and looked at the ground. "I'm sure that'll do, but first I'd like to talk to Jib. Is he here? We can chat for a minute, then it's a deal for seventy."

The man frowned again. "Whaddya want him for? I'm right here, in front of you."

"We've got some business, if you know what I mean."

The man's frown didn't dissipate. He looked at each of them in turn, as if for the first time. His gaze paused on Anuvant. "Hey, you look like my cousin," he said. "Maybe if you stand up taller."

Anuvant obliged.

"I only got a picture of him though. He had a big smile."

Anuvant smiled.

"Yeah, like that. A real likeness. Maybe you had the same mom."

It was a strange tangent, but Neeva wasn't about to interrupt the small talk. It seemed to be relieving tension.

The man turned back to her. "Anyway, sure. I'll go see if Jib's here. He works in the back."

She nodded. "Thanks."

The man popped around the wall again.

They waited.

Egan was standing still, expressionless, occasionally glancing at the *Onslaught* game with his nose wrinkling.

Anuvant wandered, examining the items on the store walls.

The plan was to hotbox Jib. First she would ask him why he was interested in buying the merchandise. If they got nowhere with that, she would start making accusations about owning crime scene evidence. Any sign of malfeasance along the way and Egan would apprehend him.

She glanced at the *Onslaught* game again. What had been paratroopers running through green meadows became a flurry of explosions, and foes firing at the player avatar from all angles. A text box came up on the screen but it was too far away for her to read. Egan was closer. He leaned in to see it, his brow lined. The two youths turned toward them with blank looks on their faces. Abruptly, they stood up and walked out of the store.

That was odd.

She didn't like odd.

It was taking too long. The man should have only needed a minute, maybe two. It had been at least three.

Her mind raced, replaying the scene. The man hadn't asked many questions. Were their disguises flawed?

It was possible there was some password to gain access to Jib, but she doubted it. Zae would have told her. She would want this meeting to go as smoothly as possible to avoid having to wear a monitor.

And why the strange comment from the store manager about Anuvant looking like his cousin? Was it genuine curiosity, or something else? The only thing he had achieved was to get Anuvant to stand up taller, and to smile. But would that show anything?

His teeth. It would show Anuvant's perfect reformer teeth. Among hedonites, only vid stars had good teeth, and those could usually be recognized on sight anyway.

It wasn't a certainty, but it could be enough to give the store owner pause, to at least *suspect* something. And then there were the youths who left suddenly. The onscreen message could have been to tell them to get out.

"Did you see what the message said?" she asked Egan.

"What message?" he asked.

"On the *Onslaught* screen. When the kids were playing."

"Oh that. Sorry ma'am. Looked like game gibberish to me. It said *You've died, you twisted slag.* Maybe the kid knows?"

Anuvant was frowning and shaking his head. "I've never seen that message before, but it's probably one of the pre-programmed notifications."

She pulled out her comm. Her node droid program was running, and the signal was good. She could see the feed from a camera in the node. The two pairs of men on the balconies had moved to converge over the Hock Pocket. They were brandishing weapons—blasters.

That sealed it.

"We've been made," she said. "Be ready."

A switch turned in Egan. His body tensed and knees flexed, ready to spring into action.

Neeva would have thought this was a small operation, perhaps with some illegal contraband or drugs, but it was all too smart. And there were too many thugs around.

"Let's get out of here," Neeva said, "but through the back. Bring the box. Quickly."

Egan pulled out his blaster and took the lead. Anuvant and Neeva followed. Anuvant held the box and Neeva also pointed her blaster ahead of her.

The space behind the wall opened up into a large room, replete with rows of shelves laden with labeled items stacked up to the ceiling. They were mostly electrical gadgets, including refurbished tablets, comm devices, miniature remote-controlled carts, light fixtures, paintings, shoes, belts, and jewelry. There were reams of reflectors, and metal cups, possibly from the Eastborough site, but none of the ornate lamps like in Zae's box.

Egan glanced down each row carefully before committing to cross it. At the last row, Egan pointed to an open door at the back.

They moved toward it.

It led into a hallway with yellow ambient lighting, giving Egan a jaundiced pallor as he poked his head around the corner.

"Stop!" he said. "PDA business. You're wanted for—"

A blazing energy pulse hit the wall in front of Egan. Blaster fire.

Egan ducked back into the room, but only for a moment. He fell to the floor and promptly rolled back into the corridor, his blaster pointing at his assailants. He fired three times.

"There's two of them," Egan said. He jumped to his feet and ran down the hallway.

Neeva followed with Anuvant close behind. They turned down a corridor where there were closed doors on each side. Any of these could open at any given moment. Her heart was pounding in her chest.

Egan outpaced them rapidly. He was stepping down a half-flight of stairs to enter a room at the far end. "Stop!" he said. "Hands up and no one gets hurt."

Neeva caught up with him and entered the room. There were four long tables, each lined with printers and monitors. These were connected with wires leading to small, hand-sized black ovoids placed periodically along the table. About twenty chairs were pulled out, most of them askew. Boxes were scattered about, filled with what looked like electronics, although Neeva caught glimpses of frosted glass and the glint of metal.

At the far end of the room was another exit. A flash of black clothing disappeared behind it. Another two men remained, staring back at the three of them, a few steps removed from the exit. One of these was older, with dull brown hair, dressed in a dark blazer over a white shirt. He was embracing a stack of tablets. The other was younger, no more than twenty, with purple hair and a flushed face. He was holding what looked like a remote control device in one hand, and a blaster in the other. The blaster was pointed in their direction.

Everyone in the room was frozen in time, until the man in the blazer said, "We've done nothing wrong here. You're trespassing."

Egan looked to Neeva.

She almost asked Egan to respond, because she had little experience with armed confrontation, but she hesitated. She was in charge, and she couldn't show weakness. Neeva said, "And yet you tried to kill us. You heard the man. Drop your weapon. Put your hands up. No one's going to get hurt, but we need to chat."

The man in the jacket sighed. He reached out his hand, while still grappling with the stack of tablets, and touched the youth's arm. "Time to join the flow," he said. He turned to Neeva and said, "Fine. Let me put these down." He bent over, and in a sudden movement slipped around the exit. Egan tensed but didn't pull the trigger in time.

The youth remained. His hand holding the blaster was slowly raising toward the ceiling, but he still had the remote cradled in the other. His face looked tight, pastier than before. His jaw was clenched.

"You watch the kid," Egan said. "I'll go after the other one." He began bounding across the room.

"No, wait—" Neeva said, but it was too late. She could tell something was wrong. The Hock Pocket people were too ready. And the boy looked scared, and yet determined.

The remote. He still had the remote in his hand.

The remote had a red button on it.

A button that the boy pressed.

The flash blinded her, and the blast threw her back. Or rather, it wasn't just one blast, it was a series of them. Small explosives had been lined up on the table, and they all blew in rapid succession, splintering plastic and shattering the electronic devices on top of them. She'd managed to throw her hands up, and thankfully so, because a piece of burning metal cut into her forearm right in front of her face.

When the cascade of destruction stopped, she peeked out from behind her wounded arm. Anuvant was unscathed, but Egan had been running through the middle of the room. He was covered in shrapnel wounds from head to foot, and his left arm was terribly mangled. Somehow he was crawling forward, his blaster in his right hand. The hedonite youth was still alive, his blaster nowhere in sight, and he had cast the detonator box aside. He had a gray shard sticking out of his thigh, and he was trying to push himself back toward the exit. Egan was gaining on him, though, a look of bloodlust in his eyes.

Searing pain shot up her arm. Her ears were ringing. She wanted nothing more than to let Egan kill the youth, but she couldn't let him. He could be useful. They needed him.

She hopped to her feet and ran past Egan, just as he put his blaster down and pulled the youth by his shoe with his one good hand.

"Stop, stop, STOP!" she said. Egan looked at her, and something snapped in him, pulling him out of his feverish state. He gawked at his mangled arm, as if he hadn't noticed it before. It was a mass of red, and aside for one finger, all the digits on his hand were missing.

He promptly vomited yellow bile on the floor.

"Anuvant," Neeva said, "we need a tourniquet for Egan's arm. Then we need to get out of here, pronto."

She turned to the hedonite youth. He had stopped inching away and was lying on his front, oblivious, moaning in pain.

"Everybody up on your feet!" she yelled. They had to keep moving.

Anuvant helped her lift the youth onto his feet. He was able to stand on one leg and limp on the other. Egan was much worse off, but he somehow managed to push himself up to a standing position.

They staggered to the exit together. Neeva led the way, blaster first. The hedonite youth who'd triggered the bomb followed listlessly, with Egan and Anuvant bringing up the rear.

The corridor turned. It turned again.

Her blaster found no targets. There was no one to be seen.

Egan fell and stood up again, leaving a smear of blood on the floor. His eyes were wide, his body shaking. He was in shock, and wouldn't last long without help.

There were branches to the corridor. Hedonites most often dug downward, so to get back out to the main tunnels of Skiddado they would have to go up in elevation. Neeva led them along whichever corridors slanted up.

Eventually they spilled out onto a tight, empty avenue, and from there they moved to the larger promenade, where a handful of people were passing by. Most were walking, but a couple were on motorized scooters. Neeva pulled three node droids out of her PDA suit pocket and threw them up in the air. "One and two, get help," she ordered. "We need a medivac. Three, set a defense perimeter." Two of the nodes sprouted propellers and flew off in different directions. The third hovered above them.

The node droids were classified Planetary Defense tools. She wasn't supposed to use their flying capabilities except in extreme emergencies. She figured this qualified.

Most people that passed by gave them a wide berth, but one stopped—a skinny woman. She had long ratty hair with subtle remnants of pink dye. "Can I help?" she asked. She had deep green eyes.

"Yes, please. We need medical assistance. A doctor, or paramedic. And enforcers, for protection."

The woman ran off. Had Neeva finally met a hedonite who had some compassion, or would she come back with thugs? In those moments of thundering panic, she wondered if the green-eyed woman would try to blow them up as well.

A large crowd gathered around to watch, standing at a distance, whispering quietly, as if watching a wedding, or a delicate racquetball serve at game point. For some reason, Neeva thought of a scene from *Sky Gate*, in which Hix's character was wounded, and the two municipal officials were in the medical frigate whispering to themselves, watching him sleep, hoping that he would survive.

She wondered if, in among the crowd, there might have been perpetrators of this debacle—thugs in disguise, their eyes filled with hate, wanting to finish them off but unwilling to test the node droid perimeter. Later, she would try to remember the faces of those watching, but she couldn't. They were just an amorphous mass of people in her memory bank.

Anuvant was holding up well. He had his blaster ready in one hand. In the other he had the box from Zae Samar-Nia against his side—he must have retrieved it from the room when Neeva wasn't paying attention. For some reason, his persistence made her laugh, even though it wasn't the right time for it.

Her laugh died as her gaze returned to Egan, who was rocking back and forth, his teeth clenched, and his mangled appendage stuck in the air.

A rush of anger overcame her, and she turned her weapon on their hedonite prisoner. "Why the bomb?" she asked.

The youth awoke from his daze to shake his head.

She grabbed his neck and forced him to look at Egan, who was still bobbing, staring at his mangled arm.

"What does *time to join the flow* mean?" she asked. "What were you doing in that back room?"

"We were... I'm sorry." His eyes were dark pools, like a baby robin she was about to slaughter. She released his neck.

It was an act that she regretted immediately, because it was then that he bolted away, limping through the crowd.

It was a risk. They didn't have any cuffs, and they couldn't exactly hold him down. She took aim with her blaster, and had a clear shot, but she couldn't bring herself to do it. He was useless dead. Instead, she said, "Node three—paralyze target."

The perimeter node buzzing above them shot after the youth, and the crowd scattered below it. The youth turned down a tunnel and the node veered in behind him.

Her node messaged her on her comm. *Subject lost behind door.*

Dammit.

She could chase him, but she wasn't going to leave Egan and Anuvant alone. Who knew how many of the people around them were sympathetic to these Hock Pocket criminals?

She typed a response to the node droid. *Return to perimeter monitoring.*

The node droid returned. The crowd still stared, but shifted to a wider circumference.

Help did arrive, eventually. The other node droids had done their thing, tracking down the nearest medivac team, and the green-eyed woman did come back, with a mangy-looking hedonite doctor who tended to Egan. The woman appeared genuinely sad. She tried to comfort Egan, telling him it was going to be alright. Egan was breathing heavily, eyes wide, trying to stay conscious.

Neeva kept thinking, *Why does this woman care?* For some reason, it bothered her that the woman had come back, even more than it bothered her that she had lost the kid. This green-eyed woman didn't belong here. A hedonist stranger wasn't supposed to help them.

Neeva didn't thank her. She didn't even get her name.

They were placed on medivac carts and rolled away. Saline drips and other fluids filled their veins. A machine beeped, serenading her with stable health signals. Egan had his own cart, where three medical personnel worked on him. His machine was beeping frenetically.

Neeva finally put her blaster away and took her tacti device from her pocket. Her hand was sweaty and her palm raw from holding the blaster so tightly, so the tacti device felt unusual. It was difficult to control, rolling in every direction between her thumb and forefinger.

It was only when they were well away from the throngs of Skid-dado that her pulse finally slowed.

11

─────

THE ZEPHYR SPEAR

Training and simulations had to end eventually. The prisoners were sent here for a reason, and Hix had a job to do. You do your job or you get sent to the clam.

So, with thirty minutes to mission prep, he was sitting on his bunk, his daypack ready beside him. He had a tablet on his lap, and the cursor blinked at him. They were supposed to leave a note before they left—a message to a loved one, or something inspirational—but he was having trouble finding the words. The message would be opened on his media accounts in the event of his death.

He swiped out of the onscreen window, looking for a distraction. In his inbox was nothing but vacuous fan mail, and from weeks ago, the letter from the PDA outlining his sentencing.

There was a letter from Shawna's sister as well, lingering in his file folder next to his sentencing. He'd never opened it, perhaps out of anger, perhaps out of fear. Now, though, he wondered if there was something in it he should know before he left on his first mission. Maybe he could find some shadow of Shawna reflected in her sister's voice.

He hovered his finger over the message and the haptic sensor opened it.

Hix,

I never told you this when you were with Shawna, but I did see you in Sky
Gate *and* Toreno Run. *I have a thing for aircraft, and Shawna wanted me
to watch the vids. I suspect that's what they'll have you doing out there in
Earth orbit. Now you get the chance to be a real pilot.*

*You will miss your stunt men and makeup artists. You will miss the scene
breaks most of all.*

*I know you were lying to me, or at least holding something back. The
symbionts are rarely wrong, and the murder determination had a high
probability score. That's why you will get what you deserve out there. We
are thrusting you into the ultimate crucible of veracity. Scientific precision,
candid collaboration and intellectual integrity are all a necessity for
survival. So maybe if you have been truthful with me—if you are who you
say you are—you might survive, for a while.*

Either way, I will never forgive you.

Neeva Nash lineage 4a

It was all gullshit—psychanthropic mind control gobble-talk
served up by the reformer's limbic chattel, the symbionts. And the
fact that she signed it with her lineage number only made it worse. It
reeked of privilege, and conceit.

Neeva had made a show of listening to him during the investigation, but she was just like all the other reformers in the end; naïve
and pretentious. Maybe she just wanted to hear him grovel, so she
could put him in the right hedonite box in her mind.

He saw what she'd said about him on the news and that was
enough: "A sterner punishment could be warranted." It was typical of
high-lineage reformers to use their position to corrupt the process.

A note popped up on the screen. It read: *Zephyr Spear crew report
to hangar 4. Mission prep in 15 minutes.*

He sighed, and navigated back to the message prompt.

He didn't like this exercise, but knew he had to do it. "You may not like reformer games, but you have to play them," Mel had said, and she'd been right.

He tapped out a quick note. It read: *You did your best to help this Falcon soar, but it always had a broken wing.*

He submitted the message, placed the tablet in his locker, picked up his daypack, and left the bunk area.

The *Zephyr Spear* had a small crew.

First there was Captain Ordan, the old reformer woman with short peppered hair who had picked Hix out of the line of *Rackshack* prisoners. She wore a transparent facemask all the time, as if she couldn't stand being exposed to the same air as the hedonite scum around her. She was the primary pilot, and Hix was co-pilot.

In one of their pre-mission meetings, Hix had seen Ordan take a break and cut off to the side. She injected a substance in her arm, which Hix later saw a bottle lying in her open bag labeled as *Stesatryptanol*. He had seen a reformer film producer use it before. It was a new drug that was supposed to boost your immune system.

Sonders was the lanky reformer who had helped Ordan select the prisoners, and was second in command. He was a geologist, of a sort. Or at least, he knew a lot about the coring operations of the ship, so that's what Hix assumed.

Tolquist was the climatologist Hix had met on the *Rackshack*. Apparently this was something of a scarce resource, so he was treated with respect by Ordan and Sonders, even though he was a criminal just like Hix. Maybe it was because he was a *reformer* criminal. He sat next to Hix, but unlike Hix he had leads running up to the base of his skull at the back, and lights flickered on his temples. It was a cerebral cortivation link—an occipital lobe channel that connected to the ship's computer. It would provide a bandwidth increase on visible content, a sort of layman's version of the symbiont collective, allowing processing of digital signals several orders of magnitude beyond what untethered humans could manage. The real-time climate modeling he would be doing required a certain awareness and level of rapid computation afforded by the device.

Finally there was Nia, the broad-shouldered hedonite machinist Sonders and Ordan had picked out of the lineup in the hangar. Hix had only seen her a couple times on the station. She was usually off doing her own training with Sonders. She would be helping Sonders with the coring work in the bay of the *Zephyr Spear*.

The mission itself was a surface core extraction, a critical step in determining how orbital operations would deploy resources in Earth's atmosphere. These ground composition scouting missions would determine the optimal location for surface-to-stratosphere shunt towers to be built next to future mining operations. In turn, this would determine where any major dirigibles would have to be located atmospherically, because these dirigibles would be stationed close to the shunt tower peaks.

The *Zephyr Spear* was a sleek vessel, unlike the blocky habitat units, with flared, adjustable wings, and numerous positioning thrusters on both sides. It had high reliability ratings, at least for Venusian surface-to-atmosphere missions. The ship was much more versatile than the *Rensselaer* in *Toreno Run*, which he'd flown on Venus for three years while shooting the movie.

Unfortunately they weren't going to be flying on Venus today.

"Are you sure you don't want me to take the entry, Captain?" Hix asked through his helmet mic.

"I can handle it," Ordan responded, her gaze didn't waver from the command console. She certainly could. Entry was substantially automated, but the lower atmosphere would be another story.

The ship jolted free of its moorings and tilted down toward the planet. He could feel the G-forces increasing.

"Zephyr Spear is away," Ordan said.

Ordan was a mediocre pilot. She'd scored in the sixtieth percentile in the simulations. Hix had the impression she was more interested in command. She always stopped once she'd attained the required degree of scenario variance, whereas Hix kept going to test the limits of the simulation system—limits that were too easy to find. There weren't enough climate permutations. Nor were there enough core extraction protocol challenges. These simulations were like the psychanthropic reports of the symbionts. They were only as good as the data they were fed, and the available data on Earth's airstreams and climate were limited.

The viewport showed the crescent of Earth's upper atmosphere approaching. Beneath the ship an iridescent glow radiated outward from the arc, where clusters of mustard, russet and tan lurked, in places revolving together in blistering hurricanes.

The *Zephyr Spear*'s trajectory slipped two more degrees, and the nose started to redden, with fiery streaks shooting around it. Ordan engaged the heat shield, and it covered the viewport. Everyone on the bridge gazed at the display monitors.

"Sonders, is everything ready?" Ordan asked. "I want to be finished site one in less than half an hour."

Across the bridge, Sonders bobbed his helmet. "Yes, Captain. I've checked it twice, and reviewed the protocol with Nia several times. Timing will be primarily dependent on climate vectors. The mission variance parameters are ninety-two percent climate related." It sounded like he was passing the buck to Tolquist, but it was true. Sonders was one of those parrot reformers. He had to state the facts all the time, no matter how pretentious it made him sound.

The *Zephyr Spear* was shaking. They were securely fastened in their seats, but that didn't stop them from gripping the armrests tightly. Tolquist had his eyes closed, but the rest seemed alert and focused.

It didn't bode well for Tolquist. This was the easy part.

"Nearing mesosphere," Ordan said. Thrusters fired, adding a low grade rumble to the shaking vessel. G-forces increased, pushing Hix down in his seat.

Hix was checking their approach on his monitor, making sure they were on the right vector. Everything appeared to be in order.

The G-forces abated, and the heat shield retracted.

"Are we still good for site one?" Ordan asked.

"Confirmed," Tolquist said. His eyes were open again and he was tapping on his monitor. "It still has the best profile of the five." The cortivation nodes on his neck were flashing blue.

"Okay," Ordan said. "Speak up if anything changes. En route now." She tapped a button and the automatic guidance system kicked into gear, angling the ship deeper into the atmosphere so they could cut into banks of yellow clouds. Hix kept a close eye on the sensors. They were essentially flying blind except for radar. There was no reason to believe anything solid would be airborne, but the lack of visibility was disconcerting.

A rattling sound started up over his head, as if something was loose and about to fall. Strong bouts of turbulence would amplify the sound on occasion. He could be comforted by the fact that the outer skin of the *Zephyr Spear* was sheer, seamless metal. Something was certainly loose, but it was probably contained in the bulkhead above.

The ship jumped. Then it dropped. Hix tensed against the G-forces. The viewing portal remained a vortex of opaque yellow and brown-hued mists blowing past.

Eventually, the rattling stopped. Hix could see on his radar readout that the surface was approaching. The ship had entered the pocket of low turbulence Tolquist had identified, and was nearing the core extraction point.

"Okay, the coring target is below us," Ordan said. "Sonders and Nia, you're up. Keep us posted."

Sonders and Nia unstrapped their belts and went aft, leaving Tolquist, Hix and Ordan on the bridge.

Sonders offered the occasional update. "Tethers away. Tether one secure. Tension good. Tether two secure. Tether three secure. Tether four secure." The turbulence was low in the atmospheric pocket, and the *Zephyr Spear* was becoming increasingly stable with the ground tethers holding them in place. The occasional rumble hit the ship, but otherwise it was hard to tell the ship was even airborne.

"Drill one descending. Angle looks good. Drilling beginning.

Drill two descending. Drill three descending. All three drills in process."

"How will we know if the extraction is a success?" Hix asked.

Ordan frowned at him. She wouldn't like impromptu questions in the middle of the mission, especially from him.

Tolquist answered for her. "We will be able to know if we obtained the cores successfully, but we won't be able to determine the geological composition until we return to the station."

"Thanks," Hix said.

"Drill two blocked. Redirecting through cavitation."

"Drill one core extraction in process."

"Captain," Hix asked, "did you want me to take the run to the next core site?"

"No," Ordan responded. Ordan had always been curt with Hix, and reluctant to relieve the controls. She was obviously suspicious of him. It was fair, given his sentencing, but it was hard to tell if it was more than that—if it was just innate prejudice. He only hoped she would be able to realize her folly when they were in the more dangerous flying environments.

"All drills up," Sonders announced. "Core two partial, cores one and three full. Stowing cores and releasing tethers."

The ship gradually became more unsettled, and Nia and Sonders marched back up from below decks. Nia had beads of sweat on her brow.

"Ready," Nia said, her suit fastened.

Sonders followed suit. "Ready."

"And we're away," Ordan said. The ship lurched down, then pulled up. The next coring location was several hundred miles away, so it wouldn't be a long trip.

"Exiting atmospheric depression," Tolquist said. He was concentrating intently on his climate monitoring interface, the lights on his neck still blinking. The *Zephyr Spear* listed left and pulled up. They broke out of the opaque turmoil of dense vapor into a region with detached pockets of cloud that were lit up by the front beams. The ship would cut through a different cloudbank every few seconds.

The crew was quiet. These individual clouds were so thick that it was hard not to imagine they were about to hit something solid. Nothing was showing up on the radar, of course.

"How does the second core site look?" Ordan asked.

"It... it's actually degrading," Tolquist said. "More in line with the fourth core site, per original mission spec. We will need to modify our course, and fly closer to a restricted area."

Ordan said, "That's fine. We planned for worse. Let's get ready for chop."

It wasn't that bad at first. It felt a lot like atmospheric entry with a few more violent bumps thrown in, but when they reached the core site, it got worse. They were just settling over the target when a gust tilted the ship a good thirty degrees. Hix was worried they might completely flip, until Ordan grabbed the manual grips and righted the ship.

The ship began descending again, but another gust pushed up the other side of the craft. Hix grabbed his own manual grips, waiting for Ordan's ridiculous hubris to relinquish its hold.

Ordan kept working at it. She wasn't that bad. She anticipated the next gust, and managed to keep the nose down this time. "Okay. Sonders, Nia, go."

Nia unstrapped immediately but Sonders was hesitant.

"That's an order," Ordan said.

Sonders stood up and followed Nia down below decks.

"Looks like a squall coming in," Tolquist said. "Two hundred miles an hour. ETA... three minutes."

"Get those tethers down quick," Ordan said.

Hix's mind raced. The squall would be higher than sim parameters, and thus higher than known safety tolerances. If this had been a sim, this was the point it would shut off for lack of data.

"Ma'am, maybe you should allow me secondary control?" Hix asked.

"We're doing fine."

Shit.

It was going to get savage, and soon.

12

RECOVERY

Neeva was only in the hospital for a few hours. Her arm wasn't seriously injured, so the doc gave her basic pain meds and bandaged her up. Anuvant was with her the whole time. Granted, he was playing *Onslaught* on his tablet for much of it, but at least there was another warm body in the room.

Gorman came to visit her as well. He brought real flowers from the Enjo hydroponic farms. They were daffodils, full of color. His hair was combed and his uniform clean.

"I am so sorry about this," he said. "I feel remiss about this happening under my care here in SoPo. Please let me know what I can do to help."

"No need to apologize. It was more dangerous than we expected, but it's part of the job."

"Get some rest. Maybe take some time off with your girlfriend. When you return from NoPo, we should talk. I can give you guidance on local dangers like these."

How did he know about Celia? She was deliberately private about her orientation, at Grandpa's recommendation. For the same reason, she didn't want to ask Gorman how he knew. But she could still challenge his presumptuous statement.

"Why would I return to NoPo?" she asked.

Creases rippled along his brow. "Because you were just in a room where a bomb went off, and because your colleague almost died. Surely it makes sense to spend time recuperating—to have the right experts analyze the situation, and to wait for additional resources from the north."

"I don't want this to go cold. Whoever did this to us is organized enough to cover their tracks if we give them enough time."

He looked at her grimly. "I understand, fine—but please, Inspector, if you will at least listen to me on this one point." Gorman took a long breath. "No more reckless flights of fancy into Skiddado, of all places. You are endangering lives, and ruffling hedonite feathers that don't need to be ruffled."

"Noted," Neeva said, and she returned a modest nod.

He only frowned.

"Goodbye, Inspector Nash," he said, and he left, summarily ignoring Anuvant. At least he didn't take her one resource away, no matter how green he was.

After being discharged, she went to check on Egan, who was in a separate trauma unit. He was unconscious and, according to the doctors, would be for some time. His face was no longer the gray-green color she remembered from Skiddado, but the rest of him was hard to assess because his entire body was covered with bandages, except for his mangled arm, which was now missing. Neeva winced at the sight. They would give him a high-grade prosthetic, at least. The PDA Special Ops Enforcers took care of their people.

Again, she had that feeling. It wasn't so much wanting to quit; it was more a sense of failure, as if she'd missed some crucial clue. Anuvant's smile couldn't have been *that* revealing. Maybe it was that she kept underestimating the threat, and the animosity of the SoPo hedonites in general.

Or maybe she was on to something that people were taking great pains to cover up.

"What do we do now?" Anuvant asked as they stared at Egan's mummified form.

Anuvant didn't look distraught. He was just following along, wanting to know what happened next. Did he realize how close they had all come to dying?

"Honestly, I'm not sure. The SoPo inspectors sent a team of enforcers back to the Hock Pocket and found that the whole store had been pillaged and abandoned. Nobody is willing to identify the missing people and they probably all scattered across SoPo anyway. The only name we have is Jib's, but there are over a hundred Jibs in the SoPo database. It would take weeks to track them all down. So, besides a few debriefs on the incident, PDA has asked us to take some time off."

Anuvant's eyes darted back and forth in contemplation. "Are you going to do as they've asked?"

Neeva smiled at him, but it wasn't a witty smile, it was more in sadness, in recognition that life must go on. "Well, it wasn't an order, was it? I'll call you when I'm ready. That is, if you're up for it."

"Yes. I'd like to continue on," Anuvant said.

It was a trapping of youth, something she remembered in herself, from not too long ago. Anuvant was enthralled with the whole investigation; the novelty, and the excitement, perhaps even the danger. Eventually, with experience, and pain, the traction of these emotions would lessen.

"Anuvant, did you tell Gorman what happened to us in Skiddado?" she asked. "And did you let him know we were here, in the hospital?"

"No," he said. "I know that's not PDA protocol."

He didn't appear surprised, or defensive. It would be a grave infraction for a PDA operative to lie to her, so she believed him.

So how did Gorman know so much about her personal life, and where she was? There wasn't any media following her, and she hadn't found anything about the Hock Pocket incident on the local news feeds. He probably had someone trailing her.

She doubted it was foul play. Gorman's file was clean. In fact, he'd been in the PDA, a well regarded verdarist, and his pay at the mine was attractive. She suspected he had her followed, to ensure the investigation wasn't going to smear his good name. Many politicians and business leader reformers hired private investigators for this reason—as a kind of early warning system on bad news.

She barely cared. Let him watch, as long as he didn't interfere.

"Let's go home," she said to Anuvant.

The confines of the hotel room were what she meant by home, but it didn't feel welcoming. It was a spartan place, full of gray cushions, beige rugs, and blocky furniture. When she opened the heavy curtains, the constant spew of ash clouds on the horizon was mesmerizing, but not uplifting.

She could have taken the train back up north, despite what she'd told Gorman. Grandpa said it would take her mind off things. But that's not what she wanted. She wanted her mind to stay in the stream of evidence, to keep revisiting the events that had played out, even if it was uncomfortable. There was a lot to unpack and ruminate on, and her analysis couldn't be done with family distractions or by walking daintily through a biocrawler. Besides, it would take a whole day of travel in each direction.

"It's lonely here without you," Celia said. They had been talking by comm more often. When they did, Neeva would be floating around the room, occasionally catching glances of the spewing ash. This time she decided to lie down on the bed. She pulled out Zae's box from Eastborough and started playing with the pieces for the umpteenth time. It was a habit she'd taken to when she was idle.

"I'm sorry. I have to finish this," Neeva said.

"Aren't you worried? You could have died."

"Yes, and yes, but this is my job. I can't just cut and run at the first sign of trouble. Maybe I can figure out what's really going on here, and maybe save some lives instead of... "

Celia finished her sentence. "...endangering them?"

"Yeah." Neeva had been spinning the reflectors on the ground.

She tried the cups. When that proved uninteresting, she pulled the light fixture over for closer examination.

"Maybe it's just a big mess that you can't clean up," Celia said. "These are *heeds*, Neeva. I know you think everything is part of some big complex machine where everything is connected, but maybe it's not a machine that can be fixed. Or maybe it's just a trash receptacle full of hate."

It was possible. She could be chasing a bunch of false leads and coincidences. Her troubles could be the result of walking down blind alleys and talking to the wrong people.

"I have to do my job," was all she said.

Celia sighed, and was quiet for a moment.

Neeva could tell Celia was tiring of their conversations. "Tell me about your trip to the gardens," Neeva said. Celia always liked to tell her about her trips to the biocrawlers. She was a Verdarist through and through.

"Like what?"

"How are the new breeds coming along?"

"We've developed a cucumber plant that can hibernate for ten days at a time, but we can't extend it anywhere close to a whole star season, and we can't splice the hibernation sequence and apply it to other plants."

"That's still progress, right?"

"It's something, but we've been here before with other plants, and gotten nowhere."

"Did you do the night tour again?"

"Me and Rathy went. The best part is the beginning, before the solar panels first cover the ceiling of the crawler. The bluebells were the feature flower this time. They were purple up close, but together as a pattern in the field they looked like a sea of blue."

Speaking of bells, the light fixture in Neeva's hands had a kind of bell shape to it. A black cap topped six frosted panels lining the sides, and between them ornate calligraphy surrounded the black connectors. The wispy calligraphy ended in the shape of a leaf, much like she'd seen in some of the old First Colony artifacts and paintings.

Neeva remembered the frosted glass she'd seen in the boxes before the room exploded around her, and wondered if it might have been from a similar light fixture, disassembled in the room.

Celia was still describing her foray into the gardens. "Some of the flowers were drooping over, almost in a sad way, but I still love the shape of them. You can almost hear them. They're like big colorful horns, calling their beauty out into the meadow."

"That sounds incredible," Neeva said. "If you Verdarists can make musical flowers, you can make anything."

"Ha ha," Celia said in an acerbic tone.

Neeva was fiddling with the top of the fixture. With a hard turn, it came loose. Underneath was a bulbous light source fastened to a gold pin. She pulled off the bulb and noticed that the pin was attached to a black ovoid at the base of the lamp. The ovoid must channel the power through to the lamp bulbs, but where did the power come from?

Celia said, "When the solar panels finish casting their shadows, the darkness is sort of romantic at first, but then, honestly it just gets kind of boring, especially without someone to share it with."

"I'll share it with you, when I get back."

"Which will be..."

"When I'm finished. What's Rathy up to nowadays?"

"Oh, she's really into these new interactive vids. She knows way too much about her favorite heed stars. She even wants to go to the premiere of *Blue Verdara*. I think she might be getting a little obsessive. I did remind her of what happened to Shawna." She paused. "Sorry, I shouldn't have mentioned that."

"No need to apologize," Neeva said, "but yeah, I hope she knows enough to stay away." She had been rolling the ovoid over in her hand. There didn't appear to be any way to open it up. She couldn't even find a seam. Then she remembered the room near the Hock Pocket. The tables were lined with similar ovoids. They had to be power sources of some kind.

"It won't matter, though," Celia continued. "Rathy won't stay away.

She says she will, but when she's watching the vids she gets that baby sparrow look—"

There was a crash as Neeva inadvertently knocked the light fixture top onto the ground. She'd been forcefully trying to open the ovoid, despite the fact that there was no visible joint, and her hand had slipped.

"Sorry, Celia. I just knocked something—"

"I could hear you the whole time," Celia said, "fiddling away. It's okay, let's talk later."

She hung up.

Eventually, Neeva did feel like she needed a break, or at least a distraction. Unfortunately, there wasn't much to do near Enjo that didn't involve being in public with lots of hedonites, and that was something she wanted to avoid. She might have made some enemies in Skiddado. People could be out to get her.

Maybe she was being paranoid, but either way, she decided to book a tour of the major dirigible. She took the premium package because she could afford it, but also to be sure there weren't any hedonites participating.

Bam Jam dropped her off at the windblown landing site close to the main fusion reactor entrance. It was star season so it was dark outside, the sky filled with constellations.

Before he left, Bam Jam said, "Hey, remember what I said. If you're lonely..."

"I'll remember that. Thank you." She sometimes wondered how people couldn't tell she was a lesbian. Or maybe he thought she was so lonely it wouldn't matter. She could use some company, but she wasn't *that* desperate.

She passed through a rectangular glass door over which hung a huge vaulted slab of metal on parabolic hinges. Inside was a lobby with chairs, and a place to stow climate gear. She took off her face-mask and strapped it to a hook.

Soon after, she was met by her guide—a fit-but-elderly reformer woman with curly gray hair. "I'm Wyneth Valonair, lineage 13b," she said. "You must be Neeva. Are you ready?"

"Shouldn't we wait for the other participants?"

"You're it," Wyneth grinned. "We don't give many premium tours. This is only my second one this year, in fact. Shall we?" She gestured away from the lobby.

Neeva followed Wyneth into the complex. It opened into a large chamber adjoined by several corridors. The ceiling must have been at least thirty feet high. It was hard to believe she was actually on a gigantic airship that used to float high above the ground. A few offi-cial-looking hedonites and reformers crossed their path, some walking purposefully, some buzzing around in carts. To her right Neeva saw a slatted gate watched by two Egan-sized guards.

"As you probably know," Wyneth began, "this major dirigible still has a working fusion reactor. It supplies about a quarter of the energy to SoPo, as well as ten percent of the longitudinal power conduits."

"I didn't know all that, actually. Are we going to see the fusion reactor?"

"No, I'm sorry. Even with a premium tour we aren't allowed to enter the power facility. It's under the jurisdiction of the symbiont collective, and we would need special privileges to enter. But don't worry, from what I hear all you can see are flashing lights, diagrams and bundles of wires. The exterior of the main containment field isn't visible to the naked eye."

"I understand," Neeva said. She suspected that would be the case. The fusion reactors were all run exclusively by the symbionts since they were the only ones with the cognitive dexterity to balance the internal magnetosphere. Thankfully, the symbionts were also smart enough to know there should be limited access to their facilities.

Wyneth escorted her through more high-ceilinged hallways, away from the power facility infrastructure. She set an energetic pace and was generous with her smile.

They were walking along the port side of the dirigible. A great glass wall arched upward on Neeva's left, several times her height, allowing her to look out onto the Venusian landscape in the direction of her hotel. The glass needed to be cleaned on the outside—it was partially covered in striations of magnesite, basalt and ash—but the sheer size of the curved bay window was still impressive.

"When they had the choice," Wyneth said, "the First Colony engineers used soft curvature in their designs over orthogonal lines. It was a byproduct of being an airborne society. Everything needed to float and be aerodynamic."

The glass soon fell away into a seamless white wall. Wyneth took her along what had at one time been a moving walkway, but was now defunct. There were recesses and doors on either side of them, but they were all roped off with thick fluorescent wire.

They entered a huge hangar. An old standard dirigible was docked inside. It appeared to be a weathered factoroid—the kind they used for exterior maintenance. It was blocky-looking with a number of arms lining the side. Beyond the dirigible, large, rounded hatches protruded from the far wall, each with a heavy metal door on the front.

"This is where raw magnesium composites were received from orbit, processed, and sent out in minor dirigibles for bombardment of the atmosphere, a process that continued for about three hundred years. It also acted as one of the eight hangar bays for a variety of other uses. You can see that along the far wall there is an arm for manipulating aircraft, construction and repairs." The arm was a composite of thick metallic rods. It had at least four degrees of freedom, and at each junction hinges folded in together to pack the arm neatly into an inset of the wall.

"Where did they dock with the shunt tower?" Neeva asked.

"That's on the other side of the dirigible. It's a specialized junction that minimizes the impact of any torque from the shunt, and allows the dirigible to easily share atmosphere with the tower."

"I see."

They left the hangar and walked toward the interior of the ship, where they passed through bunk rooms and eating areas. These rooms didn't appear to be much different than what you would see in the interior of First Colony homes in Lakshmi Central. The tour organizers had placed statues of happy children in one of the "teaching rooms". They were configured to be playing with a model of a lush Verdara scene, with bright smiles on their faces.

Wyneth said, "Most people who lived on the major dirigible spent their lives in tight quarters, but they would rotate through more spacious abodes on occasion. Great care was taken to make sure hedonites and reformers had the same rights to living space, as well as food and clothing."

"Why don't they open up the major dirigible for housing? It looks like there's enough space for a small settlement here."

Wyneth forced a smile. "It would cause too much wear and tear. The First Colony Heritage Society wanted to keep it preserved for as long as possible. And there are safety reasons as well. The inhabitants would be quite close to the fusion power facility."

Neeva suppressed a frown. The reasons had some validity, but they seemed shallow. If the First Colony people could live in the upper atmosphere on the major dirigible for hundreds of years, why not now, when it was on the surface? She suspected it had more to do with not allowing hedonites to tamper with First Colony artifacts. And of course they couldn't allow reformers to settle on the major dirigible without hedonites—the optics would be bad.

"How old is this major?" Neeva asked.

"We don't know, exactly. After the Cessation we lost most of the First Colony records. We can be sure this vessel was used for magnesium bombardment, which took place between three hundred to six hundred years ago, but it's possible it was refurbished after hydrogen bombardment—one of the earliest phases of terraforming. So in theory it should be over six hundred years old."

"How do you know how the hedonites were treated, if these records were lost in the Cessation?"

It could have been perceived as a snarky comment, but Wyneth absorbed it with an easy smile. "We do have some written records from the late Magnesite Bombardment Era, preserved by the Keeper Complex on Telliac Mountain. Mostly diaries and letters."

Neeva wondered if Grandpa had read these diaries and letters Wyneth was referring to. He would probably have enjoyed this tour, even if he already knew everything. In fact, it made her feel a little less lonely, thinking about Grandpa, as if he was there with her, asking questions with a sharp tongue and gazing at the ancient artifacts with his fiery eyes.

They navigated through hallways and chambers that were fairly innocuous, including lavatories, food stores, and defunct greenhouses. There wasn't anything that was different from what you might see in Samar City, or Lakshmi Central, until they reached the control bridge.

The entrance featured harsh cut marks in the thick walls, perhaps where the hallway had been broadened, and some atmospheric sealant scoured away. The bridge itself was two stacked arcs of chairs and terminals, one of them floating in the air on thick supports that strutted out from the main hull. Facing them was a wide expanse of glass with a jagged fissure tripping down the right side, as if the glass had split open and was later repaired.

Wyneth followed her eyes and pointed at the fissure. "The main viewport was cracked during landing. Except for this crack, and some damage on the starboard side, the whole dirigible is almost fully intact, a testament to First Colony engineers." She gestured to the topmost arc of chairs. "The main officers would be stationed on the upper balcony, so they could see out the viewport window but also watch over the rest of the crew below them."

Another fluorescent wire prevented them from walking about the bridge. Wyneth unclipped it and gestured for Neeva to enter. "The premium tour has its privileges," she said.

Neeva walked carefully along the balcony of the top arc, circling one of the raised command chairs. There were a number of panels laden with buttons, and the chair looked comfortable, but it was covered in dust. The premium tour did have its privileges, but apparently clean seats weren't one of them. Of course, if there really were only a few premium tours each year, she couldn't blame the museum for not maintaining it.

Neeva walked down the ramp leading to the lower arc of chairs. The armrests were curvilinear and even the seats weren't square but rather ovals. They were pushed up against a blue display panel.

It made her imagine Hix on his joyride with Shawna. Hix hadn't been in a major, but the chair, display and curved glass would look similar in the smaller airships. She could almost feel Hix there, sitting in front of her, with Shawna on his lap, laughing as they headed toward the vapor meteor storm.

At least Shawna was happy during the last few minutes of her life.

Neeva turned away and closed her eyes, trying to extinguish the image.

"Are you alright?" Wyneth asked.

"Yes, fine, thank you. Did they have video surveillance of the bridge?"

"Yes, they had cameras everywhere. If you look there, in the bulkhead of the upper balcony, in those black shiny nodules."

Neeva saw what she meant. They were very discreet, almost decorative.

"Do they still work?" she asked, remembering that the inspection team was only able to collect limited footage from the dirigible Hix had commandeered.

"Remarkably, yes. Almost all the cameras on the major dirigible still function. Like I said, the First Colony engineers were—"

"Would they be the same on the other dirigibles? The ones still in operation."

"They should be, although some are older than others."

Neeva had asked a number of dirigible engineers and air traffic control officials why the cameras on the dirigible Hix had commandeered hadn't worked. She always received the same response; that it was hundreds of years old and nothing lasts forever. She wondered if she should have probed further, or investigated the people who were giving her this facile answer more thoroughly.

Wyneth was waiting patiently, her hands hung together in a cribbed fashion, while Neeva noodled. She would look into this later.

"So what's next?" Neeva asked.

"Oh, I think you'll like it. It's really quite fascinating."

They left the bridge and Wyneth escorted Neeva to the starboard side. Here, a number of corridors were barricaded off with *Danger* signs posted on them.

"The major dirigible first hit ground on the side we're on now," Wyneth said. "Some of these corridors lead to rooms that have been crushed inward, and others we had to block off because they became exposed to the atmosphere."

Eventually they reached a broad set of double doors labeled *The Old City*. Inside was a cavernous hall with buildings, vehicles and trees reaching several city blocks into the distance. A walkway extended over the scene, allowing Wyneth and Neeva to view it from above.

This wasn't an ordinary town you would see on Venus, or even a historical First Colony metropolis like Samar City. Many of the buildings were made of stacked red blocks and white-silled windows. The ground was made of what looked like gray and black stone instead of the usual rubber composite. Blocky, fully-enclosed vehicles were scattered about, in a variety of different colors, and then there were the large trees. These weren't like the philodendrons, dracaena, or palms that frequented common spaces on Venus, but more like the robust sun-thirsty trees you would see in a biocrawler. They were surely fake, but still impressive. There was a grassy area with a pond as well, just off of a main road.

In the distance, a large bay window revealed the outside of the dirigible, but based on the visible cracks in the glass, it was clear the window had been destroyed and rebuilt. The farthest buildings were rubble, or crunched together, no doubt the result of the impact Wyneth had referred to.

"We believe this is a replica of a city from the original home of the First Colony people," Wyneth explained, "possibly from Mars. The

First Colony people wanted to preserve a memory of their original home."

"A museum inside a museum."

"Precisely."

Neeva wondered if Wyneth knew the truth—that the original city wasn't from Mars, but rather from Earth, before the hedonites destroyed it. Wyneth's lineage was in the teens, so she may have privileged information.

She looked into Wyneth's eyes, and her grinning face, and could see no deception, no discomfort. No, reformers didn't lie, not on purpose. She must not know. There were rumors and stories, but no one believed them. Only the Keepers knew, and Neeva, and a few others.

They arrived at a bank of monitors at the end of the walkway. Here, Neeva could see different vantages in the city: the park, an intersection, a long building with arched doorways, and even a beach that she hadn't seen from the walkway. She toggled control arrows to move the cameras around while Wyneth waited patiently.

When Neeva had seen enough, she walked back over the bridge, trying to establish her bearings relative to where she had been looking on the vid screen display. She could see the park nearby. There were trees, and also a few lamps posted about, but nowhere else where cameras could have been placed.

She stopped in her tracks.

"Can I go into the city?" she asked.

Wyneth paused. "I'm sorry, but we don't typically—"

"Only for a minute, I promise. This is the premium tour, isn't it?"

"Yes, but..." Wyneth looked around, as if someone might be watching. "Only for a minute. I'll show you the way."

Wyneth escorted her along the remaining expanse of the walkway. They moved through a secure door with a pin code entry interface, down a dusty old spiral staircase, and into the city proper.

Neeva headed straight for the park, while Wyneth rushed to keep up.

"Please don't step on the grass," she called behind her.

"Of course," Neeva said. She kept to the path and walked up to one of the lampposts. Now that she was closer she could see that it did indeed look identical to the one she had obtained from Zae Samar-Nia.

"Are these lamps new?" she asked.

Wyneth let out a brittle laugh. "No, but you may be familiar with them. They are still used all over SoPo, because so many remain from before the Cessation, and because they have a certain beauty that is endemic to the—"

"What do you mean *they are used*? These actual First Colony lamps are still functioning?"

"Yes. I'm sure there are some replicas, but why bother when there are so many working ones left, and they never seem to break?"

"Are there cameras in them? Is that how I can see the park area from the walkway?"

Wyneth raised her eyebrows. "You are very perceptive. Yes, similar to the bridge, they are in those black rounded orbs."

Neeva looked up and saw the rounded ball poking out of the bottom.

Wyneth said, "Remarkably, these lamps have their own power sources that can be given a ten-year charge."

"The power sources, are they little black ovoids?"

Wyneth's eyes widened. "Why yes, are you an energy tech?"

"No."

Neeva's heart was beating faster. She knew she was on to something, even though she hadn't quite pulled it all together. "I need to leave immediately," she said. "What's the fastest way out?"

"Oh. Of course." Wyneth began leading her back to the spiral stairs. "Please follow me. Is there something wrong?"

"No. Well, yes, actually, but it's none of your concern. I'm feeling unsettled."

Wyneth only nodded, and obliged by moving at a faster clip. Neeva didn't speak to her much the rest of the way out.

Nor did she speak to Bam Jam. She avoided his leery smile and baiting words as best she could. Her mind was still in turmoil, churning through a list of things that Gorman had said to her—what he knew, and what she'd told him.

By the time she'd made it back to the sanctity of her hotel room, her mind had settled, but not on anything good.

She stared out at the mountain spewing ash, and then at the source of her misgivings—the box containing the lamp.

Her mind was forming more connections. With each new one, another could be made, and another. Some of it was conjecture, the result of a paranoid mind, but not all of it. Some of it had to be true.

Now she knew why all these old First Colony lamps had been taken from the scene of the riot in the Eastborough settlement. They all contained durable cameras, and they were being brought back to the Hock Pocket and sold for an unusually high price, where they were being disassembled in the room in the back, by a group of highly organized, armed hedonites.

But that was just the beginning.

These were *working* cameras that were *transmitting*. How did she know? Because Gorman had been spying on her. There was no other way he could have known all the details about the foray into the back of the Hock Pocket, or even that Neeva was in the hospital. Yes, he could have had her followed, but he'd also mentioned Celia. Very few people in the PDA knew she was a lesbian, never mind the fact that she had a girlfriend. And there was no way he could have tapped into her comm. He had her under surveillance—through the lamp that came from Zae Samar-Nia.

He told her he had no camera footage, but she suspected he had plenty.

Gorman—a credentialed NoPo reformer—had been *lying* to her. He'd been watching the hedonite settlements, and now her. Who knew where else he'd been watching, and who knew what else he'd been lying about?

These lies, on their own, were serious crimes for a reformer citizen. Gorman himself had said that it was illegal to watch the settlements in SoPo, and yet that was what he had been doing. But no, this was worse. He must have footage of the riot, and much more. He had withheld this evidence from the SoPo inspectors, and now Neeva, which meant he was almost certainly in league with this criminal hedonite group. This was an act of high treason, by PDA standards. It was even possible Gorman had contributed to Neeva's near-demise at the Hock Pocket.

It was bad, but even worse than all this was the *why*. Gorman was well-respected, had a family, and a good job. There didn't seem to be any profit motive, and he didn't seem the type to do this on a whim. So it had to be ideological, or some kind of insanity. Or maybe he was being blackmailed. Furthermore, to manage the cameras and keep their use a secret would require a widespread network. Neeva couldn't know exactly how wide, but wide enough to know one thing for sure.

As soon as she exposed Gorman, her life would be in grave danger.

13

THE SQUALL

"Tether one down," Sonders announced from the aft bay.

"Ma'am, I think we should abort," Hix said. "The squall changes things."

"Let's get it done," Ordan said.

"Tether two down and secure," Sonders said.

"Even with the tethers," Hix said, "we might not—"

"Enough!" Ordan barked, "I'm not going to release control to some hedonite wannabe flyboy."

"Tether three down and secure," Sonders said.

Ordan wasn't finished. "And how dare you question—"

The squall hit. The whole ship tilted radically to the side.

"Fuuuaaahh," Nia hollered into her mic.

"Ma'am, the tethers, they're..." Sonders trailed off.

The ship lurched higher. "Tether three dislodged," Nia yelled.

"Ma'am," Hix said, "We *must* abort."

The ship lurched again. Nia said, "Tether two has snapped!" and the whole ship started spinning. The one remaining tether was pinning them to the ground and the squall was pushing them in a circle like the blade of a wind turbine turning faster and faster.

And with each turn, the centrifugal force was getting stronger.

Hix felt dizzy. He was reaching desperately for the control overrides. Ordan was plastered back in her chair, passed out, but Tolquist was conscious. "Help," was all he managed to say. He tapped something on his screen.

An icon flashed green on Hix's control display. Tolquist had given him secondary flight command. It must have automatically passed to Tolquist when Ordan lost consciousness.

Before Hix could do anything, he tried to contain the surge of nausea climbing up his throat. *Not now*, he told himself. He reached out for the controls, slowly, deliberately, and with all his strength. He activated the thrusters to counter the spin.

It helped. The force lessened, but it was still over three Gs.

"Can you remove the tether?" Hix asked no one in particular.

Nia croaked out an answer. "Broken."

Apparently not broken enough. Hix was able to think more clearly now, and an idea sprang to mind. He began angling the ship down. It was still spinning, but its rotation was slowing as they neared the surface.

"What are you..." Tolquist said, but he soon figured it out. "Below two hundred feet," he said. "That's where the squall should lessen. But be careful. There's more volatility the closer we get."

It worked. Hix was able to stop the spin completely, but he had to keep his full attention on the controls, flicking thrusters on and off in quick succession to stop the wings on each side from tilting in every direction.

Hix said, "I need that tether removed, Nia."

"Not sure how," she responded. "The force of the spin bent the release grips into the ship panel and they're not working. Sonders is out cold."

"Can you use the arm, and the N16 charges?"

There was quiet for a time. Then Nia said, "Maybe. I need access."

Tolquist tapped something on his display. His face had been flushed only a moment ago. Now it had gone pale.

"Got it," Nia said.

"What are you doing?" Tolquist asked.

Hix said, "We're going to lay explosives near the tether site, to blow apart the rock we're anchored to."

Tolquist's eyes widened, but he offered no objection. He started whispering to himself. "Float me on your river of fire, into the heart of you."

Hix recognized it. It was an old pyrolyte chant, which sounded odd coming from a buttery reformer like Tolquist.

"Okay," Nia said. "I've placed one charge on each side of the ground tether. You'll need to detonate them on my mark. Be ready. We'll come away quick."

"Check."

"Mark one." The craft shook underneath them.

"Mark two." The craft shook again and the G-forces changed dramatically.

"Hix, Hix, HIX!" Tolquist cried.

Hix didn't need to be alerted. They were being blown toward a rock massif now that the tether tension had released. He spun the craft one hundred and eight degrees, angled up and blasted aft thrusters at full burn, barely averting a collision with the massif.

There was quiet as they pulled away. The G-forces were strong, but nothing compared to what they had just endured in the spin. Hix was still concentrating on maintaining control as he navigated blasts from the squall. He could hear Tolquist tapping away on his own console.

Tolquist said, "Head to latitude 42.17 north, longitude 85.43 west. That's the best I can do for a good ascent vector."

"On my way," Hix said. His heartbeat was finally beginning to slow.

Nia said, "Well, we got our core sample."

Indeed. They were hauling a large chunk of rock that was still stuck to the tether. It whipped around, below and behind the ship, requiring Hix to make frequent manual thruster corrections to compensate for the drag. Autopilot would be useless with the foreign object attached to the trailing tether.

He was pretty sure this wasn't in the sims either.

They were gaining altitude steadily, approaching the new ascent vector. The storm bullied them with the occasional blast of wind, tilting them in fits and starts.

As the ship struck upward, his console display remained a morass of alerts, including messages for the three broken tethers, and his flagrant near-miss on the ground. Also, health status alarms were chiming regularly for Sonders and Ordan, who were both still unconscious. Their vitals were stable, though. They would live.

Tolquist closed his eyes. His lips were moving, as if he was performing some kind of internal communion. Despite their stoic nature, many reformers had hidden spirituality that would come out in times of duress. It was something Hix could appreciate, but not because it made the reformers seem less vicious and calculating. No, it was something he could exploit.

"We were lucky," he said to Tolquist.

Tolquist opened his eyes and nodded.

"But we're slated for at least twenty more core sampling missions, and then what?"

"Well... once we identify the atmospheric shunt tower locations, there will be the surface missions to prep the shunt tower installation."

"How many?"

"I don't know, hundreds, maybe thousands. What are you getting at?"

"There's too much space on the station, Tolquist."

"What do you mean?"

"I mean there used to be way more people there—both hedonites and reformers. They come every month or so, a new shipment, but how many return?"

"They don't tell us that. I'm sure those that have served their tour go home, along with those that have finished their sentence."

"Do you know of anyone who has returned to Venus?"

"Well, no, but I just arrived. I don't think—"

"The station is too old, Tolquist. What is it, a hundred years, *two hundred*? Just look at the scuff marks on the unused rings that are no longer serviced. What happened to them? Why are we still doing the same work they were doing?"

"As Captain Ordan said, they've made a lot of progress on the dirigibles, and scoping the surface remotely, but they had to cut back on operations due to budgetary constraints."

"That's all true, I'm sure, but how long do you think they've been doing coring missions? Five years, ten years, *fifty* years?"

Tolquist scoffed. "Fifty years? Come now, I don't think—"

"You saw the ship manifest from Sonders. This is not the *Zephyr Spear*, this is *Zephyr Spear 57*. I thought it might have been a serial number, but it was too short for that. No, we're in the 57th *Zephyr Spear*."

Tolquist's head receded into his helmet, his brow a skeptical frown.

"Then there is our illustrious Captain." Hix nudged his helmet over at Ordan's slouched form. "You must have seen her taking her meds. It's called Stesatryptanol. Reformers use it as preventive medicine, to avoid viruses, but it's also used for a terminal immunodeficiency disease. That's why she wears the mask."

"So?"

"So she doesn't care about living or dying, because she already has one foot in the clam."

Tolquist winced, then shrugged. He understood the point Hix was making. Or maybe he already knew and was arguing for the sake of it. Maybe there was some regular reformer powwow on Kanto Station where they shared this information while eating quail eggs and drinking spritzers.

Nia was listening in. She said, "What're you saying, Hix?" She didn't quite get it. Or maybe she wanted it to be said explicitly.

"I'm saying we were all sent here to die."

PART II

HERITAGE

Excerpt from Durrah's Proclamation.
Reformer Doctrine. Post-Cessation Revision
First Colony History Curriculum P. 173
Source: Tablet Download. Found on Major Dirigible 5A, year 765 AVL

****

Civil unrest on Mars was believed to be caused by an ineffective electoral process, and the odds of First Colony mission success were considered low, so difficult decisions needed to be made to improve Venus mission parameters.

The First Colony council, led by Commissioner Durrah and with the support of the symbiont collective, assessed the genetic profiles of those people deemed to have a negative influence on productivity. Behaviors associated with these genetic profiles included a predisposition for mental instability, hedonism, gullibility, dishonesty, and analytical nonperformance. For societal betterment, and to maximize the probability that Verdara could be achieved, people fitting this profile (colloquially named "hedonites") were excluded from executive First Colony positions and later, also had voting rights withdrawn.

Reproductive rights for hedonites would be maintained as a moral imperative, although offspring of one or more hedonites would also be considered hedonites from the date of Durrah's Proclamation onward.

Hedonites continue to be valued members of society, with important labor, service and cultural contributions, but without any deleterious influence on effective governance.

****

14
———

A MEETING REQUEST

Grandpa still had his former office on the First Colony Heritage Society premises, in one of the north-facing leaves of the fern. Although *former* may have been a misnomer, because he was there more often than not, even in retirement. This was where Neeva was heading.

The entire lift access area of the emporium was under heavy security. Neeva's retina was scanned when she first exited the train stop, and also before the shunt tower lifts. The door to the upper level executive suites were guarded by two heavily-armored PDA enforcers that were a good eighteen inches taller than Neeva. They wore helmets with orange-tinted visors, and didn't say a word as Grandpa buzzed her in.

She walked through the open-concept cubicles made up of frosted partitions surrounding impersonal work spaces. It was star season outside so it was dark, but floor lights pulsed in front of her, leading her through the maze. Grandpa was brooding under a desk lamp in his office. His eyes were closed and nodes flickered on the back of his neck. He had his cerebral cortivation link running to expedite his consumption of visible content on his tablet.

The flickering lights ceased and he opened his eyes, smiling. He rose to greet her. "It's so nice to see you," he said.

"You too, Grandpa."

He looked like a different person when he came in to work. His hair was slicked back, and he was wearing a tight gray two-piece uniform. It was quite dapper and conservative compared to her aquamarine inspector uniform.

"You've been busy," he said, lowering himself into his chair. A hint of a smile tugged at the corner of his mouth. Was it pride, or mirth? It was hard to say.

She took a seat across from him. "Yes. Thanks for seeing me. A lot has happened."

He nodded. "Are you finally taking a break? Why did you come all the way north?"

"I'm not taking a break. I came back to see you."

He frowned. "Is that what this urgent message is about?" He looked down and swiped on his tablet. The screen cast a red pall on his gray uniform. "Why couldn't you just send me the details via regular PDA channels?"

Neeva stood up, closed the door, and returned to her chair. "Is your tablet completely secure?" she asked. "No monitoring, psychographic or otherwise?"

"Yes, of course," he said.

She took out her own tablet and sent him the encrypted tight-beam message she'd prepared. He gazed at his display, unlocked the message, and began reading her detailed report. His chair rotated around slowly until he was facing the window.

The office looked down onto the eastern part of LC. This leaf was higher up than the parade of towers stretching out before it. In the distance, the Maxwell Montes chain reached up into the sky. In star season it was just a huge monolith of black, save the anti-collision strobes pulsing around the uppermost peaks, and the clot of lights concentrating high up at the psychanthropic facility on Harriet Shelf. Shuttle copters—mostly X92s, but also elongated T44 rotary copters —floated about, pulsing red, blue and green beacons of their own.

Like fireflies, Celia would have said.

Neeva tired of examining the cityscape. Her tacti device was in her pocket, but she forced herself not to play with it. Instead, she slid her finger over the rubber arm of her chair, and pressed up and down on it to feel its rigidity. Grandpa would berate her for fidgeting, so she stopped when he turned his chair around again. His eyebrows were raised, and his expression was grave. "You were right to be careful with this," he said.

"I want a meeting with the symbionts," she said. "I need to better understand Gorman's motivations—the motives of all the players, actually."

"No," Grandpa said. "You can't just hand it over to the symbionts. This is your responsibility, and you have to finish it, no matter how prickly. This level of treachery by a reformer as high up as Gorman is not to be underestimated, and the situation is too delicate in SoPo already. You should take this to the Executive Council immediately. They need to know."

She'd had a lot of time to think through options on the train ride north, and she'd also contemplated what Grandpa's opinion might be. This response was one of the scenarios she'd envisioned, and while she often bent to Grandpa's will, she told herself she was going to hold firm this time. "There are ten people on the council, plus their individual recorders. That's twenty people."

"So?"

"It's too many. I'm a PDA inspector, and I've ascertained that respected reformer citizens are not only lying, but are involved in a conspiracy. I can't rule out the possibility that there are others, possibly even at the higher levels of governance."

Grandpa's eyes opened wide. "You think *Executive Council* members could be traitors? Who could possibly... Neeva, this is silly. It's the antithesis of who they are."

"The same could be said about Gorman."

Grandpa glanced at his tablet. "He's just a normal citizen."

"He was in planetary defense for three years. He was also a Verdarist for five. That's far from typical."

Grandpa frowned and swiped down on his screen. "The Executive Council members are responsible, duly elected leaders. Gorman volunteered for his post—probably for the SoPo relocation pay."

She held firm, her mouth a straight line. "I would like a meeting with the symbionts, and I can't do it without your help."

"And what about the symbionts? How is that better than the Executive Council? You'll be connected to a thousand minds *and* their subordinate recorders."

"I want a private meeting with one symbiont, for sequestered feedback."

"Sequestered? You know how they hate being disconnected from the collective. It's extremely arduous for them to set up the necessary firewalls and security protocols. They'll be whining about it for years."

"I think the situation is serious enough—and sensitive enough—to justify it."

Grandpa frowned. He stood up from his chair and stared out the window. He wasn't used to her arguing with him. She could tell it irked him.

After a moment spent in thrall to the view, he returned to his seat and leaned back in his chair, adopting a relaxed composure. Neeva thought he was going to flat out say no, but he said something else entirely.

"There have been two other settlements that have been cleared in SoPo. Whole hedonite communities, just like Eastborough 13, vanished. One was a manufacturing center in Dione, and another was a suburban outskirt of Samar City, not too far away from the altercation you were involved in. At first we suspected this was just some hedonite fad—to cut and run from trouble—but your report suggests it could be something else. It could be that Gorman, or someone like him, is influencing these communities, and causing these migrations."

"Were there any inciting incidents at these other communities?"

He shook his head. "Yes, but nothing extreme, and nothing that warranted an evacuation. One was a theft at a Multimat, and the other didn't involve any kind of crime. They held a communal rally, and they were gone. But the disappearing isn't the problem, it's *where they're going.* The three settlements altogether are over two thousand hedonites. Some of them surely found another home, like this Zae woman in your report, but others..." He threw his hands up in the air.

"Thanks for the info," she said. "It only reinforces my argument that this could be a broader criminal sect, and thus sequestered feedback should be justified."

He snorted. "I knew that wouldn't change your mind, but there's something more you should know. I've wanted to tell you for a while now. If you're going to be a Keeper, it's important that you begin to understand our history, so that you can protect our future."

Every time she met with him it was there, this trove of information Grandpa protected. The knowledge was like a long shadow, looming over him. But was he going to spoonfeed her some unimportant trivia, or tell her something of substance for once?

"I'm all ears," she said.

He sighed. "During the Cessation, a lot of people were hurt. You've seen the statistics; thousands dead, diminished energy capacity, billions of exabytes of data lost, the Verdara delayed for hundreds of years. The common understanding is that it was caused by the viral blackout—that it was an attack, deliberate or not, by Martian machine tech which systematically corrupted all of our Mecha-AIs. Our dependency on the Mecha-AIs caused chaos, until the Planetary Defense Agency was founded and we were able to decommission the Mecha-AIs and enlist the symbionts to put us back on the right path."

"Are you saying that's not true?"

"Oh, it's all true, as far as I know. We are reformers after all, so truth is sacrosanct, but... there's more, because some truths are too dangerous to tell. What's not explained is that much of the damage during the Cessation was caused by a hedonite insurgency, one that capitalized on the disorder to fight back against what the hedonites perceived to be unfair discrimination."

Neeva had heard about skirmishes between hedonites and

reformer factions during the Cessation, but this sounded like something bigger.

"Tens of thousands of reformers were kidnapped," Grandpa explained. "Most of these were killed. Whole reformer communities were tied up along the major power conduits to suffocate, blister and die."

She was shocked into silence for a moment. He had his palms facing her in a gesture of calm, anticipating her reaction.

"Tens of thousands?" she exclaimed. "But... how?"

"It was a time of chaos, remember. In fact it's hard to imagine. Everything shut down when the Mecha-AI systems failed. Food distribution and sanitation systems all went awry. Only the primary rail lines worked, and the few manually controlled transport copters. But along with all that, major security systems failed. You've seen the thousands of mobile droids in the reclamation warehouses—some of those were enforcer drones, and they all stopped working. Areas where hedonites were once forbidden were open to explore, or pillage, as the case may be."

"Okay, but why are you telling me this? With symbiont oversight, everything has been made impervious to Martian intervention. We have a broad distribution of PDA security planetwide, and hedonites aren't given access to the network. Surely you don't think anything like the Cessation is possible again."

His contemplative expression didn't give her much comfort. He said, "There were three hedonite groups that became organized during the Cessation: the Hedonite Protectors, the SoPo League, and Mantle. These were cults, of course," his nose wrinkled as if he smelled something rotten, "but their followers were loyal, and ruthless. They had mission statements, and oaths, and rights of initiation. Many of the perpetrators weren't captured, and we can't be sure that they didn't continue on in some way, hidden in hedonite rituals and passed down from generation to generation. I know that sounds unlikely, but there was someone we found—a mad terrorist bomber that referenced Mantle just before he was caught ten years ago. Or rather, he used one of their call signs—'twisted slag'—a catchphrase for them to issue Mantle commands or identify hidden operators surreptitiously. Other references to Mantle and this call sign pop up in PDA investigations every few years, but no inspector ever puts it together because the Executive Council doesn't want them to put it together."

"Why not?" Neeva raised her voice. If she had known about this 'twisted slag' call sign beforehand, it might have made her move more quickly in the Hock Pocket. "Why is this information hidden?"

His expression turned sour. "For the same reason that we don't talk about the Cessation insurgencies. Because we don't want the hedonites to know what's possible, for their own good. They could have some misguided sense of heroism, develop a penchant for martyrdom, and attach their names to one of these groups. Basically, the reason is: why give them any ideas?"

It made some sense. History was to be learned from, but hedonites had a tendency to interpret the facts selectively. "So all this is to warn me?"

"Yes, and as you probably surmised, it could have a bearing on your investigation. If this Mantle group is out there, it could be much more organized than anything we've run across in the past, so we need to act decisively to snuff it out. Movements like these can gain followers quickly because the hedonite tribes are so impressionable and disenfranchised."

"What else do we know about Mantle?"

"Not much. Originally they were a splinter group from the pyrolytes, but more bent on killing others than suicide. Their dogma speaks of communion with Venus geology, and in particular volcanic activity. They use analogies of rising up from the tenements, like lava flowing from a volcanic eruption."

She nodded. "Well, thank you, I guess. It's a lot to take in."

"I'm trying to show you why we need to take this to the council. The other inspectors don't know about this history, but the Executive Council does. They will understand the need to apply resources to stamp out this hedonite problem once and for all."

"This isn't just a hedonite problem," she said. "Gorman is

involved and there could be other reformers. Even if there aren't, I'm not sure an aggressive approach, which I presume is what you mean by *stamp out*, is the best option. It's a different world down in SoPo. Harsh methods could have adverse consequences, either by polarizing hedonites against reformers, or causing undue harm."

He smiled at her. "You're young, Neeva, and you've been there recently, and seen the hardships hedonites face, but maybe that allows me to look at this more objectively. I can't deny that a few hedonites might get hurt if we get Middich's enforcers involved, but this is how it has to be. Someone has to do volcanic maintenance, to repair the magnetic pulse lines, to serve our food, so that reformers can be free to look to the future, to do the painstaking work of building the Verdara. And someday—man, woman, child, hedonite, reformer, and symbiont—we will be all break our subterranean shackles and enjoy the vast green spaces of the Verdara. So yes, no one likes harsh measures, but there has to be a hierarchy. There has to be strict order or we will never be free to fly into paradise together."

Seconds ticked away as Neeva rubbed the back of her head in contemplation. Grandpa spun slowly around in his chair, giving her freedom from his gaze.

When he returned to view, she said, "I do appreciate the added information. It will help me in my investigation, but otherwise I'm sorry, but my position remains the same. At the beginning of this conversation you said that this was my responsibility. It is. You want me to move quickly. I do, but this has to be done right. I still think a sequestered meeting with a symbiont is the best next step, because I don't want to rush into a council meeting without all the facts. I came to you not only for your input and advice, but because you're one of the few people that can organize a sequestered meeting. Will you do that for me?"

He was expressionless for a moment, until eventually he sighed and relaxed in his chair. "You're growing up, Neeva," he said. A snippet of laughter escaped him. "I'm just an old man. Who am I to stand in your way? I'll organize the meeting as soon as possible."

She exhaled. "Thank you, Grandpa."

He became all smiles again, and stood up to give her a hug. "Anything for you," he said. "Our future is in your hands. Don't drop it."

He said it facetiously, but his smile could not lighten his weighty words.

15

TURNING TOLQUIST

"Hey Tolquist," Hix said, "want to grab a bite at *Crushed*?"

It had been two days since the core sampling run. Hix had tracked Tolquist down at a changing room on the fifth ring. He'd heard that he liked to run the ring circuit at this time.

"Did you just go swimming?" Tolquist asked, perhaps trying to change the subject.

"No, about to." Hix tapped his swim bag.

"I don't know," Tolquist said. "I'm not a fourth ring kind of guy."

"I get it," Hix said, and set about changing.

Tolquist was sitting half-naked on the bench, immobile, looking thoughtful.

"You ready for the next coring mission?" Hix asked.

Tolquist grimaced. "I suppose so."

"Maybe you should go talk to Ordan, or Sonders. Get to know them on a personal level. When I was about to do a new shoot I would talk to the cast and crew ahead of time, to see what made them tick. It would make us a better team during filming."

It was a hollow suggestion. Tolquist would have a bad taste in his mouth for Ordan after the last core run. And besides, Sonders and

Ordan wouldn't want to fraternize with a criminal like Tolquist, reformer or not.

"Later," Hix said, leaving Tolquist to mull his words in solitude.

When Hix asked Tolquist to join him again the next day, he said yes.

Crushed was a modest eatery, but it was on the fourth ring, so it wasn't without its share of obnoxious characters. Their speciality was protein mash—it was still a prison after all—but the mash was served in a puddle of salty red water, making it look like it had actually been something alive at some point. For most people that was the main attraction, although Tolquist didn't seem to appreciate the food.

On the back wall was a mural of the Verdara—a legacy of the fourth ring's intended reformer occupants, but it had been "remastered" with hedonite touches: a giant reformer boot about to step on running hedonite children, an orgy of men and woman with octopus-like tentacles on a table replete with Verdara nutritional bounty, and a blood-soaked First Colony pioneer holding a decapitated head, his chest emblazoned with the fist-to-seed splayed hand. All of this was portrayed before the entrance to a lush, tree-lined boulevard. Some of the art was quite evocative, even though it would be too offensive for your average reformer.

Hix had deliberately chosen the early evening hours, so it wasn't busy. Most people were eating and drinking quietly. At a couple tables were solitary patrons with scornful stares, and the unsolicited entertainment for the evening was a heavy woman lap dancing on a much skinnier man in the corner. The folds of the woman's skin showed under her sheer dress, and her whole back was painted with a tattoo that made it look like she was covered in long feathers.

Tolquist was managing his expressions, but he was tense. He would tap his fingers and cluck his tongue, or occasionally bob his head. He was actively trying to appear comfortable in a setting where he clearly wasn't.

Hix began the conversation talking about the crew of the *Zephyr Spear*. He did an impression of Sonders he'd been practicing. "I have substandard tolerance for remotely factual arguments."

It wasn't very good, but it earned him a polite laugh.

"I gotta say," Hix said, "you surprised me that day on the *Zephyr Spear*."

"In what way?" Tolquist said, looking defensive.

"You did your job well, and unlike some others in the crew, you kept your cool. But that wasn't what surprised me. No, it was the whispering: *Float me on the river of fire*."

"Oh, that." Tolquist's face colored.

"My mother was a pyrolyte, and I respect their teachings. Everyone follows their own spiritual path, but I just didn't figure you for one."

"Why not?"

"I don't know, maybe because it seems so at odds with scientific principles. Not many reformers are pyrolytes. Must be less than one percent?"

"Isn't there a hedonite saying, *hedonite doesn't rhyme with stereotype*?"

"Yeah, so what?"

"So just because there isn't a catchy phrase for reformers, it doesn't mean we aren't subject to quite a few of our own. There's a lot more than one percent."

Hix gave a wry smile. "Touché, but I still don't understand why it interests you. You're a climate scientist who understands the effect of volcanic eruptions on the atmosphere. It's hard to see how the pyrolyte teachings can have some kind of spiritual connection for you."

"That's exactly why. I understand in intimate detail the profound influence geology and volcanology has on Venus. I find it moving. And yet in other aspects of life I sometimes have trouble—I feel lost. Pyrolyte teachings have helped ground me. *Float me on your river of fire, into the heart of you. There may I rest unencumbered.* The river of fire will always be there for me, waiting."

"Not for me, but I get it. So if you were back on Venus, would you do the ceremony? If you were selected, I mean."

Tolquist turned to stare at Hix, and Hix saw something different in his eyes. His irises no longer looked like muddy pools. His eyes glowed with yellow flecks. Maybe Hix just hadn't noticed it before, or maybe they were reflecting the lights of *Crushed*.

Tolquist turned back to his drink and said, "That's personal."

"Sorry to pry," Hix responded.

They both nursed their drinks.

"What does Falcon Fire mean?" Tolquist asked. He was obviously looking to change the subject.

"You haven't seen *Toreno Run*?"

"No."

"*Sky Gate*?"

"No."

It was quite unusual. *Toreno Run* and *Sky Gate* were two of the most popular films in the last five years. Although Tolquist didn't seem like the type who would enjoy action movies, or really any kind of conflict at all.

"Well, it depends on who you ask," Hix said. "My character's name is Captain Zak. Most people think Falcon Fire is a nickname related to his piloting abilities, and the producers sort of ran with that in *Sky Gate*, but its origin is more complex. Captain Zak is also a falconer. All his falcons are killed by his crawglodyte enemies—all except one—when they burn out his private aviary ecochamber. So whenever he wins an air battle, he lands his copter and burns whatever's left of his enemies' craft as a sort of revenge. At the end of *Toreno Run* he also burns up an entire biocrawler—the crawglodyte leader's headquarters—and has it reseeded as a new aviary for his remaining falcon. So while most think it's because Captain Zak is a top notch pilot, I think it's more of a statement of retribution, or catharsis."

"Is that what you were trying to do with your joyride? Was that some kind of retribution?"

"I'm not Captain Zak, Tolquist. *Toreno Run* is fiction."

Tolquist raised his eyebrows. "I bet most of Venus thinks that's why you did it."

"They're gulls."

It wasn't a topic Hix liked to discuss. He tried to think of another way to connect. When they were halfway through their mash, he asked, "So why are you really here, Tolquist? You don't seem like the average criminal."

Tolquist raised his eyebrows. "Stereotypes again?"

Hix laughed. "That's fair," he said, "but seriously."

Tolquist's cautious smile evaporated. "I haven't told that to anyone."

"I understand. Only if you're comfortable."

After a sip of his drink, Tolquist said, "Did you know you're the only one who's even bothered to talk to me, other than the grifters and bullies? So I guess it doesn't matter if I tell you. And after what happened on the *Zephyr Spear*, it's hard to care anymore."

Hix shrugged.

"It was a terrible mistake," Tolquist said. "A professor in my department slept with a woman in my climatology class. It wasn't a big deal, but he did it just because he could, and he didn't care one iota about the girl. So I punched him in the nose when he told me. It was totally out of character for me. I have a partner—someone I love very much—so it wasn't like I was jealous."

Tolquist sighed. "There was a trial and Milton, the professor, really sicked the vultures on me, adding libel to lawbreaking. He said it was evil to punch out a man for an act of love. He told my girlfriend and the symbionts that it was jealousy, that I would fantasize about the girl. And it was true, I did once, and I stupidly told Milton, but that's not the reason I punched him out. I punched him because he was petty and irresponsible. But my girlfriend—her name is Talia— she's such a fragile thing, so impressionable. All this slander about me, it broke her, especially when I admitted to fantasizing. She left me."

"Why did you admit to fantasizing?"

"Because it's the truth."

"Sorry, of course." Sometimes Hix forgot he was speaking with a reformer.

"So they gave me a choice," Tolquist said. "Ten years, which I thought was overkill, or I could volunteer for the Earth missions for four years. I wanted to show Talia that I could do good, and use my knowledge for something useful. I had this romantic notion that she would forgive me if I came back, a conqueror of Earth."

Tolquist wrapped his hands slowly around his cup, as if he could embrace his drink. He cleared his throat and said, "What about you, Hix? What happened to that girl on the dirigible?"

Hix had anticipated the question, but it still sent nerves through his chest. It always did.

"I... it was an accident," he said. "I was trying to show off, so I piloted it through a vapor meteor storm. It's not really dangerous, just water, so hitting one wouldn't damage the dirigible. But then something malfunctioned." He shrugged, deciding not to elaborate any further. It might prompt incriminating questions.

Tolquist nodded slowly. "So the joyride actually happened?"

Hix forced a smile. "Yeah, but don't pretend like it's crazy. All I did was commandeer a dirigible. You came all the way to Earth for your girl."

Tolquist tilted his head thoughtfully.

Shawna's playful smile on that day flashed in Hix's mind. It was a lopsided thing. He could still remember how her shrill laugh would tremble through him when she was sitting on his lap. He'd been another person when he was with her, and at times he wondered, was that person even real? Was it just one of the many personas he'd developed just to survive?

It seemed so long ago, and it was literally a world away.

He saw Pru lingering at the entrance to *Crushed*. He motioned behind his back for her to scram. He was to give the signal if he needed help, but he wasn't entirely confident Pru and Rav would do it his way. They had their own ideas how to conduct this meeting.

Hix leaned toward Tolquist. "Hey Tolquist, since you're a scientist and all, what do you think our chances are for surviving these core runs?"

Tolquist laughed nervously.

"No, seriously."

Tolquist shook his head, and frowned.

Hix said, "You said your term is four years. That could be as many as a hundred runs. We won't even be done setting up the atmospheric shunts by then. You think we'll still be on *Zephyr Spear 57*?"

Tolquist's look of mock amusement morphed into annoyance.

"I'm not a climatologist," Hix continued, "but I'd give us less than one percent."

"I don't..." Tolquist stuttered. He was frustrated, and he looked like he wanted to argue, but he couldn't find a good counter. He spoke quietly. "Look, you made your point on the coring mission. You're right, but why rub it in? There's not much we can do about it."

"Sure there is," Hix said.

"Like what?"

"How badly do you want to get back to your girl?"

"I... I don't know."

"You don't know?" Hix asked. He stood up and went to the restroom, icing him. The skinny man had passed out and the lap dancer was sloughed in the corner, her makeup smeared all over her face. She smiled up at Hix as she noshed her mash but he didn't return the sentiment. His face was hard, focused.

He took his time in the bathroom. Tolquist was a gentle soul—careful, thoughtful, compassionate. He didn't belong here. The answer to Hix's question was obvious, but Tolquist needed to process the implications. And yes, he could be coerced with the threat of violence, but then he wouldn't be dependable. He had to have a vested interest. He needed to feel guilt if he didn't succeed.

When Hix rejoined Tolquist, he waited until Tolquist said it.

"I do want to see her again."

Hix sighed and nodded. "You have to give me your word. We do have a way, and we could use your help, but if you're in, you're in all the way. We'll be counting on you, and people will get hurt if you change your mind." He tried to elicit a sense of earnest in his eyes.

Tolquist looked down into his drink, over at the mural, and then scanned the faces of the many patrons of *Crushed*. "Okay," he said, "but I don't want people to get hurt—us or anyone else. Honestly, I'm having trouble believing you, even though I don't think you've lied to me before." His last statement had an inflection of surprise in it. Hix was a hedonite, after all.

People *would* get hurt, but it didn't matter. Hix was pretty sure he had him. He leaned in and whispered in his ear, "There's only one way to survive, and only one way to get back. The next Venus-bound interplanetary transport. We're going to take it, and we need your help."

16

THE HERITAGE MUSEUM

Did Neeva want to be a Keeper? At times she would find herself asking the question, and then quickly dismissing it. It seemed inappropriate—shameful even—to consider saying no to such an honor.

She remembered vividly when Grandpa first told her. Shawna had a rock flute recital that day. Neeva wanted to see Shawna perform but Grandma insisted she go visit Grandpa at the Heritage Museum.

Neeva had taken a gondola up to Telliac Mountain, which was one of the largest mountains in the Maxwell Montes range—the one that loomed closest over LC. She left from a terminal at the top of an LC tower. The gondola had a shiny bronze shell, untarnished by the streaks of dust that blemished the vehicles frequenting the plateau below it. A picture of the Slanted Teeth was stenciled into it. These were the four tall buildings that made up the Museum and Keeper complex at the top of the mountain. The buildings were skinny and rectangular, but also stacked sideways together, leaning back over the edge of the mountain. Grandma had once told Neeva that if the attractions and exhibits weren't interesting enough, she could at least enjoy the feeling of vertigo when walking over the transparent floor panels.

The gondola was full, mostly with tourist reformers, and all presumably heading up to visit the museum. It was sun season, and there were no clouds in the sky. Neeva had hoped to see snow one day, but it had only fallen a few times on record on the mountain top, and never during sun season.

When she disembarked, Grandpa was waiting at the offramp, his hair peppery and slicked back, an earnest smile on his face. This was before his fall, and so before his cane. Grandpa moved efficiently, his hands behind his back, his bent torso adding conviction to his gait.

In the museum, the entryway corridors guided visitors through the stages of Verdara, and a documentary about the horrors of the Cessation, but she rushed through most of them.

"You don't like the historical exhibits?" Grandpa asked.

"Not really," she replied.

He smiled. "You're young. You will, in time."

"I want to see the transport systems floor," she said.

"Of course you do."

The copter schematics and models were interesting, but her favorite exhibit was a room-sized model of the old First Colony dirigible fleet. It was from hundreds of years ago, during the bombardment eras, and before the Venusian surface had been ready for settling. There were fifty major dirigibles, and thousands of others spanning the globe, each one serving a purpose: carbon scrubbers, transport shuttles, surface bombers, and biofloats. Most had a role in terraforming, but others formed airborne economic systems. Neeva sped the model up 100,000x speed, and the fleet looked liked ants crawling over a spherical anthill.

It saddened her, in a way. Yes, they needed to progress to the Verdara, and so the surface had to be prepared, but there was something dignified about living high in the clouds. Unfortunately, of those dirigibles that remained aloft—a small fraction of the original fleet—a good portion had been set adrift or abandoned.

She'd also toured the ancient wildlife exhibits, including the many extinct species that you could no longer find in biocrawlers. They featured massive underwater mammals called whales that weighed a hundred tons, and ridiculously fat animals called pigs that looked like they could barely walk. It was hard to believe these had ever had a place in any ecosystem.

Grandpa had been patient with her. Eventually, after more than an hour, he'd said, "I have something special to show you."

He took her through doors with complicated security protocols, and along a glass-paneled pathway that left the museum and headed toward the First Colony Keeper Complex. In the Keeper Complex the walls were made of smooth marbled stone, any corners meticulously rounded. There was no one in sight.

"I'm not supposed to be in here, Grandpa," Neeva said.

"I know," he answered enigmatically.

They arrived at the First Colony Arcade. It was as she'd heard it described—a massive hall replete with flags, model spaceships and airships, and the statues of great men and women standing three times the height of Grandpa. These were the heroes of the First Colony, from before the Cessation, preserved for antiquity. There was Durrah, and Killian, and so many more that she'd never seen before.

"Who is that?" she asked, pointing at a statue of a one-armed woman depicted with a kind of miniature symbiont's visor over her eyes.

Grandpa was watching Neeva closely, oblivious to the spectacle. "All in good time," he said, and he kept moving along. She rushed to keep up.

All along the hall, great muscled arms of brass reached out from the sides, with open hands, fingers spread wide, and in the palms were depicted mounds of seeds. There must have been a hundred of them, all identical. The arms were so thick and strong they could be mistaken for extensions of trusses—except that they weren't holding anything up.

At the end of the hallway was another door, and another. Standing before this final one was a lithe-looking female enforcer. She was the only other human being Neeva had seen in the entire Keeper Complex. She let them pass once she tested Grandpa's retina with her scanner.

Finally, they arrived in a circular room. The far wall was an expanse of glass, hanging over the cliff. Two lines of shelves contained a library of labeled plastic cases, and beyond them, just before the transparent flooring, was a statue of a man with outstretched arms. In one hand were the same seeds she'd seen in the hands in the arcade, and the other was curled upwards into a tight fist. The face featured an austere nose and angular jaw. Veins and muscles bulged from legs and arms that stretched out of a loose tunic. Even the jaw muscles appeared to be flexing.

"Have you ever seen this statue before?" Grandpa asked.

"No, but... it's Durrah, isn't it."

"Yes, that's right. You've seen him in picture books. I like this representation of him because it sends a message. It says we need to be strong to survive. The Verdara will not come without sacrifice and fortitude. Sometimes that fortitude means fighting for what we believe in. Sometimes it means holding back, preserving and being responsible—hence the seeds."

He took her hand and escorted her past the statue, onto the tinted glass flooring. A sphere had been obscured by the statue, hanging from the ceiling. It was like the Venus Verdara globes Neeva had studied as a child, but also different. There were no cities on the poles. It wasn't like Mars, either. There was much more water, and the continents weren't laid out in the same manner.

"What is this?" she asked.

"It's Earth."

"Earth?"

"Yes, from long ago, but what's important is that it's where we came from."

She almost laughed, but caught herself. His face was stern, serious.

"Our home before Venus wasn't Mars, Neeva. It was a beautiful, wondrous place that was corrupted by the misinformed. The people of Earth chose decadence, and indulgence, and refused to believe they were destroying their planet. Only the First Colony peoples had the foresight, and the *fortitude*, to place truth above all else, to establish the delicate—and necessary—separation of hedonite and reformer so that we can all live in a world governed by reason. This thinking wasn't welcome on Earth, so the First Colony peoples left to start their own world on Venus, while the Earth fractured into wars and boiled into the tempest you see in the sky today."

He allowed her time to digest this, while she circled this long-ago depiction of Earth. She had so many questions, but one of them spurred her curiosity harder than the rest. "But withholding this information about Earth... isn't that a lie? I can understand why the Reformer Doctrine is necessary—to segregate the mentally unstable hedonites, but it's also founded on the idea that a democratic society that isn't gullible to lies will fare better, because it can make decisions analytically and deductively. So why wouldn't we speak the truth about this? Maybe even the hedonites would better understand their place in the world."

Grandpa was grinning, perhaps with some measure of pride for his choice of Keeper. He said, "I can see why you would think that, Neeva, but no. First of all, there is no lie—we are simply presenting what needs to be presented, and excluding what does not. The hedonites chose to believe Mars was our home many centuries ago. It is our policy not to intervene, and so the rumor propagated such that even higher-lineage reformers believed it and wrote it into history. And yes, we could correct it. In the past we have tried to open up these tomes," his arm swept toward the shelves of plastic cases. "all of it, in fact, before the Cessation, but it only made things worse."

"How could it have made things worse?"

He came closer. His eyes were fixed on hers. "You see, Neeva, our history on Venus is long, but on Earth it was even longer. Hedonites will pluck what treasure they can from this trove of history, and then distort it to fit their misguided beliefs. Maybe there was a great martyr who died in flames that the pyrolytes can use to help recruit more poor souls to their suicidal cult? Maybe if hedonites know they were once free to vote in elections on our home planet, they will say they should be free to do so again. At the same time, they will disown the obvious negative consequences of doing so, choosing only what fits their desired narrative. So, as you will learn, it's better that the absolute truth remains here, protected, so that it can never *become* a lie."

As you will learn, he'd said. Neeva was only sixteen at the time, but she wasn't naïve. She wasn't supposed to be in the Keeper Complex, and she certainly wasn't supposed to know about Earth. Either Grandpa was breaking the rules, defying this *fortitude* he was speaking of, or...

"Why am I here, Grandpa?" she asked.

He took her hand, examined it, and cradled it in his own. He spoke slowly, his eyes reflecting the orange sky beyond the glass. "Because you may not realize it yet, but you have something inside of you, Neeva. You're like Durrah, and you're like me. You have that strength, that humility, and that probity. You are the one, out of all my grandchildren, that I have chosen to help protect us all. You'll be the Keeper. You're the one who will be given these gifts, and you're the one who will bear this burden."

It did make her feel special, at the time. He'd chosen her for a great honor. She was jubilant for weeks, and it motivated her to excel in her school assignments. But it was a heavy thing, this honor, these secrets, and this *fortitude*. To this day, she wasn't sure whether it would lift her up or pull her down.

And now she would be visiting Telliac Mountain again, but this time she wouldn't be going to the top.

Tunnels and lifts were dug out of Telliac, many of which allowed access all the way down to the LC fusion reactor far below, but only symbionts and their recorders were allowed to use them, so Neeva had to take a PDA copter to reach the psychanthropic facility on Harriet Shelf.

The craft was a brand new T44. These were longer than the X92s, and decked in blue paint, with powerful rotating props on both wings, plus an additional thruster that could flex between two aft booms. There was a slight hum when it banked, but in general, maneuverability was much smoother than the X92 she'd been using in SoPo.

Her NoPo pilot was the antithesis of Bam Jam—a slim reformer woman named Priva in a dapper gray uniform. Priva's movements were efficient and precise, and she was sparing with her words. Through the fog of her mask, Neeva could see that the T44 was taking an unusual vector, moving in parallel to the Maxwell Montes chain after liftoff, away from Telliac Mountain.

"Why the circuitous route?" she asked.

"They've closed off airspace above the LC fusion reactor," Priva replied. "It's being refurbished, and there are too many low-flying drop ships and revolving cranes in the vicinity. Plus, the sequestration facility isn't in the main psychanthropic facility. It's on the south face of Telliac Mountain."

"Got it," Neeva said. She wondered if it would be a good idea to forbid aircraft passage over any fusion reactor indefinitely. Now that she knew what organized hedonites were capable of, anything could be at risk.

The T44 banked to the left, finally veering toward Telliac Mountain. Neeva's seat vibrated and the craft bumped through a patch of turbulence.

Priva shut off the dashboard lights and the external floodlamp. "It's protocol," she explained, "to cloak our approach to the sequestration facility."

The landing pad was a dotted LED cross inlaid in a circle. It seemed to be hovering next to the mountain. Only when they were within a few copter-lengths of it was the outcropping of transparent plexmold visible. The platform lacked railings, staff, or signage, and was reinforced by huge cylindrical support beams on either side, which were also transparent.

"You'll be met inside the door," Priva said, pointing to a slab of metal cut into the mountain.

Neeva exited the T44 and ventured toward the door. It took her eyes a moment to adjust once she was inside. The interior was brightly lit, with unblemished white walls. A squat man with a beaklike nose was waiting for her.

"I am Jansis," he said, "a recorder. I will take you to VV-912." He turned and Neeva followed after stowing away her mask on one of the many empty hooks nearby.

They navigated through a series of corridors that went deeper into the mountain. A couple of shiny mounds of metal that must have been cleaning droids scurried about, but there were no people.

"How long have you been a recorder?" Neeva asked.

"Seven years."

Psychanthropic recorders were known to be poor conversationalists. They were reformer citizens, selected by symbionts from any variety of academic disciplines, and there was no formal training. It was considered an honor to be selected, albeit less so than being a Verdarist, a First Colony Keeper, or even a Planetary Defense Agent, because there was no test or feat of will required to attain the position. You simply received the message, and you accepted or declined. The pay was quite good, so few ever declined.

She tried again. "How many sequestration visits do you get?"

Jansis sighed, as if her questions had already become monotonous. "I can't give you specifics."

"What about a range?"

"There have been fewer than ten in the last fifty years."

"Only ten?"

"Fewer than ten."

"And yet you have a whole wing of the psychanthropic facility for these meetings?"

He only shrugged.

"Well, thank you for allowing the exception."

"Don't thank me," he responded sharply, as if it was a command.

The corridor opened up into a room with a high ceiling. Carts filled with metal tools and transparent canisters brimming with colorful liquids lined the wall. A large gray-tiled door barred their passage. It had several keypads, as well as a retinal scan, which Jansis used to identify himself.

"I've never met a symbiont before," Neeva said, "at least not face to face. Is there etiquette I should be aware of?" She knew that symbionts valued their privacy, but otherwise the PDA taught her nothing about how to engage with them. They probably didn't have much data to go on, since so few people ever saw one in the flesh, despite the fact that everyone's lives were influenced by symbionts' thought processes on one level or another.

Jansis said, "Engage in common courtesies as you would with your professional colleagues. Comedy is to be avoided, because even though VV-912 may find your comments humorous, he is unable to laugh without feeling pain. And do not try to access the containment room."

"Thank you. I'm glad I asked. Maybe we should give future visitors these guidelines?"

Jansis ignored her question.

They entered a sort of antechamber with a broad pane of glass. This was the consultation room. Beyond the glass was darkness—the containment room.

Jansis was hovering next to a keypad near the glass. He said, "This is very unusual, Inspector Nash lineage 4a. We would like it to remain unusual."

"I know. Apologies. I assure you it is of paramount importance."

"According to your judgement."

"Yes," she answered. Apparently, Jansis's judgement differed. He was acting a bit like a protective mother here. Maybe that was what the symbionts looked for in a recorder? Either way, Neeva could tell she was going to have to do a lot of fawning. "I hope VV-912 will agree with me. Thank you again for accommodating the request."

Jansis nodded, touched the keypad, turned about and left. The containment room glowed softly at first, and only gradually became bright enough for her to view the surroundings beyond the glass.

In the center of the room, facing her, was the skinniest man she'd ever seen. His limbs were like sticks covered in wiry blue veins, and his face was discolored to a turquoise tint despite what looked like heavy beige makeup and the green glimmer of a visor wrapped in an arc around his eyes. The back of his skull flared out to make room for an assembly of wires and tubes servicing his brain. The thickest leads snaked into his spine, brain stem, cerebellum, cerebral cortex, and frontal lobe like a steel mohawk. All of these wires and tubes reached up to mobile boxes that ran on rails in the ceiling.

Despite his gaunt limbs, he managed to stand, although it was possible he was being held up by the apparatus surrounding his head, like some kind of marionette.

It was easy to understand why the symbionts preferred to stay hidden.

"Hello, Neeva," a voice said, but the man's lips didn't move. "Welcome to our facility. I am VV-912." The visor blinked in cadence with the words, which was the only way Neeva could be sure the voice came from him. "I apologize if my corporeal form is alarming to you. In the past, others have expressed disgust when seeing me."

"No, of course not," she said. "I find your form to be interesting, but not alarming. I appreciate that you must make great sacrifices to be a symbiont, and that it places a burden on your body. I also hope that my being here does not cause undue stress—I do understand that you don't like to be separated from your peers."

"It is more than that." VV-912's visor flashed again. "The information you are providing will need to be sequestered in three ways: in my remote backup, in my personal hard drives, and also in my neuronal patterns. The biological sequestration in neuronal patterns is the most challenging, because it will require that active algorithms seek out and curtail my unenhanced human thought processes, so that they do not influence topics of broader psychanthropic concern. In essence, I will need to wear a mental muzzle, limiting my contributions to the collective for some time."

"Oh, I'm... terribly sorry. I can only assure you that you are making this sacrifice for a matter of utmost importance."

"We do understand that there are times when sequestration is warranted."

When she had first laid eyes on him, she felt some degree of guilt. VV-912 and the other symbionts had to stay in their emaciated, trapped bodies so that they could wield the necessary computational power to keep order on Venus. And now his comments on sequestration rubbed salt in the wound. She knew it would be cumbersome, but not this cumbersome.

She actively considered aborting the meeting.

"I am ready," VV-912 said.

In the end, Neeva had to consider the greater good. That was why she had requested sequestration to begin with. Despite the hardship she was placing on VV-912, he was still one man, and the lives of thousands of others could hang in the balance.

She scanned the interface Jansis had used and saw that it accepted data packets. "Can I tightbeam you the report?"

"Yes," VV-912 said.

She sent him the encrypted packet and authenticated it with her PDA code on the tablet in front of her. The surface of the tablet was red around the edges, reflecting the dull light like the shell of a ladybug. She felt the smooth surface with her index finger as she waited for VV-912 to process the report.

A few seconds later, VV-912 said, "Report received and analyzed. What is your question, as it relates to psychanthropic interrogation?"

"I would like to know what you can tell me about possible nodes of corruption associated with my case. In particular, I would like you to leverage your data feeds to see if people are exhibiting patterns of behavior akin to Gorman, or if you know of aquaintances of Gorman that should be investigated. I'd also like you to map these events, and any potential suspects, through relationship chains to the Executive Council members, to determine if any should be recused in the event of a discussion on this matter."

"I see," VV-912 said. "This will take several minutes. I have limited computational power during sequestration." His visor turned into a flashing yellow strobe and he went quiet.

Occasionally the yellow lights would flicker to orange and back to yellow on one side of VV-912's head. Colored fluids slid through the transparent tubes, to and from the access points in his skull.

Neeva tried not to fidget. The window in front of her was so clean, without any reflection. She resisted the urge to reach out and feel the smooth glass with her fingertips.

VV-912's visor stopped flashing and turned green again. "I have completed my analysis and I am sending you a tightbeam encrypted report." Neeva's tablet flashed with a new message. "There are no suspects with a high enough probability to warrant immediate apprehension, but I have found several persons of interest for you to pursue in your investigation. I can find no clear relationship chain link to any Executive Council members, or other notable reformer institutions, but such computations are notoriously unreliable when the chains originate within hedonite communities."

Even though there was nothing concrete, it was some measure of relief that his mapping hadn't given her dozens of arrest warrants, and more so that there was no link to the council. But he wasn't finished.

"If I may," VV-912 said, "I have additional information that I can provide which was not a direct answer to your query, but may aid your investigation. You will certainly be questioned by the Executive Council soon, and it may benefit you to have this information in advance."

"Of course."

She looked down at her tablet but no new message showed up.

"I would prefer to communicate this verbally," VV-912 said. "There are two considerations of note. One is that we have lost approximately ten percent of our psychanthropic data feeds in the south pole in the last two months. Half of that we lost in the last week."

"Whoa. How is that possible?"

"It was not an accident. A likely scenario is that one of these hedonite groups, perhaps the one affiliated with Gorman, has been systematically dismantling them by disabling the connective channels. It may also have been compromised through a sophisticated cyber attack."

Neeva knew something of the security and secrecy surrounding the psychanthropic data feeds. Whomever disabled them must have had advanced systems engineering capabilities and a knowledge of the feed architecture.

"That's very concerning," she said.

"Secondly, a symbiont by the name of NM-198 has gone missing in the south pole psychanthropic network."

"But—how did he... or she... go missing?" She knew she sounded stupid, but it was a legitimate question. It wasn't as if symbionts could just walk away.

"She has likely been kidnapped. Her personal recorder is also gone. One other symbiont and recorder were found dead nearby. The Sena Facility, where she was stationed, has more lax security than our Telliac Mountain facility, or any of our other facilities in the north. It is only a satellite office that principally acts as a redundancy. It has a marginal contribution to psychanthropic pattern recognition overall."

"Do you think these two things are connected—the dead data feeds and the kidnapping? In other words, could NM-198 have provided information to her abductors to enable them to cut the data feeds?"

"There is a high likelihood that these two incidents are associated, but the psychanthropic feeds began lapsing before we lost NM-198, so we do not think her knowledge was used in disabling the feed systems. The converse may be true—it may have been necessary for the perpetrators to dismantle the data feeds prior to NM-198's apprehension at the Sena Facility."

"Why would someone take her?"

"It could be that a malevolent entity intends to corrupt the symbiont collective with viral attacks using her as a vector, but that would be naïve, since we took immediate steps to block NM-198's connective nodes and we altered our security systems so that she can no longer penetrate them. The abductors could also be seeking to interrogate her, but she would be able to proactively block her own access to local data stores to render their interrogations impotent. The only practical objective we can envision is that they want to interrogate her biological form, which will only be able to dispense what is in her human brain. Hedonites may not understand that her neuronal imprint will offer little in the way of intelligence. And, of course, since her abductors are likely hedonite, it is also possible they have no intention of using her instrumentally at all, other than to make a statement."

"Could she have left of her own accord?"

"There is no logical motive for such an action, especially because symbionts cannot survive for long without supportive healthcare and nutritional systems. We are prone to infections, and need daily grooming and synthetic inputs. In fact, she may already be dead unless whomever has taken her is also supporting her maintenance needs."

"Do you want me to find her?"

"It is not in our purview to request PDA actions, but if you wish to restore and maintain order in the south, we believe it would be a desirable intervention."

It was a confusing "no and yes" type of statement, but only because of the constraints under which VV-912 operated.

"Do you know NM-198 personally?" Neeva wondered if VV-912 was showing a sign of his humanity here. Maybe he cared about this girl but couldn't say it.

But he was a symbiont, after all. He said, "I do not have any emotional connection with NM-198. If I did, that would introduce bias, and I would have prefaced this discussion with the appropriate qualifier. My knowledge of her extends only to her recorded history, biometric patterns, and minor contributions to psychanthropic determinations. I do hope you find her, though. Like all branches of Planetary Defense, the symbiont collective takes pride in keeping order, but when we are blind we are powerless. We need to bring the perpetrators to justice and restore our data feeds as soon as possible."

"I understand," Neeva said, her mind churning. It was a lot to consider, and she couldn't think of any other questions at the moment. "I will review your report," she said. "May I reach out to you if I have questions?"

"Yes. The credentials for a secure channel are already in your tablet."

"Thank you, VV-912. It has been quite helpful. I hope you agree it was worth sequestration."

The light on his visor flashed yellow for a moment. He said, "Goodbye, Inspector Nash lineage 4a," and the lights went out inside the room.

Soon after, Jansis entered and escorted Neeva out.

It would have been nice if VV-912 had at least recognized the gravity of the situation. A simple "thank you" or "good luck" for her offer to assist in finding the symbiont was all she had been hoping for.

It didn't help her already-heavy conscience. She'd almost killed Zae Samar-Mia by accident, and poor Egan had nearly died on a mission she'd led. Now she may have burdened this poor man with sequestration.

I'm doing my job, she told herself. *An important job.*

Unfortunately, at the moment it didn't feel like a job she enjoyed, and she had a feeling that her meeting with the Executive Council wasn't going to change that.

17

———

SHAWNA

Hix did think about Shawna from time to time, even though he tried to suppress the memories. The idle hours on Kanto Station didn't help. Neither did Tolquist's questions about the joyride.

He first met Shawna at a gala being held by the company that was producing *No Other Champions,* a film about a group of Verdarists fighting to refurbish an abandoned biocrawler. Hix played a supporting role in the film. He was supposed to be egging on the indecisive Verdarist protégé until she finally overcame her self-doubt. It was low budget and was panned during screenings, so never released.

The gala was a pretentious affair, held in a lavish warehouse-sized room in the fern of LC, with one wait-staff member for every ten participants. Hix was dressed in a tight-fitting gray suit with a banded right arm and crater-patterned black undershirt. He was alone, at the request of the studio head who wanted to make him "accessible". In other words, he wasn't there for fun, but rather as a spectacle.

In the spirit of making himself accessible, he had been dancing with an inebriated middle-aged woman. Her hair was gelled so stiffly he was worried it might knock him out. She was all smiles as she spun under his arm. He made sure to give her a dramatic dip or two.

It was on one of these dips when a fragment of sheer white cloth was suddenly covering her face. She jumped up in surprise, unwittingly snagging the white material with her teeth. This in turn pulled at the cloth, and sent the aberrent cloth's owner into a tumble with her.

The owner was Shawna. She was wearing a white satin dress with tassels that raised up into a windmill of flailing cloth when she spun. Hix had seen Shawna before, off set. She worked in artistic design for another production company.

The nearby dancers all stopped to gawk at the embarrasing scene.

Hix's dance partner spat out the cloth from Shawna's dress. She said, "Watch where you're going, you tramp." And she walked away.

Shawna had fallen on her front, and Hix was worried she might be hurt.

"Are you okay?" he asked, squatting beside her.

When she turned over, she was laughing. "Well, that was graceful," she said.

"Sorry about that," Hix said, giving her his hand.

She took it, and her face lit up when she saw him. "I hope you are, at least enough to dance with me."

He obliged her. It wouldn't be polite to leave her. People were watching.

If Shawna wasn't the most proficient dancer, she was a passionate and creative one. They did pirouettes, a loose jive and, finally, a feet-kicking sort of polka that Hix could barely follow. He doubted it was a real dance, and it was probably inappropriate given the circumstances, but Shawna's smile was mesmerizing. And besides, he was being accessible.

Two energetic songs later, they headed to the bar to get drinks. Shawna said, "You know, you could have just left me. I almost killed your last dance partner."

"Lucky for you you're good at guilting people."

She let out a playful guffaw. "I was genuinely distressed. And honestly, I was doing you a favor, don't you think?"

Hix couldn't help raising his eyebrows. He tilted his head to one side in a tacit acknowledgement.

"So, are you in production?" Shawna said, sipping on her drink.

Hix tried to keep a straight face. Did she really not know who he was? By this point in his career he'd already received acclaim for *Sky Gate* and *Toreno Run*, and it was a film production party. He was pretty sure everyone else knew who he was, but something about Shawna was different. She seemed so carefree. Maybe she didn't.

But of course, she did know. She was just playing. Shawna's life was an endless parade of games.

"I'm an aspiring actor," Hix said.

"Ah, I see." She cringed. "Tough gig, that. My job is much easier. I do doodles and they pay me for it."

He smiled.

"I'm also working on my professional dancing career. I could use your help."

"I don't usually rescue someone twice in one evening."

She smiled, downed her drink and made her way to the dance floor. He couldn't help but follow.

The next day she came on set. He didn't notice her at first. After he'd finished his take—a whiny commiseration with the protagonist—he went for his fermented tea, but it was gone from his chairside table. Shawna was standing across the room, sipping it. She winked at him and gave him a thumbs up.

He made his way over to her. "Are you a taste tester as well?" he asked.

"Yeah, I decided my dance career might not work out."

There was a way about her that made him feel at ease. He couldn't keep the crook of a smile off his lips. It reminded him of his days with Mel, before she got caught up with Mantle.

"It looks like you're no longer an aspiring actor," she said.

"Oh, that?" he said. "It wasn't a real take. I'm just helping the lead with her lines."

"Places!" the director said.

Shawna's eyes darted back and forth, catching the actors and stage managers moving into action. "Maybe I could help you with your acting later," Shawna said, "at my place?"

His smile waned. It had been fun banter, but now he had to decide whether to get involved with a reformer. Most reformer girls just wanted a notch on their bedpost, and it wasn't worth the publicity and tabloid attention. He didn't need to scratch some perverse itch.

"I don't sleep around," he said.

"Do you date?" she asked, blushing. "I said my place because I assumed you'd want privacy."

He was getting uncomfortable. The stage was set and he needed to take his place. "Why would you want to date me?" he said. "I can't even vote."

It was an abrasive comment, enough to send most women packing.

"Are you sure about that?" she asked, not missing a beat. "If Falcon Fire beats Representative Chauncey, people get to draw positive allusions. In *Toreno Run*, you sided with the Verdarists over the crawglodytes, and it bumped Awekwol in the polls. You do influence people. Millions of them. That's more powerful than punching a ballot."

Shawna was smart, too.

"Hix?" the director called. "Let's go."

"Sorry," Hix said, and he walked away, but he stopped and turned back after a few steps. He showed eight fingers, then pointed down, mouthing *here*.

Shawna smiled, winked and disappeared out the back exit.

There was one place on Kanto Station that would offer a suitable distraction from pretty much anything. It was hard to think about Shawna, or much of anything else.

Besides, they had work to do. Hix was still in the flow.

Scream was one of the more exclusive drinking holes on the fourth ring. It was a desperate, visceral place, full of indulgent distractions, and it made *Crushed* feel almost welcoming in comparison. There was a pricy cover charge which was readily elevated two- or threefold if you weren't already known to the bar staff. Of course, as one of Rav's "friends", Hix wasn't charged at all.

The walls were uniformly covered with projected images of explosions over a fluid starscape punctuated with flowering nebulae. Some explosions originated from circulating spacecraft, asteroids and planetoids. Other sources were not celestial bodies at all but rather human bodies, scantily clad in suggestive poses. The most noticeable feature—and it would be impossible not to notice—was that the soundtrack to this unrelenting montage of detonations was a disturbing collection of extended screams, moans and grunts. These were at times sexual, or at times flavored with pain, or longing, or fear. Occasionally, a particularly abrasive high-pitched scream would nearly make Hix drop his drink.

Hix was sitting with Pru, Rav and Iri in a booth made of soft, red cushions tightly encased in tough plastic covers. Iri was one of Rav's new recruits. He was plain-looking for a hedonite, with bushy eyebrows and undyed auburn hair. He had a tendency to lean forward, attentive, hanging onto Rav's every word.

Toward the back of the bar were the private booths, where Tolquist was sitting. He was wearing a blue button-down vest with a broad lapel. His clothes were his best attempt at impersonating the reformer guards that hardly ever left the first ring. In front of Tolquist was a curvaceous woman prancing and pulsing her hips to the screaming symphony around them. Tolquist bobbed his head to the rhythm, but all too often his eyes wandered and his smile withered. His enjoyment was far from convincing, but hopefully it wouldn't matter. Being uncomfortable in your own skin was pretty common for reformers.

"There's Loanna," Iri said. Iri had been a pilot on Venus as well. Now on Kanto Station he worked in flight maintenance in the docking bays. He knew all the transport pilots.

Hix watched her enter. It was hard to tell she was a reformer. She was stalky, with a flushed face, sporting blond spiky hair with purple tips. But they didn't need Iri to help identify her. She still wore her Transport Officer uniform, with sweat discolorations around the neck and armpits. She wasted no time at the bar and headed directly toward the back rooms.

Tolquist waved at her as if he knew her. Loanna just frowned in return. It was awkward.

Loanna was soon lost behind a curtain that led to the private rooms. A minute later, Eun—their server—collected a brutish ogre of a man, who must have been seven feet tall, from the other side of the bar and escorted him to the back rooms. Apparently this Loanna liked her men extra large, and quite hairy.

There weren't many times when Hix was glad he'd volunteered for the *Zephyr Spear*, but this was one of them. He wouldn't last being a pawn of these flesh merchants.

A particularly violent scream blared out around him, jarring him so much that his hand gripped the table.

Rav smiled at Hix's reaction. "You get used to it," he said.

Apparently Rav frequented *Scream* a lot. Or at least that's what he hoped Rav meant.

Scream was a place to get lost from the world—a distraction from the dreary hopelessness of the station, or being in some monotonous and uninteresting hedonite job, but it reminded Hix too much of home. There were times when he'd heard moans from Mel in the other room in the apartment. He knew they were fake. They were made to sound like lust, but in truth they were the moans of hardship, of endurance, and of sacrifice.

She could act, too. It ran in the family.

Eun came out of the back room area, walking stiffly with a tray of empty glasses. She maneuvered past their booth and surreptitiously slipped a comm device onto the chair next to Pru, who relayed it to Hix under the table.

Hix worked quickly, using the tabletop to obscure his actions. He took a picture of the login screen and patched it into his console for incorporation into his waterholing program. Thankfully, the comm device was standard issue, without any personalized markings or nameplates.

The program was pretty straightforward. They would give Loanna a new comm device that looked exactly like her old one, with the same access screen and function tabs. The home screen would allow access with any code she put in. When she accessed the transport hub login it would capture her credentials and send them to Hix remotely. After that, the device would become corrupted and unsalvageable.

The main concern was that the transport hub app would look different than the one she'd seen before, but it was a risk they would have to take. Hix was comforted by the fact that it was close to many of the utilitarian Kanto apps, and not too removed from Commander Ordan's login on the *Zephyr Spear*.

When he finished initiating the waterholing program he passed the new comm device to Pru, who fed it back to Eun on her next circuit of the table. Rav petted her arm as she passed, as if he was stroking a baby duckling. She flinched away ever so slightly.

Tolquist was craning his head around the dancer, looking for the sign. When Eun returned from the back rooms, Rav held his index finger up.

One minute.

Eun went behind the bar and tapped something into her register console.

An ear-splitting alarm went off, and along with it, red lights flashed on the ceiling. The explosions on the walls froze mid-detonation and the latest guttural yell cut off to silence. Tolquist moved the dancer off his lap, grabbed his own comm device, and pretended to examine it. He stepped out in front of the curtain that led to the back rooms.

Loanna came stumbling out, pulling on her Transport Officer uniform. "Everyone," Tolquist yelled, his voice cracking a little, "there's been a collision of external supply drones. They're worried one might hit the fourth ring." He pointed at his device aggressively.

"The supply drones?" Loanna asked.

"Yes."

She slapped at her coverall pockets, looking for her comm device, and dashed back through the curtains. When she returned the replacement unit was in her hand, and she moved straight for the exit. It looked like she'd taken the bait.

"Do we need to follow her?" Iri asked.

"That wouldn't be a good idea," Hix said. "She'll still be in range for a little while. All she has to do is log in to the transport utility hub to check on the supply drone activity. It's what any rational person would do."

Hix was staring at the console screen, waiting for the data packet to appear. Out of the corner of his eye he could see people streaming out of the bar, checking their own comms.

"I'm sure it's nothing," Eun said, trying to reassure them. "Don't go too far away."

"Did she do it?" Pru asked.

Hix shook his head.

Seconds passed. "I don't see anything," someone said to Tolquist. It was a lone drinker, possibly a reformer as well, but it was hard to tell. "Where did you see the message?" he asked.

"Yes, it's strange," Tolquist said. "I can't find it. Excuse me—I should go." He maneuvered around the man to head for the door.

"Why don't you stick around," Rav said, grabbing his arm as he passed by.

"I... uh. Sure, okay," Tolquist said. Now that Tolquist was closer, Hix could see sweat streaming down his neck. His face was tinted an ivy color. He looked traumatized.

The data packet finally blipped onto Hix's screen. Loanna's credentials were there.

"Got it," Hix said. They all vacated the booth and started peeling out of the bar.

They split off into twos, and then into ones, moving alone to the agreed-upon remote portions of Kanto Station.

18

THE EXECUTIVE COUNCIL

The planetary defense subcommittee meeting was being held in a large boardroom in the upper leaf of the LC shunt tower offices, not far from where Neeva had met with Grandpa days ago. There were only five of them in physical attendance, taking up no more than a tenth of the spacious room that stabbed out onto the tip of the leaf. VV-912 had also been patched in via comms.

"This is very disturbing," Quayle said. "In all my time as Commissioner, I have never seen such an organized insurgence in SoPo. We will have to do an in-depth review of our security infrastructure to see how this could have come to pass, but for now we have an urgent situation that needs action. Suggestions?"

Quayle was an elderly woman, her face ridged with wrinkles and her tight bowl of hair a wispy white. Neeva had the impression Grandpa wasn't fond of her. When he was still an active member of the Council he would speak about how a new initiative was being considered and then say, "But with Quayle, you know... I'm not sure anything will ever happen."

Middich was leaning into the table, his eyes blazing over red-hot cheeks. As Executive Director of Law Enforcement, Middich stood to bear the blame of any security shortfall, so Neeva's report was hitting close to home. "I can have a strike team ready in four days," he said, "and a full-scale intervention regiment with up to one thousand enforcers trained and ready in three, maybe four weeks. We can arrest Gorman and any possible accomplices with the strike team, and follow with the intervention regiment to assign biophysical monitoring to anyone involved. That will stop this in its tracks."

"If I may," Fisker said, his hand half-raised. He had his hair perfectly combed for the meeting, in tight parallel lines. "This is not your typical hedonite temper tantrum. They are organized, and smart. They could be ready for intervention. I think this is what you are seeing here, with these communities vanishing. Hedonites are being told to cut and run if there is any sign of being exposed."

Before the meeting, Neeva had expressed her concerns about a heavy-handed military intervention, but she hadn't been sure Fisker was really listening. Apparently he had been, and he was even brave enough to voice it.

Middich only frowned.

"What do you propose?" Quayle asked.

"We could expand our investigation," Fisker responded, "while still keeping those in the know to a limited few. It may be our best hope of finding out more about the true perpetrators—perhaps this Mantle group—before we show them that we're on to them."

Middich shook his head. "Meanwhile we could lose more symbionts, more psychanthropic feeds, and more settlements."

Representative Awekwol cleared her throat. She was wearing a green satin blouse, symbolic of her Verdarist supporters. She had brown, silver-flecked eyes and long braided hair that trailed down to the small of her back. The braided hair was an unusual style for reformers. It was an attempt to appear natural, to connect with the essence of Verdara. Unfortunately, many believed Awekwol to be overly sympathetic to hedonite advocacy groups, and the hair wasn't helping.

"Deep wounds take a long time to heal," Awekwol said. "Why inflict them needlessly? I agree with Director Fisker. We'll get to the bottom of this. Let's talk to them, find out what they want. At the very least it might allow us adequate time to prepare for effective strike team operations."

"You want to solicit their opinions?" Middich had an incredulous look on his face. "These are criminals, and even if they weren't, we can't cross that line. You know what will happen if we include the hedonites in governance, even tangentially. Democratic politics will evolve into a puppet show, driven by emotion rather than fact—fad rather than reason. This is against First Colony principles, and it will certainly lead to our downfall." He opened his hands to Quayle, as if his objection was obvious.

Quayle grimaced sympathetically in Awekwol's direction. "Yes, I know you mean well, Representative, but what you speak of is a fundamental shift in policy. It is our first imperative to preserve the Reformer Doctrine, and above all we must not allow our system of governance to be corrupted. If we give these SoPo instigators a bullhorn, it will only amplify misinformation."

"And we need to consider the bigger picture," Middich added. "Not just in SoPo, and not just with hedonite communities, but the security of the entire planet. What do you think will happen if we succumb to global unrest, or worse, hedonites are allowed to stand up their own tribal governments? How will we be seen by Mars?"

Quayle couldn't suppress a frown, and Awekwol was about to speak, but before she could, Middich answered his own question. "If the Martians see us as a threat, they might consider it an opportunity to pursue their annexation plans. With a compromised psychanthropic network we're practically inviting them to stamp us out and assert their machine-mind shackles. That's the greater threat here, and that's why we need to take immediate action to stop this before there is a large enough disruption that they can exploit."

"Really, Middich, you're bringing Mars into this?" Awekwol shook her head. "We don't have any indication Mars even remembers we exist."

Quayle put up her hand in an attempt to stop any further bickering on the subject. "VV-912," she said, "what do you think?"

All eyes turned to the table speaker. VV-912's voice crackled through. "Since Mars has blocked all of our communication attempts for over a hundred years, there is little data to evaluate your question. From our probes and telescopes we know Mars dwarfs our on-planet infrastructure at least tenfold, and they have more than a thousand times our footprint of orbital operations. Thus it stands to reason that if they chose to, they could take us by force at any given moment. Unfortunately, I cannot provide any guidance on their ideological preferences or motivations as they may relate to Venusian hedonite tribes."

When it came to Mars, it was always the same "I don't know" response reformers got from the symbionts, and yet it never stopped people from invoking Mars as a way to make an argument, as if they had the inside scoop about what a mysterious civilization millions of miles away was thinking.

"That doesn't disprove my point," Middich said defensively.

"No, it doesn't," Quayle said. "It doesn't prove anything at all."

It was a testy enough comment to make Middich hold his tongue.

Quayle descended into contemplation, her fingers tapping the table. "Mr. Nash, do you have an opinion here?"

All eyes turned to Grandpa, who was sitting with Neeva behind the main table as a guest observer.

"It's a tough call," he said, "and an important one. I see the merits of both sides, but I worry we are underestimating the threat."

"So you prefer Middich's plan?"

"No, I just think neither plan is enough. These criminals are systematically dismantling our most sophisticated surveillance systems. Thousands have been displaced. We need to do more. If we broaden the investigation, we need to dedicate more of Fisker's staff to the task. Likewise, if we send a PDA strike team, why not send two, or three, or five? Why not enlist the help of special forces as well? This is the first time we've been blind, so we need to be prepared to deal with things we haven't yet seen."

There were nods and some furrowed brows around the table. After scanning the reactions, Quayle said, "Thank you, Mr. Nash. I will render my opinion shortly."

Quayle began typing her draft decision. She would send it to the symbionts, or in this case only VV-912, for review prior to finalizing it. VV-912 would provide feedback on any significant assumption errors or risks that may have been missed by the group.

Before Qualye could finish typing, Neeva said, "Excuse me, commissioner, may I comment?"

Quayle's eyebrows were raised in surprise, but she said, "Go on."

"Having been to SoPo only recently, I have reason to believe that the biophysical monitors, should they be used, could have a detrimental effect. People who wear the monitors are ostracized, and I have evidence that some have been murdered when the monitors are removed. Thus they may have limited benefit, or could result in increased friction with hedonite tribes."

Middich was quick to contest her. "Maybe with one-off monitors, but we're talking hundreds or thousands. What are they going to do, shun all of them—kill all of them?"

"Yes," Neeva said, a little too quietly than she intended.

Middich's eyes bulged and he laughed it off. "That's preposterous."

Quayle was looking at her quizzically. "VV-912?" she asked.

"There is insufficient data to predict the outcome of widespread monitor introduction."

Quayle frowned. "Anything else?" she asked. Her eyes darted around the room, to Neeva, Grandpa, Fisker, Middich, and Awekwol. Their heads all shook in turn.

Quayle finished writing her proposal. It only took her a few minutes. She looked it over once and sent it off. Seconds later, her tablet flashed and she scanned the response. One of her eyebrows raised.

"Okay, here it is," she said. "There is little benefit to apprehending only Gorman and his crew with a strike team immediately, as it will alert the culprits to our sensitivity to the situation. So we will proceed with the expanded investigation. VV-912 has recommended seventy-two of Fisker's staff to work on this project—selected based on skills and security assurances. Two additional inspectors will be sent to the other lost settlements, each with an attachment of three PDA officers."

Fisker nodded and said, "We will move expeditiously, Commissioner."

"I trust you will, because I am only giving you five days. Middich, you will be on standby with a strike team to support Gorman's apprehension at that time. In parallel, Middich will look to enlist at least a thousand PDA enforcers, including special forces, for action in several weeks time—what you called your intervention regiment. We will make a go—no go call for rounding up all people of interest at that time. Biophysical monitors will be used on selected targets upon release, as determined by psychanthropic analysis."

It seemed that Quayle hadn't listened to Neeva about the monitors, but at least she'd allowed them to take in Gorman before their introduction. Maybe Neeva could make a break in the investigation in the meantime, or at least convince the council not to use the monitors.

"Finally," Quayle continued, "given the importance of exposing as much of the conspiracy as possible through Director Gorman, it is recommended that Inspector Neeva Nash lineage 4a be promoted to Senior Inspector, and be assigned a personal support team. In addition, VV-912 would like to assign a personal recorder to her, as an observer and assistant during her investigation. Do you accept?"

Neeva was about to say yes, but she realized Quayle was staring at Fisker, her superior.

"Of course," Fisker said. "We will make it happen."

"Good. I'm glad we all recognize the gravity of this situation. I expect daily reports to this subcommittee. Bring only those people in who need to know. Dismissed."

"I'm so proud of you—you're so *senior* now." Celia said,

"Ha ha," Neeva said with a note of sarcasm.

"You're senior like Grandpa. He must be proud as well."

She nodded. "Yeah, he congratulated me about the promotion, but he didn't seem happy. He said they still weren't doing enough. He's probably right."

"Yeah, I agree."

Neeva pushed her shoulder. Celia was just playing around. She didn't even know why the meeting was being held, only that Neeva had received the promotion.

They were sitting on the couch, eating salad bowls filled with duck protein strips and veggies. The meat flavoring was particularly spicy, enough to make Neeva sweat.

"Come on." Celia slapped her on the leg. "Should we say hello to our melancholy bird? I know that's who you really came here to see."

Celia stood up and trotted down the hall, returning with Rocket's cage. Rocket chirped energetically.

"Hi, Rocket," Neeva said. "I missed you."

Rocket was quiet.

"He's being passive-aggressive," Celia said.

He finally chirped.

"You've won him over."

"Either that or Rocket just chirps randomly."

"Hey now," Celia said.

They spent a few minutes making bird noises and sticking their fingers in the cage. Neeva occasionally caressed the base of the smooth bars, testing the cold metal, feeling it drain heat from her fingers. The polish tarnished under the residual condensation.

Celia was smiling, watching her pet the cage.

Eventually Rocket seemed to tire of entertaining them. He sat on his swinging rung and became apathetic to any noises or prodding. Celia said, "Sometimes I wonder why we got this bird. Most of the time he just poops and sits there, looking sad."

"Did you have one when you were a kid?"

"Yeah. Four, in fact, over the years. I know, I'm a hopeless Verdarist."

"Grandpa told me that it was a conscious choice by First Colony pioneers to have a broad biodiversity of bird species, not only as a food stock but also to permeate our culture—whether as pets, or tattoos. It's partially because, as far as pets go, they don't require much nutrition, but also because they help inspire us."

"You're kidding me. How is Rocket inspirational? Look at him."

"You've seen the signs; the slogans that say when the Verdara comes we can release them from their cages and let them fly away into the wide expanses of Venus. They have those so we will always be wondering what that looks like—imagining birds serenading us in spaces filled with trees and grass and rivers. Their presence helps us work harder to give them that future."

"Wow. Who knew that Rocket here was actually brainwashing me all this time? I'll be more careful next time I clean out his poop."

"Yes. Watch out. Make sure he's finished before you go in."

This time it was Celia's turn to push Neeva's shoulder.

Neeva's comm beeped twice. That meant it was urgent. She looked down at the message, expecting it to be one of the many notices she was receiving about members being added to her team, or logistical preparations for meetings and travel. But it wasn't that at all.

Inspector Neeva Nash lineage 4a,

We matched a Tetraderyx stash to an evidence sample you found in Samar City. You had noted in the file that you were looking for a Mel Redrock-Ora, and we have someone here that fits her description. She's alive but needs medtech assistance. I can hold her for 24 hours before bringing her back to NoPo enforcers for processing. We're at an abandoned biocrawler near Atlar Massif, if you'd like to question her.

Let me know. I'll send you the coordinates.

Jedol Coates lineage 151e
Lieutenant Second Class
SoPo DEA

Neeva wasn't due to head south until the next afternoon, and the abandoned biocrawler wasn't far away, so she would have time. It could be her last chance to close the case with Hix for good.

She had to go and see Mel.

When Neeva looked up, Celia's head was already cocked to the side. She might not have known the contents of the message, but she knew what was going to happen next.

Neeva said, "You know I said I was leaving tomorrow... I'm so sorry. Something came up. I have to do this and I—"

"Stop stuttering, my little sparrow. I fully expected it. Go on and find that all-important detail you're always looking for. Go on and conquer the next hedonite uprising, oh great senior inspector." Celia's smile was gracious, but also forced. She was trying so hard.

Neeva picked up her bag and made for the door. Celia followed.

"I don't deserve you," Neeva said. "I'll take some time off when this is over. I promise."

"Shhh. Fly away. Do what you were meant to do, my precious bird."

They kissed, barely more than a peck, and then hugged for a good minute.

Celia broke apart, they shared a smile, and Neeva turned and left.

19

———

THE CLAM OPERATOR

The next transport launch window was in two days, and Rav wanted to use it.

There was going to be a diversion. Then, using stolen credentials and the strategic disappearance of a few unprincipled security guards, an assault party would make its way along the snake to the main dock, and take the transport by force.

At least, that's what Hix had pieced together based on the shakedowns and blackmailing he'd been party to so far. He'd given up asking Rav for more details. People who've been impaled by scalding pipes tend to have a low tolerance for logistical minutiae.

Rav's latest request—"to see a guy about helping"—was even more obscure.

Hix and Pru were walking together on the seventh ring promenade. It wasn't well-maintained, with streaks of yellow and brown tarnishing the walls and floor. They passed a defunct cleaning droid, its parts strewn about as if a mech worker had opened it up and then just given up on it.

"What happened here?" Hix asked.

"Oh nothing, flyboy. Rav has about half of the seventh ring under his thumb. The maintenance crew got up and left for another ring because they were worried about the situation. So we've gotta take care of things ourselves."

"Must make your job easier."

"Whaddya mean?"

"You're the sanitation engineer on this ring, aren't you? If you're with Rav and he has control, it must make your job easier."

"Oh yeah. Guess so."

"You know my dad was a sanitation engineer, back in Redrock. I know it can be a tough job. You're not just cleaning up after people."

Pru glanced at him sidelong, as if she didn't quite believe him. But she said, "Sure as shit."

"So are you going to tell me where we're going?"

She smiled. "We're going to the clam for a job interview."

"Who is it?"

"Soon enough, Falcon Fire."

A gaunt-looking hedonite with orange and blue hair passed them, heading in the opposite direction. He kept his eyes down and averted away. Hix had never seen him before, but he must know Pru was one of Rav's lieutenants or he wouldn't look so meek. Maybe he was even part of Rav's tribe. He could be running an errand for Rav at that very moment.

"Didn't Rav work in reclamation back on Venus?" Hix asked.

"Yeah, me and Rav both worked at the Themis clam, but not for human waste reclamation—we did machines. We were on the lower levels where they take them apart. Some pieces could be reused, but most had to be melted down. The worst were the fluids we had to syphon out of the things: gasoline, machine oil, antifreeze, coolant, mercury, you name it. Toxic stuff."

The Themis Reclamation Center was one of the largest in SoPo, employing at least a thousand people. It was hard work, and the facility was cut off from the major cities, which sowed the seeds for violence and tribalism. It was the kind of environment that spawned people like Rav.

"I thought you were in security," Hix said.

"I was. I worked in security for the clam facility. I also have eyes."

Hix sniffed a laugh. It was nice to hear some snark from Pru instead of her constant evasions. She was an important ally, and he was glad they were speaking on less formal terms.

"Is that why you both have the hawk tats?" he asked. "Was that your tribe?"

Pru looked at him in surprise. "It ain't just hawks that have good eyes. Falcons too." She smiled. "Yeah. Me and Rav were in the same tribe in Themis. He took care of me."

"You don't seem like the type to need taking care of. Although with Rav around, I guess you need to watch your back. He seems to relish conflict."

"You getting all sentimental on me, Falcon Fire? I'm security corps, through and through, but yeah, senseless killing isn't for me. I understand the need for it, though. I do it when I gotta."

"Yeah, and I'm glad you do, Pru. We do what we have to."

"Yeah."

"Just so you know, I've got your back, in case there's any funny business with Rav."

Her eyes widened. "Not gonna happen. Rav is sinister for sure, but I've been loyal. He's not gonna do 'nuthin to me. You be good, and you'll be fine."

Hix delivered a deep frown. He pulled it right from a scene out of *Sky Gate*, when Captain Zak was gazing across the Venusian cloud-scape before going to battle.

"You don't think so?" she asked.

"Truth is, I'm not sure, but you know Rav better than I. Either way, I got your back."

"Well, thanks. Now stop this soppy gullshit. You vid stars are always trying to get all mushy. We've got a job to do."

The reclamator facility was a blocky outcrop with a single two-door entrance. Typically reclamators were guarded, but no one was here. Pru punched in her code and entered.

It was a hot, sulphurous room, with four closed furnaces and numerous labeled panels lining the walls. A rundown droid had been pushed into the corner. A grease-streaked man with a shaved head and stiff beard was working to separate the components off another droid with a ply tool on a table.

The man stepped back slowly. "What is it?" he asked. He knew something was up.

"Let's talk to Rav about it," Pru said. "He'll be here in a minute."

The man nodded. His body was as stiff as his beard. His eyes shifted back and forth between them.

"I'm Hix," Hix offered. "You look familiar."

"I know," he said.

"You never seen Kaj play?" Pru asked. "Killer Kaj?"

Now Hix could place him. Kaj was one of the better murderball players. He'd heard the name mentioned a few times on Kanto, and he'd seen him play once on Venus.

"Sorry," Hix said. "Of course. I'm always behind on murderball,"

Kaj squinted and nodded.

Rav strolled in a moment later. He was flanked by Uwy, a former hedonite male model whose career had been subverted by a missing ear and prominent scar down his cheek. Rippling muscles stretched the fabric of his shirt.

"Oh good. We're all here," Rav said. "I do hate waiting around."

Kaj took another step back from the table. "What's this all about?" he said.

Rav sat on a stool while Uwy stood with arms crossed behind him. Rav said, "Well, let's see. You can throw a ball, and you're good with tools, and you've fired a stunner before."

Kaj shrugged. "The stunner—it was just a week of training. I was security for a few months before Themis. So what?"

"Those are useful skills," Rav said. "Who you got back home?"

Kaj shook his head. "Look, I don't care what you do, but no thanks, okay."

Rav looked offended. "Hey, I'm here to *help*. We can make their lives easier. Maybe we can help you see them again."

"Please," Kaj said. "I don't want any trouble. I just want to do my job and play ball. I'm not going to stick my nose in anyone's tail feathers."

Rav looked thoughtful. "I appreciate that, but because your nose hasn't been sticking out anywhere, it hasn't been smelling what's really going on. So let me tell you. I'm running things here on the seventh ring. Everybody's business is my business."

Kaj nodded. "I know that. I wouldn't ever say otherwise."

Rav ignored him. "So you're already working for me, since I'm running things. There's been a change in management and you didn't get the memo."

Kaj's teeth clenched. "What is it you want me to do?"

"A bit of bumping and grinding on the snake."

"No, sorry. I'll do almost anything, but that's a capital offence. I've seen enough people get put in the clam for less. I can help you here on the seventh ring, no problem."

Rav looked at Uwy. "It sounds like he's negotiating with me, doesn't it? Like we're uppity reformer peacocks vying for biocrawler time?"

Uwy needed no more convincing to begin advancing on Kaj. Hix and Pru also spread out to surround him, blocking off his exits.

"Wait," Kaj said. He looked over at Pru. "Can't you stop him? You *know* me. I won't rat you out."

"Hold," Rav said, and Uwy halted his advance. "This is interesting. Pru, you *know* him? What a revelation. Tell us how to proceed here."

Pru laughed. "Yeah, I did know you, Kaj. I hoped maybe you'd changed because that was like a whole planet ago. Still too stubborn, I see."

Kaj snatched his pry tool and took one more step back.

Uwy advanced, but before he made his move, Kaj threw his hands up. "Fine, fine. I'll do it. Whatever it is." He put the tool back on the table. He knew the odds were against him.

Uwy retreated.

Rav rubbed his head and looked about the room. Hix was relieved, but Rav didn't look happy. He was cringing, in fact.

"So what is it?" Kaj said.

"You don't need to know." Rav said.

Kaj sighed. "Can I at least know *when* it is?"

"Well, unfortunately... no."

Kaj frowned. "Then how can I possibly help?"

Rav stood up and took a step back from his chair. "You see, there is a thing called *free will*. You only said yes when you were backed into a corner, so how can I trust you? If you'd said yes right away... maybe, but what this tells me—" he waved his hand back and forth between them to exemplify their recent exchange, "—is we know you *really* don't want to be involved."

Kaj's mouth hung open.

Rav flicked his hand at him and said, "Uwy."

Kaj darted for the tool again, but Uwy was too close. Uwy landed an arching downward punch to the side of Kaj's head before he could pick it up. Kaj staggered back, bewildered, until Uwy's mitt found Kaj's skull again and pounded it against the table where the tool was, leaving a bloody indentation in the side of his face. Kaj slunk off the table, dead or unconscious.

"The clam?" Uwy asked.

"Of course," Rav said. "We met him here for a reason."

Uwy dragged Kaj by the foot to the big red bio-reclamator, opened it up and tossed him in. He puzzled over the tablet commands on the side. "Anyone know how to work this?"

Hix was lingering in the back, frozen into inaction by the violent display. Kaj seemed like he could be a decent asset, if given time. He wanted to object, or at least ask what Rav was thinking, but he held his tongue. He didn't want to join Kaj in the clam.

Rav said, "Hix, help Uwy out, will you? Otherwise we'll be here forever."

Hix regained his composure and walked over. He'd never used a reclamator either, and there were quite a few command buttons.

"Try this one," Pru whispered, pointing at an orange button. She'd followed him over. He pressed the one she indicated. Inside the reclamator window, Kaj's body became covered in mini-bots that came out of tiny apertures around him. They were beginning the dissection routine. Eventually, specific body parts would be compartmentalized, valuable biomass would be stripped off the bones, and the bones would be incinerated. On the screen was the message *Human reclamation in progress.*

"Thanks," Hix whispered. "How'd you know that?"

"Hawk eyes," Pru said. She was smiling and pointing two fingers at her face.

They all left the reclamator facility after a brief clean-up.

"Two days," Rav said, before he split off.

"Two days," Hix acknowledged, and he headed back toward the twelfth ring.

Hix wondered if the heist would have to be pushed out further. Rav would need a lot of help to fight through the snake, and he wasn't sure he'd recruited enough people. It was one thing to have a big tribe, but it was another to ask them to risk their life on an unknown lark.

It wasn't until later, after he'd had time to rewind the encounter in his mind, that Hix pieced together Rav's strategy. Rav and Pru had known Kaj from Venus and so they probably also knew he would be reticent to help. Rav had wanted this conflict, and an excuse to throw Kaj in the clam. Kaj was well known as a murderball star, so word would spread quickly, if the right people were told about what happened.

Soon the whole seventh ring would know what would happen if Rav asked for help and they said no.

There would be no more dissenters.

There was only two more days, and they would be ready.

20

MEL

Given the distance from LC, and the limited time Neeva had, a jet copter was needed, so she chartered an X92. The journey granted her a few hours of sleep.

She woke with thirty minutes to spare. In the remaining time, she fidgeted with her tacti device as she looked out of the window. The unforgiving ball rolled under her fingers. The jagged lines of studs let her orient the positioning of the ball in her mind. She found the feathery tail that stuck out of the joint at end of the ball, and she let it slide over her knuckles. It would usually send a tickle down her spine, but this time it drove her senses to alertness. An image came to mind of a starving vulture about to bite her hand.

She pulled her hand out of her pocket.

They were in sun season, so the windows had heavy tinting, and it flavored her view of the surface with an orange hue. Layers of white and red basalt, with the odd seam of black magnesite, climbed up and down the basin below. The terrain was often pocked by craters or deluged by flows of hardened lava.

The Atlar Massif reached into the sky in the distance. Verdarist renderings of the Atlar ranges showed smooth curves and a breathtaking waterfall, but at the moment it was hard to reconcile that hopeful future with the profile that occupied the viewport. Neeva's vista was all sharp spires and treacherous peaks.

Egan was dwarfing the seat next to her. He'd been released from rehab three days ago. Scars pocked his face, some of which would be permanent. His amputated arm had been replaced with a high-grade defense prosthesis, commonly known as a combat arm. It was a bulky cylinder with a built-in blaster and grenade launcher, not to mention a few other neat tricks.

He was looking at his comm, until he caught her staring at him. "Ma'am?" he said.

"You sure you're up for this?" she asked.

"Yes ma'am. I was given clearance." The words ran out of his mouth quickly. His tendency for nervous chatter hadn't changed.

"I know, but this is unrelated to what happened in Skiddado. And I heard it could be messy inside."

"I'm going." He stared her down. His eyes were filled with tension, shadowed by blue bags. Eventually his countenance softened. "If it's alright with you, ma'am."

"Of course, Egan. I'm glad to have you."

The symbionts had pegged Egan at eighty percent recovered psychologically. And he was surely physically substandard relative to other PDA agents she could have chosen, but what he would have in great abundance, and what was most important for Neeva, was another quality: loyalty.

They flew past an area of undulating ledges and entered a broad canyon cut out of the Atlar Massif. This was where the biocrawler lanes were. The huge, parallel channels stretched to the horizon, circling the planet to allow the biocrawlers to stay in perpetual sunlight. Just to the east, Neeva could see a line of crawlers visible on the horizon, glinting in the sun. It was hard to tell if they were moving. They may have been pausing for harvesting and resupply near Atlar Station to the east. From Neeva's vantage point they looked like an army of metal insects waiting to charge.

Ahead was one crawler that wasn't part of the line. It had split off from the arcing tread lines of its peers, as if it had gone awol from the rest of the insect army. The outer surface was sand-blasted and a dune had built up on one side. A rough road led up to and around it.

"Yes, sir," Priva said into her mic. She pitched the X92 into an angled descent, dropping onto a makeshift landing pad next to the main dome of the lonely derelict crawler. A masked man walked out to meet them.

"This should be Officer Coates," Priva said, "I'll stay in the copter. You have two hours if you want to make it back to LC before morning."

"Thank you, Priva," Neeva said. Egan and Neeva donned their atmospheric masks and disembarked.

"Inspector Nash?" Coates said, extending a fist-to-seed salute. She returned the gesture and nodded. He sported long, unkempt locks of hair above freckled cheeks. Brown spots marked a trajectory across his chest—blood spatter. "Nice to meet you," he said. "Come with me."

The first door they entered had scratches on it, and the vacuum seal had clearly been compromised, so they kept their masks on as they entered a large vestibule. It wasn't until they'd passed through yet another door that adjoined one of the ecochambers that they had a proper atmosphere. Here, they removed their masks.

Neeva said, "Thank you for alerting me, Coates. I almost forgot I had submitted the evidence, frankly."

Coates looked frazzled. "Yeah, no problem," he said. "Our operation was pretty savage. We're still after suspects who left in ground transports, and we're low on manpower here on the crawler. Otherwise I could have delivered her to you up in LC."

"Can you describe the context of her apprehension?" she asked.

"Sure," he said. "These abandoned biocrawlers are sometimes used by hermits. Pockets of atmosphere can be maintained and it's easy to recover the leftover charge for life support operations with working solar panels. But there are quite a few of them—about seventy have been abandoned in NoPo and forty in SoPo—so it became too resource-intensive to police all the squatters. And at times they've been used by Tetraderyx dealers, but it's only been small-scale so we just let them be so we could focus on distribution hubs in major population centers. Or at least, until now." His brow furrowed.

He pointed at the ceiling. "We had a drone still doing flybys. One of them noticed a transport that was regularly coming and going from this crawler. The vehicle had an angular dent in it that the symbionts associated with a transport that disappeared in one of our ongoing investigations. So yesterday we sent a team in and found a large stash of Tetraderyx, and a bunch of runners."

"Runners?"

"People who try to avoid capture. But this, this was more than that. He sighed and looked down at his bloody shirt. "Usually on these busts you might get one or two brave heeds with contraband weapons. This was different. There were four, all with blasters, and they knew what they were doing. We lost five of our guys—top of the line enforcers." He edged his chin toward Egan. "We tried to disarm the runners who didn't make it out, but they were so aggressive, so desperate. We killed three and the last one shot himself after he was injured. These people..." He cringed and shook his head.

"How does Mel fit into this?"

"Not sure exactly. It was a big smuggling operation, and they like to have girls like her hanging around. She told us they kidnapped her, and were using her for entertainment, or to run errands. Her story matches her psychanthropic profile, and we don't have any reason to believe otherwise, but maybe you know something we don't."

Neeva nodded. "Not really. In fact, I have very little info on her. Is there anyone else we might be able to question about Mel's involvement?"

"Seven suspects fled using other transports—we're still after them. They left Redrock-Ora here. She was tied up, away from the action, and she couldn't flee with the rest. She didn't even try, although it may be because she was high or strung out. She's more lucid now, but still a wreck. We have her on step down doses of Amadone, so she doesn't go into shock."

"Good."

"What's your angle here, Inspector, if you don't mind my asking?"

"This is related to another investigation—Hix Redrock-Ren. Nothing to do with narcotics."

His eyebrows raised. "From *Sky Gate*? I thought he'd been convicted."

"Yes, well, there are still some loose ends."

His eyebrows remained raised; whether in contemplation or suspicion, Neeva couldn't be sure. Finally, he said, "Alright. I'll show you in."

They entered through a hatch with squeaky hinges and walked down a glass-walled corridor that threaded through the old ecological chambers. Most of these chambers were completely empty, but others contained rotted biomass that looked like drifts of peat. There were holey roosting walls and a bubbling stream in one, just like the Big Beetle chamber she'd been fishing in with Grandpa, but instead of the ground shimmering with green grasses, it was brown and scarred, with nothing alive. One of these ecochambers seemed to be at least marginally maintained, with sparrows and pigeons flying and twittering about, and scattered patches of sickly ferns and grasses. The floor was saturated in yellow and white feces in places, and empty seed bowls were littered throughout. Birds found perches in stone nests and the few dead trees that hadn't fallen over.

They crossed a hallway where the floor was covered with shards of transparent plexmold, most of it swept against the side walls. From there they walked into a jagged forced-opening in the glass that led into a long rectangular ecochamber stretching into the distance. It followed a meager river that was adrift with floating detritus, the water curdling with an oily texture. Along the sides were mini-stalls, behind closed glass doors where the biocrawler's former proprietors would have grown other plant species not part of the chamber's ecology. Most of these were dark, but a few ahead of Neeva had been blasted open.

They passed through quickly. One side antechamber had an orange pull line across the entrance. Beyond the line Neeva glimpsed pink tags positioned on the floor, and blood spatter in an arc across the wall. Perhaps it was where some of Coates's smugglers had been held up.

Egan's eyes were active, scanning in every direction. A hollow sound emanated from his throat. It was a bit like wheezing, but it wasn't exhaustion, or some post-traumatic habit. His new arm wasn't his only new prosthesis. He'd also had some of his trachea replaced, and every once in a while the new material would cause interference on his breathing that was just audible enough for her to hear.

Two more side stalls later, they found Mel. There were a number of cots in the room, and a few potted plants. In the center was a large gray tree without any leaves. Neeva touched the trunk as she passed by it. She liked the texture of tree bark. It usually felt like miniature mountain ridges, with rhythmic, repetitive patterns, but the bark of this tree had been stripped away, making the surface too smooth, with only small ridges and faint cracks. It was probably dead.

"I'll leave you to it," Coates told them. He was pressing on his earbud. "I'm needed elsewhere."

"Thank you, Coates," Neeva said. He was already jogging away.

Mel was sitting up in a cot pushed into the corner, staring at a tablet. Next to her was a plant with drooping leaves, and two open bags with clothes lumped across them. She was wearing shorts and a halter top that was ripped, but perhaps on purpose—as a fashion statement. Her negligible clothing exposed the jumble of angles and protuberant bones that made up her arms and legs. A chevron-shaped scar angled across one cheek, heavily caked with foundation, and her blue irises were mostly obscured by dilated pupils.

Mel had been pretty once. She wasn't anymore.

Mel wrinkled her nose as Neeva approached. "Smells like peacock poop around here," she said.

"I'd like to ask you a few questions," Neeva said.

Mel was avoiding Neeva's gaze. "Uh huh. And why would I answer? My lovable captor is already giving me Amadone. What can you do for me?"

"I could get you another plant."

Mel looked over at her mournful plant and raised her eyebrows, as if considering it. She yawned.

"Or I could tell you how Hix is doing."

Mel's eyes snapped up to meet Neeva's. "Who are you?" she asked.

"Planetary Defense. I worked on your brother's case."

She squinted. "Now I remember you. You were on the news. Where is he?"

Neeva offered her a grim smile. "I'd like your help first, if that's okay with you."

"With what? I already told them I don't know anything. The smugglers kidnapped me and didn't tell me anything."

"No, this is about Hix. I want to know who he was working with."

"What do you mean—which director? The last one he had was—"

"No. Who told him to take that joyride in the dirigible?"

Mel's eyes rolled, followed by her head. "That was all him. It *was* a joyride. Nobody told him to do anything. Yeah, he shouldn't have taken the dirigible—that was wrong—but what happened with Shawna, it was an accident. He had a thing for her. That was real."

"How do you know it was real?"

She looked thoughtful. "Because he's my brother, and because I'm his only friend. Because I saw the way they were together. It was him, but not him, you know? And I don't mean he was acting. When he was with Shawna, he always had this cheesy grin. It wasn't a smile from *Toreno Run* or *Sky Gate*. No. It made him look too stupid; they would have never allowed it on the vids. But I'd seen that grin before. It was the grin of a ten-year-old that only I knew—the ten-year-old that would come with me to swim in the pools of Samar City, or tag along on jobs. "

"But he was famous," Neeva said, "and he had money. Why would he jeopardize all that by going on a joyride?"

She sniffed and shook her head. "Love makes people do crazy things. What's that saying again? Oh yeah: 'Love changes everything, especially the psychanthropic algorithms'. That's why you 'formers are having trouble figuring this out."

Neeva nodded, trying to give the impression she was satisfied with Mel's response. She kneeled down and felt the drooping leaves of the plant, propping them up and letting them fall down again. "And what about you? Why are you doing this to yourself?"

"Doing what?"

"Prostitution. Tetraderyx. It's going to kill you. Why?"

She snorted. "Is this the part where you pretend to care? Come on. My brother is an actor, remember—I can tell what you're doing. And yeah, I know I'm washed up, but who gives a shit. I won't be missed. I might as well be a pyrolyte. I could certainly use the tan." She chuckled, but it triggered a dry cough that sounded more like hacking.

Neeva said, "I know someone who might give a shit."

Mel's eyes flashed. "Yeah maybe, if he's still alive, but he's not here, is he? I'm talking to you, and to you I'm just another data pattern for you to feed to the symbionts. You'll use my words to twist the vice, or tighten the noose, or... whatever you're doing to Hix now."

"This won't affect Hix. His case is closed. His sentencing can only be revisited if facts come to the surface that prove his innocence."

Mel shrugged.

"I'm here because there's more to the story. More that you're not telling me."

Mel just gave her a sour expression.

"Hix is in orbit around Earth," Neeva continued, "part of the terraforming operations. The Executive Council commuted his sentence on account of his community standing. It helped him avoid capital punishment."

Mel's expression morphed into a confused frown.

"Like I said, I'm the PDA inspector who investigated Hix, but I'm also Shawna's sister. Despite the fact that I hate Hix, and despite the fact that he got my sister killed, I also believe—like you—there could have been something between them, that maybe, just maybe, Hix isn't completely reckless. Maybe there is a method to his madness that I haven't found."

"So what?"

"So what?" Neeva said, raising her voice.

Mel shrugged.

Neeva stabbed an index finger at her. "Ask yourself what you're doing here, Mel. Why did you sleep with Henckels June, Wik Scorpio-Vas and Tim Samar-Ben, if not to protect Hix? And yet you can't even answer a few questions that might help him *and* you. But no, you'd rather hit Tetra into oblivion. Consider for a second that if you'd showed up to testify, Hix might not even be in Earth orbit. And don't give me your excuses. We know you were with Tim Samar-Ben, probably as one of his concubines, but also as a messenger, and—" she paused and took a breath, before delivering her last words crisply, "—that you're Mantle's whore, just as much as everyone else's."

Mel just stared back at her, her eyes burning.

"So ask yourself, are you really Hix's guardian angel, or are you just a slut looking for your next fix?"

The ridge of Mel's nose rippled. Her pale face was filling with color. "Ha!" she said, some spittle escaping her lips. "If you know all that, then both our fates are sealed, aren't they? It doesn't matter what I tell you, or how I help you, because soon you'll be on a copter, or a crawler, or even in your fancy 'former apartment and you'll hear a 'twisted slag' whispered behind you, and that'll be it, you'll be snuffed out. In fact, you might as well join me in the little time you have left. Ask your DEA buddy for some more Amadone while you can. I'm sure he has plenty."

Neeva's head slowly recoiled. She breathed mechanically, in and out, letting the emotions subside. There was no need to escalate the conversation further. She had what she needed.

Mel noticed the change. "What?"

Neeva stepped away, averting her face from Mel. It had been a hunch to mention Mantle, and she'd doubted it would make any sense, but it had. Not only that, Mel had used the call sign. It meant Mel was almost certainly involved, and could be an important asset to Neeva's investigation in SoPo. In fact, it could be that this whole drug-dealing operation was run by Mantle.

There was a slight rumbling beneath her feet. It felt like the engines turning on to move the crawler. An urgent message vibrated her comm device. It was Coates.

The suspects have returned. Vacate the crawler at once.

She passed her comm to Egan so he could read it. "We could see some heat," she said.

Neeva turned back to Mel, her eyes scrolling over her skinny limbs. She was pouting in defiance.

"What is it?" Mel asked.

"They're coming back. Why?"

For the first time Mel's face registered something other than bitterness. She blanched in fear.

"You don't have to die here," Neeva said. She took out the picture of Mel and Hix that she'd obtained from Mel's apartment, and showed it to her. "I don't think that's what Hix would have wanted."

Mel's eyes consumed the picture. Her irises darted back and forth. "You'll have to take me by force," she said. She extended her wrists out ever so slightly. One of them was still cuffed to the bed.

It was an affirmation that Mel would come with her, but only if it looked like it was against her will. Neeva resisted the urge to look around for cameras. Was someone watching? Was *Mantle* watching? It only heightened her concern about the situation.

Distorted sounds could be heard. They must have been yelling, but the voices came across as low moans reverberating against the metal walls of the biocrawler. There was another tremble.

Neeva used her comm to override Coates's cuffs. With one eye on Mel, she untethered them from the bed and reapplied the cuffs to Mel's wrists.

They left the side-stall and re-entered the larger ecochamber, heading back toward the copter landing pad. Their backs were glued to the wall and their blasters were out. Neeva had to pull Mel along occasionally, but only to make a show of it. She was moving of her own volition.

The subsequent passageway led through smaller antechambers. Here Egan stopped and kneeled down ahead of them. He put his index finger to his lips and showed his combat arm. It was fully powered up, with two barrels sticking out of the sides. On the display panel was a heat map of distorted figures crouching down and moving across the screen presumably behind the wall ahead of them. Egan had used the arm's sonic sensors to resolve the image.

The image on the display panel exploded with color as blaster shots rang out. Egan bounced to his feet and jogged to the leading edge of the corridor wall, maneuvering his arm around the corner. The display screen flashed a crisper image of several men taking position behind a small hillock in the center of the next ecochamber. They were firing periodically toward the other end of the chamber, where two of Coates's enforcers were pinned behind a dead tree. Blaster damage formed dark nebulae patterns on the wall behind them.

"I'll take the right flank, behind that tree," Egan said. "You stay here and cover me."

Egan was about to make his move, eager to jump into battle so he could help Coates and his men, but Neeva knew it wasn't right. Their first priority was to protect the valuable intelligence they'd obtained. In fact, it was entirely possible that these Mantle men were coming back for Mel.

There was another pathway. It would go around the outer perimeter of the biocrawler.

Neeva placed her hand gently on Egan's good shoulder. He flinched, his eyes shining.

"This isn't our fight," she said. "We have to get out with this asset."

His brow furrowed in confusion. He looked back and forth between her and Mel while blaster shots rang out behind the wall.

"But ma'am. These people... We can't just..." His stuttering monologue trailed off.

She just looked back at him sternly.

"Fine," he said slowly. It wasn't as definitive as Neeva would have liked, but she wasn't about to complain.

They retreated from the melee and took the secondary passage. It curled around one of the main walls, where they found a hatch that led to the perimeter causeway.

Occasionally, blaster sounds and distant yelling resonated through the walls of the corridor.

Egan was pulling up the rear. His breathing was loud and laden with reverberations caused by his throat prosthesis. It made him sound like a muffled goose.

As for Mel, her eyes were wide, watchful. She moved willingly, and quietly.

The corridor arched and opened up until Neeva saw a DEA agent pointing his blaster at them in the distance. It was Coates.

"Senior Inspector Neeva Nash here," she yelled, her blaster pointing toward the ceiling. Egan also directed his combat arm toward the floor.

Coates recognized them, but was still slow to lower his blaster. "You'd better go," he yelled back, waving them over. "The situation isn't stable."

"What about you and your men?"

He ignored her question. "Another dealer transport is arriving soon. I'm not sure..." He became distracted by a new message flashing on his comm.

Neeva pulled an atmospheric mask off the wall for Mel, and Egan grabbed one as well. Neeva paused before she put one on herself.

"Yes, retreat!" Coates said after pressing on his earbud. "Find better positioning!"

"When are your reinforcements coming?" Neeva asked.

"I don't know," Coates said, not taking his eyes from his comm.

There couldn't be many more DEA men left on the biocrawler. She would be abandoning them, but if there was a whole other Mantle transport coming, she and Egan weren't going to make much difference.

And she needed to get to the root of this. If she died, or was captured, the whole investigation could be disadvantaged. She gritted her teeth and donned her atmospheric mask. Mel and Egan were already waiting for her by the airlock.

Before they entered the hatch, she turned to Coates and said, "I'll call PDA—I'll get them to send help."

It felt woefully inadequate, but it was enough to divert his eyes from his comm momentarily. "Thank you, Inspector. Now go."

They entered the airlock, and followed the exit procedures. Priva was waiting, the X92's engine purring. They lifted off while Neeva made feverish calls and sent urgent messages, trying to get reinforcements for the DEA crew. She went all the way up the line to Fisker and Middich.

There were hundreds of responses. The PDA and the DEA went into a frenzy trying to mobilize the necessary resources, but there was nothing nearby. They couldn't get backup for at least an hour. It would take five hours for a proper strike team to reach the biocrawler.

Coates and his crew were on their own.

Neeva found out later that the whole biocrawler was set aflame, destroying all the evidence of what had happened. And the Mantle transports also got away, lost into the growing dark spots of the psychanthropic surveillance feeds that now reached into the southern massifs of NoPo.

Two days later, she would be asked by both Fisker and the DEA Director alike to be the one to go to Coates's family and explain how he died.

21

THE SNAKE

Pru and Rav looked down at their comms in unison.

"Okay, here we go," Rav said, standing up and stretching his back.

Hix and the rest of the group followed them out of the fifth ring gymnasium. They were all dressed in murderball outfits—tight fitting stretchy pants and shirts, covered in puffy jackets, with fake sweat stains around their collars and duffel bags hefted over their shoulders.

Rav led them along the main promenade to the nearest spoke. They began climbing up the ladder toward the snake.

Hix was watchful, looking out for other hedonites and reformers, but also any hints from Rav and Pru as to what the next hour might bring. They had the access codes they needed, but he still didn't know much about the plan for bypassing the sentries along the way, and he was unsure what kind of reformer presence they were likely to meet in the transport bay itself.

Although Hix wasn't so much worried about Rav having a well-thought-out plan. He was more worried about how he fit into it.

The G-forces gradually lessened the higher they climbed, until they reached the junction point. The junction was an internal ring around the snake that had a broad aperture allowing you to jump from the rotating spoke into the snake. Uwy opened the door to the aperture and a mechanical arm pulled them in, one at a time, while spinning them to counter the ring's rotation and bring them stationary relative to the snake. Hix went through with his eyes closed. It helped to reduce the feeling of disorientation.

Once inside, they paused, adjusting to the difference in spin by staring away from the aperture. Many of them held onto cleats along the wall, as if they were falling and it might hold them up. Most prisoners traversed through the snake on a daily basis, but it was still hard to get used to the changes in spin and G-forces. Pru and Uwy looked pale, and were possibly nauseous, but G-force changes usually had little effect on Hix.

All of them donned pairs of communal magnetic boots that were hooked onto the wall. These made tacking noises as they plodded down the corridor in the direction of the first ring and the hangar bays.

Rav stopped at a viewport where the rings could be seen rotating around the snake. The viewport was next to an interchange where the reformer sections of the snake were accessible.

"We wait here," Pru said.

"For what?" Vas said. Vas was a quiet fellow with bushy eyebrows, hunched posture and droopy eyes. One might get the impression he was half asleep, but he was always alert. His movements were sharp and precise, and sometimes violent.

"We wait here," Pru said again, smiling.

There were seven of them in all. Rav, Pru, Hix, Vas, Jin, Tolquist, and Uwy.

Jin was the most notable addition. Hix was surprised he'd been invited at all. He had fallen in line with Rav, but he could still be a threat to Rav's leadership given the size of his following. Maybe they had made some kind of agreement so they could both make it back to Venus. It was possible Jin was Mantle as well. Hix would be the last to know.

All in all, it was a small crew for such a daring objective.

What was perhaps more surprising than Jin's presence was Iri's absence. Maybe he had a falling out with Rav. Whatever the reason, Hix was relieved. With no one to compete against for top pilot, it meant Hix was indispensable.

Rav was still preoccupied with the viewport. Hix tried to follow the direction of his gaze as he stared out at the revolving rings. Every once in a while he would glance at his comm. Eventually, he stopped staring and nodded. "Ten minutes until we move."

Hix saw what Rav had seen. The seventh ring was spitting out atmosphere like a leaky faucet. Objects flew out: furniture, droids, and revolving human bodies. It quickly escalated as a chunk of the ring severed off, bending into space. The ring was only being held together by two skeletal arcing beams.

The explosion had to be a part of a diversion. It would call reformers from the snake and the first ring to address the issue, reducing security along the path to the transport.

Hix said, "What if the ring had split completely? What if it collided with the other rings?"

Rav smiled. "I guess our diversion would have worked even better."

The intercom blared. "This is an emergency. Incendiaries have been detonated on rings four and seven. Riots have broken out on rings four and five. Martial law is in effect immediately. All prisoners must return to their cells or be subject to penalties, including immediate reclamation."

This would certainly preoccupy the guards, but martial law would also mean the access points from the rings to the snake would be closed to prisoners. In other words, there wouldn't be any more help coming from Rav's tribe.

"Is that where Iri is?" Hix asked. "On ring four?"

"He's doing his part," Rav said.

"But won't all these people rat you out if they aren't included? It's not like we're going to be able to send for them later."

Rav frowned. He escorted Hix away from the window, out of earshot of the others, and spoke quietly. "They're gulls, Hix. They think we're trying to throw off the reformer yoke and take over the whole station. They don't need to know about our little adventure. If they're not happy about it, they can go ahead and try to catch us. We'll be halfway to Venus."

Hix nodded slowly. He was amazed at how much chaos Rav had already caused, and they hadn't even entered reformer territory yet.

They returned to the window, and a few minutes later, after watching the torn ring, Pru punched him in the shoulder. "Falcon Fire, you're up." She pointed down the hall to the access door that led to the reformer-patrolled passageways on the snake.

Hix approached the door. The others closed in behind him.

He took out his comm, pulled up the access code that they'd waterholed, and plugged it into the door control panel. This panel didn't have a retinal scan so it would be straightforward. It was the transport bay he was more worried about.

The access door opened. Pru poked her head in. She said, "Keep an eye out, but the reformer security teams should already be through. They're usually dispatched in less than ten minutes."

They moved with purpose into the corridor on the other side of the access door. This was one of the main arteries for their reformer wardens. They shut off their mag-boots and propelled themselves through the air using the rungs along the wall. Vas, Jin, and Uwy reached into their bags to grab knives and clubs, items that Rav had appropriated from his contacts on the fourth ring.

At one point, Vas accidentally side-swiped Uwy with an overzealous push down the corridor, bouncing Uwy off the bulkhead.

"Watch yourself," Uwy said angrily.

It was obvious it hadn't been intentional. They weren't trained to move in zero G, and many of them had only one free hand.

Pru was in the lead. She slowed down as they came closer to the exterior vestibule of the hangar bay and snuck a peek around the corner to recon the security situation. After she nodded back at them, Vas, Jin and Uwy maneuvered up to her and positioned themselves at the threshold of the opening.

Rav was behind Hix, at the rear of the group. He began prodding

Hix and Tolquist forward. Apparently Hix was supposed to participate, even without a weapon.

Jin, Vas, and Uwy vaulted around the corner and torpedoed themselves at the transport bay entrance. By the time Hix was out of the corridor they were already grappling with two guards, each wearing the typical Kanto Station orange helmets and black nylon suits.

"We're under attack!" one of the guards yelled into his helmet mic as he wrestled with Jin for control of his weapon. The weapon was a prod-shocker—a long barrel with a circular contour at the snout that served dual purpose as a stun rifle or a close-range shocker. "Prisoners at transport bay four!"

The other one was stronger, or maybe better prepared. He threw off Vas, activated his weapon, and shocked Uwy, blasting him across the vestibule. But Jin managed to overcome the first guard and prodded the second guard with the first guard's shocker, making him flail against the hangar hatch. At that point, Hix, Tolquist, and Pru reached the melee and helped to pin down the two guards and remove their helmets.

Their eyes bulged with fear.

Rav floated over much more casually. "It's funny," he said, "in zero G you can move through the air so much faster than sprinting. They don't train you for that, do they?"

The guards didn't answer the rhetorical question.

"What they *do* teach you," Rav continued, "is how crass we hedonite prisoners can be, how base and uncivilized. Maybe I can help you with your training?"

The two guards looked at each other, confused.

Rav smiled, withdrew a knife, and slit each of their throats in turn. Then he promptly proceeded to gouge out the taller one's left eye. Rav glanced back at Jin while he was working. "Really, what's the point of a retinal scan if you can just cut out someone's eye? Stupid."

Tolquist was cringing, his eyes wide. Hix had to look away, and when he did he caught Pru's expression. She was popping her cheeks, making squishy sounds with her mouth, as if she was bored. She picked up the extra prod-shocker and handed it to Hix with a smile.

Why couldn't she use it, he wondered? She was security. Although maybe she wasn't trained with that kind of weapon either. Uwy looked like he might have injured his hand, and maybe Vas wasn't a good shot. In any case, he didn't object.

Rav pushed the freed eyeball against the scanner and it flashed green. The outer hatch to the airlock opened and they moved inside. The door panel for the next hatch was also flashing green.

"Alright," Rav said, "after this next hatch, this is it. They've been alerted, so we need to move fast. We have the credentials to take the *Little Jaunt*," he rolled his eyes at the transport's name, "so once we're there we're home free. It's in the berth immediately across the bay. You ready to go home?"

They all nodded. Rav opened the hatch.

Hix couldn't remember if it was the same hangar bay he'd come into when the *Rackshack* arrived, but it looked similar in size. The hangars were blocky rectangular prisms that splayed out of the end of the snake like fingers from a hand. The contents were surely different, however. When he arrived in the *Rackshack* the bay had been empty, save the line-up of prisoners and the inspection team, but here there were a number of towers of floating supply containers, covered in nets tethered to the ground so they would stay in place. Two of these containers were being pushed by floating fan-powered drones toward different airlocks, presumably for redistribution to the rings of the station.

The other difference was the number of security guards. Before there had been a few of the *Rackshack* crew and maybe four more guards in the bay. Now there were twelve guards, and they were all wearing helmets and body armor, talking animatedly and looking at their comms. Four others were already jogging towards the prisoners, having been alerted by the guards at the door.

Jin and Hix fired their prod-shockers while they secured cover behind one of the supply container towers. Only one of their shocker pulses hit the mark, and it simply glanced off of the guard's armor. The guards sought cover and returned fire.

The odds didn't look good. The guards were directly in their path, and how were they supposed to overcome sixteen of them?

Hix and Jin used their prod-shockers to trade fire with the guards, while Rav and Pru receded behind them to discuss the situation. Uwy and Vas stood just behind Hix and Jin, waiting in reserve and brandishing their crude close-combat weapons.

The hangar guards fanned out, running between supply towers to improve their positioning. They would have better firing angles soon, and should be able to flank the prisoners easily.

Hix told himself not to panic. He tried to think of ways out of their predicament. This was going to end badly for them, unless they retreated. He needed to nudge Rav in the right direction.

"There's no way we're going to make it," Hix yelled, firing around the corner of the boxy supply container without looking back. "There's only two of us with real weapons against sixteen of them, and they'll have reinforcements in no time."

Two shocker pulses hit the container in front of them. Hix and Jin ducked down reflexively.

"Did you hear me?" Hix called out. "We've got to abort, or find some other way. This isn't going to work."

He risked a glance away from the melee to where Rav and Pru had been crouching down behind them.

They were gone.

22

LIGHTS, CAMERAS, TREASON

When Neeva returned from the biocrawler she was subjected to a barrage of questions from a cross-agency team hastily put together by Fisker.

"Why are you still investigating the Hix Redrock-Ren case?" asked the Law Enforcement Deputy Director.

"How is it possible that this dealer outfit had so many men?" asked the DEA Executive Director.

"How come sensor feeds have none of this recorded?" asked a PDA intelligence deployment officer.

These questions all had an undertone of disbelief. Neeva wondered if they were questioning the veracity of her report, and she tried not to be insulted—although, in truth, she found it a bit hard to believe as well. The situation in SoPo was rapidly deteriorating, and an incident like this in NoPo—where a whole DEA team was eliminated by an organized threat—only served to pull at already-frayed nerves.

Mel had been temporarily placed in one of the more discreet PDA interrogation facilities, in an LC sub-settlement. Neeva was staring into her cell at the moment. The interior was a uniformity of dull gray paint, with vertical rectangular slits as the only viewing aperture.

Mel was resting inside on a stiff-looking cot, her eyes closed. She would rub her arms on occasion under the blanket she'd been given.

What part did she have to play in this? Their conversation hadn't given Neeva the impression she was a gull. She must know more than she'd been letting on.

When Neeva was growing up, despite her lineage, and at times because of it, she sometimes felt that her life wasn't fair. When she would compete with others in exams, or sports, or in the academy, she would think they had it easy. They hadn't lost their parents, and they weren't labelled a genetic zero by First Colony preservation advocates for being a lesbian. This chip on Neeva's shoulder would give her an edge—a willingness to fight harder and do better.

But next to Mel, that all fell away. Yes, the Reformer Doctrine said Mel had a profile prone to mental instability, but that wasn't Mel's choice. And with no parents or grandparents, Mel had to help raise a younger brother on her own, while being preyed upon by all manner of hedonite trash. Neeva couldn't imagine how she would fare if she was placed in the same situation.

And there was nobody to protect Mel, except Hix.

For a brief moment, there in that interrogation room, watching Mel rub her arms, Neeva finally understood Hix a little better.

"Stop staring you 'former bitch." Neeva's contemplation was interrupted by Mel's voice. Her eyes were open, staring sourly. "I'm not about to sing and dance for you."

"How about an explanation? Did you know they would come back?" Neeva slipped an Amadone pill onto the crest of the slitted window.

Mel snatched it quickly and popped it in her mouth. "If you want a parrot to do tricks, you give them the reward afterward, not before."

"I keep hoping you're not a parrot."

"Chirp chirp," Mel said, showing yellowed teeth with her smile.

It had been like this—this kind of circular debate—every time she'd questioned Mel. Neeva sighed. "I have to go. I'm having you sent to a secure facility. Only three people will know your whereabouts, for your own security."

"Why? Where are you going?"

"I'm heading to SoPo on assignment."

"Have a nice time. And you better watch your back."

Neeva nodded slowly. She knew better than to think Mel cared about her well-being. She was probably more concerned about her Amadone supply drying up.

After a flurry of communications, briefings, and a whole day's train ride, Neeva was back in Enjo again. It had been five days since the Executive Council meeting.

She was on the same copter, and with the same pilot, as the first time she'd met with Gorman. This time, however, the back seat was occupied by Egan's considerable bulk, as well as Hedlund's much more diminutive form. Hedlund was the recorder that VV-912 had assigned to her. He had dark brown eyes and a bumpy burn mark across his neck. So far, he'd shown less snark than VV-912's other recorder, Jansis, but Neeva hadn't spent much time with him.

She'd told Bam Jam that it was another routine visit to Eastborough. Of course, it was anything but. Every agency responsible for planetary security had input into planning this mission.

The X92 angled into a steep turn, picking up speed. Neeva had the impression that Bam Jam was showing off, which was fine. He seemed capable enough. Visibility was clear and wind velocity was low. If conditions were poor, she might have had more reservations.

They leveled out once their vector pointed them toward the mining facility on the distant horizon. Bam Jam turned to her. "Did I hear right that you've got one of them psychanthropic recorders with you?" Neeva could see her own distorted form in the oily aquamarine lenses of his sunglasses.

She gestured to Hedlund, who was sitting in the seat behind her. "Yes, this here is Hedlund. He's a recorder based at the psychanthropic facility on Telliac Mountain."

Bam Jam said, "So, Hed, you gotta clean one of them things, and feed em' too? What's that like?"

Hedlund said, "I am satisfied."

"Neat." Bam Jam pulled down his shades to wink.

Neeva felt it best to change the subject. "Bam Jam, has there been a lot of work recently—flights for you, I mean?"

"It's been a bit slow. Only a few flights to the mine recently. Mostly remote supply dumps, but not many official visits."

"Why is that? Have there been any of those incidents I've been hearing about in the last couple weeks?"

"I dunno. I hear about the odd scuffle, people disappearing. But it's sun season. Makes people a bit crazy sometimes. The rock hermits come out to dance. Crime goes up."

"A four percent increase versus historical comparisons," Hedlund said. His cortivation nodes were flashing blue.

It was barely an increase, and so it didn't really support Bam Jam's argument, but Bam Jam smiled knowingly. "Like I said."

Streaks of cloud appeared in the far distance. They were frail strips of red, barely visible. Celia had seen a real rain cloud once, on the north side of Maxwell Montes. There were only a few places where the conditions were conducive for air to condense, and very rarely would these clouds spit out any fleeting bouts of precipitation. According to Celia, it would be decades until there was enough water vapor to create rain clouds with any regularity.

Neeva missed Celia.

She decided to ask Hedlund some questions, this time to distract from her own thoughts rather than Bam Jam's queries.

"So, Hedlund, where are you from?"

"Betar City."

"Did you always want to be a recorder?"

"No."

She tried another tack. "You know, there's something I've always been curious about. What do the symbionts do for fun? I know so little about them."

"They would view the concept of fun differently than you. Their utopia is to be in constant communion with other symbiont minds. In fact, they find interaction with other non-symbiont humans as burdensome, often painful. It is one of our jobs as recorders to minimize those interactions."

It only reinforced Neeva's view that she had inflicted some kind of grievous wound on VV-912 by requesting sequestration.

She decided to stop prying and instead take in the view.

It didn't look like they were passing over the major dirigible this time, so she tried to find it on the geo-locator app on her comm. It was to the south of them. She squinted in that direction, but all she saw was a plume of smoke angling off into the distance.

"Egan, what's that?"

Egan was sitting stoically in the seat behind Bam Jam. His combat arm had a telescoping function that could zoom in visuals on distant objects. He pointed it southward, tapped on his display, and showed Neeva the result.

At first she thought it might be some steam or an industrial smokestack, but it wasn't that at all. There was an open, uncontained fire.

"There's a fire near the major dirigible," she said to Bam Jam. "Did you know about that?"

Egan maneuvered his hefty arm to lie on the armrest between them so Bam Jam could see the visual up close.

"That? It's just some drilling and controlled detonations. Sometimes they let them burn a while. Nothing to worry about, but I didn't want to go through the smoke. I just had her washed." He tapped on the control console and smiled again.

"Okay, thanks. I did notice the shine, by the way."

He grinned with pride.

Curious, she searched on her comm for information about the controlled detonations, but she couldn't find anything immediately, and comm reception was getting spotty. Nevertheless, she sent a tightbeam message to Sergeant Tanner's team.

Avoid flight paths over major dirigible. Drilling and detonations throwing up smoke.

The mining facility was beginning to monopolize the front view. It looked more inviting in full sun season, and without ash clouding the environs. The windows sported some basic ornamental flourishes she hadn't noticed before, and the industrial metal lines glittered. Beyond the heliport, the interior of the facility was neat and tidy, with a dozen transport vehicles lined up in a row, and crates stacked in formation. In fact, it was virtually devoid of activity. A handful of people toiled about, and only one transport was being loaded. At her last meeting with Gorman there had been ten times as many people in the main work area.

Gorman didn't come out to meet them when they landed, but it was sun season and so Neeva didn't take offense.

The heat blasted them when Bam Jam opened the doors. They wasted no time dashing across the tarmac toward the main door of the facility.

Gorman didn't meet them in the intake lobby either. Instead, an older-looking hedonite woman welcomed them. Her skin was heavily creased by the tumults of a full life. Her long braids were dyed a teal color, but they were streaked and rooted in gray. "The director is waiting for you," was all she said.

She turned and they followed.

Egan's eyes were active, but he kept his composure. Hedlund was the picture of calm.

They soon entered the bank of cubicles and offices where Gorman worked. Neeva saw only one worker there—a young man with a rounded face. He shifted his eyes from his numerous screens to stare at them as they passed through.

Gorman was sitting in his chair, a smirk on his face. He was wearing tight-fitting mine-branded work coveralls, and his thinning hair was tightly combed over.

They all took seats across from him, and the older lady departed.

"Where is Anuvant?" Gorman asked.

"He doesn't need to be here for this," Neeva said.

"Why not? He works for me, remember. He was supposed to update me, but I haven't heard from him. Is this meeting about him?"

"No."

"Fine. Please, pray tell, why are you here, Inspector?"

"Just wrapping up some loose ends."

His eyes passed over Hedlund and Egan, and then bored into Neeva. "I get the impression you're an idealist, Inspector. You want to tie a bow around it, even if it's a goose turd. I am a realist. You should leave the turd alone and move along."

"Fortunately, the law is black and white, and has nothing to do with turds or bows wrapped around them."

"I'm not talking about reformer law, or even the Reformer Doctrine. I'm talking about *real* justice, and the greater good. I'm trying to strike a delicate balance with the workers, and yet the PDA insists on upsetting that balance."

She shrugged. "All I'm doing is asking questions."

"And the monitors?" Gorman looked at his tablet. "So far, thirty-two of my employees have been summoned. That means time away from their duties. When they do get back to work, their crew members won't want to work with them. They'll have to find new jobs. That's what I call upsetting the balance."

Neeva kept her face devoid of expression. It was the first she'd heard of it, and if it was true it was a major screw up. Middich had assured her that the monitoring summons wouldn't be put in play until after her confrontation with Gorman.

"It's only upsetting if there's something to hide," she managed to say.

Gorman shook his head. "Word is spreading. People aren't showing up for work. Mining operations are down to thirty percent today. *Thirty percent.* I've only got two hands, and you're tying one of them behind my back. That's upsetting."

He was making good points. Neeva actually agreed with him about the monitors, but she wasn't about to give ground. "Well then, let's get this over with. Who maintains your utilities in the mining settlements?"

"Marek Industries. They're one of the main SoPo utility companies. Why?"

"It's just a question I forgot to ask. I wanted to see if these service people refurbish used parts, like the reflectors from the walls. I wonder if there's some hidden economy around the pilfering of anything useful in the settlements. It would be great if you could provide some names." She was trying to squeeze a few more suspects out of Gorman before the bird was out of its cage, and the utility people were almost certainly involved.

"Marek has service people, of course, and we have service people, as well. We subcontract the maintenance guilds. But I still don't get it. How is this going to help your investigation? You already went to the Hock Pocket. Isn't that the hidden economy you're looking for?"

"It's usually the Inspector asking the questions in these situations, Gorman."

"I don't care. I'm within my rights to ask whatever I want. Your investigation is affecting our livelihoods, and putting my people in danger."

"All the more reason you should answer my questions thoroughly, so we can reach an end to this investigation quickly. Better yet, we'll just do a carpet scan and be done with it."

"You can't do that."

Gorman's comm buzzed in his lap and he glanced at it. Neeva touched Hedlund's knee. "This here is recorder Hedlund. He has been in direct contact with the symbiont collective, who have provided me with a warrant for a carpet scan, the warrant that you will now see on your comm. We will need access to all of your personal communication records, and those of all top mining officials in the Eastborough Mining Operation, by order of the PDA and the Executive Council."

Hedlund was inanimate. He didn't smile or nod to confirm her statement. Given the severity of the order it was strange but he was a recorder so maybe it was normal.

Gorman's eyes darted between them. His breathing became deeper, his voice ragged. "I... okay, fine. But by law I have twenty-four hours to collect these records. So I'll get it for you—tomorrow. Right now I need to get production back online." He gestured at the window. The last transport had left and only one person was inspecting crates. "After that I'm going to be up all night preparing this pointless carpet scan. So if you wouldn't mind—" he gestured at the exit to his office, "—you and the PDA have been enough of an intrusion."

Heads turned to Neeva. It was a desperate attempt to delay. Who knew what he would do in the next twenty-four hours? He certainly wouldn't be preparing his files. She might never see him again.

"Okay, let me call on Bam Jam," she said, smiling. "We'll get out of your hair." She took out her comm and sent a brief message to Sergeant Tanner: *Go.* It looked like they were going to do this the hard way.

"Bam Jam must be running an errand," she said. "If you don't mind, may I ask just a couple more questions while we're waiting?"

"Fine," he said, throwing up his hands.

"Actually, no more questions. It's more of a statement, really."

"And what statement is that?"

"That the gig is up."

Egan stood up and his combat arm powered on with a low purr, hydraulics pushing out the blaster barrels in Gorman's direction. Neeva pulled out her own blaster and placed it delicately across her lap.

Gorman's eyes paused on Egan's combat arm before addressing her. "What gig?" His voice had increased in pitch ever so slightly.

"The lights, the cameras, the... treason. Those two hands of yours, tied behind your back or not, have been breaking reformer law. It's time to put them up in the air."

Gorman was frowning and shaking his head. His hand at his side made a swiping motion: *cut it out.* It was an unusual reaction. She had expected shock, or denial, but not this. At first she wondered if the gesture was meant for a hidden camera or nearby guard, but it was too conspicuous. It was clearly meant for her.

Cut what out?

Gorman pulled his hand through his hair, disturbing his combover. His jaw clenched. "Can I speak to you... privately?" he said.

"Sure, but it may take a while, like as long as it takes for you to get to your prison cell in NoPo." She smiled.

A light on the control panel in the back of Gorman's office started flashing red, then another. The control panel buzzed.

"I have to see what that is," he said. "Someone could be hurt."

It was a little too convenient. "That's not your job anymore," she said.

"Fine," he said. "Take me." He thrust out his wrists. His leg was shaking under the table.

"Well, thank you for obliging, but first I'd like to know what you wanted to tell me in private."

His teeth clenched again. "We don't have much time!" He was practically yelling at her.

"Why not?" she responded calmly.

He looked at each of them in turn, then outside to the work area. The mining operation had stopped completely. A new transport that had been pulling away was parked askew, with the driver's-side door open, but nobody was around. "They'll be here soon," he said.

"Who's they?"

"You damn well know who! We have to leave. It's our only chance."

Neeva yawned and looked at her comm. She sent a message to Tanner. *Status?*

"You worry too much," she said to Gorman.

When she looked up again his hair was in disarray, sticking up like the first time she'd met him. His eyes were bulging. "Fine, I'll say it. But we have to go. Mantle. They're everywhere. I need protection."

"Protection? What you need is incarceration, but maybe we can make some kind of deal, who knows."

He stood up with his hands out, ready to be bound, but she didn't move. He couldn't know they had four strike teams moving in on the facility. They should take care of any Mantle militia in the immediate vicinity. And the more he sweated it out, the more he might reveal something in the heat of the moment.

"Fine," he said. "I'll tell you everything, but we have to leave. I think I know where the symbiont NM-198 is. My handlers are Rae Dione-Pip and Quo Redrock-Val. Rav Samar-Rav used to be involved. You already have him in custody. Now let's go."

Neeva raised her eyebrows. It was exactly what she wanted, unless he was lying. "Where is NM-198?"

"I'll tell you, I promise... when we're safe."

"The channels are down again," Hedlund said. He was tapping on his cortivation link, and his comm. "I can't confirm the names provided are valid, nor probabilistically estimate the veracity of his claims."

She could press Gorman for more, but she doubted he would be able to provide her with any evidence that wouldn't require time-consuming verification. And the channels were indeed out on her own comm, which explained why she hadn't heard from the strike teams. She decided to use the local radio bands, which had a fifty mile radius: *Status? You are authorized to proceed.*

She waited for a moment but there was no response. Was it possible Mantle could interfere with radio frequencies as well? It seemed implausible.

She kept her face free of expression. "Okay let's go," she said.

Gorman groaned with a sort of exasperated relief. Egan moved around the desk to cuff him and pad him down for weapons. He found none.

Just as they were leaving Gorman's office, her comm beeped at her.

It was a response to her radio message: *This is strike team 3. We're under attack.*

23

THE LITTLE JAUNT

"Over there," Hix, said pointing.

Jin turned to fire his prod-shocker at two guards who were running between supply container towers. Their mag-boots' attraction encumbered their gait, making their strides look forced and exaggerated. He missed anyway.

Hix was keeping under cover, his back against the floor. He could see the hangar bay window in the distance, showing the rings of Kanto Station. Debris from the ring explosions was everywhere. Service drones were also shuttling about, trying to contain the damage and prevent collisions. It was chaos.

Rav likes chaos.

That's when it dawned on Hix—why Iri wasn't with them.

Hix grabbed Tolquist's arm forcefully and pushed away from the supply box in retreat. Tolquist gaped at him, stupefied, but didn't resist.

When they reached the back wall of the hangar, Hix took hold of a railing and pulled them around through the hatch, barely evading two prod-shocker pulses. He didn't look back to see if Jin, Uwy, or Vas had noticed them fleeing.

"What are you doing?" Tolquist asked when they were clear of the doors. "Is this part of the plan?"

"No, but trust me," Hix said. "There's a maintenance airlock we need to reach, not far along the snake." He torpedoed himself down the hall without waiting for a response.

The maintenance airlock door was shut, and the display read *Occupied.*

It had to be Iri. He must have taken advantage of the confusion to steal a habitat module and maneuver it to this docking port on the snake. From here he could use the habitat module to shuttle Rav and Pru to the *Little Jaunt* without them having to blast through the guards in the hangar bay.

Hix had been part of the diversion and he hadn't even realized it.

He quickly entered his secure reformer access codes. Thankfully they still worked, and there was no retinal sensor.

"What are we doing here?" Tolquist asked as he arrived. "We don't have space suits."

They entered the airlock and the door closed behind them. There was no sign anyone had passed through recently. The next hatch opened soon after the door behind them closed.

As Hix expected, it opened to the entry port of a habitat module. Standing in it, with a prod-shocker pointed in their direction, was Pru.

A smile slowly appeared on her face as she lowered her weapon. "Right on time," she said. "Rav wasn't sure you were going to make it."

Hix craned his neck, trying to see behind her. Rav wasn't visible.

"Well, come on in, Falcon Fire," Pru said. "We don't have all day."

He lowered his prod-shocker and floated into the habitat, his eyes active as the interior revealed itself. He passed the white benches in the entry vestibule and continued into a larger room lined with labeled lockers, modular sleep pods, and two exercise bikes. There were also four angled transit chairs with command interfaces and tangles of seatbelts. Next to an exit door opposite them was a ladder that led to the upper and lower decks.

The habitats were conical ships, separated into several stacked circular levels, which meant Rav and Iri must be in the command center, up the ladder at the top of the fuselage.

An orange strobe light began flashing overhead as the airlock hatch closed behind them.

"Better buckle up," Pru said, sitting down in one of the transit chairs. "Iri's a little twitchy with the controls."

Hix and Tolquist each took one of the transit chairs.

Pru was tapping away on her comm, presumably communicating with Rav.

The room lurched, and then spun. Hix held his armrests tightly. There was no viewport, so he had no bearing on where they were heading, or which direction they might turn next.

"Was this the plan all along?" Hix asked between gravity shifts. "Did Rav have any intention of getting through that platoon in the hangar, or were we just another diversion?"

"I'm just following orders, Falcon Fire."

"Pru, please, be straight with me. The diversion worked, and we made it, so no harm done, but I deserve to know."

She glanced sidelong at Tolquist. "Not your typical meathead flyboy, is he?" She sighed and scratched her temple. "I didn't know we were going to leave you behind until we were in the hangar."

She became preoccupied by her comm again. The habitat continued to maneuver. It wouldn't be long until they docked with the *Little Jaunt*.

"'Scuse me," Pru said. She unstrapped, pushed herself to the ladder and climbed up.

The G-force shifts became less pronounced, like minor earthquakes rippling through the craft.

"How many ports are there on these habitats?" Hix asked.

"I think there's a main entrance in the back," Tolquist responded, "and then two airlocks."

"So we could be docking with the *Little Jaunt* at the other airlock?"

"I suppose so. One of the airlocks comes off the bridge."

Hix started unstrapping. "Stay here," he said.

"What are you going to do? Are you really going to trust Pru after—"

"Stay here," Hix repeated forcefully, and he followed Pru's path up the ladder.

He tried to move quietly. The ship was still in motion, making minor adjustments, but the G-forces were negligible. There wasn't much on the intervening levels, only sleeping quarters, a common room, and supply rooms. As he neared the top of the ladder he readied his prod-shocker.

He heard Iri talking. "...we have transport lock."

"Any obstacles in the transport's path?" It was Rav. "Other ships coming our way?"

"No bogies," Iri responded. "Kanto's systems still think we're debris from the seventh ring, but human monitors might see the transport leaving. Then we'd be in trouble."

"We'd better hurry up then, and let's make sure..."

When Rav's head turned to look at the stairwell, Hix was ready. He fired and the pulse hit Rav in the shoulder, throwing him back out of view.

Hix launched himself the rest of the way up the ladder into the bridge.

Rav was cringing, his body tightened into a ball, rolling through the air into the conical top of the habitat. Faint blue static pulses rippled through his body.

Iri had been facing a viewport built into the top cone. He turned around and fumbled for a hammer in his belt.

"Don't bother," Hix said, pointing his prod-shocker at him.

Pru's head poked up above a chair, along with the muzzle of another prod-shocker.

"Wait, Pru," Hix said, his left hand up. "Don't shoot. Let's talk about this."

"What's there to talk about?" she said.

"You must see that Rav will turn on you, just like he left me and Tolquist behind in the hangar, just like he sent Kaj to the clam in order to send a message. We're all pawns in his game. What do you think Wik would say? We should all be in the flow, together."

Pru frowned and rubbed the stubble on her head. "See, here's the thing. Me and Rav, we've been rollin' in the flow for a long time. Same tribe, hawk tattoos and all."

"That's all superficial. Rav doesn't care about that. Think about how many people died today who were in his *tribe*." Hix made air quotes with free hand. "Rav is a sociopath. He doesn't know compassion, he doesn't know loyalty, to you or Wik or anyone. He only knows how to survive and get what he wants."

She laughed. "Well you got one thing right. Rav does like to kill. He's smart, but he's still a rabid vulture. A rabid, obedient vulture."

The word *obedient* was out of place, especially with Rav in the room and able to hear it. It was enough to stop and make him think. Later he would realize that was what Pru wanted, because it gave her the split second she needed.

She fired at him and it was a direct hit. It was agonizing, and the force of it propelled him back to convulse on the floor and drop his own prod-shocker.

His body retracted into a fetal position and his jaw clenched as the energy coursed through him.

As the shock dissipated, Pru moved toward him, while Iri continued working the habitat controls behind her. Rav was slowly recovering from his own shocker hit. He'd managed to push himself toward the open airlock.

Despite Hix's unresponsive limbs and foggy faculties, he knew he only had one choice. He had to fight.

He had the strength to reach out for his prod-shocker, but Pru slapped it away. It spiraled and hit the metal rungs behind him.

Pru watched Rav leave through the airlock. When she looked back at Hix, her eyes were blazing. "I know more than you think, flyboy, especially about loyalty. I know that if you inflict enough pain on someone—for hours on end—that person will fear you, and also obey you. That searing, relentless pain is unforgettable. You become like the equatorial sun, the unyielding master that must never be defied."

"What are you…" It took him a moment. His mind was still clouded, and Pru was sounding different. "You… you're the one that impaled Rav with the pipe?"

She snorted and squinted at him. "It's better to be hidden in plain sight, to lead without people knowing you're leading, especially for those who might want to take your place." She nudged her prod-shocker at him and winked.

Hix remembered the cowering look from Kaj in the reclamation facility. Kaj had been with Pru and Rav at the Themis reclamation facility on Venus. Maybe he'd known that Rav was just a puppet—that Pru was the one who was really in charge. And there were the many side glances from Rav to Pru. Now it made sense. Rav wasn't giving her commands. He was checking with her, making sure he was doing what she wanted.

He had his answer. Pru was an owl.

He tried to unravel his limbs but they felt stiff, as if his joints needed to be plied apart.

"We're all set," Iri said. He'd moved from the control panel and was waiting for Pru by the airlock. "Rav said the *Little Jaunt* is secure, but we've only got two minutes in our launch window for the orbital dynamics to work."

Pru nodded. "Well, so long, Falcon Fire." She pulled out a long utility knife from her belt and stepped toward him.

He tried to push away from her but his limbs still weren't responding properly. He managed to bounce off the floor but not in the direction he wanted. His body started to spin.

Pru tilted her head side to side, as if assessing where his neck would be most accessible during his aerial acrobatics. "Iri, you're not going to tell his fans about this, are you?"

Iri said, "No, Pru."

The sound of a prod-shocker discharging came from somewhere behind Hix. The pulse missed Pru by a wide margin and glanced off the forward viewport. Pru crouched, retrieved her own shocker and fired back toward the stairwell. Hix managed to catch a glimpse of Tolquist's head popping out and ducking down again when Pru fired again and missed.

"Let's go," Pru said, and she pushed off the floor to retreat toward the airlock. Iri ducked in ahead of her.

Hix struggled to flex his limbs again. This time he managed to kick off the floor properly. It sent him into the ceiling cone, where he desperately rebounded toward the open airlock.

Just before he reached the hatch, it slid closed and his shoulder bounced off it painfully.

Orange lights surrounded the perimeter of the door. Hix and Tolquist were locked out.

"Hurry," Hix said. He pushed back off the hatch toward the command chairs. Tolquist raised his head slowly above the stairwell opening, and eventually made his way over as well.

They needed to override the airlock, but there was another program running. It was blocking other command functions.

"Try to figure out what this program is doing," Hix said. "I'm going to override."

Tolquist puzzled over the command interface.

Hix managed to find the *Abort sequence* button and he pressed it. A prompt came up: *Access code?*

He used the reformer credentials.

Access denied.

He used the Transport Officer credentials he'd waterholed.

Access denied.

He heard something break off behind the airlock. It was like a pneumatic pump firing several times in a row. *Shit.*

The same sound came again, only it was quieter, and it came from down the ladder.

Shit.

The orange lights flashed again. A stencil popped up in front of him, and a monotone voice said, "*Please secure yourselves. Launch in thirty seconds.*" A thirty-second countdown popped up on the display panel.

"I have visuals," Tolquist said. He pressed a key and the viewport came to life, showing the spinning rings of Kanto Station. The hulking *Little Jaunt* was pulling away, but it would soon be obscured, because the habitat was in motion relative to the snake. Thrusters were firing, rotating its position, reorienting it.

No.

Hix tried manual override, but access was denied. He tried a maintenance request, but access was denied. He even tried to channel fuel away from the thrusters and main boosters, but it was always the same: *Access denied*.

His mind raced. Manual override was usually less secure than other command functions. They had to ensure lower-level crew could operate it in the event of officers being dead or incapacitated. Again, he tried all his stolen credentials in the manual override prompt, and the reformer's he'd stolen finally worked, but all that happened was that the display panel slid back, revealing an inset rectangular keyhole.

The key was missing. Iri must have taken it.

Tolquist was toiling on his own console to no avail. He said, "It looks like our communications are blocked as well, both ship and handheld."

The feeling of vertigo increased. The rotation must be accelerating. Hix had to brace against the side of the chair to stay seated. He and Tolquist both strapped themselves in between frenetic taps on the control console.

Abruptly, the vector thrusters stopped. Another set of thrusters fired. There was a change in pitch, and the habitat ship stopped rotating altogether.

Hix looked up at the radar. It was covered in blips. The *Little Jaunt* was accelerating rapidly away toward Venus, leaving them behind.

And the habitat module's intended destination was clear. The conical viewport display came to life, bringing it into view. The habitat was pointing away from Venus, and away from the rings of Kanto Station, towards the arc of that beige ball of toxic windstorms —toward that lifeless hellhole.

Toward Earth.

"Dammit!" Hix was pressing buttons indiscriminately. Nothing was working.

Three, two, one.

The main boosters fired.

24

AIRSHIPS AND COMMS

Under attack by whom? Neeva messaged back on the radio bands.

There was no immediate response.

"Let's go," she said, stepping out cautiously from Gorman's office. Egan urged Gorman along. Hedlund trailed behind.

The round-faced man who had been in the block of cubicles was gone, his desk left in disarray.

It was quiet. There was nobody in the hallways. A group of workers ran across the corridor in front of them, their brows creased with concern. Another group charged out of an adjoining hallway farther down the executive offices, but they turned back as soon as they saw her party.

She passed back over the major underground artery leading to the nearby mining settlements. Here there were dozens of people running into the depths, carrying possessions, prodding loved ones along.

Other than the occasional fleeting glance, these people never looked up. They didn't care about Gorman, or Neeva, or even Egan's swiveling combat arm. All they wanted to do was run.

"What's happening?" Neeva asked. "Why are they running?"

"Someone in Mantle must have tipped them off," Gorman replied.

"Tipped them off about what?"

"Let's hurry," was all he said, with one eyebrow raised.

A low rumble rolled through the corridor, driving everyone into tense crouches. Red lights flashed from recesses in the ceiling. The intercom blared, "Please evacuate the mining facility immediately."

The warning seemed redundant. Everyone already seemed to know what was going on, except Neeva.

They made it to the main lobby that led to the helipad where two men were standing with stripped atmospheric suits curled on the floor near their feet, and blast rifles strung across their backs. They weren't wearing the tight maroon outfits of the enforcers, and their hair was long and dyed a deep navy blue.

They weren't PDA.

"Against the wall!" Egan commanded. His combat arm shifted to point back and forth at each of them, as if on a pendulum.

The men put their arms in the air and faced away from them, but before they actually touched the wall they bolted down an adjoining corridor.

"Ma'am?" Egan asked, his arm tracking the fleeing men.

"No, don't shoot. They know they're outmatched, whoever they are. Let's get out of here."

The four of them donned atmospheric masks and walked out onto the tarmac. Heavy gusts of sweltering air buffeted Neeva as she scanned the surroundings.

Nobody was around, and not one jet copter. Even Bam Jam was gone. Smoke curled up from the north, its source obscured by the blocky facility buildings.

Distant percussions sounded to the north, and also to the east, from the other side of a craggy rise.

Neeva's comm buzzed. An urgent message came in.

This is Cavish in gunship 2. 1 and 3 are down; anti-aircraft rockets. We are pursuing source to eliminate. Gunship 4 landed at north terminal but did not gain entry to facility. Lost contact.

Two strike teams down. It was hard to believe. Mantle must have been ready.

Neeva was thankful they hadn't stayed in Gorman's office any longer.

We have Gorman, she responded. *Need immediate evac, utmost priority, from south helipad. Abort securing facility.*

Confirmed, Cavish responded. *On our way.*

"They're coming," she said. Even Hedlund seemed relieved when she announced this. They all stood glaring into the distance, and occasionally pacing on the tarmac. The heat was oppressive. Sweat streamed down her face and damp patches formed around her collar.

Her main comm channel was still down. Mantle must be controlling the local routers. She walked around the helipad, holding up her comm to the sky to try to find a signal. There was nothing.

She texted Cavish again. *Need mainline comm channel. Patch me through radio. Will send access kernel.* She attached her commlink kernel to the message. This would allow Cavish to patch commlink communications through to her over the radio, assuming he had access.

Patching through.

Her comm messages started coming in, but slowly, one every few seconds.

"What's going on?" Gorman asked.

"Got somewhere to go, Gorman?" Neeva asked.

He ignored her and glanced back at the entrance to the lobby. Maybe he was having second thoughts, or maybe he didn't think they were safe.

Finally she noticed some activity. At the north end of the facility a gunship rose up and leaned toward them at a low altitude. It was kicking up eddies of dust.

She radioed them. *Gunship 4. Need evac at south helipad.*

No response. Maybe the radio was fried. Neeva waved her arms, trying to get their attention. She stepped away from the landing pad to give it space to land.

A loud explosion sounded from the east, beyond the rise. Debris flew everywhere, spiraling up over the hills in broad arcs.

Cavish, status.

Nothing.

Cavish, status.

Still nothing. She checked the kernel link. The messages had stopped transmitting.

Gunship 4 was close. These P88 gunships looked a lot like bloated X92s, except they had additional attitudinal jets that flared out below the cockpit, and they were laden with guns. This one was also riddled with holes, and part of the landing gear had been blasted off. It turned and prepared to land, the side door opening up.

A man with a gun appeared.

He wasn't wearing maroon. He had navy blue hair.

The man fired.

It was a military-grade assault blaster with an automated repeater, so it could fire at least ten pulses a second. It tore up the helipad next to her as she dived into the shallow ditches next to it, seeking cover but not finding any.

Of course, Egan hadn't flinched. He fired at the copter with his combat arm. An aileron flipped away from the tail boom and the copter immediately began churning out smoke. It pulled up, forcing the door gunner onto his buttocks, and swayed back and forth as the pilot tried to regain control. Egan continued to fire but his shots went wide. His arm wasn't designed for long-range combat.

When Neeva pulled herself out of the shallow ditch she saw Hedlund cowering on the ground next to Egan, and Gorman was...

Torn apart. A mass of red. She had to look away.

A cocktail of nausea and anger flushed through her. She felt like she was in some terrible horror vid, in which nothing would ever go right. Would she be outplayed yet again? Would this be yet another Hock Pocket, or biocrawler, where she would be tied to who knew how many deaths?

She tried to stay focused. She was still alive, as was Egan, and

Hedlund. It was her responsibility to get them to safety. She needed to think.

She checked her comm. Nothing.

Egan said, "Another copter ma'am." He pivoted to face west, where another copter was indeed heading their way. It was an X92.

"Find some cover," Neeva said, and they crouched under an awning near the lobby entrance.

Egan had his combat arm trained on the X92 the whole time, and his gaze fixed on the display. "It's Bam Jam," he said.

They stayed away while he landed. Only after he shut down and sat in the cockpit with his hands up did they approach the copter cautiously. "Where did you go?" Neeva asked.

"Hey, sorry," he said. "I saw the gunships were taking heat in the north end. I didn't want to stick around, so I hid out away from the mining facility until the air cleared."

It was plausible enough.

"If you want out of here, it's now or never," he continued. "The ground-to-air stuff I can avoid if I take the right vector, but I don't know about that stolen gunship."

She didn't really have another choice. "Let's go," she said, and they all climbed aboard.

The copter lifted up and lurched forward.

"Back to the hotel?" Bam Jam asked. "The whole mining settlement is down, but I haven't heard anything about Enjo."

"No," Neeva said. "It's not safe. Can you take us to Redrock City?"

"Sure, you got it."

The copter veered north. Smoke spiraled in tornadoes across the southern horizon, several funnels originating from around the mining facility.

As they gained altitude it lent Neeva a better view of Eastborough's northern landing pad. It was covered in debris, with bodies strewn about. Two transports were parked nearby, and a team was scouring the remains.

"Egan, capture that," Neeva said, pointing to the northern heli-pad. "Try to get faces, license numbers, anything identifying."

Egan pointed his arm toward the helipad.

To the west, beyond the rise, Neeva could only make out a few spirals of smoke, and no sign of Cavish. His gunship was almost certainly down. She checked her comm. There were hundreds of messages that she had pulled through, using Cavish's radio comm as a conduit, but they had stopped abruptly at the same time as she'd heard the explosion coming from that direction.

The messages were almost all urgent. Other settlements in SoPo were in turmoil, not just the mining facility, and she had several network blackout warnings. Nine of the messages requested situation reports.

She skipped them all and looked earlier, to a message she had received from Sergeant Tanner, before everything went haywire. It was about the detonations near the major dirigible.

It told her what she feared.

Her heart was still beating erratically, but she stayed focused. She checked the copter's vector on her comm and cross-referenced it to her mapping function.

When the copter had gained sufficient altitude, far enough away from the hot spots on the horizon, she sent a tightbeam message to Egan.

We are off course by 20 degrees.

Egan's comm pinged behind her.

So? he responded.

Bam Jam misled us about the work at the major dirigible. It was a Mantle attack. He didn't want us to know uprisings had started. I also think the airship missed us on purpose. They only shot at Gorman when they could have shot all of us. We're being kidnapped.

What do you want me to do? he responded.

She answered. There was really only one choice.

Egan's comm pinged again.

Moments later, Egan blasted Bam Jam through the back of his seat. He angled the shot up, away from the copter controls. After cutting through Bam Jam's chest, the shot sprayed his blood on the window and pierced it. The copter lost atmosphere, but everyone already had their masks on.

Neeva was ready to take the controls. She stabilized the copter and had Egan pull Bam Jam's limp body out of the pilot's seat.

She took Bam Jam's spot and corrected their course toward Redrock City.

"Hedlund," she yelled over the turbulence, "secure us a First Colony transport dirigible and send it to the Redrock City shunt tower. We'll dock the X92 there and take the dirigible north."

It was the only thing she could think of. Mantle could control the tunnels, and the settlements. Even biocrawlers were within reach, but it would be much harder for Mantle to subvert airpower, especially of First Colony origin. Aside from Hix's infamous joyride, most hedonites had never even been aboard a dirigible.

It turned out to be a good call. There was unrest in Redrock as well, but it hadn't impacted shunt tower operations, and the dirigible was safe for the three of them. It would be an airborne oasis as they deliberated frantically with PDA command.

The truth was, they were lucky. Nothing was really safe anymore, and nothing would be for the foreseeable future.

PART III

RESTRICTIONS

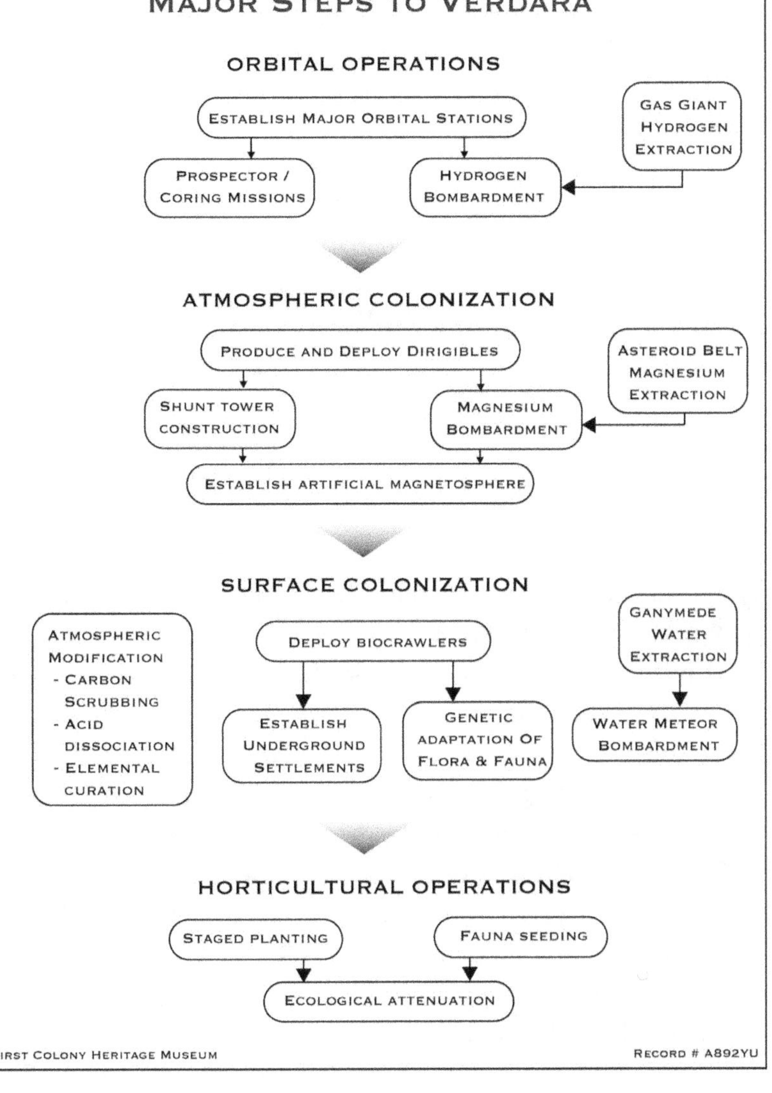

MAJOR STEPS TO VERDARA

ORBITAL OPERATIONS
Establish Major Orbital Stations
Prospector / Coring Missions
Hydrogen Bombardment
Gas Giant Hydrogen Extraction

ATMOSPHERIC COLONIZATION
Produce and Deploy Dirigibles
Shunt tower construction
Magnesium Bombardment
Asteroid Belt Magnesium Extraction
Establish artificial magnetosphere

SURFACE COLONIZATION
Atmospheric Modification
- Carbon Scrubbing
- Acid dissociation
- Elemental curation
Deploy biocrawlers
Establish Underground Settlements
Genetic adaptation Of Flora & Fauna
Ganymede Water Extraction
Water Meteor Bombardment

HORTICULTURAL OPERATIONS
Staged planting
Fauna seeding
Ecological attenuation

First Colony Heritage Museum
Record # A892YU

25

EARTH

After the main booster burn, the G-forces abated, and Hix was able to unstrap and push himself out of his chair.

"I need a wrench," he said, "or some kind of tool to open the manual override panel."

He looked in the compartments on the other side of the bridge. There were scanning devices, dried food packets, oxygen cannisters, and batteries, but no wrenches or drivers. "Do you know where..."

Tolquist was already gone down the ladder.

The arc of Earth was dominating more of the viewfinder. They would hit the atmosphere in two minutes, and their entry angle was too steep. Iri must have programmed the same entry pattern he'd put into Lon and Eta's habitat.

Hix finally found a small square-headed driver. He tried it in the screws of the manual override panel but the size wasn't right, so instead he tried to carefully push it into the manual override keyhole. It fit partway in, but it wouldn't turn, and the hard plastic had no give.

"Warning," a woman's voice said, "your entry angle is too steep. Please consider a correction. Press abort to prevent entry."

Hix tried the abort key again, but of course it didn't work.

The ship started shaking. "Entering atmosphere," the woman's voice said. "For safety, please return to your seats and strap in."

Hix didn't follow her recommendation. *Safety* was a relative term here.

The only thing he could think to do was to force the keyhole. He could jam the driver in and try to turn it, but it might break the tool, or worse, disable the manual override function altogether.

The tremors throughout the hull of the ship increased. He wondered if Tolquist would ever come back. Maybe Tolquist thought he could jettison himself out the rear airlock and have a better chance of surviving. Or maybe he was praying to his pyrolyte gods. Come to think of it, atmospheric incineration wouldn't be much different than jumping in front of an erupting volcano.

But Tolquist did return, with a whole tool belt, and even a torch.

"Give me the torch," Hix said. "You try the keyhole." He started blasting at the side panel below the manual override, hoping to melt it and lay bare the internal circuitry. They had maybe a minute left before it would be too late.

Tolquist yelled, "Got it!"

Hix got back on his feet. Tolquist had jammed the fork of a crowbar in the manual override and turned it. It could have broken it, but Hix didn't care. The display read *Manual override activated.*

"Strap in!" Hix yelled, jumping into the pilot's chair. Tolquist maneuvered into the chair next to him. Hix pulled on the yoke and the craft was responsive, firing thrusters.

This was no sleek dirigible, agile jet copter or even a Kanto drop ship. Habitats were designed for careful one-off entries, and mostly for docking with atmospheric stations that were linked to shunt towers. They allowed for surface landings as well, but that was supposed to be after terraforming, and not during hurricane-force winds.

As a result, fancy flying simply wasn't possible with the unwieldy ship. In a more versatile craft Hix might be able to use enough thrust to bounce off the atmosphere and return to orbit, but they had passed the point of no return. His only hope was to correct the entry angle, so that's what he tried to do. He pulled the yoke to maximum tolerances, firing attitudinal thrusters at full power. All the while, the habitat trembled and groaned. He managed to shave off a degree, then another, then another. The trembling worsened.

The viewfinder was being showered with fiery lines and sparks.

"Warning," the woman's voice said. "Atmospheric tolerances exceeded. Wind vectors exceed—"

"Can you shut her off?" Hix yelled over the broadcast.

"Yes," Tolquist said, tapping on his own control panel, "but she's right. We might get past entry, but we'll be hitting chop in the stratosphere soon, which could be even worse. Can you stay at this altitude?"

"Ha," Hix scoffed. He would need to correct another ten degrees, which would take several minutes—time they didn't have.

For a brief moment, the trembling lessened. Fewer sparks and heat streams were showing up in the view finder, but a wall of billowing yellow puffs was approaching.

"Brace yourself," Hix said.

The ship hit the clouds.

Hix imagined this was what it must have been like to pilot a major dirigible. The habitat felt bloated and rigid, no matter how violent or precise his maneuvering of the yoke. The turbulence spun them around, and as soon as the ship started to react, they would be in a new gust pushing them in another direction.

"Find a safe pocket," Hix said, "near the ground."

Tolquist's face was flushed and tense. Every few seconds there would be a release of G-forces and he would be able to tap on his screen, and then his body would be flung in another direction, pulling against the taut straps of his chair. He spoke through clenched teeth. "Only possible... restricted area."

"Who cares," Hix responded.

Tolquist nodded ever so slightly and tapped on his tablet.

The coordinates popped up on Hix's viewfinder.

The habitat spun, and veered, and on two occasions rolled, then finally stabilized. Hix blinked away sweat droplets coming off his forehead. His arms were tiring from making extreme movements with the heavy yoke. They broke into a low-pressure area, where there was less turbulence, but the ground was approaching fast. Hix managed to reorient the ship so that they were facing upward, and he fired the retro-rockets, jamming the craft with more G-forces. The habitat was blasted by the occasional squall, but Hix was able to correct the pitch each time with the attitudinal thrusters.

Five hundred feet, a hundred feet, twenty feet, and they touched down. The ground was on a slope, so the craft lurched, but only by a few degrees. The gusts weren't tilting the ship anymore. Hopefully it would hold, at least until it was tethered.

"Atomize this troubled mind," Tolquist whispered. His eyes were closed. He took a number of sharp breaths and leaned his head into his hands to escape from the world.

The habitat food stores had five large canisters of nutrient-rich powders and pellets. You could turn a spigot and it would dump into a bowl. To eat them you would simply add water, and they would expand into something resembling a pudding or a mealy muffin. You could also season them with herbs, salt or sugar to your liking. There was one that was pheasant-flavored. It wasn't terrible.

Hix and Tolquist were sitting in two of the more comfortable chairs in the lower hold, spooning mush into their mouths. Gusts of wind howled outside the habitat, embracing the hull with Earth's fury. Otherwise, there was only the occasional rapping of a utensil or mouth-mashing sound. These sounds were mild, and transient—a stark contrast to the cacophony of the preceding hours.

"Can we return to orbit?" Tolquist asked.

Hix didn't answer right away. He finished chewing his food and put down his bowl. "I'm not sure," he said. "The habitat is designed for one-way trips—down from orbit, or up from the ground. Either way consumes a lot of fuel, especially when we need to make so many adjustments. I'm not sure we have enough for the return trip to orbit, never mind the risks."

"So what's the alternative? A distress beacon?"

"We could set something up. Kanto surely knows we entered the atmosphere, but they probably couldn't follow us after we hit the clouds. The program Iri implemented cut off all tracking and communications, so we're hidden. And I'm not sure we could get a signal through the electrical interference of the storms. Either way, I don't think a beacon is a good idea."

"Why not? Wouldn't rescue be better than taking our chances with a launch?"

"You need to start thinking like a hedonite. We're the lowest of the low, escaped criminals who have killed reformer guards and destroyed valuable First Colony property. If we put out a distress beacon we'll be heading straight to the clam, if they even bother coming after us. Think about it. If they let us live, what message would that send to the other prisoners?"

Tolquist absorbed the words thoughtfully. "Right," he said. He finished his bowl and took Hix's to a nearby basin, spray-washing it out. "So why don't you tell me what your plan is? You always seem to have one."

Hix smirked. "I'm working on that. First, we need more info. I want to run simulations to see if we can reach escape velocity. For those simulations I need data on the weather patterns in this region of the planet, so I can find the route with the least amount of course corrections. We could certainly use the help of some friendly updrafts."

"And what do we do if we make it to orbit?" Tolquist asked.

"We'll have to find a place to dock on one of the other orbital stations, if not Kanto again."

Tolquist nodded, and cast him a dark look. "I'll take a look at the weather simulations," he said, "but first I'm going to sleep." He left the bowls in the sink and headed up the ladder, presumably to use one of the recliner chairs upstairs.

Tolquist seemed almost bitter. Come to think of it, he hadn't thanked Hix for pulling him out of the bay, or navigating them to a safe landing.

Hix shrugged it off. They'd both had a rough day.

26

A SLENDER HYPOTHESIS

The Executive Council called an emergency meeting of the Planetary Defense Subcommittee for the next day. The vids were showing hedonite demonstrations and unrest all over SoPo, and in a few equatorial NoPo communities as well. A number of major industrial facilities had been taken over, or sabotaged. Several high-ranking reformers had been kidnapped, and then let go.

It had been made to look like anarchy, but Neeva suspected the capriciousness was masking a deliberate plan by Mantle to increase their reach and control. This wasn't their big play. This was a stepping stone to something bigger.

She knew she should prepare for the meeting, or continue answering the influx of comm messages about the failed Gorman apprehension, but first she needed to go home. She felt as if she was culpable for Gorman's death. She needed grounding.

She needed Celia.

Instead, all she found was a note. It said, *I love you, but I don't love worrying about you. I feel stuck in a cage. You have the key but you won't let me out.*

Speaking of cages, Rocket was gone. Not only that, but *all* of Celia's stuff was gone: her clothes, her chairs and table, and even her bed. She didn't say where she was going. Neeva felt miffed, then betrayed, then sad.

She tried to prepare her notes for the meeting but the words felt like they were spinning on the page. Responding to her comm messages also seemed pointless.

Eventually she gave up and cried herself to sleep on the cold floor of her emptied flat.

This time Grandpa had been invited to sit at the boardroom table with Quayle, Middich, Fisker and Awekwol. He'd been reinstated as First Heritage Officer, in fact. It made sense. The council gravely needed historical context and intelligentsia, and Grandpa was both a Keeper and former PDA executive.

Neeva was sitting against the wall again, but not alone. Joining her were a dozen other deputies and operatives that were coordinating aspects of the investigation and mitigation activities. VV-912 was on the comm along with several other psychanthropes. The council had appropriately terminated VV-912's sequestration given the escalating threats in SoPo.

The backs of the council members were erect, and their voices sharp. This was not a relaxed meeting.

"It's the Cessation all over again," Middich said in an exasperated tone.

Fisker winced. "While there are indeed parallels, I do believe the situation is much less grave. Maybe it would be helpful if I were to update everyone on the latest reports."

"Please do," Quayle said, nodding.

"In NoPo we know of isolated protests in Tethus and Oatar, but no violence. We are holding steady at ninety-three percent control of psychanthropic channels, the only exception being Oatar, which we have quarantined until further notice. Enforcer reserves have been called up and we are actually seeing new reformer enlistments on the backs of reports of unrest. Psychanthropic sentiment indicators show isolated panic but mostly compliance."

"And in SoPo?" Quayle asked.

Fisker was slower to respond. "We have lost all psychanthropic network connectivity, except in Imdar, which is only temporarily quarantined. SoPo was down sixty percent when we blockaded all the connection nodes to avoid viral contamination. There have been twenty-six organized attacks on municipal governments or facilities. We have lost contact with several official bodies. The Samar City Enforcer brigade and the SoPo PDA units in Samar and Vas City are hanging on, but Samar is unstable and divided into a number of factions. Satellite readings show incendiary activity at eight locations across SoPo. There have been at least nine hundred dead and twenty-one-hundred wounded that we can tie to the unrest."

"That doesn't sound promising." Quayle said.

Indeed, it didn't. It was worse than the vid feeds were letting on.

"No, it's not, but we should keep in mind that SoPo only represents thirty percent of the population of Venus and ten percent of the economic input."

"Are you suggesting we should cut them off and leave them to die?" Awekwol asked, her eyes bulging.

"No, of course not, representative. I'm just trying to put the numbers into context."

"Even if we did cut them off," Middich said, "Mars is watching. Maybe this is the moment they've been waiting for. We become divided and they conquer."

Fisker looked down, and Awekwol clenched her teeth. Grandpa was staring at Middich, his brow furrowed in concentration.

"With all due respect, Middich, Mars again?" Quayle finally asked. "Didn't we cover this last time?"

"Last time we weren't talking about a full-blown insurrection."

"VV-912?" Quayle asked, obviously trying to put a quick end to more Mars speculation.

VV-912 said, "Our scopes do show increased orbital spacecraft and infrastructure around Mars, and these could be repurposed for an offensive. However, since it has been several hundred years since communications ceased, we have no way of knowing the motivations of Mars, and there is no evidence to suggest that they have antagonistic notions towards Venus."

"But what if the hedonites start to self-govern in SoPo?" Middich asked. "What if they become organized enough to leave Venus? Mars won't let their brand of dysfunction infect them. They will be forced to stamp them out, and us along with them."

Neeva doubted anyone in the room believed Middich, but nobody had the temerity to counter him either. VV-912 broke the silence. "If it is any consolation, Director Middich, the commissioner has allocated resources to accelerate our own orbital defenses. We will be launching the LC Beta Fusion Reactor into orbit to boost our infrastructure. We are also expanding the symbiont presence in orbit. More than fifty percent of psychanthropic personnel will be transferred to the new Haven Station."

"Yes, thank you, VV-912" Quayle said, "although I should say this was done primarily as a precaution against symbiont-targeting by hedonite insurgents, and not because of concerns over Mars. Our esteemed brain trust is safer in orbit."

"That sounds expensive," Awekwol said. She wore a cynical frown.

Quayle said, "Yes, representative, it will indeed pull resources away from Verdara activities, but this is more important and should be temporary. Once the insurgent threat is contained, we can resume Verdara activities in earnest."

Awekwol nodded. Clearly, she wasn't happy, but didn't have enough standing to argue.

Quayle said, "Let's get back to the task at hand. This insurgency needs to be quelled, and soon, not only to resume full funding of Verdara projects, but to prevent further loss of life and destruction of infrastructure. Middich has outlined Operation Amity, which is a much more significant intervention than what we discussed at our last meeting. We have all read the reports and countermeasure proposals have been prepared. This will be a final meeting to determine any adaptations we want to consider for the operation."

Middich was scrolling on his tablet. He said, "There is one thing that I find quite curious here, and I would like to explore. Inspector Nash, how is it that you consistently find yourself at the center of these new developments?"

Was it an accusation? Fisker and Grandpa had told her to expect Middich to probe further. The more Middich centered the investigation on her, the more he could blame the intelligence branch for the insurgency.

Neeva stood up to answer. "Yes, the two investigations in which I have been involved have intersected, and both have a bearing on the insurgency. I believe it to be a coincidence. With Mel Redrock-Ora, I may have uncovered new information where others wouldn't have, simply because I'm the only one who knew what questions to ask."

Awekwol said, "I for one agree with you, Inspector. At the same time, I would caution you on some of the claims made in your report. We should endeavor not to isolate and prosecute specific hedonite groups here unless we are sure they are culpable. So perhaps you could explain why you believe this Mantle group is a key actor behind the insurgency. It still seems to me a rather slender hypothesis."

Neeva looked at Grandpa. He nodded to her, acknowledging that she could go ahead.

"Based on recently declassified information," she said, "we know that this organization has been around for hundreds of years, and so may have built strong roots within hedonite tribes. And given the disparate data points connecting them to the insurgency—my interaction with Mel Redrock-Ora, the incident at the Hock Pocket, and the contemporaneous flares of unrest across SoPo following my confrontation with Gorman—we believe their footprint and influence must be large enough to facilitate an insurgency of this magnitude."

Quayle said, "VV-912?"

"The inspector's statement is credible," VV-912 said.

Not long ago, Neeva might have been offended by being subjected to open psychographic verification, but it was understandable given the stakes.

"Respectfully," Middich said, holding out his hand to Neeva in abeyance, "when you say *contemporaneous*, I wonder if there are other causal factors here. It could be that *we* are the common thread here, not this Mantle group. In other words, our investigation is simply inflaming existing tribal angst. This could be why Inspector Nash seems to be stuck in the middle of it. It doesn't matter where you wake a hungry vulture, it's still going to try to bite you. This doesn't mean the vultures are working together."

"Excuse me, Director, but I strongly disagree," Grandpa said. "Exposing a criminal does not make you a party to their crime. There are clear links with Mantle here—it's all outlined in the report. And vulture analogies are not appropriate."

Awekwol was nodding vigorously.

"That's fair," Middich said, uncharacteristically modest. "Maybe I don't know enough about the investigation. Inspector, I'm curious, please tell us more about your proposal for how we move forward." A hint of a smile pulled at his lips.

Grandpa looked down, and Quayle scratched at her neck, annoyed. Something was amiss, but Neeva couldn't say what.

"Yes, of course," Neeva said. "I have listed a number of persons of interest in my report—basically, all known acquaintances of the following people: Rae Dione-Pip, Quo Redrock-Mal, Rav Samar-Rav, Henckels June, Wik Scorpio-Vas and Tim Samar-Ben. I have proposed a plan for apprehending these people, which could give us valuable intelligence about the key agents and base of operations of the insurgency. If our efforts are successful, we could disable the Mantle command center with a strike team and minimal loss of life."

Middich said, "Very interesting, Inspector. I was wondering if there was something we missed, but I guess not. I don't think that's enough to change the opinion of the council, unfortunately."

"I'm sorry, Director," Neeva said. "Change the opinion? I'm not sure I understand."

"That's enough, Middich," Quayle said, casting him a deathly stare. "Inspector Nash, please don't take this as an indictment of your investigations. Your intelligence has been useful, but it is not customary for inspectors to provide recommendations to the council. We have, however, already considered it, and decided not to proceed with further investigations."

Now she understood. Middich already knew the outcome. He was just exposing the failure of her proposal to convince the council, to again divert attention away from his enforcers. Heat rose to her face. She couldn't help herself from objecting. "Excuse me, commissioner. I understand you must formulate plans quickly, but shouldn't we confer with the symbiont collective about this?"

Quayle's eyes opened wide. She hadn't been expecting to be challenged by an intelligence officer. Nevertheless, she obliged. "VV-912?" she asked.

VV-912 said, "On behalf of the collective, I wish to echo the commissioner's comments on the utility of Inspector Nash's investigation. It has provided a great deal of useful intelligence, and she should be commended for her work."

Neeva thanked VV-912 under her breath, but her gratitude was short-lived.

"As for her proposal," he continued, "this is a case of too many low-probability outcomes, all stacked together. The likelihood of being able to find each of the individuals named in the report, and thereafter to be able to use them to influence the insurgency favorably, is probabilistically minute. Inspector Nash's proposal is of negligible merit."

Middich was beaming, of course, while Grandpa looked stern, borderline incensed.

Negligible merit? Neeva had thought it would at least be worthy in parallel with other activities. She had been summarily shot down.

"Thank you, Inspector," Quayle said, smiling humorlessly. "You may sit."

Neeva sat down stiffly. Only then did she notice her racing heart and clammy hands.

"Director Fisker," Quayle said. "Let's review phase one of Operation Amity."

"Of course, Commissioner. In the near term, we need to preserve what we can of key population centers and infrastructure. With the council's approval, we will be sending in teams to stabilize shunt towers at Samar City and Vas City, and also to provide reinforcements for key enforcer and PDA centers in Samar City. We do not have the resources ready at this time to contain other major hedonite population centers. Expansion beyond that would spread our forces too thin, and thus would have minimal returns without lockdown and biomonitor measures."

"Good. And phase two?"

"We will be ready for phase two within a month. It will involve systematic hedonite detainment to flush out and neutralize the criminal actors. This will require a coordinated enforcer blitz and biomonitor deployment in tandem. Director Middich and I have put in place a joint task force, which is recruiting and training the operational force as we speak. We will have a hundred thousand biomonitors ready to deploy, and manufacturing expansion is underway for many more. Within a month, we should be able to produce fifty thousand per week. The symbionts assure us that we can bounce monitor data off dirigible nodes via satellite, so we don't have to use corrupted psychanthropic network channels."

Neeva waited for someone to object. She glared at Grandpa, but he was staring down at his tablet, refusing to look her way.

"VV-912?" Quayle asked.

VV-912 said, "I have worked with Directors Fisker and Middich on the aforementioned proposal. It is the most desirable way to stabilize essential infrastructure and minimize loss of life. Other scenarios have outcome profiles that are indeterminate or less favorable."

"Okay," Quayle said. "It sounds like we are all in favor."

"Excuse me, Commissioner," Neeva said, her heart beating erratically. She stood up again on shaky legs. "I wanted to make sure we have considered the impact of the biomonitors. As I have mentioned to the council before, my experience has been that hedonites have a strong unwillingness to accept them. Not only that, but those first to obtain biomonitors could be victimized. As a result, I wonder if the actions outlined for phase two might have deleterious consequences. Notwithstanding the moral considerations, it could radicalize more hedonites or draw them into alignment with Mantle's combative position."

Neeva knew she wasn't supposed to speak up, but she was feeling defensive after Middich tried to scapegoat her. It also didn't help that she was going on very little sleep.

Quayle wore an acerbic expression, which was a bad sign. She was usually too much of a politician to reveal her displeasure. Grandpa also couldn't suppress a mournful expression as his eyes locked with Quayle. He nodded ever so slightly, affirming the answer to some unspoken question.

Quayle regained a polite smile and turned to Neeva. "Thank you for your input, Inspector. We have noted your concerns and considered them, with input from VV-912, in the formulation of our plans for Operation Amity. Your experience has been an aberration. Hedonites will conform if enlisted with surveillance en masse. I mean really, Inspector, what are they going to do, commit mass suicide?"

Quayle's statement was surely rhetorical, and possibly hyperbolic, but the words felt like a fiery truth burning through Neeva's chest. "But—"

"Now really, Inspector." Quayle's voice became sharp, and her brow furrowed. "We must move on. The intelligence you have gathered has been useful, but you're no longer needed. You may go."

The room fell silent. The eyes of the council stuck to Neeva relentlessly. They were like the ends of prod-shockers herding her toward the door.

She had no option but to succumb, so her legs took her to the exit. "Thank you," she managed to utter, before the door shut behind her.

Neeva waited in the intake lounge next the Executive Council room. She tried to review reports and news bulletins on her tablet, but her thoughts were mired in the meeting, and she worried about what Grandpa would say.

She had spoken out of turn.

Her thumb pushed aggressively along the contours of her tablet.

It took the council another thirty minutes to finish. Fisker, Middich and Awekwol came out, one at a time. They ignored her. Grandpa Nash and Quayle were last, speaking to each other in hushed tones. Eventually Quayle peeled away, and Grandpa caught Neeva's eye. He hobbled over to her with the help of his cane.

"Sorry, Grandpa," she said.

He sighed. "Neeva, you can do better."

Grandpa was never one to pull punches. Nevertheless, it hurt to hear him say it. "I'll be more tactful next time. I... Celia left me and I..." She trailed off. She felt pathetic.

"Maybe that's for the best," Grandpa said.

Neeva could see how he might think it was good news. He always seemed to hope Neeva would somehow cure her lesbianism so she could continue their lineage.

Grandpa said, "Middich and Quayle wanted to demote you. I told them that you may have temporary psychological trauma, and that you should maintain your rank. My arguments were successful, but we all agreed you should be furloughed until phase two of Operation Amity begins. You need some time off."

"So am I stuck at PDA headquarters?"

"No. Stay home, or take a vacation. Either way, find a way to clear your head. And no more objections. You need to listen to the council and follow their direction. Eventually, maybe when this is all over, you will be recognized for all the intelligence you have gathered, but now is the time to keep a low profile. One misstep could mean more than a demotion. Your nomination as Keeper could be withdrawn."

"But I still think the biomonitor implementation is a bad idea. I don't think they know—"

"Neeva!" he snapped. He looked from side to side. "Enough about that. If you want to be a Keeper, you need to rein in your emotions. You'll see that the council is right. Concrete truths take time to cure." He seemed preoccupied by elaborate calculation or, perhaps hypocritically, intense emotion of his own. He simply nodded, turned his back to her and ambled away in the direction of the lifts, his cane tapping away in an offbeat rhythm.

Neeva could only guess that Grandpa was also in favor of the biomonitor deployment, since he hadn't spoken out against it.

Eventually, she moved away to the lifts. Her heart felt numb, and her feet leaden. Nothing seemed to be working. Every time she followed her instincts, it led to tragedy.

Her hand pulled aggressively at the feathery tail on her tacti device in her pocket, but it didn't offer any comfort.

It had been a long time since she'd felt this helpless.

It had been a long time since Rykers Town.

27

———

SIMULATORS AND DRONES

Hix was sitting on the bridge, toggling input values into the display and taking notes on a tablet sitting next to him.

The flight simulator functions on the habitat weren't nearly as good as the *Zephyr Spear*, or even the jet copters on Venus. It could field a limited number of parameters, and had constraints on wind velocity because you weren't supposed to fly it in anything over a hundred miles per hour. He had to attenuate the simulator scores on certain outcomes based on his own estimates for extreme variables.

He was still waiting on hard data from Tolquist, but based on the dummy variables he was using, no launch route was looking good. They would have to get lucky and find an updraft which—according to Tolquist—could change by the hour. The habitat had enough lift with the boosters but they might not have enough fuel for the attitudinal thrusters.

Tolquist came up the ladder. He was moving slowly, his expression ponderous.

"Did you get the probe results?" Hix asked.

"Yes, here." Tolquist handed Hix a data card, which Hix slipped into the port for uploading.

Tolquist said, "Do you remember when I said I was worried about our location? We landed in a restricted area that is off limits for core missions, so I thought it might be more dangerous."

"Yes. Did you find something? Radiation?"

"No. Let me show you." Tolquist sat at the terminal and pulled up one of the files on the data card. It popped up on the screen. It was a patchy topographical map that the console had created based on data from the probes. Tolquist scrolled rapidly across the landscape, then stopped and zoomed in. The ground rose in a smooth arc between craggy hills and mountains.

"What's that?" Hix asked.

"I don't know."

"Then why are you showing it to me?"

"The arc you see is the shape of an upper contour of a sphere. The curvature is perfect, and ten thousand feet in diameter."

"Tolquist, come on, help me out. Why does this matter, and how does this help us get off this planet?"

"The violent winds and harsh temperature contribute to a lot of scouring of the planet surface, creating smooth hills and ranges, but this is different because it's completely symmetrical. There are no dips, and no cracks. Perfect doesn't happen naturally. It has to have been made by someone, or something."

He had Hix's full attention now. "What do you think it is?"

"Like I said, I'm not sure. I thought it could be a reformer supply depot, or maybe a terraforming station. Maybe the orbital stations already have surface access, but they're keeping it a secret. There are no signals coming from it, though. Maybe we should send the probes out again, to do a more thorough pass?"

Hix glanced back at the most recent simulation score. He was in no hurry to rush into space with those odds. And if the structure was some kind of supply depot, and it had fuel, it could make all the difference.

"Let's do it," he said.

The probes were nimble aerial drones that weren't designed for extreme wind velocities, but they seemed to recover quickly in the volatile weather, perhaps due to their low weight. Tolquist had only lost one out of the five he'd sent out the last time.

The display showed a rolling span of topography before each drone. The data feed was added to a master map being built in another panel. The drones also recorded windspeed, temperature, barometric pressure, and humidity.

When the lead drone reached the smooth curvature, it dipped and came closer, scanning for apertures or imperfections, but there was nothing. It was one continuous arc, contoured by windswept dunes and rock.

"Can you show a visual?" Hix asked.

"Sure, but you won't see much."

Tolquist toggled his controls and a window came up showing a frenzy of rippling gases blowing past. He was right. There wasn't much to see.

"Whoa," Tolquist said. "Look here." He was pointing at the panel of one of the drones on the perimeter, at least a mile beyond the smooth surface. It was passing a huge monolithic object at least a hundred feet high.

"That doesn't look natural either," Hix said.

"I better make sure the drone sonar is configured to point ahead as well as down. We don't want them crashing into these things."

Tolquist went back to toggling the controls. Meanwhile, the drone on the perimeter passed another monolith, even taller, and another that was wider.

"Communication towers?" Hix asked.

"Could be," Tolquist said, "but why the variance in size? And why would there be more than one? I think... look."

Another curved surface arched up beneath the perimeter drone.

Tolquist was typing hurriedly. "It's the same curvature as the other one."

"This complex is big, whatever it is, or was. Do you think the reformers could have tried settling on the surface and then abandoned it?"

"It's possible," Tolquist said. "It could also be Martians."

That gave Hix a jolt. Of course machine-mechs wouldn't care about living in this environment. This could be a mine, or even a military base.

"But there are still no detectable electromagnetic or radio signals," Tolquist continued.

That calmed Hix a bit.

Abruptly, the perimeter drone feed blacked out, and then returned. The feed revealed a great deal of heterogeneity on the surface, and no more curvature.

"Pull up, maybe?" Hix said.

Tolquist obliged and the drone rose, revealing the topography in greater detail. The drone had been instructed to stay thirty feet above the surface, and so when it reached a cliff, it fell right off. The arcing curvature was broken underneath, and the new floor's only distinct feature was a long rise of sediment reaching toward a stubby monolith just outside the circumference of the depression.

"A tower must have fallen," Tolquist said.

It was a logical assumption. It also meant the curvature material wasn't of sturdy construction. Tolquist was already redirecting the drone back down. He turned it toward the cliff face it had just come over, at which point the sonar revealed that it wasn't a cliff face at all —it was hollow.

"Can you..." Hix trailed off, because Tolquist was already one step ahead of him. He had turned on the drone's front lamp and camera. The curvature above protected the drone from the gusts of wind and thick eddies of gas. Hix could now see a good thirty feet ahead.

The drone moved slowly, deeper and deeper under the overhang. As it did, visibility further improved.

At first the ground was covered in sediment, blown into knolls and ridges over the years, but gradually other shapes emerged: tall rounded pillars, blocky buildings with vacant windows, and what looked like an elevated rail system.

More buildings appeared on the display. Proper avenues became discernable. The skeleton of an old vehicle sat idle, its features indented and melted away on one side. The buildings had tight curves and lined windowsills, much like those in Samar City. The dunes were gone, and instead everything was covered with more uniform layers of yellow sediment. Hix wondered if this is what snow would look like, if it were yellow.

The drone passed a five-story stack of disks that dwarfed another abandoned car. At one point it had perhaps been a fountain. This marked the beginning of a broad expanse free of buildings—a main transport conduit. Tolquist commanded the drone to follow the avenue deeper into the ruin.

As the drone proceeded forward, the buildings grew more densely packed, and taller, until at the end of the avenue a great door was revealed, at least four stories high.

Tolquist said, "Based on our location data, this shouldn't lead to the outside, but rather deeper underground."

Beside the door was a great statue, made to look as if it was stepping out of the face of the wall. It was of a woman, dressed in a flowing gown, and holding her palms up in the air. In one hand was a plate of food and in the other a semblance of lightning bolts and star-like energy blooms. Her gown fit tightly, accentuating sultry curves and exposing the top of her bosom.

The drone hovered while they both gawked at the huge statue.

"Well, I doubt this was built by the Martians," Tolquist said. "It looks more hedonite than anything else."

Hix frowned and said, "Hedonite doesn't rhyme with stereotype." But he couldn't deny the truth of it. Or at least, you wouldn't see a statue like that in any NoPo settlement.

Tolquist said, "I'm going to pull the other drones in here, to do a comprehensive sweep, and..."

"And what?"

"And..."

"What is it?"

"I wasn't looking at the temperature readings." Tolquist tapped on his console, commanding the drone to approach the big door. "There's been a big drop, the closer we get to the door. It's down to 350 Kelvin here, that's a differential of almost a hundred degrees from the outside."

"So there's cold air. You think it's coming from there, behind the door?"

"Yes. Behind the door is probably much cooler than 350 Kelvin. It could even be room temperature. Maybe a cooling system was left on by the former inhabitants."

Hix nodded. "And if there's a cooling system, there's a power source."

Tolquist raised his eyebrows. "Yes. I suppose it's possible."

Hix couldn't help laughing. He slapped Tolquist on the shoulder, which Tolquist took in stride, despite the fact that it was a hedonite gesture. "This could be our lucky break," he said.

"I'm not sure how we can get through that door, but we can try. If we can move the habitat closer, we could walk in with atmospheric suits. They should protect us for a few hours, and much longer if we can get to cooler temperatures."

"Let's make it happen," Hix smiled.

Tolquist nodded. He still seemed resigned, even mildly annoyed. Was it a reformer quality to be so morose about obviously good news? Most hedonites would be dancing with joy across the habitat.

In any case, they went to work. Tolquist recruited the other drones to map out the rest of the ruin, looking for easy entry points or anything else that might be interesting, while Hix started charting a course to the ruin for the habitat. He would need to run a number of simulations to find the best route.

A concern lingered in the back of his mind. It was unclear how long this shell had been broken, but he suspected at least a hundred years. For a power source to be left on for this long, it must have been built to last—built to protect what was inside. And presumably the reformers knew about this settlement, and had purposefully kept it under wraps.

Whatever was behind those doors, it wasn't supposed to be found.

The flight over to the broken egg, as they now called it, was short and uneventful. Tolquist chose a time of day when prevailing winds were light, and the habitat was able to stay close enough to the surface to avoid big squalls.

Hix and Tolquist walked through the exposed city without distraction, the only sounds being the airflow ventilating their full-body atmospheric suits. There were no people, or animals, alive or dead. Small square plots were evident, where trees might have grown at one time, but with no sign of any wood remains. The heat and acid would have destroyed them a long time ago. Hix supposed the same would have been true for people, although perhaps some clothing would survive.

They entered through a small door a block from the statue of the scantily-clad woman. The door handle was a mechanical latch that opened easily when turned. Inside was just as dark. Hix shined his floodlamp in an arc to reveal their immediate surroundings. It was much like the broken egg environment, except without the prevalent dust and decay. The buildings inside were blocky six-level condominiums, closely packed together, each level with its own balcony.

The street turned and broadened into a large avenue. Every corner was rounded, and the rooftops had half-domes that arched up to the ceiling. Unlike the outside ruin, some windows here hadn't corroded away. Others had been smashed, with the remaining shards still glittering the reflections of their headlamps. Clothing lay near the one of the entryways—pants made of a shiny material covered in a powdery residue—but nothing that would indicate who they belonged to, or why they were there.

At the next intersection were street signs with arrows: *Raupost* and *Previhall.* There was another sign pointing down Raupost saying *Center*, featuring a silhouette of a man walking up broad steps into a large building. Hix headed in that direction and Tolquist followed.

They passed a few broken-down droids. These were disc-shaped and low to the ground, with two spindly arms that reached out the sides, and trash receptacles sitting on the top. Hix could have sworn he'd seen one of these cleaning up Samar City, although perhaps it was just a practical design. Maybe there were similar droids on Mars as well.

A large building loomed at the end of the street. It was striped in colorful fuchsia and blue pastels, and at the top was a fenced-in platform that ran over the edges of the main building, forming a sort of parapet. The front entrance was dominated by a broad, inverted v-shaped array of steps leading up to a columned atrium.

Hix had placed his prod-shocker in a belt holster behind his back. He decided to rotate it around to the front for easier access. If anyone was left in the ruin, this could be where Hix and Tolquist would find them.

On a three-story wall inside the atrium was a mosaic depicting a sweating man on his knees, fists clenched and yelling. His cheeks were raised in a broad smile, as if he was victorious, but it was unclear what the man had won. The image could have been something Hix might see in SoPo. It could easily pass for a promotion featuring a famous murderball player.

After glancing up at the mosaic, Tolquist raised an eyebrow at Hix.

"Yeah it's like some weird parallel universe," Hix said. If it wasn't for the dark, the silence, and the hum of his suit, the city could very well be in SoPo.

A few things did seem alien, or at least unusual. The ground was rubbery and soft, unlike the hard rock of Venusian underground passageways. The overhead ceiling was made of what looked like a transparent polymer, but one that was probably covered in thick sediment. Transparent roofs were difficult to maintain, and thus rarely used on Venus, aside from the occasional skylight. Furthermore, the sunlight would have to be reduced by filters during sun season, and these filters were cumbersome to maintain.

They reached a set of lifts. To the one side was a panel listing what was on the various floors: *City Maintenance, Permits, Transporta-*

tion, Municipal Offices, Entertainment. Tolquist pressed the lift button, but it didn't work. Hix found stairs close by.

At first they took opposing directions when they entered the stairwell, with Hix heading down and Tolquist heading up.

Hix paused on the staircase. "Maintenance is down. I'm betting power sources would be there. Or at least we can see what's cooling the place."

Tolquist said, "And the Municipal Offices are on the sixth floor. Don't you think we should find out what this place is before we start stealing from it?"

Hix was curious, but only moderately so. The familiarity bothered him, and he wanted to get out quickly. At the same time, he needed to keep Tolquist happy, as he'd seemed more than a little grumpy lately. "Fine," he demurred, "but let's not stay long."

Tolquist frowned and acknowledged him with a nod.

Hix soon realized they wouldn't need much time anyway. When they arrived on the sixth floor, the area was charred, and the doorways misshapen. It looked like there had been a big fire, or explosion, or both. The ground was mostly free of debris, probably because cleaning droids had resolved to do their job after what happened.

To access the area, Hix had to duck under a fallen metal beam.

Inside was a circular room with huge wall screens that were scratched, torn, and blackened. The control panels below were similarly burnt and melted. He tapped on the console buttons and displays. Nothing was working. There was no clue as to who the previous inhabitants were, or how they had managed the city.

"Okay, let's go to maintenance," Tolquist said, before Hix could prod him.

City Maintenance was a gallery of different rooms, some of which were locked. One was full of decommissioned droids that had been pulled apart, another was covered in empty boxes that had toppled onto the ground. The largest room was at the end of the hallway, and it bore some resemblance to the torched Municipal Office, except that it was still in decent condition. One display panel had been cracked but two others remained intact, and the control console looked dusty but otherwise undamaged.

Hix found a button labeled *Wake* on the outside of the control panel and pressed it.

The monitor flickered to life.

Warnings in bold red text began flashing on the screen

- Main Banbury dome compromised to atmosphere.
- Severe damage noted to air filtration system. Breathing support recommended.
- Banbury sections 2–15, 19, and 23–31 unresponsive.
- Fusion power offline and main reserves depleted. Emergency power reserves minimal at 10%, supported by GeoTherm TY820 unit.
- 100% of CIF droids unresponsive. Autocontrol override in place.

Recommendations:
1 Remove autocontrol override
2 Enable auxiliary power
3 Commission and deploy new air filtration and repair droids.

What is your command? __

Tolquist looked at Hix.

"Do you mind?" Hix asked, pointing at the console.

"No," Tolquist said, "but... just don't break anything."

"Don't break anything?" Hix laughed. "I think we're long past that."

"I mean, we need to preserve what is left of this site as best we can. It could have incredible archeological significance."

"Gotcha," Hix said. "I'll do my best."

It amazed Hix that Tolquist could care about such mundane things when they were fighting for their lives. Preserve it for whom? The PDA inspectors who jailed them? The reformers who had kept the place secret for hundreds of years while it fell into disrepair?

The login screen asked for a *DCID number*, obviously some sort of credential, possibly confidential in nature. But he could *Login as guest,* so he did.

The interface was unfamiliar to him. Instead of a circular menu that would expand prompts as he passed over them, the screen featured simple rounded-corner squares with icons on them. A number of them were grayed out, presumably indicating they were secure applications requiring the right credentials.

"Check the calendar," Tolquist said. He was hovering over Hix's shoulder.

Hix tapped a couple times, but it was difficult because his gloved hands had fat fingers. Eventually, he managed to pull up the application.

The calendar was empty of events. It showed the usual days of the week, but the year was different. It read *3854 CE*, rather than *1123 AVL*.

"CE was used before AVL," Tolquist said. "See how far back you can go."

Hix scrolled back months, and then years, but the application wouldn't let him go more than a hundred years back. There was nothing on the calendar, although quite a few days were highlighted in bright colors—Banbury Municipal Holidays, Labor Day, and Patriot's Day, but also some unfamiliar observances like Mourning Day, Memorial Day, and several Spirit Days.

Hix navigated to the map application. It hit him with warnings: *Network access disabled,* and *Geolocator offline,* but it still pulled up the most recently cached map. It was like the aspirational Venusian Verdara map but for Earth, because it showed imaginary green spaces, lakes and even immense oceans. They were able to find Banbury and get their bearings. The other domed city nearby was named Perth, and it featured a greater urban expanse, although much of the area was marked red which, according to the legend, meant "uninhabitable". No kidding.

"See if there's a log," Tolquist said, "some information that would tell us who these people were, and what happened to them."

"Sure," Hix said. He could care less who these people were, but maybe the log would say something about the power systems. Hix closed the app and found an application named *Municipal Communications*. When clicked on, it displayed a series of messages. The most recent was a video message, from *2404 CE*, whenever that was. He clicked on the triangle icon to start it.

A man's face appeared on the screen, before a green pastel background. He had shiny silver hair, and his skin was a beige hue, almost as if he was made out of wood. He had a plastered-on smile that revealed a long scar disfiguring the wrinkles on his forehead.

"To whomever is listening," he said, "this is Mika Higram, interim Mayor of Banbury. We need your help. Please come to our coordinates and we will welcome you. We have ample space for protection. You can run free with Laela Ayana until the end of your days."

The man took a deep breath, looked down in front of him, and his eyes returned to the screen. "Perth," he said, "honorable, peaceful Perth, we plead with you to forgive us. We never meant to steal from your stores. The perpetrators were criminals who acted independently of our government, and when they returned we gave them to the heat. We are only sixteen strong, and only have a month of stores remaining, and we have not heard from any other cities in a year. Come and join us! We still have our *nooyah*. We will dance and sing through this year and the next, together." His eyes darted back and forth retrieving some lost, hopeful memory. His enthusiasm waned. "Please," he concluded. "You're our last chance. Talk to us. Send someone. We need your help." The video ended.

Hix looked up at Tolquist, who was frowning under his mask. "It's perplexing," Tolquist said. "Clearly there was some kind of a societal breakdown in this settlement, and perhaps even more broadly. But if these dates are correct, this video could be from fourteen hundred years ago. Why would these people be here? I wonder if Martians tried to settle Earth before they settled Venus?"

"Could be," Hix said. He was scrolling through the applications. Within a *General* folder he found one named *Facility Information*. This contained a number of documents, one of which showed maps of the facility. He found the power center several pages in. It was in the bowels, a few more levels down.

"Look," Hix said, pointing to the diagram. "This shows spare fuel cells. It connects to a geothermal power source, which is probably what's keeping some level of power on. Let's go."

Hix stood up and took several steps away, but Tolquist hesitated.

"What?" Hix said.

"We still have time," Tolquist said.

"We have maybe an hour," Hix said, "if we're being careful, to collect any fuel cells. Who knows if they're compatible with the habitat. We may need to test them, or recharge them at this geothermal source the doc is referring to."

"I'd like to stay here," Tolquist said, "to review the files more before we go."

"No. I might need you. I don't want to have to go back to the habitat to replenish our oxygen and refurbish our atmospheric suit filters. Remember, Kanto Station could come after us. Let's get out of here."

Tolquist frowned. "Imagine the possibilities. Maybe this place could be a better base of operations for coring missions? We could start again down here. And people deserve to know."

"Who cares!"

"That's just the problem, isn't it?"

"What?"

"That you don't care."

"Tolquist, for fuck's sake, I helped you escape, and this is the gratitude I get?"

Tolquist was staring, deadpan. "Gratitude? I know why you did those things. You needed me to help you get aboard the *Zephyr Spear*, and you needed me to steal the transport hub credentials. You needed me to help you find this place, and now you say you need me to help you find the fuel cells. That doesn't mean you care. For all I know, you'll kill me when you're done with me. How do I know you're not like Rav? How do I know you won't cut out my eye if you need it to get wherever you want to go?"

Hix scoffed. "That's ridiculous. If that were true, I would have left you in Kanto's shuttle bay with Jin, Uwy, and Vas, but I didn't."

Tolquist sighed. "No, you needed me to help you stop Pru. To you, I'm just a tool. I understand that. It's fine. When I was on the habitat I came to realize it would be nice if I had someone real to talk to, since we're probably going to die together. It's true that you're not a flyboy on a plastic billboard, but you're something worse—a scheming criminal who doesn't care about anyone or anything but himself."

Hix was momentarily at a loss for words. The words angered him more than they should have. "Fine," he said. "I'll do it myself." He turned his back to Tolquist, leaving him at the terminal.

As he stomped away, Hix knew there was some truth in what Tolquist had said. He *had* used Tolquist, but did that mean he was callous? Did that mean he didn't care about Tolquist? He was just trying to survive. *Choose life*, Father had said.

Hix wondered if, given the choice, he would put himself at risk for Tolquist. Would he have left Tolquist in the shuttle bay if he wasn't going to be useful?

The question echoed in his mind, finding no purchase or probability. This form of thinking was alien to him.

It was true. Tolquist *was* a tool.

But Tolquist was wrong about one thing. Hix did care.

There was still one person that mattered—one person he cared about.

She was still in the flow, and he had to get home.

28

THE LITTLE DETAIL

Neeva's forced vacation was torturous. There was no way to clear her head, or get grounded. Her mind would reel, recalling the events of the investigation, endlessly sifting through the evidence. She wrote detailed dossiers on everyone involved, but she dared not consult the symbionts. Then they would know she was working.

She had to find it. It was there, somewhere. She had to find that little detail that everyone was missing.

When Neeva was a child, she'd lived in Rykers Town in SoPo with her family. It was a small but relatively affluent metropolis with shunt tower access, and prevalent First Colony architecture. The population was split evenly between hedonites and reformers, yet there was rarely any friction, probably because the municipality saw fit to ensure hedonite wages were considerably higher than elsewhere.

Rykers Town inhabitants had no shortage of work. It was the main shunt tower access point for Themis, near expansive biocrawler service tunnels, and not far from the Themis reclamation facility, which was the largest recycling center in SoPo. There was also a busy Verdarist contingent. It was the second most active SoPo massif behind Samar City, from an economic standpoint.

Or at least, it used to be.

Themis was an active volcanic sector. Neeva remembered when she'd travelled through nearby Pareya Canyon on a mini X31 twin-turbine turbo-copter with her mom. The area's geology featured cascading igneous pillows frozen in time, some curling down walls that were steep and proud, some embracing solitary monoliths and others frozen in mid-drip off precarious arches. Unlike the great Venusian basins, only a few islands of magnesite remained visible, peeking out of the hardened lava flows.

The First Colony settlers had contingency plans for cities in active volcanic sectors, of course, and Neeva's father—Lealson Nash—was well aware of them. He was the local First Colony historian, operating a small museum, and also served as magistrate for legal issues involving First Colony legal code. He would have been Keeper after Grandpa.

She woke with a start that morning, as echoing sirens blared across the city. Mom immediately came in and gave her and Shawna tablets prepared with lists of items for each of them to pack. The lists were stenciled with Dad's legal letterhead. Mom told them to not worry, that the sirens usually meant they had several hours, if not days, to vacate the area.

With an imminent volcanic eruption nearby, in a town like Samar City there might be mass hysteria, but not in Rykers Town. Within minutes, transport carts arrived in neighborhood hubs, and minutes afterward they were filled with labeled bags and boxes of valuables. These would be catalogued automatically by their identifying tags. Valuables and essentials would be sent to the copter port, and other bags would be routed underground to the tramline that led to the service tunnels.

A calm voice replaced the droning sirens, soothing Neeva and her family with progress updates and lists of action items, both executed and pending.

It wasn't as if the people of Rykers Town were robots. When they left home to transport their own bags to the drop-off locations, an elderly woman's eyes were red, and a young man's forehead was wrinkled with worry. People moved with uncommon speed. At that point it really hit home for Shawna, and she began to cry. "I don't want to leave," she said.

Mom knelt down, wiped away Shawna's tears with her thumb, and said, "Home is in the heart. We can make a new one together, if we have to."

The words seemed to pacify Shawna.

After dropping off their bags, they rushed down the broad First Colony avenues, and arrived at the tram stop. There was only one other family on the tram. Most had pickup locations within walking distance of their homes. The speaker preached to them as they boarded. "This tram will cease operation in twenty minutes. Family Nash, please disembark in sector 19e for pickup."

The stop was only a hundred feet from the museum and Dad's office. He was outside, sitting on a bench, where Neeva and Shawna often went to meet him for lunch. He was engrossed in his tablet, tapping at the screen frenetically.

"Love?" Mom said to him.

He only glanced up at them briefly. "Good," he said. "The children's transport will be here in three minutes. Is everyone ready?"

"Yes, we're fine," Mom said. "Everything going according to plan?"

"So far so good," he said, but without looking up at them. His hair was in disarray.

"What are the chances Rykers Town gets hit?" Mom asked.

He frowned, and his eyes darted to Shawna and Neeva. "We're not supposed to talk about that, but we have plenty of time to evacuate. That's what's important."

"Okay, let's give Dad some space," Mom said. She pulled Neeva and Shawna away, toward the tram stop.

At the time, Neeva was annoyed that Dad had to work, but she didn't know how important he was to the evacuation effort. The plan had been pulled from First Colony archives, and he had helped facilitate drills and organize contingencies.

A transport bus arrived. The word *Children* was stenciled in red on the front display panel.

"Okay, girls," Mom said, pulling them back to Dad. "Time to say goodbye."

Neeva said, "I want stay with you." She was a notoriously quiet child, and always compliant, so it must have come as a surprise to her parents.

Dad took a brief moment away from his screen. He smiled. "We have to follow the plan, Neeva." He waved his tablet in the air, as if she hadn't seen it before. "That's the way we'll be sure everyone is safe. So the children go first. We'll see you at the meetup in Clifton." He hugged her, and Shawna as well.

Shawna was crying again, but quietly. Dad's head tilted to the side. "You worry too much, Shawna," he said. It could have been patronizing, but his gentle smile softened the edge of his words.

Dad's tablet was flashing at him.

Mom pulled them away, and she also hugged them both in turn. "We'll see you soon," Mom said.

Neeva and Shawna stepped up the folded-out steps of the blocky transport bus.

"Shawna!" someone yelled. It was Shawna's friend Dillon from school, sitting three rows back. Shawna's face lit up and she joined him on his bench seat. Neeva took the seat behind them.

Neeva didn't know Dillon well, but it was nice to see a familiar face. It felt less like they were leaving home forever and more like they were going on a field trip.

The bus pulled away.

"At least we won't have to hand in our homework assignments," Dillon remarked.

Neeva and Shawna laughed nervously.

Only a few clusters of adults remained on corners as the bus threaded through the residential streets. When the bus reached the copter field, it lined up next to dozens of other vehicles that were unloading in sequence.

Shawna and Neeva were ushered into an older copter model with fifty other children and two adult chaperones. The pilot didn't greet them or say any reassuring words. It lifted off and followed a tight line of others heading north, hovering barely above the surface of the Themis Massif. To the west, another continuous line of copters was already returning to pick up more people. There was no sign of volcanic activity that Neeva could see.

"Do you think it's a false alarm?" she asked an adult chaperone. The man was tall, with a long face.

He smiled and said, "We won't know for a little while."

When they arrived in Clifton—the main town in North Themis—all the children were temporarily housed in warehouse rooms. They watched a vid of a news crew covering all the activity. The reporter was in a copter hovering over the spiky terrain of the massif where Rykers Town was located. A crevasse had opened up just to the east, and smoke was pulsing out.

The onscreen copter started rising to a higher altitude. The reporter said, "I'm getting word that an eruption is eighty percent likely, so we're going to pull away. I've also heard that as of now, all the copters have evacuated. Rykers Town is clear. Let's hope that any damage is limited."

About thirty minutes later, when the children were restless, playing games and teasing each other, the distant speck of smoke turned into a monstrous geyser. There was a thunderous explosion, and the shock wave rippled through the building moments later. The vids showed a huge portion of the massif exploding, showering the nearby atmosphere with rubble and pyroclast. Flows of lava poured out of the new caldera.

The children were awed by the spectacle, including Neeva. Shawna cried.

Parents started coming in to collect their children. It only took about twenty minutes, but Mom and Dad never came. The chaperone, a woman with orange braids and dressed in monochromatic blue coveralls, looked annoyed. "Let's see if I can find them," she said, and she took them by the hand.

The search took many hours, and then went into the next day. Their chaperone and other city officials combed over manifests, checked schedules, and spoke with several pilots. It wasn't until they found Mr. Tarkin, a colleague of Dad's, that they figured out what had happened.

The evacuation crews had miscounted the number of copters they needed. An elderly man had fallen off a transport, and so he needed an evac with a medivac crew who took the place of several other people on the manifest. These displaced persons took an additional copter. So, in the end, there was one missing—the last one—the one that Neeva's parents were supposed to be on.

Of course, this possibility had been foreseen. The plan had contemplated that the number of copter runs might need to be increased based on injuries, miscounts, or copter failures.

But Rykers Town power management had decided to disconnect all power from the city when the full allotment of copters had left, according to their tally, which was not updated for changes based on copter failures or other unforeseen circumstances. The power had to be shut down as a safety precaution, since there were no people manning the utility, and to prevent fires and, of course, to avoid wasting energy.

Dad had been busy all day ensuring the plan was running smoothly. He would have been using his tablet and comm frequently. And so, as the city officials later surmised, his tablet and comm had probably run out of power, and he had nowhere to recharge them when citywide power was shut down.

So he couldn't have even called for help. The many protective blast doors would have been down, so he wouldn't have been able to navigate through the city to restart the power utilities, or to find powered comm devices.

Later, Shawna would complain about how she and Neeva had distracted Dad for too long at the bus stop, or that Mom had never told them she loved them before they left. Shawna imagined all the ways their parents could have died, some horrifically, some poetically. She had written a whole comic book that depicted the many things Mom and Dad might have told Neeva and Shawna if they knew how it would all end.

But not Neeva. That's not how her mind worked. She only thought about that one little detail. If the city officials had just reviewed the plan one more time, looked at the situation from one or even two more angles, maybe, just maybe, they would have seen that they needed to coordinate copter delivery with power management, or ensure power remained for the last people to evacuate. That way, tragedy could have been averted.

If they had just taken care to not overlook that one little detail, she wouldn't have lost her parents forever.

29

WISHFUL THINKING

The thought that Hix and Tolquist could leave Earth quickly was perhaps wishful thinking.

The fuel cells in the geothermal power plant were cracked open and lined with crystalized acid. They must have had some kind of expiry date which was well past due. Hix would have to find some other way to transfer power from the plant to the ship, but a mile-long power cable wasn't available, and he could find no working batteries. A battery boost might not offer enough power delta to make a big difference on launch success probabilities anyway.

So, he and Tolquist spent the next several days searching through records and exploring places where there could be alternative caches of fuel.

At one point, Hix thought he'd found what he needed. There were incendiary fuel pellets tucked away in a storage bunker near a landing pad overtaken by dunes, far removed from the broken egg at the end of a long tunnel. But when he returned them to the habitat ship, he found that the pellets were encased in a control cylinder that didn't match the habitat's control tube size. Also, each control cylinder from the settlement had a maintenance display panel that he couldn't access, despite his best hacking efforts. So even if he could make the control cylinders fit into the habitat's fuel tubes, he couldn't be sure the fuel pellets were calibrated to the habitat engine's thermodynamic environment. Furthermore, if they had some kind of expiry date, they would be useless at best, or deadly at worst.

He was in over his head. Wik's little Mantle academy had helped teach him how to hack Venusian IT systems, but this was something completely different. He was no aeronautic or thermodynamic engineer.

Nevertheless, when he and Tolquist failed to find any other sources of fuel, they searched for documentation and tools that might help Hix fit the control cylinders into the control tubes, or access the control cylinder display.

They didn't have much luck. They did find a few portable consoles that could be charged from the ruin's geothermal power systems. These contained thousands of files, some related to facility equipment. When Hix wasn't puzzling over the control tube problem, he flailed for inspiration amongst the files and data stored on the portable consoles.

Days bled into weeks. Hix and Tolquist had plenty of food stores in the habitat, and enough power to subsist in relative comfort. They could last for months if they had to.

If they didn't go mad first.

Tolquist wasn't speaking to him much. Hix hoped he would cool off, and see the reality. Sure, Hix had been manipulative, but he was just trying to survive. Sometimes to do so you had to influence people. All owls did it, some more tactfully than others.

They worked on different levels of the habitat, which was probably for the best. Tolquist claimed he was combing the records for information related to the fuel problem, but Hix suspected he was also satisfying his curiosity about the ruin, or studying the local climate and geography. When Hix would visit the bridge, he would often see copious notes on Tolquist's tablet, while at the same time Tolquist had "nothing new to share."

Until he finally did have something to share.

Tolquist had taken to making the occasional trip into the ruin on his own. He didn't seem to want company. They had covered the accessible area inside the broken egg a couple times, so Hix wasn't sure what he was looking for. He'd thought maybe Tolquist was just trying to get some exercise.

One day Tolquist returned, sweating profusely. He looked spellbound, in a daze. He said, "I want you to come and see something."

"What is it?"

"There's a lull in the storm patterns today, so I managed to gain access to one of the communications towers."

It had proved problematic to explore the communication towers because they weren't accessible by tunnel, and the only way to reach them was outside of the broken egg.

"Is the tower operational?" Hix asked.

"Somewhat. There are more records there, much more than in the Maintenance Office. They're... It's better for you to see it yourself. I want to make sure I'm not seeing things."

"Sure," Hix said. He needed a break anyway.

Hix donned his atmospheric suit and followed Tolquist out of the habitat. Tolquist took a roundabout route, hugging the circumference of the egg to avoid the exposed aperture. Once on the other side, he scaled a ladder that led up to an open hatch.

"It's not far," Tolquist said before exiting the hatch. "But it's best if we go quickly."

"Got it," Hix said.

When they exited, they were beyond the protection of the egg's curvature. The heat and wind were still quite intense, even if this was some kind of lull. Hix's atmospheric suit started beeping at him. *Unsafe conditions. Atmosphere exceeds temperature tolerances.*

Tolquist didn't care. He was already jogging forward, into the swirling maelstrom. Hix vaulted onto a windswept knoll, fearful of losing him.

Tolquist blinked in and out of existence between dense squalls of russet air that pushed and pulled at him.

Eventually the dark tower also blinked up ahead of Tolquist, and soon it loomed over both of them, shielding them from the winds. They entered via a hatch that Tolquist had found. It was on a balcony to which Tolquist had fixed a rope ladder.

Once inside, the howling died down, as did the incessant beeping of Hix's suit, which meant it had to be cooler inside the building.

"The tower is connected to the same geothermal power source as the ruin," Tolquist explained, "but I had to reactivate it."

Hix was glad. He was sweating profusely, and he wouldn't have been able to stay in the heat much longer without risk of stroke. It reminded him of when he had worked with Mel on volcanic remediation as a teenager.

He didn't stop sweating, though, because Tolquist led him up at least twenty flights of stairs. Along the way, he had to pause periodically. They hadn't been getting much exercise in the habitat.

At one of the rest stops, Tolquist asked, "Why are you so good with IT systems?"

"I showed some early aptitude and so I went to an intensive camp."

"A Mantle camp?"

Hix was slow to respond. "Yes."

"You're not telling me everything, are you?"

"I'm not sure what else you need to know. If we ever get out of here, you won't want to know. It's better this way."

Tolquist gave him a sour look. They continued up the stairs.

Finally, they reached what was obviously some sort of control room. Computer consoles lined the walls below broad windows. There was no view, as the panes of glass were constantly buffeted by brown gusts. They were covered in scratches after being pounded with corrosive particles over hundreds of years.

Tolquist sat down at an active terminal and pulled up a number of windows with a few finger swipes. He'd become fluent with the settlement's navigation subroutines. He stood up and gestured to the seat, with one eyebrow raised.

Hix obliged and pulled up one of the windows. It was a communication from Mars.

RF satellite recording received from Martian Orbital Infrastructure.
Auto-translate Output 2821.678 CE
Content Record:

****

People of Earth,

It is recommended you avoid contact with a group of wayward colonizers that go by the name of "Reformers" or "First Colony Reformers". Their sigil often utilizes a symbol of an outstretched hand bearing seeds.

They have been banished from Mars due to their culture of bigotry, and a doctrine that disempowers an arbitrary caste of people. They are seeking refuge and may appropriate your resources for their own ends.

Automaton Zylts Reiny
Martian High Command

****

Tolquist's eyes were wide.

"Okay, why are you showing me this?" Hix asked.

Tolquist raised his hands in agitation. "Can't you see it? If this is true, it undermines the historical narrative about our origins on

Mars. This reads as though the First Colony people were refugees, or even criminals."

Hix couldn't help shrugging his shoulders. He always knew the Reformer Doctrine was gullshit. Wik and Mel had told him countless times. "I see that, but I have to say, I'm not surprised."

"You don't think this is important?"

Hix tilted his head side to side. "Who's going to believe it? And I'm not sure how it helps us get off this rock."

Tolquist's face was turning red, as if his head was about to explode. He paced around the room, scratching his temple. "I can't believe you don't care about this," he said.

"Look, it's interesting, but first of all, this communication could be fabricated. Even if it is true, we don't know if Mars is just slandering the First Colony because the Martians lost the war. They could be lying."

"But there's more," Tolquist said, "a lot more." He started pulling up dozens of other windows. They were additional communications, from different years, different agencies and representatives, all from Mars. "But I want to make sure they aren't fake. Since you know about hacking, I thought you might be able to help me."

Now Tolquist's question in the stairwell made sense. "I can take a look," Hix said, "but it will take time away from my work on the fuel cylinders."

Tolquist threw his hands up in the air again. "I can't believe… Will you please just give me a day here, or at least the next few hours?"

"Sure," Hix said. He wasn't sure why Tolquist was so irate.

Tolquist nodded and settled into another terminal, taking notes on his tablet while Hix tried to see if any standard hacking tricks could have been used to forge the communications. It was a foreign system, so he couldn't access the underlying code, but you could usually tell by patterns forming: stories that fit together too neatly, the lack of random qualifiers, and discrepancies in cataloguing.

He couldn't find any evidence of tampering, and there was indeed more to the story, including pictures of huge, four-legged animals he'd never seen before, bizarre allegations about the First Colony having rogue ornithologists that pilfered avian fetal stock, and warnings about Durrah and other First Colony heroes as being dangerous terrorists. It would be enough to ruffle the feathers of die-hard reformers, but Hix had never believed the reformer rhetoric anyway, and Venus was so far away. This new information wouldn't help them get back home, and it wouldn't help him protect Mel.

"Looks legit to me," Hix said. "I'm going back to the habitat."

Tolquist frowned and nodded. "I'll meet you back there."

Hix headed back on his own.

Several days later, Tolquist called on him again.

"Hix," Tolquist said over the comm. "We got a message. You should come see this."

Hix climbed up the ladder and joined Tolquist on the bridge.

"A message? From one of the settlements?"

"No." Tolquist laughed nervously. "I would be surprised if anyone is left at any of these settlements. This one is from orbit. From Kanto Station."

"How is that possible? I thought we couldn't send or receive under all that storm cover and electrical interference."

"We can receive, if we go above the interference. I sent a probe up to the stratosphere to listen. It came back with this."

The display flickered on. The image was dominated by Captain Millicent, his bulging eyes just as prominent as Hix remembered them. He looked haggard, and unhappy.

"Hix Redrock-Ren and Tolquist Spitzaner lineage 32b, if you are still alive, this message is for you. You have committed a capital offence, stolen Kanto property, and therefore by order of Kanto command, you have been sentenced to immediate reclamation. This would be a merciful end considering what your fellow prisoners might do to you, and it's certainly better than dying of starvation or exposure on that awful planet." He sighed and looked down and offscreen, as if reading from a script. "And now I'm told by Venus that if you return to the station of your own accord in the next five days, *and* provide us with useful information relating to capturing the escaped refugees Pru Themis-Ana, Iri Montkerot-Kal, and Rav Samar-Rav, you will have a right to trial, and a minimum stay of execution of three years." He scoffed at his own words after he read them. "Unbelievable. I didn't think it was possible for the PDA to become even softer." Millicent shut off the video.

"It has to be a hoax," Hix said. "It implies that Pru, Rav, and Iri made it past Venus orbital defenses, which is unlikely. And why would they need us? No, this has psychanthropic manipulation written all over it. They're trying to convince us to reveal our position. Then they'll obliterate us, so there isn't any trace of us finding something we weren't supposed to find."

Tolquist answered quietly, "What's the likelihood that we can get the fuel cylinders to work?"

"Reasonably likely."

"Don't insult my intelligence."

"Okay, fine, I don't know."

Tolquist said, "You can't just re-engineer fuel cylinders from a thousand years ago on your own, in a few days. Those are manufactured to precision, and fit for purpose, but if we channel enough power to one of the communication towers, we might have enough signal to reach Kanto Station."

"You want to put our lives in the hands of Captain Millicent? The man who reigns over a station built on lies? The man who uses his prisoners as expendable pawns? No, trust me. We've done too much. We've seen too much. Take your pick. Whether it's Kanto Command, the PDA, or the enforcers. They simply *cannot* let us live."

"Trust you?" Tolquist said, frowning skeptically. "Don't you think what we've learned down here is important? Maybe even more important than the both of us?"

"Oh, not this again. They won't let us reveal what we know. It's too damning. Listen, I'm sorry I... influenced you before. You may not trust me, but you know I want to live, just like you do. We're aligned in our goal of survival. If I thought we had a better chance with this ridiculous charade, I would tell you."

Tolquist looked away. He paced to the airlock that Pru, Iri, and Rav had escaped out of weeks ago, then returned to Hix.

"How about this," Tolquist said. "I'll give you five days. If you don't figure out the fuel cylinders in that time, we signal Kanto Station."

Hix couldn't very well say no. If he didn't agree, Tolquist might just do it without him.

"Fine," he said.

🔥

Three days later, Tolquist asked if Hix could come with him to retrieve an artifact from a building in the broken egg. He said it was a music hall, and he wanted to recover an instrument called a harpsichord that was housed here. He needed Hix to help him move it.

Even though his time was running out, Hix agreed to the diversion. He was going cross-eyed scrolling through reams of text and countless charts and diagrams.

They walked leisurely through Banbury's streets. They'd become familiar with the layout, and could plot their route based on the shapes of certain dunes, or the way buildings had desiccated into unique ruinous forms.

"Any progress yet?" Tolquist asked.

"Not really," Hix said.

A stiff breeze hit them, throwing up dust. They were close to the aperture in the egg, so the weather would occasionally find its way to them.

The music hall was a round building, the side closest to the aperture fully caved in. Its open doorway was framed by metal. At one time the door had probably been made of glass, which had melted away or shattered. Inside Hix saw an auditorium, and there was indeed a piano-like instrument. When they inspected it together it became apparent that one of the legs had snapped and its keys were fused together.

"Do you still want it?" Hix asked.

"No, but thanks for coming."

"Sure."

On the way back, Tolquist was whispering over the wind. At one point, Hix heard, "...into the heart of you." It could have been part of the pyrolyte parable.

"Should I be worried about anything?" Hix said.

Tolquist checked his comm. "No, I'm... just coming to terms with the fact that we might die here, is all."

Tolquist began moving more quickly through the ruin.

"What's the rush?" Hix asked. "I'm pretty sure your calendar is free of appointments."

Tolquist slowed. "Sorry," he said.

"No, I'm sorry," Hix said.

"About what?"

"Look, you were right. I was being manipulative. I've been fighting for survival my whole life. I don't know any other way. You deserve an explanation."

Tolquist stopped. His eyes were wide.

Hix said, "My sister Mel. She raised me, and she protected me, but now she needs me. She's an addict, caught up with Mantle. I need to get back to her."

Tolquist remained attentive, but his frown revealed some skepticism. "Is she with this Wik person—the one that Pru mentioned?"

Hix said, "I'm not sure, but she was before I was sent away. Mantle is more powerful than you realize. They want to start a revolution, and they have the resources to do it. They've taken over the entirety of Rykers Town—the old volcanic ruin. They even have plans to hack into the psychanthropic network and get a symbiont under their control. People are going to get hurt, and Mel is in the heart of it."

Tolquist looked thoughtful.

"Now imagine if I had told you about this on Kanto Station, and word got out. Think of how Rav or Pru might use it against me."

Tolquist might not have believed him, but he nodded slowly. "Thanks for telling me, Hix."

"Will you give me more time?" Hix asked.

Tolquist's eyes darted back and forth, then focused on the ground. "I'll think about it."

It was progress.

They continued back through the ruin. Beyond the aperture was a continuous tumble of brown clouds, roiling and folding over each other.

The habitat was positioned just outside the aperture. It was only exposed to the weather when the squalls happened to dip low enough, but it had already started to accumulate small dunes against its main struts and ladder. They would have to dig it out if they stayed much longer.

Hix climbed up the ladder first.

It was once he was inside that he realized why Tolquist was rushing back. In hindsight, Tolquist had seemed cagey on the way back from the music hall, and he usually only said his pyrolyte prayers when he was nervous.

It was because Tolquist hadn't told Hix that he'd already enabled the communications tower and turned on the distress beacon. He hadn't told him that a party was already coming to pick them up and take them back up to Kanto Station.

This realization came quickly, soon after the first prod-shocker pulse hit Hix square in the back. Sonders and Ordan—of all people —appeared, holding their prod-shockers along with two brutish PDA officers. They must have entered the habitat and hidden on the upper floors when Tolquist had led Hix away.

The harpsicord excursion had been a diversion, to lure Hix out of the habitat so the others could enter.

Hix didn't bother struggling. He was in no small amount of shock; his body was reeling from the energy pulse, and Tolquist's deception had caught him off guard.

The PDA officers sat him down in one of the habitat's portable chairs, then tied his wrists to the arms. The rippling shocker pangs gradually began leaving him.

"What is this?" Hix asked. He was breathing heavily.

"You heard the message, flyboy," Ordan said. "We're here to pick you up."

"Listen to me," Hix said. He still didn't have full control of his facial muscles, and drool was pouring out of the corner of his mouth. "They'll kill you all. You know too much. In fact, as soon as you signal to the station that you have us, they could launch an attack from orbit. We need to get out of here right away."

They all looked at each other, seeming unconcerned. Tolquist was taking off his atmospheric suit. "Thank you for coming," Tolquist said to Ordan. "On the way here I was thinking Hix may have a point. How can we be sure we'll be safe?"

Captain Ordan shook her head. "In other circumstances, I might be worried, but we've got rank. They aren't going to kill one of their own."

Hix said, "Captain, no offence, but you're a nobody. A terminal patient who can easily be counted as killed in action on a coring mission. They won't want our secrets about the restricted areas of Earth revealed. And the rest of you are even more expendable."

"I wasn't talking about me," Ordan said, a smirk showing on her face beneath her clear oxygen mask.

That was when Hix saw her. She was climbing down the ladder. Her hair was still a colorless jet black, plastered to her head. She had a jawline much like Shawna's, and she wore her blue PDA uniform, just like the day she'd interrogated him in the garden.

It was her. The one who wanted him dead. The one who had separated him from Mel.

"She's talking about me," Neeva said. "I didn't come all this way to be blown up by my own people."

A surge of anger rushed through him. He bolted at her but stumbled because his wrists were still tied to the chair, and he landed awkwardly on his side. He wasn't sure what he was going to do anyway. Bite her? He was overcome with rage, and wasn't thinking straight.

And soon he wasn't thinking at all.

Another prod-shocker pulse rippled through him, this one rendering him unconscious.

PART IV

EXTRACTION

Intelligence Report – Confidential

****

*To: **Enran Fisker lineage 7e, Director of Planetary Intelligence***

cc: Rorian Middich lineage 30b, Executive Director of Law Enforcement
cc: Chusana Quayle lineage 11c. Executive Council Commissioner

Re: Machine Moons Concerns

Sent: 1122.878 AVL

Dear Mr. Fisker,

In response to your query, the Outer System Task Force has analyzed the latest intelligence and has developed a recommendation, which is outlined hereinbelow and in the attached report and addendums.

The vast majority of our mineral mining facilities in the belt and on the gas-giant moons have failed, and without an understanding of the Mecha-AI tech that is the basis of those automated operations, we cannot reconstitute them. Ganymede remains in operation, but we dare not intercede, even for an inspection, for if it should also fail it could stop the flow of water meteors to Venus, which could be catastrophic for Verdara attainment.

Should we be concerned about Mars throttling our resources? Yes and no. Yes, in that Martian control of the gas-giant moons and most resource-rich asteroids is comprehensive (see attached Machine Moons Report). Mars has greater access and their output is much higher than we could hope to achieve, even if we had the necessary Mecha-AI tech. And no, in that Martian probes have made no attempt to expropriate our defunct opera-tions, or even encroach upon them.

Therefore, it is our recommendation that minimal investments be made in outer system infrastructure. Resources should be focused solely on monitoring Martian operations and protecting Ganymede. It is the task force's opinion that incremental resources would be better utilized for accelerating the Verdara or even supporting orbital operations on Earth, despite the limited probability of success.

Sincerely,

Waylena Mackwell lineage 22c
Project Lead, Outer System Task Force

30

EARTHHOPPER

The way Neeva saw it, there hadn't been any other choice. She'd been sidelined with nothing to do. Fisker had assigned another operative to investigate her leads on Venus, but the one lead she felt strongest about wasn't on Venus. Rav Samar-Rav had been mentioned by Gorman, and he had a big hedonite following before he was captured. He had to be critical to the investigation.

So, she'd flown to Earth orbit to interrogate him, only to find that he had escaped and nearly destroyed all of Kanto Station while she was in transit.

It only made her more certain of his importance.

And then there was Hix. She was increasingly certain of his involvement as well, given Mel's connection to Mantle. Based on the description of Rav's escape attempt, it was clear that Rav and Hix had been working together. But Hix had fled to Earth's surface, so she'd asked—or rather, *threatened*, after pulling rank—Captain Millicent to send the message to Tolquist and Hix, offering them leniency if they returned. Millicent wasn't happy then, and he wasn't happy now.

"Let me see if I understand you correctly," Captain Millicent said, glaring at her with bloodshot eyes. "After appropriating the *Zephyr Spear* and her crew without my permission, and traveling into restricted territory to pick up two wanted criminals that should have been atomized a long time ago, you now want to take these prisoners back to Venus?"

Millicent wasn't the only one glaring at her. So were the deck officers and guards on the bridge of the station.

"I've done nothing illegal," Neeva said. "I used the new martial law edicts to appropriate the *Zephyr Spear*. As a senior PDA inspector, I am within my rights."

He scoffed. "*The new martial law edicts*. How convenient. Formulated when, two weeks ago? May I remind you you're orbiting Earth, far from your edicts. As you can see," he gestured at the display panel, "we are still getting systems back to within normal operating parameters after the brazen attack of these criminals and their accomplices weeks ago. What do you think will happen if we allow the other inmates to see that these transgressions are a pathway to returning home? If we do not mete out justice on the perpetrators, there will be more riots, and I'm not sure Kanto's rings can survive another self-inflicted wound. No, Inspector Nash. I will allow you to take the next shuttle back to Venus, *alone*."

It was true that it wouldn't send a good message if she took Hix and Tolquist back with her, but Kanto Station didn't matter in the grand scheme of things.

Neeva looked thoughtfully at the bridge display monitors, as if giving serious consideration to Millicent's diatribe about the damage. The station wasn't First Colony manufacture, and so the consoles and panels were all sharp angles and exposed rivets. The main display on the bridge was filled with gauges, charts and graphs monitoring the station's operations. Two small porthole-style windows offered the only view of space, where occasionally the stacked rings or the broiling surface of Earth would spin by.

"That's quite a dashboard you have," she said. "Eighty people dead during Rav's daring escape, and forty-two wounded. Two of the rings without atmosphere. One ring almost split in two. I assume core missions and atmospheric dirigible development are on hold until you adjust security protocols?"

Millicent nodded.

"Whereas on Venus," Neeva continued, "we have lost all communication with SoPo. There have been, as far as we know, at least a thousand dead and three thousand wounded since this insurgency began. A symbiont has been taken hostage. Over a hundred billion credits in damage has been inflicted, which is about a thousand times the value of this decrepit station. Our very system of governance is in jeopardy. And you won't permit me to take back key people that can put a stop to this?"

"Come on. Hix Redrock-Ren and Tolquist Spitzaner? A washed-up actor and a deluded scientist aren't—"

"Enough!" Neeva yelled. "Just who do you think I am? Only weeks ago I was in the Executive Council meeting with Quayle, Middich, Awekwol, and Fisker. I provided input to Commissioner Quayle personally."

"You met with the Executive Council? Please."

"If you will not believe my words, believe your eyes." She held up her PDA suit lapel, showing three stars. "I *outrank* you, Captain. If you do not grant my request in the next sixty seconds, I will tightbeam Fisker, and Randol Nash—my *grandfather* and the First Heritage Officer. I will happily wait with you for the fifteen-minute turnaround time to elapse so that I can watch you be removed from duty and put on coring missions."

Millicent's brow adopted a frown of consideration. He tapped on his tablet, perhaps looking for some way to corroborate her claims. He wouldn't be able to use psychanthropic feedback in this situation, since it would take at least fifteen minutes to communicate with Venus. But he would be able to verify her involvement with the council, as well as Grandpa's reinstated position.

Gradually his expression soured. It looked like he wasn't going to call her bluff.

"Fine," he said. "I want you out of here on the next outbound interplanetary, but keep a low profile. All of you should be sequestered on the first ring until departure."

"I wouldn't have it any other way," she said.

The return interplanetary transport shuttle was called *Earthhopper*. With barrel seats, nested sleeping berths, and private toilets, it was more accommodating than the ship she'd taken from Venus. It was used primarily for Kanto command transport rather than prisoners.

When the Earthhopper achieved max burn, Neeva unstrapped and grabbed three food trays from their magnetized berths in the common area. Sonders, Ordan, and Nia were already up, sitting together at a table with Malthon and Griffith, the two PDA officers Neeva had brought along for backup. They were all playing rocks—a game of twelve-sided dice made of polished basalt.

She'd turned the mission into a package deal. Once she'd commandeered the *Zephyr Spear's* crew, they'd become "contaminated" by knowing about Earth's restricted area, and so Millicent allowed Neeva to take them with her, along with Hix and Tolquist. Besides, she didn't want to be alone with Tolquist and Hix, even when backed up by the two men she'd brought with her, and so Sonders, Ordan, and Nia could act as a kind of extra security detail.

The trio didn't react negatively to the assignment. Maybe they wanted to break the monotony, and maybe they knew this rogue PDA agent could offer some excitement. Or maybe they were hoping that getting back to Venus would be a better fate than Earth could provide. With the current state of affairs on Venus, Neeva wasn't so sure.

She navigated around a faux wall to where Hix and Tolquist typically slept. They were up as well, sitting on their beds, reading tablets. She had cuffed their wrists and linked them to wall hand-holds by a silver nylon tether. They both looked feral. Tolquist had long, mangy, red hair and a similarly unkempt beard. Hix had obviously paid more attention to grooming, with a trimmed beard, but his light brown hair was still several inches long, flopping back and forth, and its faded blue dye only remained at the tips.

"Grub time," Neeva said. She handed each of them a food tray as their eyes probed her warily.

She sat down on a bed in an unoccupied berth, unstuck the spork on the side of her dish, and peeled back the silver covering to reveal three tubs of mush. She knew from the ride over that one of them would taste like pigeon shanks butchered with a rusty knife, another like a sort of tasteless yogurt, and the third like potatoes so finely mashed that she could drink them.

She rolled the spork between her thumb and forefinger, feeling the edges of the handle, watching the prongs spin. "So I guess we should talk," she said.

They didn't reply. Tolquist opened his meal. Hix placed his tray beside him on his bed, and stared at her with loathing.

"I could use your help," Neeva said.

"Ha," Hix said. "You're beyond help—a deluded reformer in way over her head. I saw your signature on my sentencing document. First you send me to Earth to die, then you decide to bring me back? Make up your mind."

"You forgot the part about killing my sister."

"I didn't..." Hix's arm flexed and the nylon strap tensed against the handhold. He was visibly trying to control himself. "I'll never help you," he said through clenched teeth. "You're wasting your time."

"You already have helped me."

"Sure," he said with an underpinning of sarcasm.

"You helped me by talking to Tolquist. He told me where the Mantle base of operations is. Did you know Shawna and I used to live in Rykers Town?"

Hix ignored her question and turned to glare at Tolquist. "You're just like every other reformer."

Tolquist wouldn't meet his eyes. "At least I believe in something," he said.

Hix frowned. He was seething. It reminded Neeva of her first meeting with Mel in the abandoned biocrawler. Hix had similar fine facial features, as well as long, but more defined, arms. Unlike Mel, when enraged his face was full of color, whereas Mel's more limited constitution had robbed her of that.

Hix said, "I guess I'm not needed. You should have left me on Earth."

"We know the base is near Rykers Town, but it's a big geographical area, compromised by quakes and lava flows. You're going to help us get inside, and navigate us to our target."

"And why would I do that?"

"Because you'll be coming with me, and I know you're not on good terms with Rav. He won't have any qualms about taking you out, so the best way for you to survive is to help me do my job."

Hix's eyes darted back and forth in calculation.

"And if that's not enough..." Neeva pulled out her comm and swiped over to an image she'd received from Mel's caretaker. Mel was looking healthier, her skin less blue, her arms a tad meatier, and the dark bags under her eyes were dissipating. But she certainly didn't look happy.

Neeva passed the comm to Hix.

When Hix looked at the picture, his veneer of hate fell away. For those brief seconds he was like a child, his bright eyes filled with wonder.

The hateful frown returned only moments later. "I'll think about it," was all he said. He passed the comm back to her slowly, grabbed his tray, and turned his back to her.

Neeva raised an eyebrow at Tolquist, who just shrugged. She nodded and turned away as well.

She ate her meal at an empty table in the common room.

31

THE JOYRIDE

Hix hadn't killed Shawna. Or at least, that's what he told himself.

He was staying in Imdar at the time. They were shooting a sequel to *Toreno Run*, and the atmospheric station on top of the Vas City shunt tower had desirable shooting locations for aerial maneuvers. Shawna had snuck in to visit his hotel in the middle of the night, as she would often do during his shoots. He couldn't say no.

Shawna had always wanted to fly with him, but he was only allowed to fly the X92s and P88s under flight crew supervision, and half the time there was a stunt pilot for his dogfight scenes anyway.

That didn't stop Shawna from teasing him. "Oh, I see, Ana the Swan can fly with Captain Zak, but not his proper girlfriend. That seems fair."

Then Wik gave Hix his assignment, and it made for a convenient alibi.

They packed a lunch and left the hotel near the end of sleep schedule. It was the morning after the first dawn day of the year, and almost everyone was in a deep slumber or hungover after the celebration. Hix and Shawna took the shunt tower lift up to Imdar atmospheric station, under the guise of sightseeing. Discarded cups and even a sleeping hedonite lined their path.

The sun hadn't finished rising, so the sky was a deep yellow hue. Long, thin, magenta clouds stretched to the horizon below them. Gray spots drifted above the clouds in the distance—First Colony dirigibles.

"We should leave the hotel room more often," Shawna said, admiring the panorama.

Hix only smirked. Another couple was approaching the viewing area, so Hix turned away to avoid being recognized.

"Am I such an embarrassment?" Shawna asked.

"I just don't want the hassle. Even if you weren't with me, I wouldn't want anyone to know I was here."

"Why not?"

He smiled and took her by the hand. She followed willingly. Besides Tree Walk and a secluded restaurant in Samar City, it was the only time they'd been out in public together. She must have been excited.

At the door to the station's docking bay, Hix swiped his pass on the reader. Hix and the crew had filmed here before dawn day and he still had clearance. One of the dirigibles was in the hangar, and two were docked in their berths for maintenance. Shawna split off to inspect the one in the hangar. It had a sleek silver sheen, with arched outcroppings housing bladders that had shriveled inward, relieved of their buoyancy. She touched the outside fuselage. "It's so smooth. My sister would love this," she said. "She's geeky about airships."

Hix was distracted at the main terminal, entering the credentials Wik had given him. *Welcome, Officer Prinzi*, the onscreen message read. He looked over the status of the two docked dirigibles. One needed fuel, but the other was ready to go. It was a smaller vessel, not a water barge, factoroid, or colonial life float, but one of the nimbler carbon scrubbers, with a long aerodynamic fuselage and a half-dozen powerful thrusters in the stern. It would do just fine. He activated it.

"What are you doing?" Shawna asked, approaching him. He swiped the screen clear.

"Come on," he said. He put his hand on the small of her back, guiding her toward the carbon scrubber. The door opened and they stepped inside.

"Are you allowed to be in here?"

"Don't you want to fly with Captain Zak?"

"You're going to *fly* it?"

"We filmed here just two days ago. It's First Colony—they practically fly themselves, and there are a ton of safeguards."

It took all of five seconds to convince her.

The dirigible's bridge was typical—a two-level arch, with command chairs above and piloting chairs below. Not that they were needed. The dirigibles had been running automated flying patterns for hundreds of years. Thankfully, this one had recently been cleaned. The seats were shiny and soft. The material had a faint sparkle to it.

"I'll need a minute," Hix said. He was in the foremost pilot's chair, navigating through command screens. He accessed the dirigible network interface, and overrode the flight pattern, then stuck in the First Colony flash drive into the upload port. He couldn't be sure how reliable it would be. Wik never told him his source for the program.

Hix held his breath until the display read *Network command module upload initiated.*

Shawna gave him his privacy. She always did. When he wanted time alone, she left. When he was busy rehearsing lines, she never interrupted. And she was probably enjoying the surprises today, anyway. Why spoil them?

He initiated the unmooring process for the dirigible. It was substantially automated, only requiring a few button presses. When that was underway, he found the stealth packet uploaded from the flash drive and tried a number of commands to execute it. It asked for his credentials again, which he entered. *Compiling network update*, it read. There was a one-hour countdown. He minimized the windows and stood up.

There was a subtle tremble in the walls, and a woman's voice said, "This vessel has been unmoored. Bearing sixty-seven point six degrees southwest. Minimal airstream interference is anticipated. Enjoy the ride."

Shawna was standing with her face right up against the window, the curving glass wrapping around her. When she turned to him, her smile was gone. "This is fun, Hix, thank you, but it can't be legal. Maybe we shouldn't be doing this."

"There's one more thing I want to show you."

She frowned.

"Look, it's harmless. I really can fly, and I'm about to show you, if you'll let me."

Her head was tilted to the side, and a smile pulled at her lips. "I suppose I should thank you for not calling me a prude." It was a reformer stereotype that she hated.

He took her hand, and pulled her close. They kissed gently at first, and then passionately. Shawna caught herself and drew away. "Aren't there cameras on this thing?"

"I turned them off." It wasn't true, but he would be able to erase the video cache once Wik's update had loaded.

They settled in the pilot's chair, with Shawna in his lap. Hix showed her how to select the various commands. He turned on manual override, and let her turn the yoke to the right a few degrees, and back on target to the left. In the distance, tall, spindly white clouds were coming closer. Another formed in front of them from high up in the atmosphere—a cascade of billowing vapor.

"Are those…"

"That's right. Now you'll see some real flying."

"But is it safe?"

"The water meteors are slowed in orbit and parsed into small packages that can be delivered at just the right speed to dissipate once they reach the lower stratosphere. The term 'meteor' is a misnomer—they're not traveling fast. If one were to collide with us it would be like getting hit with a water balloon."

"Yeah, every reformer knows that," she quipped. "I was just testing you."

They watched cheek-to-cheek as they approached the oncoming vapor storm.

"Okay, Captain Zak," Shawna said, "let's see what you've got." She had the presence of mind to move over to the other chair, to give him freedom to operate the yoke.

Hix tested the yoke and felt that familiar rush of adrenaline. Flying was more than a childish fancy for him—it was one of the few things he could really control. Yes, there was turbulence and the occasional mechanical failure, but it was the only time he wasn't subject to the capricious fancies of directors, the whims of fans, or the inequity of reformers.

Hix could make out the individual meteors fizzling down, even though they were still at a distance from the main storm. The scrubber moved nimbly for a dirigible, and once they were closer he easily dodged two meteors on the periphery. Soon they were in a jungle of vertical contrails, and it was hard to see them coming. He deftly avoided one that sliced through an older contrail. The meteor bristled as it fell in front of the glass. They were close enough to see it losing volume. Two more were converging on the scrubber from above, and Hix steered the dirigible into a steep descent—steep for a dirigible, at least —and pulled up just in time for the meteors to cross in front of them.

When the scrubber reached the center of the storm it became chaotic, and he gave up trying to outmaneuver every meteor. He heard two of them slap against the hull, making an eerie sound, like the echoes of a damp lava tube. He thought Shawna might be afraid, but she was giggling with delight.

As they exited the core of the storm, he banked hard to the right, avoiding another meteor. Clear skies were just ahead.

A warning light flashed on the display panel. It read *Guidance System Failure.*

Shawna noticed it. "Um, should I be worried?" she said.

Hix pressed the warning icon on his screen. It showed a schematic of the dirigible with one of the tail thrusters blinking red. *Bladder 3 compromised. Maintenance required.*

He pulled into a hard turn. It would be best to get on a vector back to the shunt tower station.

When he let go of the yoke, the dirigible didn't stop turning. Hix wondered if a tail fin was stuck in place. Two more *Guidance System Failure* warnings came up. The dirigible had changed pitch, down two degrees. The yoke was unresponsive.

"What's wrong?" Shawna asked.

"I'm not sure. The whole guidance system is breaking down."

"Was it the water meteors?"

"I don't think so. We were fine until that last turn. The First Colony engineers built these to last, but they do break down eventually. Many fall to the surface every year. Those maneuvers I did might have forced an old part to seize up or break."

"Temperature, rain, winds, acidity, carbon density... and falling dirigibles. It's just another form of weather forecasting for Planetary Defense."

"This is serious, Shawna."

"Sorry. I was just paraphrasing something Neeva told me."

They weren't in immediate danger, but Hix was unable to change course. It would take them in a circle, back through the vapor storm.

Wik's data packet was still uploading into the network. Hix wondered if the program had something to do with the failure. It wasn't supposed to interfere with navigation, but maybe it had caused some kind of system overload.

"We should call for help," Shawna said.

Hix tilted his head as he considered this. It would jeopardize everything. He needed enough time for the program to load, and their joyride would prompt an investigation. But if they could somehow get off the dirigible before it crashed, it would be the ideal situation—the program would load into the network and any evidence of its use would be destroyed.

"I'm not sure they'd get here in time," he said. "We need to find another way off the dirigible."

He scanned the layout schematic. There were no escape pods.

They could try the parachutes, but they would be stuck in the middle of the equatorial wastes.

He ran a plotting simulation of their current course. Based on their current pitch, it would be thirty minutes until they reached the troposphere. At that point other bladders might fail, since they weren't designed for pressures that high, and their descent could accelerate.

Hix's mind raced. There had to be another way.

He opened the window showing Wik's program. Connectivity to the entire dirigible network had been established, even though the program was still uploading data packets. He scanned the radar and found a factoroid. These were squat, slow-moving dirigibles that were used for periodic maintenance and supply logistics. This one had a number of mechanical arms and docking ports for fuel distribution and supply module exchanges. It was inactive, but functional, and there was space for four crew.

It would do.

In order to call the factoroid he would need to communicate via First Colony command code through the network link. He opened up a prompt and started working. In a second window, he pulled up the code reference manual.

"Hix?" Shawna asked.

"Sorry, Shawna. I figured out a way off the dirigible, but I need to concentrate. I'm going to call another dirigible to come to our aid."

"Oh," she said. It was a less hopeful response than he would have liked. Her eyes were wide, vivid pools. She was frowning with resigned worry.

"We'll be okay," he said.

He continued working, testing code string snippets occasionally. The dirigible passed through the vapor storm again. Several water meteors splashed against the hull. One sprayed into vapor across the front window.

Shawna walked up beside him and placed her hand on his arm. "Hix, I had fun today. This was great, and it meant a lot to me. Maybe it was irresponsible for us to take this dirigible, but this guidance system failure, it's not your fault, and now we need to be responsible —to call for help. I can take the blame. Otherwise we could get hurt, or get into even more trouble."

"No," Hix said, still trying to concentrate on the code. He was almost finished. "I can do this."

"Is this about your public image? Or is this about not letting people see you're with me?"

"No—why would I care about that?"

"Because I'm a reformer."

That surprised him. It had crossed his mind when he first met her, but he rarely thought about it anymore. "That's ridiculous," he said. "I can fix this. Just trust me, please."

She blinked, clenched her teeth together, and nodded.

He finished, tested the code string, and when he was satisfied, executed the command.

Command acknowledged. Factoroid 89IDL moving to vector of Scrubber 45IDL for window cleaning.

He sighed with relief. "You see?" He pointed to the response.

"Window cleaning?" she said.

"These water meteors aren't as clean as you think."

If the situation hadn't been so tense, she might have laughed.

"We still need to buy more time," he added. "If we dump the cargo it should reduce our downward pitch. Let's go."

He unhitched the detachable component of the command display, which folded out into a small laptop, and they made their way to the back of the scrubber. There they donned earmuffs and opened a heavy airlock door leading into the carbon scrubbing chamber, a room with huge hydraulic pipes and coiled tubes stacked in layers against both walls. It smelled of fermentation and there was a constant hammering sound.

Hix pointed to the back of the room, where another airlock hatch opened into the cargo bay. Once through, the hammering noise diminished. Large, cylindrical piles of graphite mash—almost pure black graphite but tinted with yellow effluent from the scrubbing process—was being pushed out of a hole in the wall. The cargo bay was only about half full, but it would still make a difference to the weight of the craft.

"We need to move the graphite over the cargo bay doors," he said.

"What if it hits someone?" Shawna asked.

"We're over the equatorial wastes. Very unlikely."

She squinted, nodded, and looked away.

Luckily, when they moved closer Hix could see wheeled pallets buried under the mash. They managed to dislodge them and maneuver several over to the bay doors. Without the wheels it would have been difficult to displace all the cargo.

After they had both donned atmospheric suits, Hix strapped each of them to the wall with safety belts and used his console to open the cargo bay doors.

The air howled from the opening, pulling at their limbs. Hix almost lost hold of the laptop console. The graphite load fragmented as it dropped into the opening, turning into a rippling sprawl of black debris raining across the landscape below.

Hix checked his console. The pitch had improved 0.3 degrees, giving them a few more minutes. The factoroid dirigible was fifteen minutes away. It would arrive just before they were due to descend into the troposphere.

They moved to the main airlock, and waited for the factoroid to approach. After the scrubber passed through the water meteor storm one more time, Hix opened the door. The factoroid was in the distance, turning to match their trajectory and arc.

Shawna looked downcast. "I saw the program you were running," she said. "This joyride wasn't for me, was it?"

Hix's heart jumped. "That's silly," he said. "You know I'm good at hacking. I had to prepare a navigation program in advance."

"Why would you need to do that? You said it's mostly automated."

He shrugged and avoided her eyes.

"And I don't understand why you wouldn't call for help," she said. "We could have had a fleet skiff here in ten minutes. This factoroid rendezvous is way more dangerous."

Aside from white lies and playful jokes, he had always been truthful with Shawna. It was remarkable, given that he had to lie and maneuver with virtually everyone else. Until now, Shawna had never crossed the line, had never forced him to expose his private life or even his feelings. As a result, when faced with a need to create a convincing story, he found himself falling short.

"I... look, Shawna, maybe you're right, but it's too late now."

The factoroid was getting closer. It was an ugly, dark-gray craft, smudged with grease stains, and it made an annoying beeping noise set on a repeat pattern. Hix and Shawna took a step back as it pulled up alongside. The factoroid was constantly course-correcting, which was understandable given the difficulty in maintaining a parallel circular arc with the carbon scrubber.

Hix checked on his console. He couldn't pilot the factoroid remotely, so he would have to rely on the automated pilot. He wasn't sure he could do much better anyway.

A short gantry on the factoroid had been extended out. Beyond it, the airlock door opened. The gantry would occasionally come within a few feet, only to retreat a second later, shifting away as the factoroid changed course.

"We're going to have to jump," Hix said. "I'll go first, and I'll catch you on the other side."

"Hix, no. It's too dangerous. We need to call someone."

"It's too late," he said, grabbing both her shoulders and looking into her eyes. "We have to jump."

She could only look on, her eyes wide with apprehension. Hix checked the console one more time. Wik's program had almost finished downloading. He confirmed that the program would delete the video footage, then folded up the console and placed it under his arm.

He watched the pattern of the factoroid's movements closely. It was tacking to stay close with the scrubber, but not in a predictable way. After it moved away, he stepped back, took one step forward, and hurdled through the air.

He'd timed it well. He landed on the opposing gantry, but his momentum took him too far to the right, into the wall instead of the hatch, and it knocked him down. He dropped the console so that he could arrest his fall with his hands. Another foot to the right and he would have tumbled over the edge of the gantry. But the console didn't make it. It slid off into the void.

Shawna screamed. "Hix! Are you okay?"

"I'm fine," he said, getting to his feet. "I made it, and you can too. You just have to time it carefully. Make your jump when the factoroid is at its farthest point from you. It will turn back in time."

She was looking to her left and right, and down into the void below. Her eyes were wide, filled with fear. She grimaced and squinted, as if she was about to cry.

She said, "You're not going to catch me, are you?"

"Shawna, don't be silly. Of course I will." He held his hands out, motioning for her to come into his arms. He even leaned out over the gap.

"You're lying to me," she said. "I saw the program you were running. I'm not stupid, but I just want to know why. Why would you risk our lives for this? I know you're not careless, Hix. I've seen you rehearse, and your exercise routine, and the way you watch out for Mel. *Why are we here?*"

The water meteor storm was approaching again. They had maybe a minute left.

"Shawna, we're running out of time. Jump and I'll tell you."

"Why?" she said in desperation.

"Shawna, please." He motioned again for her to jump.

She shook her head.

He still couldn't think of a good story, and if he told her the truth, would she come to hate him? Worse, would she reveal his connection with Mantle to the enforcers?

Would Mel be left to suffer the consequences?

It was his turn to cringe. "Shawna, please. I'll tell you later. Please, please, jump. We're running out of time."

Her face was pained. "I love you, Hix, or at least I thought I did.

Tell me who you really are, Hix Redrock-Ren. All I want is the truth, and nothing more. Then I'll jump."

"Shawna, please."

The water meteors started falling. They were noisier outside of the bridge. One fell close to the factoroid and it was like someone was whispering "Shhh" as loud as they could in Hix's ear.

Red lights flashed, first on the scrubber, and then on the factoroid.

Shawna stepped back and held onto the edge of the hatch. Hix reached back to hold on to the factoroid as well, but he still kept one hand extended, ready to catch Shawna. The water meteors tumbled down around them. One impacted the factoroid, but with little effect.

The scrubber lurched abruptly and tilted down out of its arc. The factoroid nearly collided with it before it pulled up in a deft evasive maneuver.

The two craft had separated.

Now above the scrubber, Hix could see why. One of the stern bladders in the scrubber had failed. They must be entering the troposphere, and the pressure had ruptured it.

The factoroid wouldn't pursue it. In fact, it was climbing, pulling up out of the troposphere. This would be an automated safety protocol, which Hix couldn't override even if he tried, since he no longer had the console.

He watched helplessly as the water meteors continued to fizzle around him. The scrubber spun down, arcing in a counter-clockwise direction, in and out of view behind a series of vertical contrails.

He caught one more glimpse of Shawna before she was gone. She hadn't even bothered returning inside. Instead, she was on the gantry, hanging on to the hatch entrance, peering up at him.

For a long time afterward, he'd tried to understand that look on her face. She hadn't been afraid. She hadn't even seemed disappointed. It was like a confusing riddle had robbed her of emotion.

And then the scrubber steered away, veering downward, and she was lost into the void.

Shawna did jump, eventually, just before the dirigible crashed into the ground. Neeva had showed Hix a picture. The enforcers had found her body sprawled on a steep grade, her skin red and mottled, contrasting with the brilliant white magnesite dunes around her.

The carbon scrubber's video footage was indeed wiped, and he'd even managed to delete the factoroid's feed, but he didn't know the factoroid had a backup that was saved to a separate maintenance server. And why would he have known? He'd never planned on hitching a ride on one.

According to Neeva, the factoroid footage didn't show there was any gantry standoff, since it had limited visibility in three stationary cameras: internal, fore, and aft. Nor did the factoroid have any record of Hix and Shawna's conversation, because they were blocked by the fuselage, and the noise drowned it out.

It didn't matter. Hix knew they would blame him anyway. Shawna was dating a hedonite, so there would be an immediate presumption of guilt. Neeva would bring the full resources of Planetary Defense to bear until Hix was found and convicted.

So he'd called in sick to his next shoot, and went into hiding with a friend in Samar City. He didn't check in with Wik, because he suspected Mantle might be looking to eliminate him after having been exposed. He reasoned the best way to protect Mel was to distance himself from her.

It took the PDA a few weeks to find him. Later, Neeva told him that the symbionts analyzed the grocery purchases of his friend, and matched them to Hix's dietary tastes.

The PDA took him in a raid in the middle of the night. It was only at that point, at the moment of his capture, when the outcome of his joyride was explained to him in full, that he realized what he'd lost. He didn't fight back, or try to run. Instead, he blubbered and cried like a child while he let them drag him away.

It was true—he loved her. He did miss their laughing, and banter, even if it was superficial, even if Shawna hadn't really known him. He yearned for her at times. And maybe, in another world, one in which he wasn't always fighting to survive, one where he didn't have to protect Mel, it would have worked. Maybe in another world, the gap between them was traversable.

32

CP STATION

Colonial Pride Station, otherwise known as "CP Station", was the largest Venusian orbital space station, and one of the oldest surviving pieces of First Colony engineering, having been built before the major dirigibles and the shunt towers. Its outermost perimeter was octagonal, with every second segment in the octagon comprising a giant, revolving habitat cylinder. Spokes reached inward from the other segments into an amorphous mass of bolted-on modules. If one were to blur one's vision, it was almost like a spider's web.

The *Earthhopper* pulled into an oversized hangar earmarked for interplanetary craft. Maybe at one time, hundreds of years ago, this hangar had more regular use, but now only Earthbound shuttles occupied it. The back wall of the hangar showed the sign of the First Colony—a circle made of directional arrows, almost like an orbit, surrounding an outstretched hand containing seeds, illustrating the fist-to-seed salute. The seeds were shown in immaculate detail, such that a trained Verdarist could easily identify which plant each one represented.

Celia would have been able to name them.

Processing took over an hour. Neeva had to submit three detailed forms and endure two different security reviews. A recorder also inspected the ship for good measure. They were assigned an additional CP station security detail, even though most of Neeva's crew was technically a security detail to begin with. She suspected it was less about protecting them, and more about keeping the group out of station affairs until they could be granted passage to the surface.

The new protocols were undoubtedly because of the unrest on Venus, but also because CP Station was the main logistical hub for the construction of Haven—the massive station being built by the symbiont collective. When Neeva was finally allowed to pass through the viewing area of the segment she was in, she could make out its construction on the other side of CP Station.

The collective had made substantial progress in only two weeks. When Neeva had left for Earth the massive docking ring had been half built. Now the docking ring was finished, and two spinning habitats thrust out from it, like stubby, rotating horns. It was remarkable how fast it was coming together. The symbionts used a great deal of drone-assists compared to PDA projects, and it seemed to be working.

"Is it ready?" she asked Captain Larkin, a young enforcer officer who was the leader of the CP Station security detail assigned to them. He had spiky short hair and a stiff gait.

"I hear it should be ready in four days," he said, "once they launch the fusion reactor from the surface and connect it to the docking ring."

She nodded in appreciation. It was nice to see some real ingenuity. For too long reformers had become complacent, relying on antiquated First Colony engineering because it was easy and available.

The group was transported along moving walkways, secured to the floor by magnetic boots. The long corridors were bustling with engineers, recorders, and PDA officers, most busy on tablets or comm calls. Many felt it was a privilege to work on CP Station, since the habitation cylinders had idyllic gardens and active social clubs. In truth, there wasn't much difference between living here as compared to, say, Lakshmi Center. Many reformers rarely left the confines of their habitats, so whether the outside was the harsh pre-Verdara environment of Venus or the vacuum of space mattered little.

She kept an eye on Hix and Tolquist. They were quiet, compliant with instructions, and avoided eye contact for the most part.

The group entered the neighboring habitat cylinder, deactivated their mag-boots, and adjusted to the return of gravity. Soon after, they reached their assigned lodging—the Spotel—which was a three-story, u-shaped complex featuring porthole windows and rounded archways.

"Captain Larkin," she said, "I have business to take care of. Please have your men watch this man closely." She pointed to Hix. "He's crafty and has broken out of jail at least once. His companion Tolquist as well. Ordan, Sonders, Nia, Malthon, and Griffith, stay in your rooms tonight. We will take the first re-entry shuttle at oh-six hundred tomorrow."

"We can't go into the hub?" Malthon asked. His mouth was open in a guffaw, and Griffith was also frowning in disappointment. The hub was where the CP Station action was—it had a busy social scene, with a variety of restaurants and clubs.

Neeva was about to put her foot down, but Larkin saved her. "The hub is closed due to increased security measures," he said, "by order of the collective." He turned to Neeva. "We will need to shadow you and your crewmates, for your protection."

There was dead air for a moment. Neeva had been hoping for privacy, but she couldn't fault Larkin for doing his job. "Fine," she said.

Larkin distributed their room keys and they split off.

Neeva's room was a quaint, minimalist cube with ambient wall lighting. Shortly after she entered, she understood why Larkin had insisted on stationing a man outside.

Her comm registered a recorded video message from Fisker, and it wasn't friendly.

"Neeva," he said, his face contorted by the convex lens of his camera, "I received an irate message from Captain Millicent. We have enough to deal with without you meddling with Kanto Station, of all places. Is it true you commandeered a drop ship and went to the surface?" He shook his head reprovingly. "And pulled rank to take prisoners back to Venus? Honestly, if everyone here wasn't so distracted, this would be grounds for a reprimand or even a demotion. Instead, I'm having you shadowed because I can't deal with any more of your surprises."

One of Fisker's subordinates appeared onscreen, interrupting him, showing him a tablet. Fisker's eyes scrolled over it and he nodded. The subordinate left and Fisker returned his attention to the camera. "No more goose chases," he continued. "No more distractions. Operation Amity is only four days away. Stay out of trouble and return to LC for prep immediately, or you won't have a job to get back to. I don't care who your grandfather is." He shut off the video abruptly.

Neeva gritted her teeth. She had been expecting the reprimand, but it was unnerving that Fisker had asked no questions about what she'd found, or even why she was at Kanto Station in the first place.

She'd been synthesizing her new leads and formulating a proposal the entire trip back. It was twenty pages long, containing detailed profiles of Hix, Mel, Rav, and Tolquist, and the Kanto escape. The tools they had used, including remarkable IT proficiency and hacking, showed the depth of Mantle's cyber capabilities, and in turn hinted at how additional information systems could be under their control. Most importantly, she had outlined what she learned from Tolquist and Hix about the heart of Mantle operations being in Rykers Town.

Her proposal was to send a strike team to take it all out before Operation Amity could be put in play.

The audacity of her suggestion would inflame Fisker even more, but this was too important. The PDA could save millions of lives by chopping off the head of the insurgency. So screw him. She didn't care. She was doing her job as best she could. If he fired her, it would be his loss, and she could live with it.

And even if Fisker refused to see the merit of her findings, even if she was a pariah to the Executive Council, and even if Grandpa was losing confidence in her, the proposal had a good shot at being accepted. The symbionts would sort the council out. They were too logical to do anything else.

She reviewed her proposal document one more time, fixed a typo, and hit send.

In the morning, one hour before their re-entry shuttle was due to leave, she received a response. The symbionts had come through for her, but with a few surprises. They wanted to extract the symbiont NM-198 to safety with a smaller, nimbler team before the strike team would attack. And they wanted Neeva to lead the initial extraction.

It would be extremely dangerous.

Maybe it was some sort of compromise. The council would allow her proposal to proceed, but only if they could rid themselves of her once and for all.

She had twelve hours to prepare.

33

———

FLARING NOSTRILS

"This one?" Neeva asked, pointing up at the top of the cavernous biocrawler tunnel.

Hix looked up. There was a square hole in the ceiling, and reaching out of it were massive metallic arms at least a hundred feet long, askew and dangling into the void. A gantry led from the hole to the side wall, where a precarious-looking metal ladder descended to the bottom of the tunnel.

It was the second supply stop in the fourth tunnel, and it looked exactly as Hix remembered it. "Yes, that's it," he confirmed.

Neeva nodded, frowning. Tolquist and the eleven special ops commandos surrounding them shifted their feet.

"You're sure that's the only way in?" the big brute called Egan said. He hovered near Neeva protectively, and wasn't shy about raising the barrel of his arm cannon from the floor to emphasize a point.

"No," Hix said. "There are two other ways to access Rykers Town: a copter pad on the top of the massif, west of Rykers Gap, and on Bain Canyon there's a road that leads up the massif, with quite a few switchbacks. Both ways are heavily guarded. Very few people know about this way."

"And why do *you* know about it?" Captain Tilly asked. He was the leader of the group of commandos that the PDA had assigned to Neeva. He had a round face, gray hair and dark, penetrating eyes.

"I've only been to Rykers Town twice, about five years ago. I flew a shipment in for Wik, and also helped with a ground transport. This was when it was just a reclusive space for Wik to call his own, before he used it as Mantle's headquarters. Mel and I used to run down the lava tubes and supply rooms, and we found this exit. I'm not sure if Mantle would bother guarding it. As you can see, it's not exactly easy to access."

"It's our only shot at getting in unnoticed," Neeva explained to the group. "Isn't that right, Hix?"

She tilted her head to the side with one eyebrow raised, a mannerism that reminded him of Shawna. It was the likeness of sisters, because they had grown up together, but Neeva was very different—less carefree, more controlled. Shawna had her issues, but she was nothing like this PDA reformer.

He flared his nostrils, trying to suppress his anger. "Yes," he said, "that's right."

He would play the part, helping her—for now. She had Mel, so he had no choice, and who knew, Neeva might be as callous as Wik. But there were gaps in this reformer's understanding. They could be exploited. He would be watchful, looking for an opening.

He was reminded of what Mel had said: "Know them, but never, ever *become* them."

Neeva said, "Okay, Captain, you're up."

Captain Tilly assigned two of the more burly commandos to split off and climb up the ladder. They were laden with spools of rope and dangling clips that hung from their belts. The climb wasn't particularly treacherous but they took their time anyway, testing the rungs, and occasionally waving scanners before them. They made it to the gantry, walked across it stealthily, and scampered up into the square hole.

Neeva touched her ear bud. "Good," she said. "And the EMP? Okay, good."

Two harnesses tied to ropes fell down from the square hole.

These were taken by other commandos, and two by two they were pulled up into the supply depot aperture without incident.

"Is it how you remembered it?" Neeva asked Hix when they'd all been pulled up.

The supply depots were large warehouse-like rooms with lines on the ground for the organized placement of crates and storage modules. A cockpit was recessed into the floor, with controls for the mechanical arms and visibility to the biocrawlers passing below. Hix didn't remember much about this particular room, only that it had an exit point to the Venusian surface. It was unique because the atmospheric hatch was gone, probably having fallen into the tunnel below and ground into the dirt by passing biocrawlers long ago.

He said, "Nothing looks out of the ordinary. The exit doors are usually in the back." He waved toward some open crates blocking the view of the other side of the room. "We'll need to take the auxiliary tunnel across to the fourth supply stop. When Mel and I were here most of the other exits were barred by lava flows or caved in."

A subtle cringe crossed Neeva's face, as if she'd eaten a rotten fruit, but she nodded.

Hix was near the front of the column, behind two of the gun-toting enforcers, with Neeva following him. Tolquist was toward the back of the line, walking quietly. It had taken Hix a while, but on the journey from Venus he had come to terms that Tolquist's actions in betraying him were understandable. Hix might have done the same thing, in Tolquist's shoes. No, Tolquist's problem was that he was naïve to think the information he provided would do him any good. Hix knew Neeva wouldn't be that trusting, and Tolquist's inclusion in this extraction mission proved that he wasn't getting off easy.

The tunnels were layered with dust, but empty. There had been nothing here five years ago, and there was nothing here now. The inhabitants had done a good job of cleaning out their belongings, although Wik's people could have scavenged what was left, as well.

"How did you meet Wik?" Neeva asked.

"As you probably know, he has a big stake in Halico Corp—the company that makes *Onslaught*. He was also a film producer. He met

Mel at a party, and they... hit it off. They were dating for a while. He invited her here, and eventually she asked me to join them. At the time, I thought Wik was your typical idealistic hedonite packrat and recluse, although maybe overly cautious. Many wealthy hedonites fit that profile. You don't stay rich in SoPo without a healthy amount of paranoia."

"Were you in any of his films?"

"No." Hix scratched his temple. "Maybe he thought it would look bad, casting the brother of his girlfriend in a movie."

Neeva raised an eyebrow. "I thought that was pretty typical."

It could have been a bigoted comment, but there was some truth to the stereotype, so he didn't call her on it. "Wik was different," he said. "When I first met him, he had dozens of people here doing his bidding. They seemed to follow him willingly, without the infighting you would normally see in heed tribes. As one of his rituals, Wik would run through the ruins every morning, and everyone would follow him. That's how I know where the symbiont is most likely being held. He told us this grand vision of repopulating Rykers Town, which was basically to create a utopian hedonite community without reformers. One part of that was to have his own dedicated symbiont set up in one of the old fitness facilities. He'd already thought through how the life support apparatus would be installed."

"Just a minute." Neeva pressed her finger in her ear, listening to her earbud. "Okay, let's proceed."

Around the next corner the walls had partially caved in and the corridor became tight. They had to continue through single file.

When they were through the narrow passage, Neeva said, "Sorry, please continue."

"There's not much else," Hix said. "The second time I visited, Mel had broken up with Wik, but she was still working for him. He was hording weapons, and his vision had evolved. That's when we all became disciples of Mantle."

"Is that what you wanted?"

He squinted at her. "I wanted change, yes. My father died because he was made a hedonite scapegoat, and Mel had to sacrifice many things—her life, really—just for us to survive. She wouldn't have to do that as a reformer. So, yes, I wanted a better life for hedonites. Or at least a place at the table."

"Do you think that's what Wik can give you?"

"I don't know," he said. He decided not to elaborate. He was doing what the reformer wanted. He doubted Mel would come to harm just because he didn't explain his political opinions.

He did want a better life for hedonites, but the truth was he had joined Mantle for Mel. When Wik started subjecting people to atmosphere for minor transgressions, he knew they were entering dangerous territory, but Mel believed in Wik, and Hix believed in Mel.

Wik's ruthless methods did have some promise. SoPo Hedonites need a strong leader, and he rapidly recruited a devout following. His threats were often subtle, but ever-present, and the constant fear inculcated loyalty in his disciples. Hix was okay with all that. "It was the price of change," Mel said, and he followed her lead.

They held onto that thought, even as Mel fell out of favor with Wik. Even as she was demoted to a common thug, then a harlot, because they both knew that anything else—defection, flight, or even apathy—would be considered betrayal, and Wik wouldn't accept betrayal.

And maybe Wik could change things. His methods were harsh, but it was better than complacency, or the ill-conceived tribal demonstrations led by deluded attention-seekers.

There was more light ahead. The labyrinth of supply depot access tunnels ended at a large intake corridor, about thirty feet wide.

"Egan?" Neeva asked.

Egan pointed his combat arm ahead. "No warm bodies for at least the next hundred feet."

Neeva said, "Keep your scanner on maximum range. Let us know if you see anything."

Egan stayed at the front of the line as they proceeded along the intake corridor. It would eventually open up into a sub-settlement called Angus, if Hix recalled correctly. Across from them were old three-story-tall buildings with white windowsills, inlaid with patterned brown brick formations. It wasn't authentic First Colony architecture, but it was a good replica.

The street here had been covered by a huge slope of congealed lava, which had come down from a lava tube in the ceiling. A rough path had been hewn into the flow, to make the surface flat for walking.

"Take the path," Hix said, and the group did so without objection. The path split off in several directions, leading into old streets. "Stay close," he said. "I suspect Wik has placed cameras in some of the sub-settlements, although probably only in the main common areas."

The path curled around the slope and deposited them at the end of another old street. It was more of an alley, really. Trash receptacles lined the way, one of them overturned but with nothing in it.

Pictures were posted on the wall here with big, industrial spikes. They were black and white, made of thick laminated paper, curling up at the edges. One depicted a woman with two big ponytails and a cut across her cheek. Another was of a man with dark bags under his eyes, striped hair, and a long beard. Both people had loose-fitting clothing, and not much of it. They were unmistakably hedonites. Serial numbers were written in big block letters at the top of each picture.

"What are these?" Neeva asked.

"I've seen these kinds of images before," Hix answered. "Wik had thousands of them on the walls of one of his secret rooms that he liked to frequent on his runs through the city. They're pictures of hedonites that were executed during the Cessation. All of them were left to die in the atmosphere. He must have decided to post them throughout Rykers Town."

"How many does he have?"

"Over a hundred thousand."

Most people would express shock, or frustration, but Neeva just frowned. "Are you sure they're real?" she said. "How did Wik obtain them?"

"He said they were preserved by Mantle disciples, going back generations, so we wouldn't forget—so reformers couldn't take our past away from us. They knew the PDA would destroy the evidence."

"Look, the Cessation was a mess. Lots of terrible things happened. I'm sure some hedonites were exposed to atmosphere, but a hundred thousand? My grandfather is a Keeper, and he has access to Cessation-era records, and I can tell you it didn't happen. In fact, it's the other way around. Hedonite cults were the ones who did this to reformers. There were tens of thousands of murdered reformers, and the authenticity of the records has been verified. So while I acknowledge that records were lost during the Cessation, one hundred thousand dead hedonites is not something that would just slip through the cracks."

Hix flared his nostrils and breathed in slowly, trying to stay calm. He looked away and said, "I guess it's the word of a heed against the word of a 'former. We all know who people are going to believe. That's what 'formers have counted on for centuries. That's what you're counting on today."

She didn't immediately respond.

He considered telling her what he'd learned on Earth, but he doubted she would listen. She probably wouldn't even give him time to explain it.

They entered a broad tube, bored out of the lava flow. If Hix recalled correctly, it would lead to the westernmost part of the main Rykers Town settlement.

Neeva moved ahead and whispered something to Egan, who nodded and checked his combat arm display again. They continued on.

Hix watched Neeva carefully as they navigated the ruin. Occasionally she would stop and place a node droid into the wall—possibly as a signal repeater so they could maintain a line of comms out of the ruin. She would often reach out and feel the walls as if she needed help to walk in a straight line. Her steps were tentative around corners, her face a mask of concern. A creature this delicate could only be a reformer.

He flared his nostrils and breathed in slowly, one more time.

34

NM-198

As they advanced through the ruins, Neeva often spoke with Egan and checked the readings on his combat arm. It was sensitive to noise and heat disturbances that could signify people ahead. It could also identify electromagnetic signals. She could be reasonably sure they hadn't passed by any cameras or sensors.

They were all moving cautiously, but Neeva was doubly careful. She kept thinking they were going to turn a corner and her parents' skeletons would be staring back at her. Her childhood nostalgia didn't mix well with dangerous combat operations.

After the volcano hit, Neeva took the city officials' word for it that her parents were dead. According to follow-on coring and probes in areas where there was no collapse or lava, the pyroclast had burned through the city, leaving no one alive. Even in areas where the pyroclast didn't reach, the water reserves had transmuted to a scalding steam that baked the interior. So anyone in an open space with exposed lava flows would have died.

But what if her parents were cut off? What if part of the massif had collapsed, and blocked the lava flows altogether? If her parents had been in one of these sections, maybe a sub-settlement, they might have survived, at least for a few days. No one had been allowed in to check this possibility. The ruin was deemed 'unstable', and the volcano remained active for years.

Neeva preferred to believe her parents had been alive those few days together in some remote sub-settlement. They would have had more time to come to terms with their fate, rather than those few hours of desperation.

Years later, Wik bought the whole ruin for a pittance. The survivors wanted little for a life they had let go of a long time ago. Selling to Wik was a form of catharsis rather than a business transaction. Neeva remembered getting her check. All of eleven credits for her childhood home.

Neeva nearly ran into Hix when the column stopped. Up ahead, Egan was waving his arm in a broad scan. He continued on after gaining comfort with the results.

She was just as nervous about Hix leading them astray. The more he spoke, the more she sensed his innate hatred of reformers, and her specifically. And she would never trust the man who'd killed her sister. She could only hope she'd gauged him correctly—that he wouldn't sacrifice Mel on his altar of hate.

The borehole they were navigating dumped them into another back alley with more black-and-white pictures of unsmiling hedonites posted on the walls. Neeva could see how this would have a powerful psychological effect on Wik's disciples. It was a brilliant fabrication that would act as a constant reminder of what they were fighting for.

In this alley there were more waste bins, some of them detached from their wall berths. One was tilted over and an old Verdara globe had spilled out, turned over among discarded packaging, and covered with dust. It must have been left behind during the evacuation. Neeva couldn't help herself—she stopped to examine it. It was an older version, with conservative greens and blues. The topography of Maxwell Montes rose up in ridges from the surface, as well as the larger massifs. Neeva spun the globe and felt the ridges sliding under the pads of her fingers.

When she looked up, the group was staring at her. Hix was frowning.

They moved on and reached a proper city corner, with street signs and defunct lights hanging from the ceiling. Egan motioned for the group to stay back while he scanned the area. "Warm bodies, and voices, about a hundred feet that way," he whispered. He pointed across the intersection toward another alley.

Hix whispered, "That leads to the back of the fitness center, where the symbiont should be located."

Neeva pinned another node droid into the wall, making sure it was exposed enough to receive signals. "Everyone quiet from now on," Neeva whispered. "Check your weapons again. And let's pause before entry into the fitness center."

They crossed the intersection quickly, keeping low. On the wall of an adjacent building Neeva noticed the symbol of Rykers Town—an R with a sloped line through the top oval. It was meant to symbolize the biocrawler tunnels, even though Rykers Town had a diverse array of other industries. She hadn't seen the symbol since her youth. The sight of it sent a shiver through her.

This next alley was bare, with no trash receptacles. It looked as though its main purpose was to allow the servicing of utility stations and supply depots for what was probably a plant or warehouse, given a gray door halfway down and the lack of windows. At the end of the alley was another door, painted black. *Hally's Fitness* was written on it in small, faded lettering.

"This is it," Hix whispered. The whole group of fifteen gathered close to the door.

Neeva watched Hix closely. There were no shifty movements, and no inflections in his whisper, but Hix was a talented actor.

"Remember," she whispered back. "Mel is waiting in an attack copter. She's protected now, but if something happens to us, I can't guarantee her safety."

Hix's jaw muscles flexed as he nodded. "This is what you wanted," he said quietly.

"Okay, cuff him," Neeva said. Getting them where they needed to go was one thing, but trusting Hix in a firefight would be something else altogether.

The lock on the door wasn't electronic, so they couldn't deactivate it. Instead, one of Captain Tilly's commandos brought out a laser cutter and sliced slowly through the bolt. There was a pungent odor of melted metal, like the smell of tarmac but with a much stiffer kick to it.

When the cutting was complete, Captain Tilly pushed through first, followed by the bulk of the commandos, Egan, Tolquist, Hix, and Neeva, with one last commando pulling up the rear.

Blaster shots rang out as they scrambled in. Neeva's teeth clenched and her heart raced. She reflexively lifted her spare hand to cover her ear, as if that would make a difference.

The fitness center was a large oval room with a raised platform in the middle. The perimeter of the oval was a soft rubbery textured floor, possibly a running track at some point, but much of it had been torn up, leaving holes down to the bedrock. There were a few old benches and exercise machines pushed off to the side. This was where she sought cover.

On the platform was NM-198, the symbiont. She was shirtless, her ribs showing, more like a skinny child than an adult, with a number of red chafe marks and ulcers on her body. She was so emaciated that any feminine curves she might otherwise have had were no longer evident. Above her an apparatus hung from the ceiling, servicing the pipes and tubes emanating from her skull. Unlike the ceiling apparatus Neeva had seen for VV-912, this was a lumpy mass of varying pipes and wires, with no small amount of rusted chains and even industrial duct tape jury-rigging it in place.

On the far side of the room were four doors along the arc of the oval, two of them open, and three guards. One of these guards was already dead, face first on the ground in front of one of the open doors, his back a mess of blaster hits. The other two had taken positions behind thrown-over desks and were firing back at them.

One of Tilly's special ops commandos was positioned behind a portable generator on a table that had open wires reaching up into the symbiont's ceiling apparatus. He disconnected the power to the symbiont's apparatus, just in case it could endanger her through some kind of electronic surge.

Neeva ran behind the center platform, through a barrage of blaster fire. Her heart was racing, but she was hopeful their numbers advantage would allow them to prevail. Thankfully Hix and Tolquist weren't interfering. They'd found cover behind the symbiont's apparatus to wait out the fight.

After trading rounds back and forth, Egan's combat arm blew back one of the tables, which revolved around the discombobulated man behind it, leaving him exposed. He was taken down quickly by sniper fire.

The other guard dashed for the door. He made it, even though a blaster shot clipped his arm on the way out. He was yelling at the top of his lungs. "'Former's attacking! 'Former's attacking NM-198!" Two of the commandos lunged after him and stopped at the open doorways to level their rifles. A few shots were fired, and they resumed their pursuit, only to drag the dead guard back into the room moments later.

Neeva jogged over to the open doors. They led to a broad patio overlooking a major street that had numerous entry points. If there was anyone else in the city at all, they'd surely have heard, and unfortunately Tilly's team would have multiple access points to protect in order to defend their position.

"We need a lookout here, and there," Captain Tilly said, pointing at the two doorways at the left- and rightmost parts of the main entrance to the fitness center. He finished circulating around the track, his head swiveling, and joined Neeva again. "The room is secured," he said. "We have one injured—Rittik. But he's mobile and can make it out."

"Thank you, Captain," Neeva said. She tapped on her earbud. "Inspector Nash here. Target acquired. Need immediate extraction."

"Acknowledged," a voice chirped in her earbud. "Be there soon."

She allowed herself a weighty exhalation as she walked up to the center platform.

NM-198 was inanimate, slumped in her chair. Blaine, a medic on her commando team, was taking her vitals. When he was finished, with his finger he traced the paths of tubes stuck into the top of her headpiece, as if trying to figure out a puzzle. NM-198's visor was dark, so it offered no sense that she was aware of their presence.

"Is she okay?" Neeva asked.

"She has signs of malnourishment," Blaine said, "but her vitals are okay. She should be able to hear you."

"NM-198," Neeva said. "We're here on behalf of the PDA. We've come to rescue you. Can we carry you out?"

NM-198 didn't raise her head, but she was able to speak. Her voice was quiet and raspy. "I can't thank you enough for coming to my aid, Inspector Nash. I have been the subject of much depravity here, and will gladly leave with you."

Neeva nodded. "Our medic is going to detach you from this... contraption, and make sure you're stable for the trip out. Can you help us with instructions, to ensure you can be removed safely?"

"I can, but first I should warn you. There are hundreds of Mantle operatives nearby. They have been alerted to your presence and will be upon us soon. They will also be able to access the sub-settlements you came through, to cut off your escape."

Neeva said, "As we speak, we have a fifty-man attack team coming to pull us out. They can take care of anyone trying to surround us via the sub-settlements. They're only twenty minutes away."

"That's not fast enough. Please listen closely, Inspector Nash. My captors usually have me connected to a throttled channel into the psychanthropic network. It offers limited amperage, and only allows me to answer their questions and perform a few unimportant functions. If you can remove the throttle, and allow my unencumbered access to the mainline, I can buy you time by locking doors, setting off mock alarms, and sending fraudulent communications."

Neeva looked up at Blaine, who had a perplexed look on his face.

He had been charged with keeping the symbiont healthy, and knew nothing of psychanthropic network technology. He just shrugged.

They could have used the help of a recorder, but the symbionts hadn't offered one up this time. Perhaps the op in Eastborough had been too traumatizing for Hedlund.

NM-198 continued, "All you have to do is return power to the apparatus, and exchange cable 78C with 45A."

Blaine examined the ends of the various dangling and connected cables. "Found them," he said, looking at Neeva expectantly.

"Please, Inspector," NM-198 said, "I cannot stand being in this house of torment any longer, away from the collective. And if you connect me to the network, it will allow me to gather critical intelligence about Mantle activities in SoPo in the time we have remaining."

It made some sense. Neeva had to make a call.

"Fine," she said. "Do it."

Blaine returned power to the apparatus, and switched the cables. NM-198's neck straightened up and she sat upright, as if the electrical power was restoring her physical state. Her visor was facing Neeva, and it emitted a thin green line of light, which periodically shifted to yellow.

"Please keep us updated, NM-198," Neeva said. "Do you have camera access?"

"Affirmative," NM-198 responded, but in a loud metallic voice that echoed across the room. She was using her amplified voice now that power had been restored.

Neeva stood waiting, hoping for some kind of report, but there was no immediate response. The symbiont must be busy.

Neeva did a circuit of the room. The captain was pacing, too. Hix and Tolquist were sitting behind the raised platform, still cuffed, watching her every step. Neeva knelt next to Rittik. His arm was in a sling, covered in bandages. "We'll get you home soon," she said.

He nodded, but his teeth were clenched. "Yes, ma'am," he said.

"Please close the front doors," NM-198's voice echoed across the room. "I will lock them electronically."

Captain Tilly glanced at Neeva.

"It's probably safer," she said.

Before Tilly shut the door nearest to Neeva, she glanced out one more time, into the streets of Rykers Town. There was no sign of activity. Maybe NM-198's diversionary efforts were working.

She pressed on her earbud. "Extraction team—report."

There was no response

A prickle of nerves assailed her. It reminded her too much of the Gorman mission.

It could have been her comms. The shortwave signals were weak to begin with, greatly diminished by having to navigate the circuitous rock tunnels, and the repeater node droids didn't always work. She was trying to thread a signal needle through opaque, igneous rock. If only one node droid was misplaced, that thread could be cut and she would lose the connection.

She walked back up the stairs to NM-198. "I lost contact with the extraction team. Do you have eyes on them?"

NM-198 didn't respond immediately. After a delay, her visor flashed from yellow to green and she said, "I have no visibility of that part of the facility. Based on Mantle communications, the extraction team is likely two minutes delayed, but should make it through due to the diversionary tactics I have implemented. Their communications may be compromised, however."

"And what about here? Should we expect any company?"

"There are several Mantle security contingents gathering nearby. I have diverted them by alerting them to a number of other fictitious PDA cells in other parts of Rykers Town, but I will not be able to keep them occupied indefinitely."

"Understood," Neeva said. "Thank you." She looked down at her comm. "When should we begin removing you from your apparatus?"

"In ten minutes."

Neeva stood at the edge of the platform to relay the news to the team. "NM-198 is holding off Mantle forces until the extraction team arrives. We leave in ten minutes."

There were some nods. Those in defensive positions in front of the closed doors shifted their weight and clicked their necks. Captain Tilly stopped pacing. Weapons were inspected again. Water flasks were used and stowed away in packs.

Neeva pressed on her earbud. "Extraction team—report."

Again, nothing.

Two minutes later, all five doors opened at once, and dozens of screaming hedonites poured in with weapons blazing.

35

THE PRICE OF PREJUDICE

I t was mayhem: five surges of Mantle disciples against four defensive commando positions, in close quarters. There must have been ten Mantle men for every commando. Only a few of the disciples had blasters, and they used them judiciously, perhaps fearful of wounding their symbiont prize. Or maybe they were worried about friendly fire.

Hix couldn't do much of anything. He stayed low against the back of the raised platform and covered his head with his cuffed hands to protect his face from stray blaster shots. It may have seemed cowardly, but there wasn't much choice. *Choose life* was an easy decision in this situation.

Hix glanced to his left and saw Tolquist sitting back, his head exposed and resting against the platform, as if in some kind of meditation.

The medley of grunts, groans, and gunfire only lasted for a few minutes. It was followed by cheers, which could only mean Mantle had won. Hix uncovered his face and looked around. He had a view of the rear exit door, where two enforcers were on the floor, weighed down by a pile-on of intertwined hedonite bodies. One of the commandos was moaning. A hedonite stepped on his head and he fell silent.

Hix put his cuffed hands in the air and stood up slowly, taking in the rest of the scene around him. All the doorways had been taken by Mantle disciples. Three of the enforcer commandos were being held, and several others were bloodied on the floor. Neeva was next to NM-198, held by two hedonites. In front of her, Egan was unconscious, bleeding from a blaster shot to his chest, his head down. Disciples were pulling at his combat arm, trying to remove it, or at least disable it.

A handful of disciples ran over and manhandled Hix and Tolquist, pushing them up onto the platform next to Neeva.

"Careful," Hix said. "I'm Hix Redrock-Ren—I was their prisoner."

Tolquist said nothing.

A moment later, Rav strolled into the room, trailed by Pru and two other barrel-chested hedonites. Rav immediately made his way up onto the stage to stand in front of Hix and Tolquist. For a brief moment he just shook his head in disbelief. "I should have known you treacherous leeches would survive."

Hix couldn't know what Rav and Pru had told Mantle about the escape, but he was fairly certain it wouldn't paint Hix in a good light. So he would represent a threat to Rav—a threat that needed to be eliminated.

"You're the traitor." Hix spoke loud enough that the other hedonites could hear, and turned away from Rav to catch their attention. "Rav abandoned me after I helped him escape. He sent me spiraling down to Earth." He didn't mention Tolquist. Any association with a reformer would only weaken his case.

His plea was met with confused frowns. None of these hedonite gulls would care about what happened millions of miles away. It looked like they were all under Rav's—or maybe Pru's—thumb.

Rav lifted his blaster and placed the barrel against Hix's forehead. "It sounds like quite the story," he said, "to Kanto Station, then Earth, then back to Venus again. But we just don't have time to listen to fairy tales. Maybe they'll make a movie about it. You can watch it in your next life."

Rav glanced over at Pru, and Pru sniffed. It must have been a sign—some sort of confirmation. Hix was done for.

"Wait," a man said, entering through the back door. It was Wik. He was still fit, walking nimbly in his all-black utilitarian nylon pants and shirt. A tattoo of a slanted ellipse with a silhouette of a man running was imprinted on his neck, stretching partially onto his pock-marked face. It was the logo for *Onslaught*. Wik was followed by a tall, curvaceous woman and a dead-eyed youth with purple hair.

Slowly, Rav lowered the barrel of the blaster from Hix's forehead.

After assessing the scene, Wik said, "Everyone out, except Rav, Pru, Kri, Zor, and Bez. Lock up all the 'formers except this one," he pointed to Neeva, "and these two," he gestured to Hix and Tolquist.

Hix suppressed a cringe. Being lumped in with the reformers wasn't a good sign.

There was a slow exodus, leaving only six of Wik's group. The doors closed behind the last to leave.

Hix said, "Wik, please hear me out. They betrayed me, and..." He trailed off. Wik was wincing, as if the words were wounding him. He put his hand up and looked down at the floor. Hix felt it was best to not continue.

Wik sighed, walked up onto the platform, and placed his hand on Hix's shoulder. "I know what happened," he said. "It's okay. It was savage, but Rav and Pru were doing what they could to survive. They didn't trust you, and I wasn't there to smooth things over—to tell them you were one of us. But we're all owls here. You must understand that the story of Rav's escape from Earth has become something of a legend. It's a powerful allegory, and inspirational for the flow. I need Rav and Pru to rally more hedonites to our cause. Besides, no matter what they've done, they remain loyal to Mantle. No, the real question here is, do you?"

"Absolutely," Hix said. "I've never wavered. I was brought to Rykers Town against my will, by this PDA inspector." He cast a scowl at Neeva. "They've taken Mel hostage and are holding her in a copter outside. In fact, we're all in danger here. They're sending an attack team in through an access port in the biocrawler tunnels, and there's a whole squadron ready to attack the facility via the copter pad."

Wik nodded slowly, thoughtfully. Part of his charisma was derived from his careful listening skills. He gave weight to everyone's words, or at least appeared to. "I see," he said. "That's unfortunate—about Mel, I mean. And you needn't worry about the PDA attack force. We've taken care of that."

"You have no idea," Neeva interjected. "You have a few minutes left as a free man, if you're lucky."

Wik laughed. It was hearty, and voluminous, the sound filling every corner of the room. "You must be Neeva Nash *lineage 4a.*" He said her name wistfully. "The granddaughter of Randol Nash, Keeper and First Heritage Officer."

Wik gestured toward her and turned to address the room. "You see, everyone, right here in front of us is a perfect example of reformer bigotry. For one, she thinks we are too incompetent to counter her feeble PDA attack force. What's worse, she assumes that she has the moral high ground—that an arbiter of truth and justice would obviously pick her side."

"What are you talking about?" she asked. "What arbiter of truth and justice?"

He didn't answer, because he didn't have to. Heads and eyes turned in one direction, to NM-198.

Wik laughed again. "Yes, you presume that a symbiont *must* be on the side of the venerable PDA and their precious Reformer Doctrine. A symbiont would *never* see the plight of the hedonites, would *never* see the flow as a righteous cause."

He shook his head reprovingly. "When you plugged her back in, she told us everything in an instant. We knew exactly where your extraction force was. It allowed us to surround you and counter your little attack, both within Rykers Town and outside of it."

Neeva was slack-jawed with shock.

Hix had to admit that he was surprised as well. When Wik had told them he would have a symbiont on site, Hix never assumed one would be there of their own free will.

Wik was relishing the look on Neeva's face. "This my dear, what you feel now, this is the price of prejudice."

36

———

DESTINY

Two of Wik's Mantle cronies dragged Neeva through Rykers Town. Hedonites cursed and spat at her along the way.

At first, she had a relatively plush abode in west Rykers Town, and Wik's guards gave her a tasty meal of egg noodles with synthetic juice. Wik came and sat down across from her and watched her as she ate.

She pushed the tray away. "Why don't you get it over with?" she said.

"Tell me, Inspector," Wik said, "is it true what they say about the three-letter hedonite naming convention—that they had to cut down space on a major dirigible docking manifest so they truncated all the hedonite names?"

"Our records indicate that the hedonites preferred it that way. They took to the three-letter convention of their own volition. There's no evidence that the reformer names weren't truncated on the manifest as well."

"*No evidence.* I have heard those two words so many times. It seems convenient, doesn't it? Two simple words to placate a simplistic people who have simple three-letter names. It is much easier to take what you want from a simple person."

"Not simple—dangerous."

"Yes, yes, but even if we are inherently dangerous, as you say—which is ridiculous, of course—even if we are mentally unstable, shouldn't we still be granted a seat at the table? A democracy that is selective isn't a democracy at all. As soon as you exclude one person, that person is chattel to the system, and must stand in opposition against it."

"It doesn't have to be an *us against them* dynamic. Reformers think of ourselves more as parents having custody over immature hedonite children. We want the best for you. The doctrine recognizes that hedonites have complex emotions, hopes, and dreams. But hedonites are also people that can be manipulated into making calamitous decisions. You know this all too well, and you've used it to your advantage."

She thought he would become angry, but instead he looked thoughtful. He said, "It's funny, because I also see myself as a parent, in pursuit of a completely rational objective; better lives for my kin. You would label me a sociopath for doing so, whereas you would claim to have impeccable morals for the same goals. No, Inspector, you are the unstable one, since you fail to see the harm you have done by driving a wedge between us over a thousand years, and by continuing to rationalize an unfair system."

He stretched his arms and yawned. "And now I'm sure you're wondering, what does this deranged madman want of me? Surely he needs me to cough up some information for his obsessive cult. Surely he will threaten or even torture me because I am such a very important person. Well, let me show you what it's like to be a hedonite."

He stood up, walked away, and never returned.

Her food was unceremoniously removed and her accommodations downgraded.

Her next stop was at the mental health wing of the old Rykers Town hospital. Here Mantle had access to straitjackets and binding rope that her captors never put on her quite right. She wasn't exactly beaten, but her guards slapped her, and spat on her again. The lead guard—a round-bellied man with a greasy beard named Daw—threatened her with all kinds of creative atrocities; slowly roasting one limb at a time in the lava flats, hanging her from her arms above the biocrawler tunnels, and gouging out various parts of her anatomy. But the threats weren't transactional. He didn't ask her any questions about the PDA. He simply wanted to see her squirm.

Mantle would kill her, eventually. She could only be a liability to them.

They would probably make a spectacle of it. Why not use the pathetic death of a well-known inspector, and a future Keeper, to inspire a new generation of insurgents into Wik's army? Why not *thicken the flow*, as Daw described it?

Twenty-two attack copters were down, and two hundred enforcers dead—according to Daw. The numbers were too close to the total attack force number for them to be fabricated. Neeva had no idea how Mantle could have contended with that much airpower. There was a tangential mention of the shunt tower, which must be in use again. Maybe Mantle had rockets, or guns on the shunt tower, but that still didn't explain it.

She could only hope that the PDA still had Mel. The copter was supposed to abort and fly Mel north at the first sign of trouble. Maybe it was one of the three that made it back.

Neeva felt terrible about the casualties, but something stopped her from expressing real grief. She didn't want to show weakness in front of her captors. She also knew this was just the beginning. When Operation Amity went into effect, the casualties would be orders of magnitude higher.

She wondered if Hix had known about the symbiont. She could have held it against him if she'd asked him, but she never had. She felt stupid, but also not the least bit confused. Why didn't VV-912 tell her the symbiont could have gone rogue? Embarrassment? Ignorance? Hubris?

The whole operation would have worked if it wasn't for that one thing—if she hadn't plugged in the rogue symbiont again. And maybe, with the symbiont back under PDA control, and Wik neutralized, they might have turned the tide against the insurgency. Millions of lives could have been saved.

It was the little detail. She had missed it, just like her father had missed it.

It seemed fitting, to be left here to die. Maybe it had always been her destiny to die in Rykers Town with her parents.

Maybe she had cheated that destiny for too long.

37

AN IMPORTANT JOB

Hix was sitting in a makeshift canteen not far from the fitness center. Opposite him was a lithe Mantle disciple named Cha. Cha had shifty brown eyes and a long scar down her arm, which had been supplemented with tattooed ink to make it look like an aerial view of a long canyon. Maybe it was a landmark from near where she grew up.

"So you found an old ruin on Earth?" she asked. "I thought there was nothing on the surface." Cha was supposed to be getting him up to speed, to reindoctrinate him into Mantle, but she had also been gently plugging him for information.

"I thought so too. It was from fourteen hundred years ago. They must have been colonists from Mars."

"You don't think…"

"That we came from Earth? That's a fairy tale. Believe me, no one could live there. It makes Venus's atmosphere feel like a luxury biocrawler."

She smiled. There was something wistful about her. Maybe she was a fan.

But then her smile faded. She gathered her tablet and left the table abruptly, saying, "We'll finish this later."

"Sure," he said.

He was relieved to finally be alone. It was the first time since the melee in the fitness center. But by the time he stood up and turned to leave, he realized his solitude would have to wait. Wik had been approaching from behind.

He sat back down again. Now he knew why Cha had left so quickly.

Wik circled around to take Cha's seat. Zor, his young purple-haired friend, was with him, standing several feet away. Hix had met Zor before. He was a damaged individual, obsessive about fighting routines—actually, all forms of violence—and was not to be trifled with.

Wik placed a reassuring hand on his own. "Hix, my friend, I need to tell you, I'm so glad you've rejoined us."

"Thank you. Rav and Pru—"

Wik put his hand up. "No, Hix. I don't need to hear it. Nor do I want to hear it. They were doing what they needed to do to survive. We have to let it go. I've told Rav and Pru that they must rejoin the flow. I trust you will as well."

"Of course."

"It's all the more important now, because it's our time. Tomorrow, the flow quickens. Tomorrow we rise up to flood the massifs and form a new foundation for Venus. These reformers, they are all like this Neeva Nash—blinded by their own prejudice—and it will be their undoing. They won't be ready... for you."

"For me?"

"For you," Wik repeated with relish. "For Hix Redrock-Ren, also known as Captain Zak, also known as Falcon Fire. I know your nickname is more about catharsis, and rebirth, but either way, I have always thought your likeness to a Falcon was appropriate. Falcons are known for their hunting skills, for being ruthless—dominant predators within their environment. They hunt their prey from the skies above. This is you, Hix, through and through, and these talents are wasted making films, as a servant to some bogus reformer narrative.

Falcons can be trained, but not domesticated. You aren't anyone's pet, Hix. Your choices are your own."

"What choice is that?"

Wik smiled. "I have a job for you. It's an honorable role, and one fitting your skill set. It's a commission you deserve after having been mistreated by Rav and Pru, a commission that will bring you glory and redemption..." He looked off into the distance, enthralled by his own visions.

"What is it?"

Wik's focus returned. "I will tell you, but first I must level with you on another matter. It's about Mel."

"Do you know where she is? Cha said her copter escaped, that they flew her north."

"Cha wasn't telling you the whole truth. I wanted her to check your story first, to make sure you were still with us, before letting you back in."

Hix's heart started hammering in his chest.

"Mel is in the infirmary," Wik continued. "Her copter was shot down in the battle. She was rescued by our valiant ground crews, but she was gravely wounded in the crash."

Hix tried to control his breathing. In, out. In, out. Every part of him wanted to stand up and run to the infirmary.

"I'm so sorry, Hix. As you know, Mel and I, we grew apart, but I did love her for a time. I still do. It tears me apart what they did to her —using her as leverage in a game they should never have played."

Hix couldn't stand it anymore. He stood up and marched away toward the infirmary.

"Yes, Hix," Wik said behind him. "Go to her. She needs you. Then come back to me. Tell me if you want redemption. Tell me if you want revenge."

Much of Mel's body was bandaged. Her torso and left leg were in a large, composite cast, and what was visible of her arms and neck glowed pink. Her face was beaded with sweat and her skin colored with jets of black and red, some of it blistering. Her eyes were barely open, but her irises still shone with life.

Hix sat down next to her.

"Where's Falcon Fire when you need him?" she said weakly.

"I couldn't get to you. It was the 'former. She set all this up. I did what she said, and still—"

Mel wasn't paying attention. Her eyes were searching the expanse of the warehouse-sized infirmary. "What did the doctor say about me?" she asked.

"That you're strong. You'll make it through this."

She nodded ever so slightly. "At least they're giving me the full pain buffet, and I took another Amadone pill from the 'former bitch as well. Makes for a nice cocktail."

"Just hang on."

"Come on. If I don't survive, no big deal. What did you say to me that time? *You're always too busy playing the part to enjoy it.* Maybe you were right."

"You were too busy protecting me to enjoy it." He said it through clenched teeth. A surge of emotion was trying to well up from deep within him, but he quelled it.

Mel tried to smile, but he could tell it was painful for her. She settled for a smirk. "Remember when we used to run through the Clarendon biocrawler after work? You must have been, what— eleven? We thought it was empty but that geriatric caretaker was still there, talking to his flowers and tending his flock of geese. He chased us off into a dead-end aviary. I thought we were cornered for sure until you knocked down his roosting wall. There must have been a thousand of them that went swarming. I'm never seen an old man run so fast."

"I remember." Hix tried to smile, but he found that he couldn't. Watching Mel's once-beautiful face, lined from Tetra overuse and now ravaged by burns, and listening to her nostalgia—it was too much. And what the medic had told him weighed on him, the words too recent for him to muster any display of positive emotion, real or contrived.

"And remember that party after the *Sky Gate* debut?" Mel asked. "There were like a thousand fans outside, so I dressed you up like a girl so you could get away."

"I think I broke your bra."

She sniffed, a substitute for a laugh. "We didn't fool anyone, but I think the shock value gave you a head start."

"Those were good times."

"They were *great* times. It's what I lived for—watching you break through the ranks of the pandering actors and stuffy sycophant businessmen. They were hard times, too, and at times downright savage, but I loved it. What we did together—it was the only thing that was real, the only thing that was sure and true."

"There'll be plenty more times like that. We're back together."

Her eyes gave him a once-over. "You know Hix, you're a good liar, but not that good." She took a deep breath and her body trembled. Her eyes blinked, and when they opened they were smaller slits than before.

"We'll get through this," he said. "The 'former is our prisoner, and Wik says we're about to make a big push. Maybe this is our time. Maybe you were right about Wik. He has an important job for me."

He searched her eyes for approval, or at least acknowledgement, but they were hard to read, drifting across the room again. The Mel he knew was buried under layers of torment and pain drugs.

A nurse entered at the opposite side of the room, to check the vitals of another victim from the crash.

"Do you need the medic?" Hix said.

"Sear away this sinful flesh..." Mel said. She paused, grimacing.

"You're losing it, sis," Hix teased. "Snap out of it."

"I think I finally understand Mom," she said. "What's the rest of it? Incinerate these brittle bones... atomize this troubled mind."

She was reciting the pyrolyte parable, from the ceremony. Hix's image of his sister blurred as tears welled in his eyes.

"Stop it. You have to fight it," he said. "Fight it," he repeated angrily.

"Float me onto your river of fire," Mel said. Her eyes were staring into the distance. "Into the heart of you..." Her eyes closed.

"Mel," he whispered. "Mel," he said, louder. He pulled at her hand, but she didn't respond. She was unconscious.

He finished the parable for her. "There may I rest unencumbered."

He knelt by her bed, resting his head against the mattress, his tears dampening the sheets. He couldn't let go of her hand. Minutes ticked away and turned into hours, until eventually, the only person who had ever truly known him, the only person who had ever cared about him, faded from the world.

The grief swallowed him up, and then cast him into a furnace of rage.

The anger imbued him with new energy, forcing him to his feet. It fueled his steps back to Wik, where he would accept whatever job he was offered.

PART V

ERUPTION

Highly Confidential – Keeper Complex Record # 87295RB

Last words of Tal Samar-Van, suspected Mantle operative. Recorded by Inspector Baliri Quaburn lineage 8c, 856.237 AVL

****

"Right now Mantle is nothing; a distant memory beneath your feet, a dense metallic cocktail constrained by the fragile crust, pressed and oppressed, into obscurity. Or, just maybe, we are the flows of scalding lava that are ready at any given moment to rise up and melt the massifs of Venus into oblivion."

****

38

———

SNEERING HEDONITES

In the morning Daw allowed Neeva a proper shower. She'd been wearing rough coveralls which were removed from her cell and replaced with her PDA suit, neatly pressed and folded. Next to it was a plate of hot food—potato biscuits, protein mash, and even a vitamin supplement. It was far better than the stale gray mush she'd been eating for the last three meals.

She tried to enjoy the flavor, given that it could be her last meal, but any sense of satisfaction proved elusive.

Two sneering hedonites came for her after her meal. They were tall, broad, and riddled with disfigurements—missing teeth, a slanted nose, a half-bitten ear. They were the kind of hedonites that weren't satisfied with their day unless they had at least one good scuffle. One of them was chewing sheck-gum. "Time to go," was all he said, and he popped a bubble in Neeva's face.

She was cuffed and escorted out of the mental health facility.

The men took her to one of the main promenades. There was no more spitting and yelling. Few people were about, and those that were walked quickly and paid her no mind. The black-and-white images of long-dead hedonites were on every wall: a skinny child with a vacuous look, a frightened woman with a shaved head, a resigned old man with a flat nose. In some cases, the placards were drooping down, or were torn off. The disrepair made the pictures seem less staged, and consequently more impactful.

They entered Rykers Central—the huge hall at the administrative center of Rykers Town. Before the evacuation it had provided access to the Rykers Town copter port and shunt tower, although now it wasn't laid out how Neeva remembered it. When she was a child she had run around the stout columns of Ryker Central with Shawna, playing hide and seek. There had been intricate mosaics in the marbled floor, and statues leaning out of the walls. The columns were gone, replaced by metal pillars with exposed rivets, and the walls and floor were made of the kind of generic paneling you might see in a tenement community center. Neeva suspected the hall must have collapsed during the eruption, and Wik had it rebuilt.

Her handlers exchanged information with one of the guards in the main hall, and the three of them entered an open-air carriage in a skeletal lift shaft. The carriage itself was supported by a shock of exposed cables that were each half a foot thick. The carriage ascended the wall of the main hall and penetrated the ceiling. From there, it traveled through what had surely once been the old municipal work spaces of Ryker Central, but were now chock full of sediment. Eventually, the texture of the shaft walls changed to sleek silver paneling.

They kept going higher, and higher still.

It could only mean one thing. They were in the shunt tower.

"Here you go," one of her handlers said. He had a large pill in his hand. After some hesitation, Neeva put it in her mouth. When she did, she realized by its sweet taste that it wasn't a pill at all. It was sheck-gum, which she promptly began to chew.

They continued up. Pressure built in her ears, only to be alleviated by swallowing—hence the gum.

Finally, the silver shaft wall she was facing fell away to glass, revealing the expansive sky and mottled Venusian surface reaching into the horizon. Below the carriage was the Themis Massif, already dwindling from view. The topography revealed no towers or other signs of human habitation. She saw a few plumes of smoke farther away, but they could have been volcanic as much as insurgency-related.

The carriage passed a number of intermediary shunt stops and kept rising all the way to the top platform. Here, her hedonite handlers pushed her out of the lift, where she was met with a flurry of activity. Dozens of Mantle disciples were rushing by, most wearing atmospheric suits with pulse rifles strapped to their backs.

Neeva was escorted through the crowd quickly, past another ID verification point, and into a giant airlock.

On the other side of the airlock, the walls stretched several stories high above her. They were made of clear glass curved into an arc, as if she was inside a huge bubble. It seemed familiar, but she couldn't place it.

"Where are you taking me?" she asked.

"You're already there," one of her handlers said.

It came back to her. The only other time she'd seen such huge walls of tall, curved glass was during the tour she'd taken near Enjo.

She had boarded a major dirigible.

They maneuvered her past three aircraft hangars, all filled with copters and dirigibles cradled in massive arms, with fuel and power lines attached, and with tablet-wielding technicians circulating around them.

She passed a window through which she saw a familiar sight. NM-198's sprawling ceiling apparatus had been set up. Neeva veered closer to the window, catching a view of a large room with NM-198 in the center, her visor pulsing with activity. It made sense that they would need NM-198. The major dirigible's fusion power source would need close symbiont oversight.

Neeva had little more than a cursory glance before she was shoved along with no small amount of force. Her neck felt strained and stiff afterward, as if she might have whiplash.

The implications of what she was seeing were harrowing. Mantle had control of a major dirigible with its own airborne fusion power source. This meant they could service a whole fleet of smaller dirigibles and copters from the air without needing ground support. No wonder the PDA's strike team had failed. And there was no way they could have anticipated this.

Finally, they arrived at the bridge.

Her museum tour of the grounded major dirigible had been during star season. The seats had been dusty, and the front window had a huge crack down the side. The layout of this major dirigible was the same, with two broad arcs of command chairs, but the bright Venusian sky lit up the room, and the consoles were alive, glittering with status reports, detailed maps, and diagnostics.

She was pushed along to the top arch of chairs, where she was met by a number of familiar figures.

Hix was at the broadest console, facing the front window and tapping away. His overgrown hair was askew, and his face had taken on a reddish pallor, with bags under his eyes. He performed a half-turn when she arrived, enough to catch her eye. His nostrils flared and he turned back to his console without a word.

Tolquist was in a chair off to the side, his hands cuffed and his eyes downcast. Eight other Mantle disciples were present, all wearing atmospheric suits, tapping away at the consoles dutifully—all except one, who was facing her and grinning, a man with chipped teeth and orange braids. She'd seen his picture before—it was Rav.

"What have we here?" Rav said. "Another one of Falcon Fire's adoring fans?"

"Why am I here?" she asked.

"This bridge," Rav said, making a show of looking around, "Falcon Fire, Tolquist, all this First Colony gullshit, it feels oh so much like Kanto Station all over again. It brings back memories. And one of the beauties of the majors is that, just like Kanto, it has reclamators. Some damn fancy ones at that. So, to answer your question, you've come here to die." He stood up, rubbed his palms together with satisfaction, strolled over to her and put out his hand, as if offering her the next dance. "Shall we?"

"No, Rav," Hix said. He had turned around in full to face them. His eyes were burning with a fervor she'd never seen before.

Rav nodded to Neeva. "He's had a bad week, you see. His Tetra-fixed slut sister died." Rav turned to Hix. "I'm going to forgive that comment because you're under duress, but this is how she dies. You stick to what you know, flyboy."

Rav pulled her along, and Neeva's two handlers fell in step behind them.

A blaster shot rang out above her. Neeva ducked and turned to see Hix with his blaster pointed at the bulkhead ceiling. He said, "Wik placed me in command of this vessel, and by association, our fleet—a fleet which we wouldn't possess if it weren't for sacrifices I made. That puts me in command of you, Rav, *and* all the rest of you. And so I say the 'former bitch stays here. Bring her back, or the next shot won't miss."

Rav's eyes were active, scanning the faces around him. A few disciples were checking their tablets or comms, as if to verify Hix's statement, or simply to avoid his gaze. Pru was scratching her head, her eyebrows raised.

Eventually, Rav said, "Fine. He's so testy today, though. It's not good for ratings." He released Neeva and strolled back to his seat as if nothing had happened.

Neeva's handlers nudged her closer to Hix. "Thanks," she said quietly.

Immediately Hix lashed out and grabbed her neck. "Don't you dare thank me," he said. "You *will* die, reformer, just not yet. I want you to witness the full extent of your failure before you're cast into oblivion."

He released his grasp and took a deep breath. "Your chair," he said, pointing at the empty seat next to Tolquist.

Neeva's handlers nudged her toward the chair and fastened her to it with cuffs and a cinch.

The officers around her were busy—Hix occasionally asking them questions about this hangar or that fuel port—except Rav, who kept spinning around in his chair like a child. Eventually he tired of it and said, "Come on, Pru, let's see what this bird has to offer," and he and Pru sauntered away.

Neeva could really have used her tacti device at that moment, but she couldn't put her hands in her pockets. Of course, she didn't have it anyway. Daw had thrown it away in Rykers Town. She settled for massaging the smooth plastic of the seat of the chair with her fingers.

"Okay, we're ready," Hix said. "Airlocks?"

"All clear and secured," a young officer on the lower arch said.

Hix pressed a button and took a step back from the console. A woman's voice called out from around them, "This vessel is now departing the Rykers Town shunt tower, berth 1A. Enjoy the trip." Neeva felt a low tremble beneath her. The window perspective tilted a few degrees.

They were away.

39

SUBSTANTIALLY AUTOMATED

Several hours into the journey, many of the officers on the bridge had been relieved. The major dirigible was substantially automated, so once Hix set their course there wasn't much to do. Hix would need to rest as well, but it was another hour until Baz—his replacement—would take the helm.

They had crossed into star season, and the dirigible was running with red internal lighting at low ambient settings so they could stay hidden. It made for a quiet, sleepy atmosphere. The faces of people on the bridge were imbued with long, somber shadows.

Even the reformer had been quiet. Perhaps she was resigned to her fate, or simply spellbound by the view. Eventually, she said, "I'm sorry about Mel. She didn't deserve to die."

He was preoccupied, preparing an answer to a question on fuel capacities for one of the fleet captains. He only glanced at her, and then returned to typing his message.

"Do you ever think about Shawna?" Neeva asked.

This time he tried to stare her down. She didn't look away. She was just trying to get under his skin. He went back to typing.

"Why am I really here, Hix? I know you well enough. This isn't about revenge."

"Ha," he mock-laughed. "You don't know me. You know only what the symbionts spit out at you—data, and probabilities. Maybe I thought it would be fitting that if our mission fails, you die."

"That doesn't make sense."

"No, it doesn't, but it certainly sounds familiar. I'm sure that's what Mel thought before her copter was shot down."

Neeva bit her lip.

Hix added, "By the way, if our mission succeeds, you'll also die."

"And what is your mission? You know, so I can bet on which way I'm going to die."

"We're going to shift the balance of power toward SoPo. Once your ilk are dependent on us, you won't be able to deny our basic rights."

Her eyes darted back and forth. "The biocrawler channels?"

He nodded. "And NoPo fusion reactors. And of course, we can't forget about the PDA. An archaic, sickening institution that needs to be eradicated."

"I get your gripe with the PDA, but the biocrawlers... with the channels damaged they can't move, all the flora and fauna will die out. Countless people will starve and we will lose untold genetic diversity. Even in the Cessation the biocrawlers were spared."

Tolquist chimed in beside her. He'd been so quiet Hix had forgotten he was there. "She's right. And if you compromise enough of the fusion reactors, it may decouple the transglobal magnetic field, resulting in a loss of atmosphere. What you're doing now—co-opting the dirigible network—could also cause delays in achieving Verdara. All of this together could demote the climate to a less desirable homeostasis."

Hix frowned. He understood what Tolquist was saying, but climate science had always seemed like a silly pastime for those that didn't have to fight for food or medicine. Many hedonites thought the whole idea of the Verdara was a fairy tale that would never come.

Neeva said, "What Tolquist said is all true, but just the biocrawlers alone—so many will die, so much will be lost, and they have no military significance."

Hix said, "If they provide nutrition to our oppressors, they are a weapon, and therefore need to be destroyed. And besides, everything you know is built on lies. Biocrawler diversity and transglobal magnetic fields? It's just more reformer gobble-talk—obfuscation and excuses."

Neeva shared a look with Tolquist. It was the same condescending expression he'd seen on the faces of so many reformers, as if he was some poor lost child. "You have to be kidding," she said. "We're telling you the honest truth, and yet you refuse to believe it. You must understand that you live in a cloud of misinformation. This is why we have to keep a separation between hedonites and reformers, so that at least some of us can reason clearly and make decisions to benefit us all."

"Sometimes it's only one lie that matters."

"What are you talking about?"

He finally finished his message and sent it off. Then he turned to give her his full attention. This may be the one time in his life he could properly tell off a reformer without facing any consequences.

"The lie that the First Colony immigrants defeated the Mecha-AIs of Mars," he said, "and then left to find a better home. And the only way we could survive was to establish an underclass of hedonites. That's not true, is it?"

Even in the red ambient light, he could tell her face took on some color. "It's all true," she said, "except... where we came from. I'm sure you know by now, we originally came from Earth. We needed the rigid order of the Reformer Doctrine to survive. Its necessity has been proven time and again, during the Cessation, for one, and on Earth, because we allowed irrationality and indifference to taint our voting pool. That's why we destroyed our planet, and why we came here to start again with a better recipe for success."

Hix rolled his eyes. "Please," he said.

"That's the truth. My grandfather is a First Colony Keeper. He has access to all the old records."

"She really doesn't know?" Hix was looking at Tolquist.

Tolquist was frowning, shaking his head. "I didn't tell her. I thought maybe you were right. Maybe they would kill us, and suppress the information."

"Know what?" Neeva said.

"Amazing," Hix said. "Let me tell you what we found on Earth. The settlements there were abandoned fourteen hundred years ago, whereas the First Colony arrived on Venus a thousand years ago."

Her brow furrowed in confusion. "That's not possible. You're saying... the First Colony did come from Mars after all?"

"Yes, but there's more. Tolquist and I accessed old recordings from a communication tower on Earth. It was picking up messages from Mars for over four hundred years after the Earth people perished. One of the ideologies that grew from the divide on Mars was that of the First Colony reformers, who believed—just as you do—that some people needed to be oppressed for the greater good. A great war was fought between factions, and the First Colony reformers lost."

"You're confused. There was a great war, but the people who stayed were the losers."

He rolled his eyes. "You're wrong. The reformers lost, and they were *banished* from Mars, but not just because they lost, because of what the Martians called, 'A culture of bigotry, and a doctrine of deceit that disempowers an arbitrary caste of people with hedonistic tendencies.' Sound familiar?"

"Predictable. Now you're saying that the Reformer Doctrine is flawed as well?"

"Absolutely. The justification for the Reformer Doctrine is based on fictitious historical records. The truth is there isn't one shred of evidence that society is better off with hedonite segregation. In fact, there's evidence to the contrary, since Mars has been prospering ever since the First Colony left. Think about it. Mars was able to complete terraforming in a much shorter timeframe, which proves that it can be achieved without a boot on someone's neck."

Neeva's eyes were darting back and forth. She clearly didn't believe it, but she was at least digesting what he was saying. "That's... ridiculous. For that to be true it would mean—"

"Yes."

"It would mean that—"

"That all your precious First Colony records have been falsified. That the Cessation was used as an excuse to wipe out any trace of our past, so that this false history could be put in its place. That you reformers are hiding the secret of Earth behind your *restricted area* lies for the same reason. And yes, that you will be a Keeper, Neeva Nash—a Keeper of the most monstrous, terrifying, all-consuming lie. One lie that is bigger than all the lies every hedonite has ever spoken combined."

Neeva looked like a lost duckling, her head swiveling between Hix and Tolquist. Tolquist nodded in affirmation.

Neeva opened her mouth, then closed it again.

"Hix, time for break." It was Baz, who'd walked up behind him. Hix had been so engrossed in the debate that he hadn't noticed that all the officers were staring at him, just as slack-jawed as Neeva. Even Pru, Rav, and Iri were there, on the lower level of the bridge, all ears.

Hix was perspiring, and dreadfully tired. The fighting would begin in a few hours, and he needed to be alert. "Yes, of course," he responded. "I'll be back in a few hours. Watch these two, and don't believe a word they say."

He marched away.

40

VERTIGO

The major dirigible was the smoothest ride you could find on land or in air, especially when locked on a flight path, but Neeva still had a distinct sense of vertigo.

What Hix had said couldn't be true. And yet, she couldn't disprove it either.

"You're a scientist, Tolquist. You don't really believe this, do you?"

"I saw it with my own eyes."

"Couldn't the communications from Mars be fake?"

"Why would different leaders and representatives send fake communications over hundreds of years? The messages were full of other information, much of it quite tangential, but in no way contrived. And believe me, I'm a scientist, and a reformer, if I had any doubts I would tell you. They showed the First Colony people with a symbol showing an outstretched hand with an array of seeds, just like we saw in the docking bay of CP Station. The video was authentic and the depiction identical. And you know what, in hindsight it doesn't make sense that Mars would have been radio silent with Venus for almost a millennium. My guess is that First Colony officials have been blocking their communications so that no one can find out the truth."

His explanation was elaborate, and yet Tolquist wasn't a good liar, according to his psychographic profile. It was hard to see how it could be a fabrication.

It was more and more disturbing.

As the dirigible continued to float north through the starry sky, Hix's argument churned in her mind, spreading like a tenacious vine. Butterflies fluttered in her chest.

Had Grandpa known about this? Could he actually have a hand in blocking Martian communications? She had thought it strange that he didn't know there were old ruins on Earth. The fact that she couldn't bring herself to rule out his deceit knotted her chest with anxiety, and then with rage.

"Which side are you on, anyway?" she asked Tolquist. It was a little too loud. She caught an annoyed look from Baz, who was trying not to pay attention.

Tolquist looked thoughtful. How could he be so calm? He said, "All I've ever wanted was to find some way to contribute to the greater good. When I was a professor I wanted to accelerate the Verdara. I chose Kanto Station as punishment for my crime, because that way at least my skills could be put to good use. Then, on Earth, I responded to Millicent because I didn't think we would survive without your help, and also because I didn't want all the knowledge we had gained to be lost. And now, well, a good scientist evolves his beliefs when the information changes. So you see, it may seem like I keep changing allegiance, but this has nothing to do with *sides*. It's about helping people—whoever they are—find truth, so that I can make a difference."

His response further undermined Neeva's view of the world. What once had been bright lines between hedonite and reformer were fading from view.

She held her head in her hands, replaying Hix's troubling narrative over and over again. She tried to reconcile it against all she'd learned from the Heritage Museum about the Cessation, and with the images of thousands of murdered hedonites she'd seen on the walls of Rykers Town. She tried to reconcile it with all she had been told about Mars, and with the strange secrecy around the ruins on Earth. It fit. All of it. The First Colony story could be a big fat lie, and by connection, so could the Reformer Doctrine.

But finally, she found a fault line running through the story. It was a fault line that only she could have seen, and she followed it until it formed a fissure, and then broadened into a treasonous chasm of deceit.

Hix was right. The Reformer Doctrine was a big fat lie, but there was still one little detail he was missing.

41

———

INCOMING

Hix was awakened by a beeping sound that wasn't his alarm. It was Baz on his comm.

"Yes?" Hix asked.

"Incoming."

"What's incoming?"

"Twenty supersonic jet copters on the radar. Probably P88 airships. They're not ours. Come to the bridge at once."

"On my way."

He slid out of his sleep pod and made his way to the bridge. PDA command only had about a hundred combat copters for the whole planet. It was a token armada to defend against an attack from Mars. They never would have contemplated needing them for an airborne insurrection. Which meant either somebody had tipped them off, or a patrol got lucky.

Hix could see nothing out of the windows except a few faint concentrations of light on the surface below. Based on the pattern it looked like Oatar Massif, which meant the biocrawler channels were still at least thirty minutes away.

Red strobes began flashing around him, and the intercom buzzed loudly. It was Baz. "Everyone to your stations. Enemy copters approaching."

Hix jogged the rest of the way.

Baz wasn't reluctant to give up the helm. "We'll have to counter," he said. "I'm needed in hangar seven."

"Just a minute," Hix said as he digested the course and speed diagnostics. The PDA jet copters were coming in hot. "How did they find us?"

"Not sure. We were supposed to be in the clear until after the biocrawler run."

It was disappointing, but not that surprising. Mantle had stolen one of the few major dirigibles and pointed it north. All the reformers had to do was look. Wik had hoped they wouldn't until it was too late.

"Okay, go," Hix said. "I'll buy us time." He called out to the officer on the lower arc, "I need external comms directed at the PDA birds."

"Granted," the officer said.

Hix held up the mic and pressed the activation button. "Attention, PDA attack squadron. We have commandeered this major dirigible as a peaceful act of protest. We have reformers on board, including PDA Inspector Neeva Nash lineage 4a, and the symbiont NM-198. If we are fired upon, it may result in decompression and a crash that could rupture our fusion reactor containment fields."

There was no immediate response.

"Are you sure they got the message?" Hix asked.

"I sent it on all channels," the officer said. "If they're listening they got the message."

The blips on the radar separated into two groups. "Shit," he said, "give me Baz on internal comm." The officer nodded. "Baz, they are in attack formation. You better—"

"Incoming object, Captain," an officer interrupted. "Supersonic speeds."

"That's what you call a missile," Hix said. "Hard to starboard, full, incline ten degrees." The dirigible's vector began changing. "Baz?"

"One minute until we're away," Baz responded.

They were powerless to stop the missile. The major had been outfitted with guns, but the PDA copters were out of range. Hix could only hope it was a warning shot.

"Brace for impact," he announced.

The viewfinder showed a small, rapidly moving dot, but it was only visible for a split second before the missile hit. The floor trembled and there was a loud explosion.

"Impact below hangar four," another officer called out, "near the rear stabilizers. Damage assessment ongoing."

"A message from the PDA," another officer said.

"Patch it through," Hix said.

"This is Lieutenant Vail Reigard, leader of the PDA attack squadron. You have been warned. If you do not immediately return all dirigible network control within one minute, we will shoot you down."

Hix held the mic in his hand, but didn't press the button.

"Sir?" the officer asked. "The mic is live."

He nodded. "I know."

"Sir?" the officer said again.

Hix put his finger up. Ten seconds later, he initiated the communication. "Message received and understood, Lieutenant Reigard. We will need at least five minutes to disconnect the network."

The PDA squadron flew by, rattling the dirigible, then split and arched back in two separate sub-squadrons.

"We're away," Baz said.

Numerous blips started forming on the radar beside the dirigible. It was the Mantle fleet dumping out of the major's hangar doors. Mantle had two supersonic fighters, but most were transport copters retrofitted with guns and launchers.

The PDA forces were slow to respond. The appearance of the major was probably enough of a shock, and they likely hadn't contemplated that it could be transporting a whole fleet of aircraft.

Once the PDA copters were in range, the Mantle fleet unleashed its weaponry all at once.

The sky around the dirigible became a flurry of explosive

ordnance. Shockwaves rolled underneath Hix's feet. Hix's display panel showed the major's fore and aft gun turrets coming to life in sporadic bursts. There were explosions in the distance. A burning PDA squadron aircraft squealed past the viewfinder, curling down into the clouds below. Another passed by and then arced back, directly toward the major dirigible. Everyone on the bridge ducked down until a veering Mantle copter perforated the aircraft with blast pellets and it began losing altitude.

"This is your best movie yet, Falcon Fire," Rav said. He was in one of the lower chairs, leaning toward the window.

On the radar it was hard to distinguish winners from losers, or even friend from foe. Most of the fighting was taking place between the two squadrons on the starboard side, leaving the dirigible out of harm's way.

Until one of the PDA copters spun out of control, directly toward them.

An officer called out, "Brace for—"

It hit on the starboard side and exploded. This time, the hulking dirigible really did move. It started listing, and Hix had to compensate with a number of thrusters to right the vessel. The red strobe lights were flashing more frequently. Alert messages popped up all over the command consoles.

"Damage report," Hix said.

"Extensive damage," the officer to his right said. "We lost one of the main bladders. There could be... it hit close to the fusion reactor containment area."

A message came through. It was from NM-198. *Reactor core damage is a possible outcome. Given system complexity, I will need time to process.*

He focused on the radar again. The number of blips were diminishing. Two broke off and headed north.

"Remaining PDA bogies retreating," Baz said.

Cheering and hooting came from all around the bridge, but Hix didn't participate. He was too focused on the incoming status reports. The collision had impacted countless systems, and the major dirigible was a complex piece of engineering.

He made a shipwide announcement. "All medics and engineers to hangar bays to tend to returning copters. We need to repair bladders 3C, D, and F. I've also lost thrusters 78Y and 82Y. What's the status with the reactor?"

There was no response from NM-198. He sent her a message: *Please report.*

Processing, she responded.

When the reports stopped coming in, Hix took the opportunity to sit down in his chair. It would take time for the teams to assess the situation thoroughly.

🔥🔥🔥

The flight crews had been working to repair the damaged Mantle copters. Their course was set, and the dirigible's flight path was stable. Hix was still waiting on NM-198's report on the fusion reactor. There was nothing else he could do to help, for the time being.

"You won't survive the next attack," Neeva said.

"Stay out of this," Hix said, "or I'll muzzle you."

"We've all been muzzled," she said.

He ignored her and did another sweep of the status displays.

"You were right," she said. "Or at least, I can't disprove it. The Reformer Doctrine is a lie. Our whole history is a lie."

He couldn't help raising his eyebrows. He never thought she would admit it.

"I'm prejudiced against hedonites," she continued, "and yes— that's why I never suspected NM-198 could be a traitor. But there was another reason. The collective never told me it was even possible. I had checked NM-198's profile. She was completely loyal to the collective before this, and in actuality a key contributor."

"Are you going to make a point?" Hix said, frustrated. He stood up and reviewed the new status reports one more time. They'd lost ten of their aircraft out of thirty, which could impact their plans. He started punching out a summary report for Wik.

The reformer continued her monologue. "But if they didn't think NM-198 was a traitor, why wouldn't they send a recorder with me? It was like they knew she didn't need one."

"I don't have time for any more reformer gobble-talk."

"It's the symbionts," she said. "They're behind this. All of it."

"Oh, come on," he said with a laugh. He didn't tell her to shut up, though. Part of him was genuinely curious what ridiculous story she would concoct to deflect her guilt.

"It was Wik's statement about arbiters of truth that got me thinking. That's supposed to be the symbionts. If the hedonite genetic separation algorithms are false, the symbionts must know about it. They were the ones who formulated the original algorithms, and so they are clearly propagating this lie. And then I wondered what else could they be lying about."

"The symbionts are shills for reformer loyalists," Hix said, "always have been. They're tools of oppression to be wielded by your corrupt government."

"Yes," she said. "I know that's the common hedonite belief. I suspect NM-198 reinforced that belief with Mantle as well, but let's look closer. Where would your insurrection be without NM-198? You wouldn't have access to the SoPo psychanthropic network. You wouldn't have the ability to fly this major dirigible because you couldn't manage the fusion power source. This whole gambit was made possible by a single symbiont."

"Yes, the symbionts are powerful, but Wik is calling the shots."

"Is he? I once asked a recorder what a symbiont wants. He said, 'To be alone, away from non-collective minds.' You see, symbionts find our incessant questions to be intrusive and even painful. Now think about what the outcome of this insurrection will be. The majority of the collective will have moved into orbit. They will finally be self-sufficient, with their own fusion power source, away from prying humans. I suspect this is something they have been wanting to do for hundreds of years. Our dependency on them, enabled by our internal divisions, has allowed them to gain increasing levels of influence, first during the Cessation when they encouraged us to eliminate the Mecha-AIs once and for all, and now during this insurrection in which, once again, Verdara progress is being hamstrung while the collective's power is increasing. And guess who controls our communications satellites? The symbionts are the ones blocking communications from Mars."

She made some interesting points, but it still seemed so outlandish. "That's preposterous. You're just trying to deflect blame. Someone would have figured this out already."

"Are you sure? You, me, and Tolquist are the only people on Venus who could put all the pieces together, because we're the only ones who've been to the restricted area of Earth. We're also the only ones who can stop them. We're the only ones who can give our planet —our people—the courage to see beyond the stories they are born into."

The major dirigible was listing again. Simple wind pattern changes could no longer be compensated by automatic guidance. Hix would have to continually adjust thrusters to maintain stability. After a few adjustments, the tilt corrected. He said, "Actions speak louder than your misguided words. NM-198 is helping Mantle, and that's all that matters."

"Let me guess, you're supposed to attack PDA forces in LC, the biocrawlers and fusion reactors, but for some reason you're *not* supposed to attack the symbiont headquarters on Telliac Mountain. Doesn't that seem strange to you? If the rest of the collective is lying about the Reformer Doctrine, wouldn't NM-198 want to eliminate or at least bring to justice those people that enforce the doctrine?"

"You're insane. We aren't attacking psychanthropic facilities because they control the fusion reactors. It would be too dangerous."

"But you just said you were going to destroy the fusion reactors."

"That's enough!" he yelled. It was just too much, and he couldn't see the relevance of it. He was on a mission to turn the tides against their First Colony oppressors. That was what Mel wanted, and it was that simple.

He scanned the incoming damage reports, but his mind was in turmoil. He adjusted thrust vectors again, trying to maintain stability.

Then he returned to preparing his report for Wik, but he was having trouble concentrating.

"Hix, listen—"

"Enough!" he yelled again. "You there." He pointed to one of Neeva's handlers, who was tapping on his tablet nearby, oblivious to the conversation. "Gag her. I can't stand the sound of her voice."

The man pulled a rag from his pack.

"Hix, please," Neeva called to him. "Think about how many people will die today. You'll just be another tool. You'll be... you'll be just like us." Her head was pulled back forcefully, the cloth covering her open mouth. She squirmed for a brief moment, but soon gave up fighting.

You'll be just like us. Her reformer gobble-talk further confused Hix's frenetic thoughts. He tried to block her out. He needed to focus on the task at hand.

One of the main bladders had been patched and was reinflating, but there was another that was out of commision. It would hamper lift and also affect the drag coefficient on the starboard side. The thrusters were seriously damaged, too. The automated guidance systems couldn't adjust for them, but Hix could do so manually. An additional six copters had been found to not be airworthy, which would further reduce their ability to conduct a bombing run on the biocrawlers.

But what Hix was most worried about was the fusion reactor, and there was still no word from NM-198.

He finished his preliminary report to Wik and sent it off. Only a moment later, a personal message from NM-198 popped up on his screen: *Urgent private discussion required re: fusion reactor. Bring Tolquist Spitzaner lineage 32b.*

It was a strange request, but the fusion reactor was the highest priority, so Hix didn't question it.

"Iri," he called out. Iri was sitting next to Rav and Pru on the lower arc. Hix didn't trust him, but he was the only other pilot around. "Keep her steady," he said, and offered no further explanation.

Iri joined him at the console and took the con. His eyes were active, scanning the open reports on the main console. He would figure it out.

Hix uncuffed Tolquist from his chair. "Let's go," he said.

Tolquist came along without objection. Hopefully he would keep quiet.

NM-198 had been set up in an old lecture hall in the major's schoolhouse area. It was close to the peripheral walkways so that NM-198 didn't have far to go to get in and out of the dirigible. Her chair had been placed on a dais on an elevated stage at the back of the room, where her head apparatus reached up into a series of pulleys and channels that, before she arrived, had probably been used for shifting props or moving curtains.

NM-198 didn't look good. She had urinated on herself and her guards were trying to wipe it up. One of the fluids coming out of her headpiece was a cloudy brown color he hadn't seen before. Her visor was pulsating with an almost strobe-light intensity.

"Is there something wrong?" Hix asked the guard.

"Sorry, Captain, I'm not sure. She hasn't spoken since the fighter crashed into the major, but she's been trembling a lot. And she went and peed without warning."

"NM-198," Hix said. "I'm here with Tolquist. How can we help?"

There was no reply.

Tolquist said, "Symbionts who are under stress sometimes have their external senses shut down. She may be unable to speak or hear."

Hix tried sending a message to NM-198 on his comm tablet. *We are here. Are you ill?*

She responded: *There is a breach in the outer containment field of the fusion reactor. I need to maintain the magnetosphere at precise homeostasis conditions to prevent leakage. This has caused physical duress and requires my uncompromised attention. I cannot support other functions. I need*

Tolquist to relieve me of flight modeling functions including climate modeling.

Hix wrote: *What happens if there is a leakage?*

The reactor will melt down in less than thirty minutes.

It was very disconcerting. NM-198 was their only hope of keeping the reactor under control, and she looked like she could keel over at any moment.

Hix didn't like the idea of handing any kind of control over to Tolquist. He was about to ask NM-198 why it was necessary, but Tolquist anticipated the question. "I'm the only one with cortivation nodes," he said, pointing to the back of his neck. "This won't be much different than what I was doing on the *Zephyr Spear*. I'm probably the only one on the major who can do it."

"Why is the climate modeling necessary?"

"We will be heading through some complicated air currents. They are difficult to predict unless you use real-time modeling. They could cause your trajectory to be thrown off or you could even risk turbulence damage. With the ship guidance system already compromised, it's better that I find the best route through the weather to minimize risk."

Hix considered it. He typed another message. *Can Tolquist damage you or the system if he is connected?*

No.

Tolquist witnessed the exchange. He said, "I could change our course, but you would notice significant deviations from your objective almost immediately. Ordinarily NM-198 would take over the task easily, but to do it now might kill her. All I want to do is help. That's all I've ever wanted." He looked down and away sheepishly.

This is urgent, NM-198 messaged.

"Fine," Hix said. "Plug yourself in."

Tolquist walked up the steps to the dais, just below NM-198's chair. There was a nest of cables and electrical boxes on a table. After fumbling through the mess, Tolquist found a visor and placed it over his eyes. He untangled two cables that led up to a mainframe next to

NM-198's chair and fastened the leads behind his head. His visor started thrumming with light.

Hix checked his tablet, and navigated to the onscreen control console. While they had been talking with NM-198, there had been an exchange between NM-198 and Wik which he had been copied in on. Wik said: *Abort biocrawler run. Instead focus on PDA installations in LC. Use entire payload.*

It made sense. The major's position had been revealed, and could easily be intercepted by another PDA squadron. Also, with Mantle's diminished copter fleet they might not be able to bomb out enough channels.

They were forty-five minutes away from LC.

Hix would need to go back to the bridge, but he didn't quite trust Tolquist. He wanted to stay and watch him work. On his tablet he tried to follow Tolquist's analysis and commands. He assessed the minor shifts in course that Tolquist proposed and found them to be reasonable enough.

Meanwhile, NM-198 was still slumped in her chair, her visor a constant blitz of pulsing light. *It's the symbionts,* Neeva had said. It was hard to believe this pathetic, wasted creature could be so manipulative. He wondered why she had to be naked and emaciated, and why the headgear was so cumbersome. They'd had a thousand years to figure out a less off-putting means of existence.

It reminded him of an event during the filming of *Sky Gate.* A prison-break scene had to be reshot because the prisoners weren't ragtag-looking enough. The cast had to tear their clothes and bring in skinny hedonites in order to invoke a more sympathetic reaction in the audience.

Could the symbiont's appearance be for show—to make people pity them?

It was true that Neeva had made some points that couldn't easily be refuted. The collective was certainly complicit with the reformers in facilitating the oppression of hedonites. So the real question was, was NM-198 in cahoots with the rest of the collective?

He couldn't resist typing a message to NM-198. *Why are we not targeting the psychanthropic facility on Telliac Mountain?*

No time, she responded. But that didn't make much sense. It was right next to LC, close enough to PDA installations, and it was a concentrated target. Maybe she meant she had no time to answer him?

"What is this, an *Onslaught* tournament?" It was Rav, who had entered the room behind him. Pru stepped in next, followed by Iri.

"Who is piloting the major?" Hix asked in alarm.

"Baz will do a fine job." Pru said.

"What are you doing here?" Hix asked. He was standing up, his hand hovering near his blaster.

Pru said, "Will you just calm down, flyboy? Yeesh. Falcon Fire is supposed to have nerves of steel. We're on the same side."

"Why. Are. You. Here."

"Send him the order," Pru said, and Rav punched something on his tablet.

"Wik said we need to move NM-198 off the major," Pru said, yawning. "She's at risk here."

"But the reactor will melt down."

"Yeah but... Hix, you knew this was a one-way trip, right? And, well, you're getting off before the last stop anyway. Just read it, will you?" Her head nudged in the direction of his comm.

The message from Wik popped up in his inbox moments after Rav forwarded it.

This order overrides all priors. NM-198 is crucial to the flow and must be saved. Rav, Pru, and Iri are to take her by copter prior to LC assault. All others are to evacuate the major during attack. Set vector for major to collide with LC.

Hix nodded slowly to Pru. It looked legit. Then he reread the last sentence. *Set vector for major to collide with LC.*

That was new. They weren't going to just destroy PDA installations; they were going to drop a fusion bomb on a million people.

"Why do we need to collide with LC?"

Pru laughed. "I dunno, ask Wik. What did you say on the bridge?

Whatever keeps my oppressors alive is a weapon? Very poetic. You still got it, Falcon Fire."

He'd said it, but he had been talking about the biocrawlers, and he didn't really think they'd be able to destroy all of them. There were plenty of food stores and biocrawlers in SoPo as well. It would have been a strong message, but this was something more. This was something the reformers would never forget, or forgive.

Pru and Iri were already collecting cables while NM-198's guards helped to disconnect her head apparatus. One of them was about to disconnect the main power source. Hix said, "Can you wait until the last minute? Take all her accessories first. We need to keep the fusion reactor stable as long as possible."

They did wait, but only a couple minutes more.

Tolquist had already disconnected his cortivation nodes. There was a pained look on his face. His head swiveled between the dismantling of NM-198's apparatus and Hix. He was whispering something to himself. Hix only caught a few words "...sear away this sinful flesh."

"What's wrong now?" Hix asked.

"I was able to mitigate some risk, but not all of it."

"Why did you stop, then?"

Tolquist looked pained again. "Can you tell Talia—my girlfriend —I did this for her?"

"Did what? Wik asked everyone to evacuate. You can tell her yourself."

He closed his eyes, as if in deep concentration.

They shut down NM-198's power, and her visor went blank. The main ports from her skull piece had been disconnected and capped to keep fluids contained. The three guards bent over to lift up her chair and place it on a trolley below the stage.

That was when Tolquist made his move.

It caught them all by surprise, because Tolquist was not by nature a violent person. He had been acting strange, sure, but Tolquist always acted a bit strange.

He bolted up the dais, and in one fluid motion twisted NM-198's neck until it snapped. Even though Tolquist was cuffed, and even though he wasn't strong, it was easy. The symbiont's neck was devoid of muscle, a toothpick on a rack of bones.

Tolquist didn't last long after that. He was hit by blaster shots from Rav and Pru in quick succession. Both shots hit him square in the chest, throwing him toward the back of the stage to land tangled up in wires. He died instantly.

"Dammit!" Rav raged. "What just happened?" He turned to Hix. "You did this!"

Hix put up his hands. "NM-198 asked me to bring Tolquist here. We needed him to help. I had no idea he would do this."

"You two are always scheming," Rav said. "I smell something fishy." He walked up to Hix and fixed his blaster barrel to Hix's forehead.

"Are you sure this is what Wik wants?" Hix asked. "Who's going to pilot the major into LC?"

Pru scratched her temple and began typing on her tablet. She had to be messaging Wik. Hix had to wait with the cold barrel against his forehead.

Finally, Pru said, "Easy, Rav. Wik is mighty disappointed, but he can't see how it's Hix's fault. He wants us to join the fight when we hit LC. Hix is going to pilot the major until the last minute, then evacuate."

Rav smiled. "Of course he will," he said, and he pulled away his blaster.

Pru looked thoughtful for a moment. "It's really quite fitting, ain't it, Falcon Fire? Kind of like that last scene in *Toreno Run* where you burnt out that biocrawler. Only now you get to burn out all of LC."

Hix could only frown in response.

Rav, Pru, and Iri glanced up at NM-198's emaciated corpse, and Tolquist's body behind it. They were passive, uninterested looks, like people walking past a dead rat in the tenements. Then they made their way out the door, with the three other guards following closely behind.

Hix needed to get back to the helm, but he lingered a moment more. He walked up to Tolquist's body and kneeled next to him.

He checked Tolquist's pockets but there was nothing—no message for his girl Talia, or even any comm device. It must have been taken away in Rykers Town.

Hix felt a rush of emotion at seeing Tolquist's lifeless body up close, but he wasn't sure why. Tolquist was a reformer, and one that had betrayed him. Why did he care?

Maybe it was because he'd never met a reformer like Tolquist. He always did what he thought was right, often to his own detriment. Tolquist had refused to learn the hard lesson that most hedonites learned: that you always do what you can to survive. You "choose life".

The floor shuddered beneath Hix's feet.

He rolled his fingers over Tolquist's eyes, closing them, and returned to the bridge.

42

LAKSHMI CENTRAL

Neeva woke to the major dirigible entering dawn day. While there were still stars visible above, the horizon was glowing with an orange-to-pink gradient, illuminating wispy fuchsia clouds. Below, the major passed over craggy walls of rock. A shining line of dots became visible on the horizon, its base glowing with distributed light, and beside it dark monoliths of stone rose up. It was the metropolis of LC next to the Maxwell Montes range.

Baz was frantically tapping buttons. They were slowly losing altitude, and were now firmly in the troposphere, but Neeva couldn't be sure if it was deliberate. The dirigible tilted and veered every few seconds, as if Baz was driving on Tetra.

"Somebody needs to fix those thrusters," he called out in frustration. The remaining officers looked at each other with clueless apprehension. Others had periodically picked up and left, presumably to go to the hangars to man the attack copter fleet.

Neeva's jaw was aching from the gag. She couldn't fully close her mouth around the rough cloth, so bouts of saliva dribbled down her shirt.

Hix walked back up the gangway. He was moving slowly,

absorbed in thought. When he saw her, he frowned with what could only be described as vitriol.

"Hix, good," Baz said. "Everything is in order here. I'm due for copter flight prep." He walked away briskly.

Hix took up the helm. He tapped away slowly at first, and then with verve. The course disturbances continued, but they seemed less abrasive.

Rav, Pru, and Iri marched their way onto the bridge next.

Rav sat down next to Neeva. He said, "Don't worry, it will all be over soon. You're going home." He wrinkled his nose and squinted his eyes, trying to be cute.

Neeva pointed to her gag with her cuffed hands. Rav obliged by pulling it down. "You want a kiss, sweetheart?" he said.

"You have to stop this," Neeva said. "You're all being used."

Rav broke into a cackle, followed by a full-throated laugh.

Hix said, "Shut it, 'former, or I'll sit you in the back next to the reactor."

"Oh, please don't," Rav said. "She's so much fun."

Pru rolled her eyes. She said, "Wik wants me, Rav, and Iri to take our copter out to shadow the major. We'll have company over LC, for sure. Hix, you're to take the last copter off before you scuttle."

Hix expanded a display pane with his thumb and forefinger. "How come I didn't get the message?"

"I'm sure it will come through soon. Some comm issues now, with NM-198 gone."

Hix frowned. "And I thought we'd have company sooner. We're only ten minutes from LC and so far, nothing."

Pru raised an eyebrow. "You sound disappointed. Maybe NM-198 cloaked our approach before Tolquist snapped her neck."

"How could she possibly do that?"

"I dunno. She hacked into the collective or something. Who cares? Now get this bird back to her nest, flyboy." She slapped him on the buttocks and the three of them strolled out of the bridge.

Neeva said, "If you believe that, maybe there is some truth to the Reformer Doctrine."

"Shut it," he said.

"There's no way NM-198 could have hacked into the collective on her own. They were working together."

He just shook his head. Neeva couldn't be sure how much he was paying attention. His fingers were active on the display.

"Where's Tolquist?" she asked.

That made him pause. He said, "You poisoned his mind and got him killed."

"What? How?"

"He killed NM-198." He snorted after he said it, as if he couldn't quite believe his own words.

She felt a surge of hope at first, but it was quickly extinguished. It would have little effect on the outcome. A feeling of malaise then set in. Tolquist didn't deserve to die—not like that.

"That should tell you something," she said.

"Keep quiet."

"Venus is a morass of corruption, but there *are* good people, people that deserve to live. There are many people like that in LC— people you are about to kill."

"Many more have died, or lived brutal lives in SoPo, because of these so-called good people in LC."

"Or because of the symbionts. Ask yourself why Tolquist did what he did. I studied his profile. He was extremely sharp, objective to a fault, and had scrupulous morals. You know this about him. He believed that the symbionts were the problem, so much so that he was willing to sacrifice his life for what he believed."

"He was always looking for a way to die. He was a pyrolyte."

Hix's counter wasn't convincing, and he might have known it, but he didn't seem to care. He was focused on his screen. The dirigible tilted more than before. Red lights flashed, but were soon extinguished.

An officer called up. "Multiple bogies launched from LC airfields. We've been spotted."

Hix used the external comm. "Attack formations, everyone."

"Sir, should we..." one of the officers said. The others were looking at him expectantly.

"Yes," Hix said. "Join the flow. Support the attack fleet." The officers left the bridge. Neeva's handlers had left a while ago.

Only Hix and Neeva were left.

From this distance, the many towers of LC looked like a bed of perfectly straight grass stalks surrounding the fern, with the upper stem stretching away from the leafy, viny base to reach high into the atmosphere. Dots of light were breaking away from behind the towers, and growing brighter. They had to be PDA defense copters, coming toward the dirigible.

She was running out of time. Her only hope was to stop Hix, but she couldn't use force. There was no way out of her chair, and Hix was armed. If she could only convince him about the symbiont threat, it might at least give him pause, but he was intransigent, unwilling to consider what he surely thought was reformer propaganda.

And it didn't help that he was trying to fly a heavily damaged major dirigible.

"Do it for Mel," she said.

"Ha," Hix said without humor, "Mel would never want me to listen to you, much less help you."

"This isn't about me. This is about the million people who are about to die. What about them? Is that what she would have wanted for you?"

"She hated reformers. She wanted us to throw off our shackles. Rise up."

"Did you know that Wik got you your part in *Toreno Run*?

That pulled his eyes from the screen. "What does that have to do with anything? And no, he didn't. I told you he wasn't like that. I got that part fair and square."

"Yes, I remember what you said in Rykers Town. You're a talented actor, and I'm sure you auditioned well. But no. Wik knew the director. He lobbied to get you on. Remember, I have access to a great deal of information, and this was something I found in my investigation of

Shawna's murder. He gave you your big break, and you know why? Because Mel wanted it for you."

She could tell it angered him. "So what?" he said. "Why does that matter now?"

"It matters because Mel didn't care about Mantle. She cared about one thing—you. She wasn't with Wik because of his ideology. Sure, she hated reformers, and I don't think she disagreed with the cause, but the reason she joined Mantle was to get you your big break."

Hix just shook his head and made more adjustments. The dirigible tilted. The red strobes came on again. He picked up the mic. "The reactor is destabilizing. It will begin melting down in ten minutes. Remaining personnel should now be off-ship."

The fleet of Mantle copters that had been flanking them advanced beyond the nose of the dirigible, going out to intercept the LC defense force. One of the sleeker P88 copters had been adapted with a gun-bubble hanging off the bottom. Neeva could see Rav inside it. He offered a jubilant wave as he passed.

"Dammit, Hix!" she said. "Are you just another dumb hedonite? Do you want to be known as another misinformed gull that will fade away without having provided any real benefit for anyone?"

She had been trying to get his attention, but it backfired.

Hix flared his nostrils and breathed in deeply through his nose, much like she'd seen him do frequently in Rykers Town. He made a few adjustments on the console, walked over, and forcefully reapplied her gag.

He said, "Hedonite doesn't rhyme with stereotype."

She tried to pull away from her chair but she couldn't. The metal cuffs cut into her wrist. She yelled into the gag, but it only came out as a muffled moan.

The sky ahead lit up like dawn-day fireworks. The copters circled and arced in their airborne dance. Puffs of smoke and contrails merged to form an expanding cloud. Explosions concussed and sent aftershocks through the dirigible.

The PDA force had at least fifteen aircraft. It would have been easy for them to evade the Mantle fleet and reach the major. They could take it down with a few well-placed shots to exposed bladders, but they didn't. They stayed engaged with the rest of the Mantle fleet. Maybe they thought the major wasn't a threat, or maybe they hadn't contemplated that it could be used as a fusion bomb.

But the collective would surely have contemplated it.

Neeva would have pointed this out to Hix, but she was gagged.

The major punched through the growing cloud of smoke, and when they emerged on the other side there was only one PDA copter left. It was listing to the side, trailing fumes. Two Mantle copters strafed it and it exploded.

Mantle had won, with eight copters remaining. No more blips of light came from LC, but guns on the surface started firing. They were antiquated things, built a hundred years ago during one of the periods of Martian attack paranoia. Again, they focused on the rest of the fleet and not the dirigible.

LC was minutes away.

43

AN INVASIVE SPECIES

Well done, Hix. Time to evacuate. Leave the reformer.

The message was from Wik.

Hix plugged in some weather contingency adjustment macros and double-checked the major's trajectory. They were heading straight for the base of the fern. According to Wik's weapons expert, the dirigible would level all of LC and topple the shunt tower as well. The meltdown was due to begin in five minutes, so even if the reactor didn't explode on impact, it would shortly thereafter.

Neeva was glaring at him, eyes wide open in alarm, or maybe exasperation. He had to leave her. That was what Wik wanted.

He turned away and didn't look back. Neeva moaned loudly behind him. He was thankful she was gagged.

Just before he left the bridge, an image of Shawna flashed in his mind. It came out of nowhere. She was sitting on his lap, laughing as they went into the water meteor storm.

It was just one more distraction. He shook his head, forcing the memory out, and jogged toward hangar five.

He did have a few seeds of doubt. They were like seeds of the First Colony flag, growing into invasive tendrils with every step he took toward the hangar. It was the reformer's fault. She had used her gobble-talk and conspiracy theories to fill his head with a cloud of conflicting thoughts. But he had a job to do, and he couldn't let her get in the way.

When he arrived at the hangar, he was relieved to see the last escape copter was still there, fully fueled up and ready to go. It was a small, two-man X31 craft with mini wing-thrusters. It was nimble enough but could be easily spooked by turbulent airflows.

He jumped into the copter and checked the exterior radar. The Mantle fleet was flanking the dirigible, escorting it in, and there was no sign of any more PDA forces. Occasional flak came from surface guns, but it was sporadic.

It was strange that the PDA wouldn't try to shoot down the major. Did they really not see what was about to happen?

The knot of anxiety tightened in his chest. The reformer's crafty words flooded through his brain again, but he flushed them out.

This was what Mel wanted.

He sent a broadbeam message to the fleet. *Be advised: new friendly coming out of the major. Hix here in X31 Copter serial number BY89C8.*

We got your back, Falcon Fire, was the only reply.

He hesitated only momentarily, and then initiated takeoff protocols.

44

———

EVERYTHING AND EVERYONE

The fern was rapidly approaching. Neeva could make out the long leaf housing her old PDA office. Another, higher leaf, one that extended out the farthest, was where she had met with the Executive Council not long ago.

She couldn't be sure the fern occupants had been alerted to the risk. Either way, she doubted they could evacuate in time.

The fleet was leading the dirigible on either side, in a broad formation. The flak had stopped. Maybe the dirigible was out of range, or maybe the gunners realized it was pointless.

She again tried to pull off her cuffs, but she would literally have to rip off her hand.

Maybe this was what it was like for Shawna, before she jumped off the dirigible. Did she see the ground approaching as if it was about to swallow her up? She must have been terrified.

Neeva wasn't fearful, though. She didn't care about dying. No, she was absorbed by bitter anger, at the symbionts, at Wik, at Grandpa, and at Hix. At everything and everyone. She'd finally uncovered the truth, but it wouldn't matter.

That was when she saw Hix's X31 leave the hangar and pull up alongside the rest of the fleet.

She was alone, on a gigantic bullet about to tear an enormous hole in Lakshmi Center, and the only person that could save them was running away.

Rav's P88 copter fell back and took position behind Hix's X31. Neeva knew immediately what that meant.

She yelled into her gag.

Rav's gunpod came to life, ravaging the easy target. Hix's flimsy X31 leaked smoke, and after absorbing a dozen more rounds, caught fire and exploded into pieces that spiraled away toward the plateau below.

45

KNOW THEM, BUT DON'T
BECOME THEM

"We got your back, Falcon Fire," Hix parroted with no small amount of snark.

After he'd set the X31 on autopilot, he'd let it take off without him. He watched from a starboard window as Rav fell behind and destroyed the copter.

It was just a feeling—and that anxious knot inside his chest.

But was the attack just Pru and Rav acting on their own, or did Wik order it? Hix had a bad feeling that it was Wik; all the 'delayed' communications, and Wik always dealing with Pru and Rav directly. Pru and Rav wouldn't kill Hix without Wik's permission, not after Wik had told them to work together.

Hix wasted no more time. He opened the wall lockers and found the parachutes. They were dreadfully old, with mildew eating away at the straps, but he had no choice. He fastened on his atmospheric helmet as well, and opened the airlock.

On three. One, two...

He paused. He had air-jumped in *Toreno Run* twice before. Most people used stunt doubles, but it made for a more immersive audience experience.

One, two...

The well of anxiety hadn't left him. It held on, like a snake coiling in his chest, holding him firm on the hangar deck.

"Choose life, dammit," he yelled out. "Come on!"

One, two...

He paced backward, teeth clenching, breathing in a forced rhythm.

Why would Wik want him killed? He'd shown his loyalty time and again. He'd done his job well. He had many talents that were valuable to Mantle. He could only think of one reason, and it played right into the reformer's hand. It had been planned beforehand. NM-198 wanted Wik to kill off Hix because he knew too much.

"Dammit!" he yelled. Tears formed in his eyes but he willed them away.

The reformer couldn't be right. It was impossible.

"For you, Mel." He took two paces forward to the edge, and receded again.

It didn't feel right when he mentioned Mel's name. In fact, since she'd died he'd felt different; set adrift, as if he was lost in an unfamiliar tenement. For so long, all he'd wanted to do was protect Mel, but she was gone. Now what did he want?

He could still honor her.

Know them, but don't become them, she'd said.

If Rav were in this situation, he would jump in a heartbeat. And so would Pru. He suspected Wik would as well. That director who molested him would jump. The reformer officer who framed his father—he would jump.

But his father wouldn't have jumped.

Tolquist wouldn't have jumped.

Shawna wouldn't jump.

"Dammit!" he yelled.

46

A STEEP TURN

"Shut it."

The words startled Neeva, and it startled her even more to see Hix stomping onto the bridge behind her.

"Just shut your mouth," Hix said.

With the gag in her mouth, it was easy to comply.

Hix started tapping on the main terminal. The attitude of the major began changing immediately. They were close enough that Neeva could see people in the windows of the fern, most of them running away from the windows in alarm. The dirigible started swerving up and away.

"Warning," a female voice called over the intercom. "Steep grade turn in progress. Find a seat and attach a safety harness immediately."

"I hate it when reformers are right," Hix snarled. He mumbled a few more incoherent words.

The turn was indeed steep. Neeva had to hold onto the arms of her seat. Her cuffs strained painfully against her wrists. A display screen next to the front window showed the major colliding with one of the Mantle copters before the smaller craft could take evasive action. The copter's rotary blades seized up and it tumbled out of sight. Another screen showed a copter on the starboard side be pulled abruptly by the massive air displacement to crash into a neighboring airship. The two vehicles got caught up together in a mass of twisted metal, spinning down toward the surface.

Suddenly there was flak. Lots of it. Ordinance tore through the floor and through the front window, cracking it.

"The symbionts must have been holding back," Hix said. "Any ideas?"

"Mmmm."

He finally realized she was still gagged. He removed it with a painful lack of finesse.

"It's nice to be able to stop drooling—thanks," she said. "Now do you mind telling me where we're going?"

He was preoccupied with the controls again, but alert enough to point at the top left corner of the window. Telliac Mountain—and if she was to follow the vector of his arm more precisely, the main psychanthropic facility on Harriet Shelf.

It looked different than she remembered. A huge platform jutted out from the mountain, with four towers and cargo containers surrounding them. Dangling below was a massive scaffold, partially obscuring the oblong form of a surface-to-orbit rocket. It was the Haven Station launch site, but it looked to be mostly vacant except for one remaining rocket.

Alarm bells started going off, adding to the cycling red lights. The cacophony was almost enough to make Neeva sick. Her fingers rubbed at the seat fabric aggressively.

"Containment breach in fusion reactor," the woman's voice announced. "Meltdown imminent. Please evacuate the dirigible immediately."

"We might be able to handle the flak," Neeva said, "but if the copters get wise to what's going on they can target the attitudinal thrusters and redirect us."

Hix frowned. "I guess we'll have to attack them first."

"Right."

"Well? Go."

She pulled her wrists up as far as they would go to reveal her cuffs.

He uncuffed her, sighing with annoyance. "Now go!"

Something hit the dirigible hard; it lurched, sending her to the floor and Hix into the seat next to her. When Neeva was able to get to her feet, she could see more alert messages had popped up on the terminal next to the dozens already listed.

She got back on her feet and staggered off the bridge. There was a lift just outside but she didn't trust it, so she took the stairs. She was thrown against the wall on one of the landings as the dirigible shifted again, but she kept on.

The gun turret was built into an old safety airlock. It was essentially a cockpit bubble that was cut out of the floor at the end of a hallway. Neeva could tell it had been a rush job due to the exposed rivets and rough seams around the exterior curvature.

She jumped directly in, put on her headgear, and grabbed the barrel handles.

"Hix, you hear me?" she said, tapping on her headgear controls. "I'm in the turret."

"Yes. I've been discussing the situation with our escort, but I don't think they're buying it. They're hovering over the bridge, and threatening to attack."

"I've got no line of sight," Neeva said. "Can you bring them underneath the dirigible?"

"Um... yeah." He didn't sound confident.

"What are going to do?"

"Just hold on."

The major wasn't like a jet copter, or even a typical dirigible. It could only change direction so fast, but she decided to strap herself in anyway.

She was glad she did. The major started turning—no, *rolling*—rapidly. It was still facing Telliac Mountain, but turning upside down.

The copters came into view. The straps held her in, but it was still hard to maneuver the gun placement, and it certainly wasn't designed for negative G. She targeted the first copter in her viewfinder and fired, only to realize the safety was on. By the time she found the safety and removed it, the first copter was out of target range and the rest of the copters were coming into view. They were shifting about, trying to steady themselves after the turbulence caused by the massive dirigible's revolution.

She fired. At first she did a couple of quick stray bursts, but then she got a feel for it and kept her trigger finger down for a continuous stream. One small copter's propellers were blown off, and another exploded in a ball of flames, pushing two of the other copters—including Rav's—into a swerve.

The dirigible's rolling continued and the remaining copters revolved out of sight.

Percussions rattled the turret; whether from flak or copter attacks, she couldn't be sure.

The revolution slowed, but didn't stop.

"Hangar five," Hix said. He sounded strained.

"What do you mean?"

"Go to hangar five."

"Okay. How about right after you stop trying to make me lose my lunch."

"Go now. Attitudinal thrusters are shot."

Neeva struggled out of the cockpit and did a kind of drunken walk toward the hangar bay, veering from the floor, to the side wall, to the ceiling, to the side wall, to the floor.

The stairs were hard—literally. She knew because she fell down on them several times. Ceilings were also hard, apparently.

By the time she got to the hangar bay she was feeling battered, nauseous, and disoriented. She held on to a door frame at the entrance, sloughing gradually from surface to surface. She closed her eyes, trying to ward off the vertigo.

"There," Hix said. He'd arrived behind her, and was pointing to a side panel halfway along the hangar. "That's where the chutes are. Take the side wall—hold on to the robot arms, or the equipment hooks."

The hangar wasn't like the small, enclosed stairwells and corridors. She and Hix would surely fall and be crushed if they were to try to run across the expansive floor while the dirigible was turning, so they needed something to hold onto.

"We've got about two minutes left," Hix said. He was already moving ahead, along the side wall. The transparent hangar bay doors beyond him revealed a steep cliff face tinted with the amber light of the dawn-day sun.

She followed him. They moved methodically, pausing to ensure they had good handholds when the ground was about to fall from underneath them. A few shiny wall cleats served her well. These must have been used to moor equipment or supplies during turbulence.

They arrived at an offset airlock door, semi-enclosed and next to the chute panel. Hix handed her a helmet with an attached oxygen pack, which she put on. All of a sudden, a rush of nausea that she couldn't contain overtook her. She scrambled to pull up her face shield and vomited bile on the floor, only for it—and her—to slough from the wall onto the ceiling.

When she looked up, Hix had already put on his chute. He was opening the airlock.

She closed the face shield again, despite the acidic stench of her breath, and went to grab her chute, only to realize there weren't any left in the cupboard.

Hix was gesturing at her with one hand. "Hurry up," he said.

"There's only one chute," she said.

He rolled his eyes.

"You go," she said. "I don't deserve—"

"Oh, shut up," he said. When gravity was toward the floor, he grabbed her arm, hoisted her over his shoulder, then turned and ran into the airlock. Before the next quarter turn, he'd sent them hurtling off the dirigible.

They were tumbling, or at least that's what Neeva thought. She couldn't help but close her eyes. There was too much spinning. She just wanted it to stop.

She heard a ripping noise and she was pulled down hard against

Hix's shoulder, knocking the breath out of her. The tumbling stopped.

She opened her eyes. They were floating rapidly forward, and the ground was staying below her for once. Her vertigo started to wane. Hix was pulling straps on the parachute, directing them away from Telliac Mountain, toward an outcropping in the cliff face.

Neeva craned her neck to see the dirigible behind her careen toward the mountainside, trailing a massive plume of smoke. Two nearby copters were fleeing from it, tilting away along perpendicular trajectories.

The major crashed into the mountain, clipping one of the rocket towers and bursting into a ball of flames.

"Don't look," she said, and she followed her own advice by turning to face the bulge in the mountainside.

The cliff in front of them lit up as if it was the middle of sun season, and a terrible snapping noise reverberated around them, as if a giant was clapping next to Neeva's ear. Then it felt as if that same giant was pushing at her back, accelerating them toward the ground.

Hix pulled on the control straps deftly. They skirted behind the outcrop of the mountain as the ground came ever closer.

Neeva said, "I think it's going to be hard convincing them this was another joyride."

She felt Hix snigger underneath her. "I would worry about your own sentence," he said.

It was true. The symbionts would spin this against her. She had no idea what tomorrow would bring.

Once they were behind the cliff face, the force at Neeva's back diminished. She closed her eyes and felt the wind against her exposed skin. It was hot, but gentle. It was probably the first time she'd truly appreciated the Venusian outdoors.

Parachuting like this would have been something Shawna found fun. She was always more of a thrill-seeker than Neeva.

"I still don't get why Shawna didn't jump," Neeva said.

Hix was targeting landfall near a future agricultural plot, one which had been neatly segmented. There was a settlement tower to the north, about a half-mile away. Neeva resisted the urge to look behind her. The mountain would impede the view of the blast anyway.

Her comment could have been perceived as a rhetorical question, but Hix answered it anyway.

"Because she didn't know who was on the other side," he said.

PART VI

FALCON FIRE

"Do 'formers make Lada laugh? Do they sing savage songs? Are they brave enough to mine in Montkerot, or to dance in the dunes of Dione? Let them vote in their pointless polls. When Mars is watching, we're all they see."

Hedonite parable

47

GOBBLE-TALK

Hix followed Neeva into an access port in the nearby tower. This led down a connector hallway to SS-98LC, which was reformer gobble-talk for the name of an LC peripheral sub-settlement. The downtown of SS-98LC—or maybe it was more of a mall—consisted of a few white-walled shops and an administrative building, all circling a fountain dumping its water over an oversized Verdara globe. Strobe lights flashed above them as some form of alarm, faint blue in color, and a reformer woman's voice tried to pacify them in an absurdly calm monotone.

No one was in the courtyard area outside the shops, perhaps due to the state of alarm.

Hix followed Neeva as she marched into the administrative building. The only person in attendance was a young clerk woman with long, glittering, silver braids, the kind that would cost a few months' salary for a hedonite. Neeva gave her an earful about the urgent state of affairs, and her need of a room and tablet access for PDA business. The wide-eyed young clerk would readily have given them the keys to the safe if they'd asked for it.

Neeva worked feverishly on the tablet, typing away for over an hour. Hix didn't interrupt. Occasionally, he drifted out of the room, making his way to the middle of the mall courtyard to place his hand in the water of the fountain. It was crystal clear. They didn't have many fountains like this in Samar City.

He collected two cups from a nearby shop and brought water back to the room.

Neeva drank hers in several big gulps. "Thanks," she said.

Hix was finally about to ask her what she was doing, when she said, "Okay, this is the best I can do." She turned her tablet to face him.

"What is this?"

"It's what happened. It's about the Reformer Doctrine being a sham, and it explains why the symbionts can't be trusted."

"Who are you sending it to?"

"Everyone. The council, the PDA, the media, municipal leaders. In both NoPo and SoPo."

"Isn't that going to upset your bosses?"

"Probably. They should be used to that by now."

"Why do you want me to look at it?"

"It's your story too. You can change it."

He nodded, and read it through. It was gobble-talk, and used all sorts of stuffy annoying PDA protocol terms, but it was balanced. It was even fair. He pushed the tablet back to her. "It's fine."

Neeva looked down her nose at him. "If I send this, it's not going to help you with diehard reformers. They could come after you."

He shrugged. "Wik already tried to kill me, remember."

"So?"

"Send it," he said.

She hesitated for a brief moment, took a breath, and hit send.

Hix and Neeva were probably safe underground, but fusion reactor meltdowns weren't something they had any experience with, so they took a tram out of the area. Neeva warned the people they came across as well. Most were already evacuating.

Nobody recognized Hix. Maybe it was his long hair. Or maybe they were too preoccupied with the alarm.

They stopped at a small park in SS-12LC. The sub-settlement looked virtually identical to SS-98LC even though it was several miles away. No one else was in the park.

Neeva received a message on the tablet she'd taken from the other sub-settlement. After reviewing it, she said, "Fisker wants us to come in to the fern in LC."

"What are you going to do?"

"I'm going think about it."

He couldn't be sure why the reformer wouldn't take him in, or what she was thinking about, but he didn't blame her for taking her time. The world was different today than it had been yesterday. It was hard not to question everything.

So they paid for a motel room, to rest, and clean up, and think.

Hix tapped on the vid screen to turn it on. Maybe he shouldn't have.

It showed the major dirigible slamming into Telliac Mountain. The news reporters were calling it the *Telliac Mountain Tragedy*. Countless video feeds played over and over again, from every angle. The impact had caused a huge, tilted crater, and the surrounding rock had collapsed and sloughed off the mountain not long after. The reporters said there were over ten thousand dead.

And of course, the talking heads were going off about Neeva's message. It was on every network. They were questioning the veracity, debating the points. It didn't look like many people believed it.

"Typical," Hix said.

Neeva was staring at him, watching his reaction to the news. She said, "Do you want to run?"

"No," he said. "Where am I going to go? Everyone knows what I look like. Wik is out to kill me. For all I know, Rav and Pru might still be alive as well. But also..."

"Mel is gone," she finished for him.

He nodded.

"You have someone?" he asked. "A boyfriend?"

"Girlfriend. Or at least I did, for a while. Not anymore."

"Maybe you can make it work now."

"What are you, a symbiont?"

"That's a bad word, you know."

She grinned, and tried to stifle a yawn.

It didn't work. He yawned as well.

"Tell me, Hix, if this hadn't happened—if you weren't famous, and now infamous—what would you want to do?"

"I want... I know it sounds strange after all we've been through, but I want to fly again."

"You're insane."

"I'm a hedonite."

"Exactly. Are you sure you want to go in to the fern with me?"

"Who knows, maybe things have changed?"

She didn't look optimistic. "Let's wait until morning. Maybe things will cool down. And besides, I'm exhausted."

They only slept for a few hours. Someone had probably recognized them, or maybe they were picked up on a feed. This wasn't SoPo. There were cameras everywhere.

Five enforcer brutes busted down the door and held them both. Neeva was pushed against the wall while the other four took their turns pummeling Hix. They concentrated on his chest, mostly. Usually these enforcers would get into trouble if a hedonite's face was too pulpy for suspect processing.

"Stop it, you idiots!" Neeva yelled. "He's with me!"

For a few hours, at least, Hix thought things might be different.

48

——————

OPTICS AND SHADOWS

A handful of people were watching from outside the motel when the enforcers finally pulled them out of the door. "It's her," Neeva overheard one of them whispering.

Hix was grimacing from the bruises they'd inflicted. He wasn't struggling. He appeared resigned to his fate.

They were manhandled onto a tram, and shuttled all the way to the fern. On the tram people gawked, whispered and took pictures.

"Looks like I've got adoring fans now, too," she said to Hix.

He cringed. She couldn't blame him.

In the LC emporium there was a huge crowd, well over a thousand strong. A man was yelling into a bullhorn, "We want justice! We want truth!" The crowd was chanting along with him. Signs were hoisted above them. One had *Reformer Doctrine* scrawled on it with fiery lines drawn through it. Another had a picture of the splayed, seeded hand, but the seeds were on fire.

Their enforcer escort avoided the crowd, and instead took little-used avenues to the back of the shunt tower. Here, they could access another entryway into the security lift.

On the PDA office floor, three of the enforcers split off, pushing Hix ahead of them.

"No," Neeva said, "Hix stays with me. Hey!" They weren't listening, and she was already being pushed away in another direction as well, into the offices. People in their cubes stopped what they were doing and stood up from their desks. They stared at her with blank faces as she passed by. Neeva wondered what they were thinking. Was it shame, or was it pride?

Judging by her treatment thus far, she guessed the former.

Egan, of all people, was standing outside Fisker's office.

"Excuse us," One of Neeva's handlers said. It was the brute named Brock. Egan gave him a look that could have melted his face off, and it gave Brock pause.

"You made it back," she said to Egan, giving him a once over. He had a bandage around his chest, but otherwise he was in one piece. Except, of course, for his missing arm.

She expected him to spout his usual nervous chatter, but all he said was, "Thank you, Inspector." His brow rippled in confusion, as if he was wrestling with emotions he didn't know he had. Then he lumbered off, letting them pass.

It was an odd exchange. Who knew, maybe there was at least one person who appreciated what she'd done.

"Thank you, Brock," Fisker said from inside the office. "You can remain outside."

Brock obliged. Fisker closed the door behind Neeva and pulled out a chair for her.

It was as if there had been a minor explosion in his office. The neat stacks of tablets had multiplied and had been redistributed to toppled towers on the floor. His hair was unkempt, his face flushed, and his eyes weary. He reminded Neeva of Gorman, of all people.

"What your men did to Hix," she said, "that's not okay."

"Neeva, you're not in a position to be telling me what's okay or not okay. I don't know if this shitstorm you've created is ever going to clear."

"You're welcome."

He scoffed and leaned back in his chair, shaking his head in disbelief, as if he was watching some surreal murderball maneuver.

"Let me fill you in on what's going on here. I'm sure you've seen the vids." He waved his hand toward his windows, in the direction of the crumpled mass of basalt that lay where Telliac Mountain used to be. "Ten thousand dead at Telliac, most of our records lost at the Keeper Complex and Heritage Museum, the psychanthropic facility destroyed... shall I go on?"

"Better ten thousand than a million," she said.

He ignored her. "And the symbionts," he continued. "Granted, we are coming around to your... bizarre experience. There are some, including me, who see merit in your claims, but that's just not how things are done."

"Some? They should look around. It's all verifiable. Check communications from Mars. Check the records from Earth."

His complexion darkened considerably. It looked as if his head might explode. "Maybe," he said, "but sending that message to everyone on Venus was reprehensible. The symbionts... many died in the tragedy, but the rest... in psychanthropic stations we've found two of them murdered. Others have committed suicide. In fact, we have yet to find one alive."

"Haven Station is conspicuously not on your list."

"It left orbit at quite a clip, using the fusion reactor to support its propulsion systems. We're unable to reach it."

"Doesn't that tell you something?"

"The only thing it tells me is this madness won't stop for a long time. Half of our communications networks are offline, and a good deal of manufacturing as well. We have no idea how long it will take to figure out how to manage our automated operational systems without symbiont assistance. Worst of all are the fusion reactors. So far, we've been able to keep them stable, but we're not sure if we can for long. The symbionts were always able to correct reactor homeostasis imbalances. We may not be able to anymore. This is a major threat."

"Are we sure those reactor imbalances are really that challenging an engineering problem? They could be another fabrication of the symbionts to justify their need for control. In any case, we'll just have to learn how to do it ourselves. And if not, that's why we're also building the new wind and solar stations."

He ignored her again. "There are demonstrations." He waved his hand at the window. "You probably saw one at the base of the fern, but that's nothing. There are ten times as many people in LC center, and Quelway, and Newik. First Colony monuments are being vandalized. People want answers—answers we can't give them."

"Well... good."

"No, Neeva, not good. And then there's SoPo. Have you ever heard of the Independent Republic of Samar, or the Redrock-Scorpio Cooperative, or the Dione Federation?"

He answered his own question before she could respond. "Well you better get used to them, because they're nation-states that are about to declare independence. Entire geographical areas—whole massifs are forming their own governments. They no longer trust us, or even SoPo central authority. Some are calling it the 'New Dawn'. Redrock-Scorpio is calling it 'The Age of Falcon Fire', after you-know-who, like he's some kind of celestial superhero."

"Can't say I blame them. What about Mantle? Wik?"

He frowned. "Egan was just briefing me. We were able to pull out the remainder of your extraction team, but we couldn't take the whole facility before we had to fall back, and Wik eluded us. And as you may have guessed, Operation Amity has been cancelled. It was being substantially planned by the symbionts, so we don't even know whom we're supposed to attack. The one positive is that Mantle is in disarray as well. They are surely lost without NM-198, and with SoPo so fragmented. They will have the same problems with unrest, communication and control we have—probably worse."

"So am I in trouble?"

"In trouble?" He gawked at the apparent understatement. "Surely you can see that much of this turmoil around the globe, this 'Age of Falcon Fire'," he rolled his eyes, "has been caused by your actions, and your ill-conceived, anti-symbiont, anti-Doctrine manifesto. Venus was barely hanging on, and you just might have pushed it over the cliff."

"Hopefully we'll land in a better place."

"Neeva!" he yelled in frustration. He paused to quell his anger before resuming. "Look, fine. From what we know, based on the evidence we have now, it's possible you helped save LC. You definitely uncovered... something significant, but your insubordination and carelessness have gone too far. The optics are, well, painful. The council thinks your report should have been kept confidential, so we can control the flow of information, minimize the damage, perhaps retain some support from the symbionts."

"The symbionts would have killed me before I could expose them, and you know it."

"I don't think..." His pause made her realize he actually hadn't considered it.

He gathered himself and said, "Neeva, you're better than this. I thought you'd learned your lesson."

"Learned my lesson? I've learned a lot, for sure. The most important thing I learned is this: how the truth is delivered is a lot less important than it *actually being delivered*."

"Well, I..." Fisker stammered. "That's just not the view of the council."

She almost laughed out loud. Once again, the council was worried the "optics" weren't good. Sure they weren't. The whole Reformer Doctrine was a sham, but that wasn't Neeva's fault. So she just sat there and took it. There was no sense laughing, or even arguing. Instead, she felt at the outline of her cuffs. The cool metal sapping the heat from her fingertips felt good.

Fisker said, "Look, I'm sorry, Neeva, but there are going to be repercussions, and more than just a slap on the wrist. There's going to be a hearing. You will be punished for releasing your manifesto."

"Fine," she said slowly. "Do your worst."

"Good. I'm glad you understand. We will still need your support, given all the leads that need to be verified. If you want any lenience, I would keep that in mind."

"Of course you will," she said in an acerbic tone. "What about Hix?"

"He's a criminal, a terrorist. He will be dealt with accordingly."

"No."

"What?"

"No. Everything has changed. We need him more than you can possibly realize—for the investigation, but also to mend relations with SoPo. If you want my support, you'll damn well leave him out of this."

"Neeva, you're not in a position—"

"Yeah, yeah, we'll see about that."

Fisker shook his head again. His expression was a mixture of consternation and disbelief.

She said, "I guess we're done here. Do you want me to wear these forever?" She held up her cuffed hands. "I'm not sure the optics are good, as you might say."

He considered it. "No, I guess those aren't necessary, but you'll be shadowed."

"Fine."

He applied his token to the cuff interface and deactivated them.

There was an uncomfortable silence. Fisker was glaring at her.

She stood up walked out. When she was at the door, Fisker said, "Neeva?" She thought he might finally thank her, or at least acknowledge her effort, but instead he said, "Close the door behind you, please."

She was reissued her comm device, although her outbound transmissions were heavily controlled by filters and bots. She had plenty of inbound to deal with, in any case—thousands of unread messages. One of them was from Grandpa.

Come to my office after you've spoken with Fisker.

That was where she found him. He was in active communion with his Cortivation device.

The two enforcers that were shadowing her squeezed into the office behind her.

Grandpa pressed the disconnection button at the base of his neck and pulled out the leads. His face couldn't hide a scowl as his eyes followed the two enforcers, but he still put his arms out to hug her.

It was a curt embrace. "Neeva, I'm so glad you're safe. This mess..." He shook his head. "I wasn't sure you'd make it, but I've made a few calls. I think you're going to come out okay."

"What did you think about my letter?"

He grimaced. "It was something else. When I chose you as Keeper I knew you had talents, but... wow. Such piercing insights. I just wish..."

"I never did have much tact."

He forced a smile that died a quick death. "Don't worry about that. What's done is done. I'll speak with the council, try to urge leniency. I can have you assigned to help us protect the remaining First Colony heritage assets. There is talk of rebuilding the museum and Keeper Complex."

"Oh," she said. Her heart sank. She had been hopeful that this conversation would go differently than the one with Fisker. Those hopes may have been misplaced.

Grandpa wasn't finished. "In the chaos, some of the new nation-states haven't yet bought into the—"

"It was the hedonites," she interrupted, "wasn't it? They were the ones that were cast into the atmosphere during the Cessation, not the reformers. Hundreds of thousands of them. Did you know about that?"

He collected himself before responding. "Yes, Neeva. But imagine if that was the narrative. Hedonite tribes would constantly be trying to find some reason to upset a system that works. We can't trust them to—"

"Did you know about Earth?" she interrupted again. "The ruins in the restricted areas. The fact that we came from Mars."

His teeth clenched and he took a step away from her to look out the window. The demolished mountainside monopolized the vista.

"Yes," he said, turning back to her. "I'm sorry, Neeva. Our past was not always pretty. Sometimes a precious gem needs polishing. But I didn't know that the symbionts could be so deceptive. That was a crucial insight. They were holding us back from the Verdara. Good riddance, I say."

"But you must have known about the flaws in the Doctrine—the fact that the genetic algorithms for hedonite selection couldn't be trusted."

"I wouldn't say that. In the Cessation, tough decisions were made to ensure we could maintain—"

"So you still can't see it."

"See what?"

"We're not Keepers, Grandpa. There are no Keepers. There never were. What we were keeping were lies—a fantasy that corrupts all of us. It's time to move on."

"Neeva," he said, mouth agape. "Our heritage is strong. It unites us, it's... who we are."

"Concrete truths take time to cure," she said. "You told me that once. Maybe we need to change. I've seen people do it. You can too."

He was at a loss for words.

She embraced him again. His arms were like dead branches, unable to bend around her back. "Goodbye, Grandpa," she said. "I love you."

She left his office, and her shadows rolled out behind her.

There was another message buried in her inbox. She didn't find it until two days later. It was from Celia. All it said was *Thanks for doing that. I'm glad you're alive.*

The words probably meant nothing. Maybe the message was a fleeting gesture after Celia saw her manifesto on the news. Either way, Neeva almost collapsed when she read it.

It wasn't hard to find her. Neeva still had access to PDA directory records, including video footage, and Celia wasn't trying to hide. Her new apartment was in a quaint sub-settlement in north LC.

Neeva procrastinated for a day, and then another, and finally worked up the nerve to make her way over. It was mid-morning, and people on the tram still whispered and pointed at her, but most were discreet about it. Since she hadn't blown up any mountains in the last couple of days, or sent out any civilization-disrupting communications, the PDA had decided to remove one of her shadows, and so it was just her and Brock.

Brock didn't talk much.

Occasionally someone on the tram would call her "hedonite trash", or a "traitor". On the previous day, someone had charged at her, his fist recoiled in preparation for attack, and she'd been thankful she still had a shadow. The man was hospitalized with several broken ribs. Brock had been happy he could be put to good use.

It wasn't all bad. Anuvant had messaged her and gushed about her being an inspiration—how he hoped to be as effective as her someday. A few times, people had approached her cautiously and wanted to hug her, or just to thank her, as Egan had thanked her. It was a non-specific form of gratitude. It was as if Neeva had given them back something they hadn't known they'd lost.

And she hadn't seen any fist-to-seed First Colony gestures since she'd been back. At the very least, people had doubts.

Celia's sub-settlement was a lively strip, with a long stretch of bars and eateries. A colorful theater took up the corner at one end, topped with blue crenelations, and windows and doorways lined with bronze trim. Celia lived in a flat next to the theater.

She found Celia before reaching her apartment. Neeva was just turning onto the main stretch and she saw Celia sitting down, having a drink at a cafe. She was with another woman, laughing and touching her arm. The woman was pretty, with full-bore blue-dyed eyelashes, and cuts in her sleeves. She was leaning toward Celia, all smiles, engrossed in their conversation.

She was more than a friend.

Neeva couldn't move. She stayed at the corner, hiding behind a wall and sneaking peeks at the couple as if in a childish game of hide and seek.

It was as she watched Celia giggle and smile with this woman that it crystalized. Neeva could never be like this other woman. It was what Neeva had already known in her heart, and what Celia had already rationally concluded.

They were never meant to be.

Celia wanted a constant companion, and Neeva was always going to be obsessive about work. All those times when Neeva had been away, she had deprived Celia of so much joy.

Their relationship was a trap, for both of them.

Maybe someday, after the interrogations, after whatever punishment the PDA doled out for their token scapegoat, Neeva could find someone more compatible, someone that she loved as much as Celia, but who also relished her independence.

Her hopeful thought was undermined by a solitary tear. It fell to her cheek and she batted it away with an aggressive swipe.

She backed away from the corner, retreating toward the tram stop.

"Where are we going now?" Brock asked, his first words of the day.

"Back to work," Neeva answered.

Before they reached the tram stop, she paused and texted a one-line response to Celia.

Thanks, but we still need to set Rocket free.

49

———————

NOT WHAT I SIGNED UP FOR

Beyond the *Zephyr Spear's* front viewport, the yellow and brown gas storms swirled in arcs on Earth's surface down below. It didn't look any different than the last time Hix had seen it, or even the first time, but it felt different, maybe because he knew what lay underneath.

"Let's start the checklist, Hix," Ordan said behind him. She had easily relinquished piloting duties to him this time.

"Yes, ma'am," he said, and he began testing the *Zephyr Spear's* launch systems.

Sonders was also on the bridge, scratching his head next to Ordan, engrossed in his tablet.

Califf was tapping away at his console, too. He was their new science officer. He tended to ask Hix a lot of questions, and often with an eager inflection in his voice. Califf was remarkably well-qualified, even more so than Tolquist had been, with both a climate science specialization and a technical degree in systems engineering. His crime had been "supporting the hedonite insurgency", which had apparently resulted from him leaving his SoPo post during the 'New Dawn' mayhem. It seemed overly harsh to send someone to Kanto Station for that. Thousands had done far worse with no penalty.

It had been almost two months since the major dirigible had careened into Telliac Mountain. Since then, Hix had bounced from interrogation to interrogation, and from safe house to safe house. He had cooperated willingly, corroborating Neeva's letter and offering additional information about Wik and Mantle. But he drew the line when the PDA wanted him to make a statement urging SoPo residents to submit to monitoring and return to rule of law.

He said he might consider it if Neeva was going to make the same statement. They stopped asking after that.

He'd come around to the idea that as far as reformers went, Neeva wasn't all that bad.

The council must have had a hard time figuring out what to do with him. Two different SoPo massif communities had declared him a national hero and were demanding his safe return. At the same time, the more hardline First Colony reformers wanted him killed for his role as a terrorist.

His celebrity status hadn't really diminished.

Ultimately the council must have decided it was better to remove him from the equation altogether. Out of sight and out of mind. So here he was again, sentenced to five years of drop-ship runs on Kanto Station. It was a neat way to effectively give him a death sentence without the new SoPo governments realizing it was a death sentence.

"Hey, Hix," Califf said, "I heard they're making a movie about Tolquist. Do you think that's true?"

Ordinarily, Hix would be suspicious of Califf as a possible PDA plant. He did have a tendency toward invasive curiosity, but Hix gave him the benefit of the doubt. His assignment to the ship was more likely the result of some clerk's incompetence, or simply bad luck.

"I would certainly watch it," was Hix's response. "Tolquist was a class act. He led by example. Whoever plays him has big shoes to fill."

He hoped they would do Tolquist's character justice. He also wondered who they would cast for Neeva, or even Hix himself. It didn't matter. He probably wouldn't live long enough to find out.

He finished the checklist. "All systems ready," he said. "Coring targets plotted. Ready to drop, but safety belts first."

Ordan didn't respond immediately. Hix looked back to see a frown occupying her brow as she read her tablet.

"Hold," she said. She punched on her tablet and, simultaneously, his display froze.

Ordan had retaken control of the ship.

Hix didn't feel he had sufficient standing to question Ordan, but Sonders apparently did. "Captain, I thought we had established through both star ratings and, um, prior experience, that Hix is the most appropriate pilot."

"It's not that," Ordan said, still focused on her screen. "I've received word we're to hold the drop. There's a pre-launch inspection team coming aboard."

Sonders frowned in confusion.

The upper airlock opened, and the inspection team came aboard. They were clad in black coveralls similar to the agents Hix had seen on the *Colonial Pride*, and they were pushing bulky, unlabeled, cylindrical bags. The first few men went directly below decks to the lower-level coring operations without acknowledging any of the crew.

By the time the fifth person arrived, it was safe to conclude this was no regular inspection team. This one had the rank of lieutenant. His eyes passed over each of them in turn, until he addressed Ordan. "Captain Ordan, I'm Lieutenant Glarmer. There has been a change in plan. We are going to commandeer this vessel."

"By whose authority?" Ordan asked. Most people would be peeved, but Ordan didn't care much about anything. She looked mildly curious at best.

"Mine," said a familiar voice, coming from the airlock.

Her hair was dyed a darker shade of black, but it was still close-cropped and matted. She was floating down from the airlock with her own cylindrical bag. She landed neatly on the floor of the bridge with her mag-boots activating in tandem.

It was Neeva.

For some reason, Hix wasn't surprised.

Sonders sure was. "Oh no, not her," he whispered, shaking his head. Neeva was still an inspector, the highest rank on the ship, so his comments could be considered insubordination. Neeva's appearance even set off a rare bout of annoyance from Ordan. She threw her hands up in the air and rolled her eyes.

"Is there a problem, Captain?" Neeva asked.

Ordan replied, "Inspector, with all due respect, we have already escorted you to the planet once before, and then all the way to Venus. I wonder if you have better things to do than to fraternize with a bunch of drop-ship criminals. And besides, these coring missions can be quite dangerous."

Neeva only glared at her with one eyebrow raised.

Ordan sighed and reconsidered her words. "Pardon my objection, Inspector. I will of course comply with your request."

Neeva smiled. "No need to apologize, Captain. And I do recognize the risks associated with coring missions. I've seen the records. Ninety-five percent of crew members eventually die."

Califf glared at Hix with wide eyes. Hix simply nodded in confirmation.

Neeva continued, "We will need to change that, but that's not what I'm here for. In fact, I'm not here to conduct a coring mission at all."

The crew shared quizzical looks. Captain Ordan asked, "Excuse me, Inspector, but what *are* you here for?"

Neeva was looking up, her eyes following the path of the last man entering the airlock. It was Egan, the enforcer brute with the combat arm.

"Airlock secured," Egan said.

Neeva returned her attention to Ordan. "This vessel has been appropriated by Venus PDA for a confidential mission. We're going to the restricted area."

"But why?" Ordan asked.

"The engineers on Venus are having trouble maintaining homeostasis on the fusion reactors. It's a delicate job requiring a great deal of computational power and constant troubleshooting. The symbionts were lying about us not being able to do it ourselves, but we could still use some help."

"Help... from the restricted area of Earth?"

"Remember the Mecha-AIs that were destroyed during the Cessation? We need blueprints to rebuild them, and we may be able to find those blueprints in the abandoned ruins of Earth. The Mecha-AIs can fill the role of the symbionts, not only to help us with the reactors but also to advance our progress toward the Verdara. And, well, I'm looking for a few other things as well, but that's the first order of business."

Califf whispered to Hix, "Is she crazy? This is not what I signed up for."

Hix chuckled. "Yeah, she's crazy. Or at least, she's pretty anal, even for a 'former. Don't bother trying to get reassigned, though. I'm pretty sure you were specifically chosen for this mission, just as I was."

The new crew members finished stowing their gear in the wall lockers and found their seats.

Neeva took a chair behind Hix and focused on her console. Mission control was passed to her from Ordan, and Neeva eventually patched through new coordinates to Hix. It was a different restricted area than Banbury, and there would be some serious chop on the way down, but the path she'd plotted looked navigable. Hix accepted the course and loaded it into the computer.

Everyone was buckled and seated. The display showed all systems ready.

Neeva said, "Alright Hix, are we all set?"

"Yes, ma'am."

"I've heard about your reckless driving on Venus. Try not to crash this one, please."

Hix smirked and initiated the launch sequence. The familiar surge of adrenaline rushed through his veins as his hands gripped the contours of the yoke.

"*Zephyr Spear* is away," he said as the ship fell toward Earth.

ACKNOWLEDGEMENTS

Falcon Fire is inspired in part by a speculative extrapolation of today's political misinformation campaigns. To thrive, or even just survive, societies might prejudicially disempower those who are susceptible to lies. If we do not take steps to mitigate growing problems like the algorithm-driven echo chambers on social media platforms, I worry that this disconcerting fiction could become premonition.

Of course that was just one seed, and Falcon Fire became much more than that. I would be the first to admit it is more entertainment than social commentary. I particularly enjoyed researching scientific papers about terraforming Venus, and should acknowledge two bodies of work that helped my ideation process; Steve Hurley for his writings on magnetic fields, and Mark Bullock and David H. Grinspoon for their work on atmospheric bombardment.

I would like to thank my editor Tim Major, who not only helped me improve the manuscript, but his praise also encouraged me to push it forward. My brother Karl's words motivated me as well—Falcon Fire may have remained a short story without his positive feedback. And I cannot forget my family for allowing me the time to pursue such whimsical diversions as writing about other worlds, thousands of years in the future.

If you enjoyed Falcon Fire, I would greatly appreciate a review on Amazon or Goodreads. As a self-published author, there are limited options for reaching online reviewers, and they are so critical to achieving even moderate levels of readership.

Thank you for your interest in my work. I hope I can be inspired to write again, for this world or the next.

Erik A. Otto

ALSO BY ERIK A. OTTO

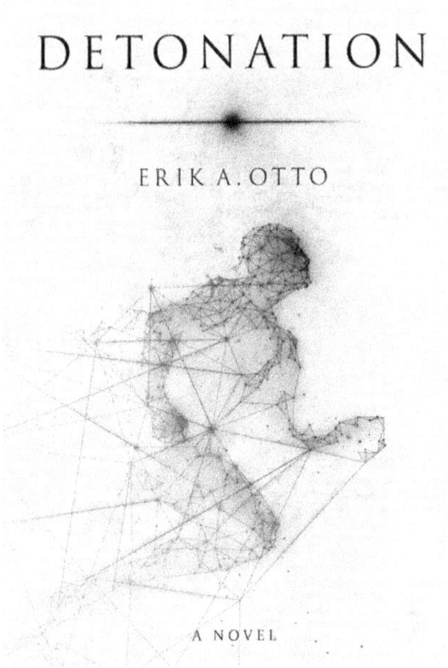

An epic dystopian tale that is a cautionary reflection on our own innovation-obsessed culture. It follows two societies that are connected, but centuries apart, and their struggle against a superintelligent machine.

Named to *Kirkus Reviews* Best Books of 2018

"A highly entertaining and absorbing combination of philosophy and action featuring robustly individualized characters."

"...a future world that vibrates with conflict and ideas."

— Kirkus Reviews (starred review)

ALSO BY ERIK A. OTTO

An epic fantasy series that deals with prejudice and political intrigue in a medieval setting, with prophesied gravity-defying events and stories of mythical beasts as regular undercurrents to daily life. It follows outcasts and pariahs who not only face a desperate fight for survival, but who are also the only ones who can save their imperiled world.

"Rich, layered and thoughtful world building..."

"...characters are well developed and intriguing."

— *Kirkus Reviews*

Finalist for the Foreword Indies Book of the Year Award.

ABOUT THE AUTHOR

Erik A. Otto is a former healthcare industry executive, now turned science fiction author. His works of fiction include A Toxic Ambition, Detonation, Proliferation, Subjugation and the Tale of Infidels series. Detonation has been named to Kirkus Reviews Best Books of 2018, and was a finalist for the Foreword INDIES Book of the Year Award for 2018.

In addition to writing, Erik is currently serving as the Managing Director of Ethagi Inc., an organization dedicated to promoting the safe and ethical use of artificial general intelligence technologies.

Please visit Erik's website at erik-a-otto.com for more information or to sign up for updates on new releases.